Reginald Hill █████ ████ dent of Yorkshire, the setting for his outstanding crime novels featuring Dalziel and Pascoe, 'the best detective duo on the scene bar none' (*Daily Telegraph*). His writing career began with the publication of *A Clubbable Woman* (1970), which introduced Chief Superintendent Andy Dalziel and DS Peter Pascoe. Their subsequent appearances, together with the adventures of Luton lathe operator turned PI Joe Sixsmith, have confirmed Hill's position as 'the best living male crime writer in the English speaking world' (*Independent*) and won numerous awards, including the Crime Writers' Association Cartier Diamond Dagger for his lifetime contribution to the genre.

The Dalziel and Pascoe novels have now been adapted into a successful BBC television series starring Warren Clarke and Colin Buchanan.

By the same author

Dalziel and Pascoe novels

A CLUBBABLE WOMAN
AN ADVANCEMENT OF LEARNING
RULING PASSION
AN APRIL SHROUD
A PINCH OF SNUFF
A KILLING KINDNESS
DEADHEADS
EXIT LINES
CHILD'S PLAY
UNDER WORLD
BONES AND SILENCE
ONE SMALL STEP
RECALLED TO LIFE
PICTURES OF PERFECTION
ASKING FOR THE MOON
THE WOOD BEYOND
ON BEULAH HEIGHT
DIALOGUES OF THE DEAD
DEATH'S JEST-BOOK

Joe Sixsmith novels

BLOOD SYMPATHY
BORN GUILTY
KILLING THE LAWYERS
SINGING THE SADNESS

FELL OF DARK
THE LONG KILL
DEATH OF A DORMOUSE
DREAM OF DARKNESS
THE ONLY GAME

REGINALD HILL

ARMS AND THE WOMEN

A Dalziel and Pascoe novel

HarperCollins*Publishers*

HarperCollins*Publishers*
77–85 Fulham Palace Road,
Hammersmith, London W6 8JB

This paperback re-issue 2003

5

First published in Great Britain by
HarperCollins*Publishers* 2000

The HarperCollins website address is:
www.fireandwater.com

ISBN 0 00 651287 9

Typeset in Meridien by Palimpsest Book Production Limited,
Polmont, Stirlingshire

Printed and bound in Great Britain by
Clays Ltd, St Ives plc.

Extract from 'Marina' from the *Collected Poems 1909–62* by
T.S. Eliot (published by Faber and Faber Ltd) reproduced by
permission of Faber and Faber Ltd

Lines from 'Girls' by Stevie Smith from *The Collected Poems of
Stevie Smith* (Penguin) © James McGibbon 1975

Extracts from *The Englishman's Flora* by Geoffrey Grigson
(Phoenix House 1987)

Extract from *A Celtic Miscellany* by Kenneth Hurlstone Jackson
(Penguin 1971)

This one's for
those Six Proud Walkers
in whose company the sun always shines bright

Emmelien

Jane

Liz

Margaret

Mary

Teresa

who most Fridays of the year . . . *on distant hills*
Gliding apace, with shadows in their train,
Might, with small help from fancy, be transformed
Into fleet Oreads sporting visibly . . .

and, of course, laughing and talking and eating
almond slices,
with fondest greetings from
one of the trailing shadows!

What song the Syrens sang, or what name Achilles assumed when he hid himself among women, though puzzling Questions, are not beyond all conjecture.

SIR THOMAS BROWNE: Urn Burial

With my own eyes I've seen the Sibyl at Cumae hanging in a pot, and when the young lads asked her, *what do you want for yourself, Sibyl*? she replied, *I want to die*.

PETRONIUS: The Satyricon

Girls! although I am a woman
I always try to appear human

STEVIE SMITH: Girls!

PROLEGOMENA

When I go to see my father, he doesn't know me.

He's away somewhere else in a strange land.

I tell myself it's not all bad. He missed all that suffering when we thought Rosie was going to die. And all those refugees in Africa, and in Europe too, that we see streaming across our television screens, he doesn't have to worry about them. Global warming, AIDS, the Euro, none of these impinges on his consciousness. He doesn't even have to feel anxious about his roses when gales are forecast in July.

He sits here in the Home, like ignorance on a monument, smiling at nothing.

At least he's content, the nurses tell us, and we tell them back, yes, at least he's content.

Content to be nobody and nowhere.

But I have seen him outside of this room, this cocoon, with memories of somebody and somewhere still intermittent in his mind, staring in bewilderment at the woman who is both his wife and a complete stranger, pausing in the hallway of his own house, unable to recall if he's heading for the kitchen or the garden and ignorant of which door to use if he does remember, crying out in terror as the dog which has been his most obedient servant for nearly ten years comes bounding towards him, barking its love.

Seeing him like this was bad.

But worse was waking in the night during and after Rosie's illness, wondering if perhaps what we call Alzheimer's – that condition in which the world becomes a vortex of fragments, a video loop of disconnected scenes, an absurdist drama full of actors pretending to be old friends and relations – wondering whether perhaps this is not a disease at all but merely a relaxing of some psychological censor which the self imposes to enable us to exist in a totally irrational universe.

Which would mean that dad and all the others are at last seeing things as they really are.

Unvirtual reality.

A sea of troubles.

Confused.

Inconsequential.

Fragments shored against a ruin.

Oh, Mistress Pascoe,
Laud we the gods, and let our crooked smokes climb to their nostrils for glad tidings do I bring and lucky joys. No more I fear the heat of the sun, as time which all these years has wasted me now sets me free, most

happy news of price, but not for all, for does not time's whirligig bring in revenges? Thou'rt much in my mind, nor shall I be content till I have seen thy face, when my full eyes shall witness bear to what my full heart feels. May my tears that fall prove holy water on thee! I must be brief, for though my enemies set me free, in freedom lies more danger than in prison, for here through thee and thine the world knows me in their care, but once enlarged, then am I at the mock of all disastrous chances and dangerous accidents by flood and field, with their hands whiter than the paper my obits are writ on and so must wear a mind dark as my fortune or my name. Fate leads me to your side but gives no date, for I must journey now by by-paths and indirect crook'd ways, but sometime sure, when you have quite forgot to look for me, a door shall open, and there shall I be, though you may know me not, but never fear, before I'm done you'll know me through and through. Till then rest happy while I remain, though brown as earth, as bright unto my vows as faith can raise me.

Close by the margin of a lonely lake, shag-capped by pines that speared a lowering sky from which oozed light unclean whose lurid touch seemed rather to infect than luminate, a deep cave yawned.

Here four men laboured with shovels, their faces wrapped with scarves, not for disguise but as barrier against the stench of the decaying bat droppings they disturbed, while high above them a sea of leathery bodies rippled and whispered uneasily as the sound of digging and the glow of bull-lamps drifted up to the natural vault.

Outside two more men waited silently by a truck which looked almost too broad to have navigated the rutted track curving away like a railway tunnel into the crowding trees. Several yards away on a rocky ledge jutting out over the unmoving, unreflecting waters stood a dusty jeep.

Away to the east, dawn's rosy fingers were already pulling aside the mists which shrouded the sleeping land, but here the exhalations of the lake still hung grey and heavy over the waters, the vehicle, and the waiting men.

At last from the cave's black mouth two figures emerged, labouring under the weight of a long metal box they carried between them.

They set it down on the ground behind the truck. One of the waiting men, his thinning yellow hair clinging to his brow like straw to a milkmaid's buttocks, stooped to unlock the container. Glancing up at the other man from black and bulging eyes, he paused like a vampiricide about to open a coffin, then flung back the lid.

The other man, slim and dark with a narrow moustache, looked down at the oiled and gleaming tubes of metal for a moment, then nodded. The first man snapped his fingers and the diggers closed the box and lifted it onto the back of the truck. Then they returned to the cave, passing en route their two companions staggering out with a second box.

Many times was this journey made, and while

the labourers laboured, the watchers went round to the front of the truck and the slim man opened the passenger door, reached inside and picked up a large square leather case which he set on the seat and opened.

The straw-haired, bulging-eyed man produced a flattened cylinder of ivory and pressed a stud to release a long, slightly curved blade. Delicately he nicked two of the plastic containers which packed the case, licked his index finger, inserted it into the first incision, tasted the powder which clung to his damp flesh, repeated the process with the second, and nodded his accord.

The dark man closed the case then took the other's outstretched hand.

'Nice to do business,' said bulging eyes. 'My best to young Kansas.'

The other looked puzzled for a moment then smiled. The older man too had a speculative look on his face as he held onto the other's hand rather longer than necessary. Then he too smiled and shook his head as though to dislodge a misplaced thought, let go and took the grip to the jeep where he laid it on the back seat.

By now the loading of the truck was complete and the four diggers stretched their aching limbs in the mouth of the cave and unwound their protecting scarves. Two were ruddy-faced with their exertions, the other two flushed dark beneath their sallow skins.

The first pair went towards the jeep while the

second pair joined the slim man who was securing the tailgate of the truck.

These two looked at each other, exchanged a brief eye signal, then reached for the holsters beneath their arms, drew out automatic pistols, and moved towards the jeep, firing as they walked. The two ruddy-faced diggers took the bullets in their backs and pitched forward on their faces while ahead of them the straw-haired man fell backwards, his eyes popping even further in astonishment under the fillet of blood which wrapped itself around his brow.

One of the gunmen continued to the jeep and leaned into it to retrieve the grip. His companion meanwhile turned back to the truck where the slim man was standing as if paralysed.

'Chiquillo!' he called. *'Recuerdo de Jorge. Adiós!'* And let go a long burst.

The slim man felt a whip of hot pain along his ribcage which sent him spinning like a top behind the truck. The rest of the burst went straight through the mouth of the cave where the bullets ricocheted around the granite walls and up into the high vault, triggering first a rustling ripple, then a squeaking, wing-beating eruption of bats.

The gunman paused, looking up in wonderment as the bats skeined out of their rocky roost and smudged the dark air overhead. So many. Who would have thought there would be so many?

Then as they vanished among the trees he resumed his advance.

But the pause had been long enough for the slim man to reach under the truck and drag down the weapon taped beneath the wheel arch.

He shot the gunman through the leg as he passed by the truck's rear wheel, then through the head as he crashed to the ground.

The second gunman dropped the grip and crouched low with his weapon aimed towards his dying companion.

But the slim man came rolling out of the other side of the truck, and gave himself time to take aim and make sure his first shot found its target.

The second gunman held his crouching position for a moment, then toppled slowly sideways and lay there, gently twitching, his visible eye fixed on the trees' high vault. The slim man approached carefully, one arm wrapped round his bleeding side, and emptied the clip into the watching eye.

Then he sat down on the grip and pulled open his shirt to examine his wound.

It was more painful than life-threatening, flesh laid bare, a rib nicked perhaps, no deeper penetration. But blood was pouring out and by the time he'd bound it up with strips of shirt torn from the dead gunman at his feet, he'd lost a lot of blood.

He opened the grip, took out one of the packets the pop-eyed man had nicked, poured some of the powder into his hand, raised it to his nose and took a long hard sniff.

Then he took out a mobile phone and dialled.

'*Soy yo* . . . *si* . . . I did not think so soon . . . *si* . . .

poco . . . not so wide as a barn door . . . the CP . . . it has to be . . . I am sorry . . . *dos horas* . . . *quizá tres* . . . *si* . . . at the CP . . . *si, bueno* . . . *te quiero* . . . *adiós.'*

He put the phone away and picked up the grip, wincing with pain. As he moved away, he thought he sensed a movement from the vicinity of the jeep and turned with his gun waving menacingly.

All was still. He hadn't the strength for closer investigation. And in any case, his gun was empty.

He resumed his progress to the truck.

Getting the grip into the driver's cab and himself after it was an agony. He sat there for a while, leaning against the wheel. Did something move by the jeep or was it his pain giving false life to this deadly tableau? Certainly in the air above, the bats, reassured by the return of stillness, were flitting back into the mouth of the cave.

He dipped into the grip again, sniffed a little more powder.

Then he switched on the engine, engaged gear, and without a backward glance at the gaping cave, the gloomy lake or the bodies that lay between them, he sent the truck rumbling into the dark tunnel curving away through the crowding trees.

High on the sunlit, windswept Snake Pass which links Lancashire with Yorkshire, Peter Pascoe thought, I'm in love.

Even with a trail of blood running from her nose

over the double hump of her full lips to peter out on her charming chin, she was grin-like-an-idiot-gorgeous.

'You OK?' he said, grinning like an idiot till he realized that in the circumstances this was perhaps not the most appropriate expression.

'Yes, yes,' she said impatiently, dabbing at her nose with a tissue. 'Is this going to take long?'

The driver of her taxi, to whom the question was addressed, looked from the bent and leaking radiator of his vehicle to the jackknifed lorry he had hit and said sarcastically, 'Soon as I repair this and get that shifted, we'll be on our way, luv.'

Pascoe, returning from Manchester over the Snake, had been behind the lorry when it jack-knifed. Simple humanitarian concern had brought him running to see if anyone was hurt, but now his sense of responsibility as a policeman was taking over. He pulled out his mobile, dialled 999 and gave a succinct account of what had happened.

'Better set up traffic diversions way back on both sides,' he said. 'The road's completely blocked till you get something up here to shift the lorry. One injury. Passenger in the taxi banged her nose. Lorry driver probably suffering from shock. Better have an ambulance.'

'Not for me,' said the woman vehemently. 'I'm fine.'

She rose from the verge where she'd been sitting and moved forward on long legs, whose slight unsteadiness only added to their sinuous attraction. She looked as if she purposed to move the lorry single-handed. If it had been sentient, she might have managed it, thought Pascoe.

'Silly cow'd have been all right if she'd put her seat belt on like I told her,' said the taxi driver.

'Perhaps you should have been firmer,' said Pascoe mildly. 'Who is she? Where're you headed?'

No reason why he should have asked or the driver answered these questions, but without his being aware of it, over the years Pascoe had developed a quiet authority of manner which most people found harder to resist than mere assertiveness.

The driver pulled out a docket and said, 'Miss Kelly Cornelius. Manchester Airport. Terminal Three. She's going to miss her plane.'

He spoke with a satisfaction which identified him as one of that happily vanishing species, the Ur-Yorkshireman, beside whom even Andy Dalziel appeared a creature of sweetness and light. Only a hardcore misogynist could take pleasure in anything which caused young Miss Cornelius distress.

And she was distressed. She returned from her examination of the lorry and gave Pascoe a look of such expressive unhappiness, his empathy almost caused him to burst into tears.

'Excuse me,' she said in a melodious voice in which all that was best of American lightness,

Celtic darkness, and English woodnotes wild, conjoined to make sweet moan, 'but your car's on the other side of this, I guess.'

'Yes, I'm on my way home to Mid-Yorkshire,' he said. 'Looks like I'll have to turn around and find another way.'

'That's what I thought you'd do,' she said, her voice breathless with delight, as if he'd just confirmed her estimate of his intellectual brilliance. 'And I was wondering, I know it's quite a long way back, but how would you feel about taking me to Manchester Airport? I hate to be a nuisance, but you see, I've got this plane to catch, and if I miss it, I don't know what I'll do.'

Tears brimmed her big dark eyes. Pascoe could imagine their salty taste on his tongue. What she was asking was of course impossible, but (as he absolutely intended to tell Ellie later when he cleansed his conscience by laundering his prurient thoughts in her sight) it was flattering to be asked.

He said, 'I'm sorry, but my wife's expecting me.'

'You could ring her. You've got a phone,' she said with tremulous appeal. 'I'd be truly, deeply, madly grateful.'

This was breathtaking, in every sense.

He said, 'Surely there'll be another plane. Where are you going anyway?'

Silly question. It implied negotiation.

There was just the hint of a hesitation before she answered, 'Corfu. It's my holiday, first for years.

11

And it's a holiday charter, so if I miss it, there won't be much chance of getting on another, they're all so crowded this time of year. And I'm meeting my sister and her little boy at the airport, and she's disabled and won't get on the plane without me, so it'll be all our holidays ruined. Please.'

Suddenly he knew he was going to do it. All right, it was crazy, but he was going to have to go back all the way to Glossop anyway and the airport wasn't much further, well, not *very* much further . . .

He said, 'I'll need to phone my wife.'

'That's marvellous. Oh, thank you, thank you!'

She gave him a smile which made all things seem easy – the drive back, the phone call to Ellie, everything – then dived into the taxi and emerged with a small leather case like a pilot's flight bag.

Travelling light, thought Pascoe as he stepped back to get some privacy for his call home. The woman was now talking to the taxi driver and presumably paying him off. There seemed to be some disagreement. Pascoe guessed the driver was demanding the full agreed fare on the grounds that it wasn't his fault he hadn't got her all the way to Terminal 3.

Terminal 3.

Last time he'd flown out of Manchester, Terminal 3 had been for British Airways and domestic flights only.

You couldn't fly charter to Corfu from there.

Perhaps the driver had made a mistake.

Or perhaps things had changed at Manchester in the past six months.

But now he was recalling the slight hesitancy before the sob story. And would a young woman on holiday really travel so light . . . ?

Pascoe, he said to himself, you're developing a nasty suspicious policeman's mind.

He turned away and began to punch buttons on his phone.

When it was answered he identified himself, talked for a while, then waited.

In the distance he heard the wail of sirens approaching.

A voice spoke in his ear. He listened, asked a couple of questions, then rang off.

When he turned, Kelly Cornelius was standing by the taxi, smiling expectantly at him. A police car pulled up onto the verge beside him. An ambulance wasn't far behind.

As the driver of the police car opened his door to get out, Pascoe stooped to him. Screened by the car, he pulled out his ID, showed it to the uniformed constable and spoke urgently.

Then he straightened up, waved apologetically to the waiting woman, flourishing his phone as if to say he hadn't been able to get through before.

He began to dial again, watching as the policemen went across to the taxi and started talking to the driver and the woman.

'Hi,' said Pascoe. 'It's me. Yes, I'm on my way but there's been an accident . . . no, I'm not involved but I am stuck, the road's blocked, and I'm going to have to divert . . . yeah, take me when I come . . . give Rosie a kiss . . . how's she been today? . . . yes, I know, it's early days . . . it'll be OK, I promise . . . love you . . . 'bye.'

He switched off and went back to the taxi.

'What the hell do you mean, I can't go?' the young woman was demanding. Anger like injury did nothing to detract from her beauty.

'Sorry, miss,' said the policeman stolidly. 'Can't let you leave the scene of an accident where someone's been injured.'

'But I'm the one who's been injured so if I say it doesn't matter . . .'

'Doesn't work like that,' said the policeman. 'Need to get you checked out at hospital. There may be claims. Also you're a witness. We'll need a statement.'

'But I've got a plane to catch.' Her gaze met Pascoe's. 'Corfu. It's my holiday.'

A sharp intake of breath from the policeman.

'Certainly can't let you leave the country, miss, that's definite,' he said. 'Here's the ambulance lads now. Why not let them give you the once-over while I talk to these other gents?'

Pascoe caught her eye and shrugged helplessly. She looked back at him, her face (still beautiful) now ravaged with shock and betrayal, as Andromeda might have looked if Perseus, on point of rescuing her from the ravening dragon, had suddenly remembered a previous appointment.

'Well, if you're done with me, Officer, I think I'd better start finding another route home,' he said, looking away, unable to bear that devastatingly devastated expression.

The constable said, 'Right, sir. We've got your name in case we need to be in touch. Goodbye now.'

As he made his way back to his car, Pascoe reflected on the paradox that now he felt much more guilty about Kelly Cornelius than he had before, when it had just been a question of simple reflexive desire.

Women, he thought as he sat in his car and put the necessary enquiries in train. *Women*! All of them queens of discord, blessed with the power even on the slightest acquaintance to get in a man's mind and divide and rule. Look at him now, sitting here when he should be heading home, checking out his vague suspicions like a good professional, uncertain whether he would be bothering if he hadn't felt so ready to submit to this lovely creature's control, with part of him hoping even as he started the process that he was going to come out of this looking a real dickhead.

Women. How come they didn't rule the universe?

COMFORT BLANKET

Arms and the Men they sang, who played at Troy
Until they broke it like a spoiled child's Toy
Then sailed away, the Winners heading home,
The Losers to a new Play-pen called Rome.

Behind, like Garbage from their vessels flung,
– Submiss, submerged, but certainly not sung –
A wake of Women trailed in long Parade,
The reft, the raped, the slaughtered, the betrayed.
Oh, Shame! that so few sagas celebrate
Their Pain, their Perils, their no less moving Fate!

But mine won't either, for why should it when
The proper Study of Mendacity is MEN?

BOOK ONE

'Your pretty daughter,' she said, 'starts to hear of such things. Yet,' looking full upon her, 'you may be sure that there are men and women already on their road, who have their business to do with *you*, and who will do it. Of a certainty they will do it. They may be coming hundreds, thousands, of miles over the sea there; they may be close at hand now; they may be coming, for anything you know, or anything you can do to prevent it, from the vilest sweepings of this very town.'

CHARLES DICKENS: *Little Dorrit*

i

spelt from Sibyl's leaves

Eleanor Soper . . .

The little patch of blue I can see through the high round window is probably the sky, but it could just as well be a piece of blue backcloth or a painted flat.

licks up the blood from the square where a riot
   has been . . .

Distantly I hear a clatter of hooves. They're changing guard at . . . I've heard them do it thousands of times. But hearing's as far as it goes. They could be mere sound effects, played on tape. You don't take anything on trust in this business. Not even your friends. Especially not them.
   I who know everything knew nothing till I knew that.

what does it mean? . . .

The only unquestionable reality lies in the machine.

But while reality hardly changes at all, the machine has changed a lot. It grows young as I grow old.

Shall I like my namesake grow old forever?

My namesake, I say. After so long usage, am I beginning to believe as so many of the young ones clearly believe that my name really is Sibyl? Strange that the name my parents gave me also labelled me as a woman of magic, but an enchantress as well as a seer. Morgan. Morgan Meredith. Morgan le Fay, as Gaw used to call me in the days of his enchantment.

But now my enchanting days are over. And it was Gaw who rechristened me when he saw that I had no magic to counter the sickness in my blood.

A wise man hides his mistakes in plain sight, then over long time slowly corrects them.

My dear old friend Gawain Clovis Sempernel is a wise man. No one would deny it. Not if they've any sense.

Aroynt thee, hag. Ripeness is all. And I have work to do.

When I first took on my sacred office, the machine loomed monumentally, like a Victorian family tomb. Thirty years on, it's smaller than an infant's casket, leaving plenty of room on the narrow tabletop for my flask and mug, and also my inhaler and pill dispenser, though generally I keep these hidden.

Sounds silly when you're in a wheelchair, but I was brought up to believe you don't advertise your frailties.

That's a lesson a lot of folk never learn, which is why so many of them end up frozen in my electronic casket where there's always room for plenty more.

If I wanted I could ask it to tell me exactly how many people had passed through my hands, or rather my fingertips, for that's the closest I get to actually handling people. But I don't bother. This isn't about statistics, this is about individuals.

Eleanor Soper . . .

My casket is also an incubator. Here they make their first appearance, often looking completely helpless and harmless. But, oh, how quickly they grow, and I oversee their progress with an almost parental pride as their details accumulate and their files fatten out.

Some live up to their promise. (By which I mean threat!)

Others, apparently, change direction completely. Such converts I always regard with grave suspicion, even if – especially if – they make it to the very top. They're either faking it, in which case we're ready for them. Or they're genuine, which means the contents of these files could be a serious embarrassment.

It's always nice to know you can embarrass your masters.

But the great majority merely fade away, become ghosts of their vibrant young selves.

married a cop, had a kid, didn't march any
   more . . .
what was it for?

Let's take a look at your protesting career, Eleanor Pascoe née Soper.

Amnesty – member, non-active; *Anti-Fascist Action* – lapsed; *Campaign for Nuclear Disarmament* – lapsed; *Gay Rights* – lapsed; *Graduates Against God* – lapsed; *Greenpeace* – member, non-active; *Labour Party* – member, non-active; *Liberata Trust* – member, active; *Quis Custodiet?* – lapsed; *Third World United* – lapsed; *Women's Rights Action Group* – lapsed; *World Socialist Alliance* – lapsed.

Once you squawked so loud in your incubator, Eleanor, now you rest so quiet.

Gaw Sempernel (let no dog bark) says there is nothing so suspicious as silence. Must have watched a lot of cowboy films in his youth. *It's quiet out there, Gaw . . . too damn quiet!*

Certainly neither sound nor silence gets you out of my casket. Once inside, there you stay forever. And if your presence is ever needed, you can be conjured up in a trice, like the wraiths of the classical underworld, which, as my classically educated Gawain likes to remind me, were summoned to appear and to speak by the smell and the taste of fresh blood.

For machines may change, and fashions change, and human flesh, God help us, changes most inevitably of all.

But some people, *my* people, have at their hearts something which refuses to change, despite all that life shows them by way of contra-evidence. Perhaps it is a genetic weakness. Certainly, once established, like the common cold, no one has yet found a way of eradicating it.

Which is why I, practising what I preach, have demonstrated to the world (or that section of it which shares this remote and lonely building in the heart of this populous city), that there is life after death by staying in gainful employment all these years, Sibyl the Sibyl, sitting here in my solitary cell, hung high in my lonely cage, laying the bodies out neatly in my electronic casket, and, when necessary, conjuring them back to life.

My poor benighted ghosts scenting blood once more . . .

Like Eleanor Soper.

All these looney people, where do they all come from?
All these looney people, where do they all belong?

ii

who's that knocking at my door?

*. . . why should it, when
The proper study of mendacity is MEN?*

Chapter 1

It was a dark and stormy night.

Now, why has that gone down in the annals as the archetype of the rotten opening? she wondered. It's not much different from *It was a bright cold day in April*, though, fair do's, the bit about the clocks striking thirteen grabs the attention. Or how about *There was no possibility of taking a walk that day*, with all the stuff about the weather that follows? And even Homer's jam-packed with meteorology. OK, so what follows in every case is a lot better book than *Paul Clifford*, but even if we stick to the same author, surely the dark and stormy stuff isn't in the same league as the opening of *The Last Days of Pompeii* (which, interestingly, I found on Andy

Dalziel's bedside table when I used a search for the loo as an excuse to do a bit of nebbing! Riddle me that, my Trinity scholar!).

How does it go? '*Ho, Diomed, well met! Do you sup with Glaucus tonight?*' said a young man of small stature, who wore his tunic in the loose and effeminate folds which proved him to be a gentleman and a coxcomb. Now that is positively risible, while the dark and stormy night is simply a cliché which, like all clichés, was at its creation bright new coin.

So up yours, all you superior bastards who get on the media chat shows. I'm sticking with it!

It was a dark and stormy night. The wind was blowing off the sea and the guard commander bowed into it with his cloak wrapped around his face as he left the shelter of the grove and began to clamber up to the headland.

The darkness was deep but not total. There was salt and spume in the wind giving it a ghostly visibility, and now a huge flock of white sea birds riding the blast went screeching by only a few feet over his head.

The superstitious fools huddled round their fires in the camp below would probably take them as an omen and argue over which god was telling them what and pour out enough libations to get the whole of Olympus pissed. But the commander didn't even flinch.

As he neared the crest of the headland, he

screwed up his eyes and peered ahead, looking for a darker outline against the black sky which should show where the wind wrapped itself around the sentry. There'd been grumblings among the weary crewmen when he'd insisted on posting a full contingent of perimeter guards. In the forty-eight hours since they made landfall, they'd found no sign of human habitation, and with the storm which had made them run for shelter blowing as hard as ever, the threat of a seaborne attack seemed negligible. With the democracy of shared hardship, they'd even appealed over his head to the Prince.

'So you feel safe?' he'd said. 'Is that more safe or less safe than when you saw the Greek ships sail away?'

That had shut them up. But the commander had resolved to make the rounds himself to check that none of the posted sentries, feeling secure in the pseudo-isolation of the storm, had opted for comfort rather than watch.

And it seemed his distrust was justified. His keen gaze found no sign of any human figure on the skyline. Then a small movement at ground level caught his straining eyes. Cautiously he advanced. The movement again. And now he could make out the figure of a man stretched out on his stomach right at the cliff's edge.

Silently he drew his sword and moved closer. If the idle bastard had fallen asleep he was in for a painful reveille. But when he was only a pace away, his foot kicked a stone and the sentry's head turned and their eyes met.

Far from showing alarm, the man looked relieved. He laid a finger over his lips, then motioned to the commander to join him prostrate.

When they were side by side, the sentry put his mouth to his ear and said, 'I think there's someone down there, Commander.'

It didn't seem likely, but this was a battle-scarred veteran who'd spent ten years patrolling the Wall, not some fresh-faced kid who saw a bear in every bush.

Cautiously he wriggled forward till his head was over the edge and looked down.

He knew from memory that the rocky cliff fell sheer for at least eighty feet down to a tiny shingly cove, but now it was like looking into hellmouth, where Pyriphlegethon's burning waves drive their phosphorescent crests deep into the darkness of woeful Acheron.

Nothing could live down there, nothing that still had dependence on light and air anyway, and he was moving back to give the sentry a tongue-lashing when suddenly the wind tore a huge hole in the cloud cover and a full moon lit up the scene like a thousand lanterns.

Now he saw, though he could hardly believe what he saw.

The waves had momentarily retreated to reveal the figure of a man crawling out of the sea. Then the gale sent its next wall of water rushing forward *and the figure was buried beneath it. Impossible to survive, he thought. But when the sea receded, it was still there, hands and feet dug deep into the shingle. And in the few seconds of respite given by the withdrawing waters, the man scrambled forward another couple of feet before sinking his anchors once again.*

Sometimes the suction of the retreating waves was too strong, or his anchorage was too shallow, and the recumbent body was drawn back the full length of its advance. But always when it seemed certain that the ocean must have driven deep into his lungs, or the razor-edged shingle must have ripped his naked chest wide open, the figure pushed itself forward once more.

'He'll never make it,' said the sentry with utter assurance.

The guard commander watched a little while longer then said, 'Six to four he does. In gold.'

The veteran looked down at the sea which now seemed to be clutching at the body on the beach with a supernatural fury. It looked like a sure-fire bet, but he had a lot of respect for the commander's judgement.

'Silver,' he compromised.

They settled to watch.

It took another half-hour for the commander to win his bet, but finally the crawling man had dragged himself right up to the foot of the cliff where a couple of huge boulders resting on the beach formed a protective wall against which the sea dashed its mountainous missiles in vain. For a while he lay there, still immersed in water from time to time, but no longer at risk of being either beaten flat or dragged back into the depths. Then, just when the sentry was hoping he might claim victory in the bet by reason of the man's death, he sat upright.

'That sod must be made of bronze and bear hide,' said the sentry with reluctant admiration. 'What the fuck's he doing now?'

For the figure on the beach had pushed himself to his feet, and as the waters drew back, he emerged from his rocky refuge and, to the observers' amazement, began a kind of lumbering dance, following the receding waves, then backpedalling like mad as they drove forward once more. And all the while he was gesticulating, sometimes putting his left hand in the crook of his right elbow and thrusting his right fist into the air, sometimes putting both his thumbs into his mouth, then pulling them out with great force and stabbing his forefingers seawards, and shouting.

'I've seen that before,' said the sentry. 'That's what them bastards used to do under the Wall.'

'Hush! I'm trying to hear what he's saying,' said the commander.

As if in response, the wind fell for a moment and the sea drew back to its furthest point yet, still pursued by the dancing man whose shouts now drifted clearly up the cliff face.

'Up yours, old man!' he yelled. 'Call yourself

earthshaker? You couldn't shake your dick at a pisspot! So what are you going to do now, you watery old git? Ha ha! Right up yours!'

'You're right. He's a Greek,' said the commander.

'Better still, he's a dead Greek,' said the veteran with some satisfaction.

For in his growing boldness, the dancing man had allowed himself to be lured far away from his protective wall by this moment of comparative calm, so when the ocean suddenly exploded before him, he had no hope of getting back to safety. An avalanche of water far greater than anything before descended on him, driving him to the ground, then burying him deep. And at the same time the renewed fury of the wind sewed up the rent in the cloud and darkness fell.

'If he was talking to who I think he was talking to, he was a right idiot,' said the sentry piously. 'You gotta give the gods respect else they'll chew you up and spit you out.'

The commander smiled.

'Let's see,' he said.

They didn't have long to wait. As though the storm also wanted to look at the results of its latest onslaught, it tore aside the clouds once more.

'Well, bull my bollocks and call me Zeus!' exclaimed the sentry, his recent piety completely forgotten.

There he was again, almost back where he'd started but still alive. Once more he started to struggle back over the beach. Only now as the waves retreated, they didn't leave any area of visible shingle but a foot or so of water. This made the anchoring process much more difficult, but at the same time, by permitting the man to take a couple of swimming strokes with his muscular arms, it speeded his return to the safety of the boulders. Here he squatted, his head slumped on his broad chest which rose and fell as he drew in great breaths of damp air.

'He's game,' said the sentry grudgingly. 'Got to give him that. But he's not out of trouble yet. How high do you reckon the tide comes in here, Commander?'

'Normally? I think it would just about reach the bottom of the cliff, a foot up at its highest. But this isn't normal. I don't know whether it's a very angry god or just very bad weather, but I'd say the way this wind's blowing the sea in, it will be thirty feet up the cliff face in an hour.'

'So that really is it,' said the sentry with some satisfaction.

'Not necessarily. He can climb.'

'Up that rock face? Get on! It's smooth and it's sheer and there's an overhang at the top. I wouldn't fancy my chances there at my peak on a fine day, and that old bugger must be completely knackered.'

'Double or quits on what you owe?' said the commander casually.

The sentry turned his head to look at the officer's

profile, but it was as blank and unreadable as the cliff face, and not a lot more attractive either.

Then he looked down. The man was up to his knees in water already.

'Done,' said the sentry.

Below, the Greek was examining the cliff face. His features were undiscernible through a heavy tangle of beard, but even at this distance they could see the eyes shining brightly in the reflection of the moonlight. He rubbed his hands vigorously against the remnants of his robe in what had to be a vain attempt to get them dry, then he reached up and began to climb.

He got about three feet above the water level before he lost his grip and slithered back down. Three more times he tried, three more times he fell. And each time he hit the water, it was higher than before.

'Looks like we're quits, Commander,' said the sentry.

'Maybe.'

'What's the silly old sod doing now?'

The silly old sod was ripping the sleeves off his tattered robe, and tying them to form a rough sack which he hung on a jag of rock protruding from one of his protective boulders. Next he knelt down in the water facing the boulder, took a deep breath, and plunged his head beneath the surface. When he emerged, he tossed what looked like a stone into the dangling sack. Again and again he did this.

'I know,' said the sentry. 'He's digging a tunnel.'

He laughed raucously at his own wit till the guard commander said coldly, 'Shut up. You might learn something.'

The sentry stopped laughing. Shared hardship might relax the bonds of discipline slightly, but he and his comrades knew just how far they could go.

Finally the Greek stood upright once more, slung the sack around his neck, put both hands into it, then reached up the cliff face. He seemed to lean against it for a long moment, almost as if he were praying. Then he began to climb again.

The sentry waited for him to fall. But he didn't. From time to time he dipped into his sack, then reached up again in search of another handhold. As on the beach, progress was painfully slow, and occasionally one of his holds failed and he'd slip back a little, but still he kept coming.

'How in the name of Zeus is he doing that?' said the sentry. 'It's just not possible!'

'Molluscs,' said the commander.

'No need to be like that, sir,' said the sentry resentfully. 'I was only asking.'

'I said, molluscs. Clams, mussels, oysters, anything he could find. He's holding them against the wall till their suckers take a hold. Then he uses them as a ladder.'

'Clams, you say? Them things couldn't hold a man, surely?'

'Three might. He only moves one foot or hand at a time. And he's using any holds he can find in the rock face too. He's a truly ingenious fellow.'

The sentry shook his head in reluctant admiration. As if taking this as confirmation that their prey was close to escaping them, the waves hurled themselves with renewed force against the cliff, breaking over the climbing man and spraying flakes of spume over the watchers above.

A harsh grating noise reached them also.

'The bugger's laughing!' said the sentry.

'Of course he's laughing. He wants the cliff face to be as wet as possible. That's the way the molluscs like it. The wetter the surface, the tighter their grip.'

The wind closed the gap in the clouds once more. This, coupled with the fact that the climber was now approaching the overhang, took him out of the watchers' sight. The sentry pushed himself back from the edge, squatted to his haunches and drew his sword.

'Let's see if he's still laughing when he sticks his head over the top and I cut his throat,' he said, testing the metal's edge with his thumb.

The guard commander said nothing but squatted beside him. They had to lean into the wind to avoid being blown backwards and from time to time their faces were lashed with salt water as the ocean rose to new heights of fury in its efforts to wash the climber free.

Minutes passed. The watchers didn't move. They

had had years to learn that patience too is one of the great military arts.

Finally the sentry's face began to show his suspicion that the sea must after all have won its battle against the climbing Greek. He glanced at the guard commander. But his was a face as jagged and pocked as a city wall after long siege, and quite unreadable at the best of times, so the sentry didn't risk speaking and returned to his watch.

A few moments later he was glad of his self-restraint. A new sound drifted up the cliff face amidst the lash of water and howl of wind. It was the noise of laboured breathing, getting closer.

The sentry began to smile in happy anticipation. He decided not just to slit the throat but to have a go at taking the whole head off. It would be fun to go back into the camp and toss it down among his half-waking comrades and say negligently, 'Got myself another Greek while you idle sods were sleeping.'

The breathing was loud now. The sentry moved his position so that he was right above it. An arm like a small tree trunk was swung up to rest on the edge of the cliff, and then a shag of salt-caked hair appeared, and finally the man's head came fully into view and a pair of deep-sunk, intensely blue eyes took in the waiting men.

'How do, chuck,' said the Greek.

The sentry rocked forward on his toes and shot out his left hand to grab the grizzled hair. But

*quick as he moved, the Greek was quicker. His
other hand came into view, grasping a large jagged
clamshell. It snaked out almost faster than the eye
could follow, and the next moment the sentry's left
wrist was slit through to the bone.*

*He fell backward, shrieking. His right hand
released his sword as he grasped the gaping wound
to staunch the spurting blood. The Greek dropped
the shell and reached out to pick up the fallen
weapon. Then a heavy-shod foot crashed down on
his forearm and pinned it to the ground.*

*He looked up at the unreadably rugged face of
the guard commander and smiled through his
tangle of beard.*

*'Thanks, chuck,' he said. 'Saved me from a
nasty fall.'*

*'Kill the bastard, Commander,' urged the ashen-
faced sentry. 'Chop his fucking arm right off!'*

*The commander was aware of the blue eyes fixed
quizzically on his face as he debated the matter.*

*'Not yet,' he said finally. 'Not till we know if
there are any more of his kind about. Besides,
the men need cheering up after what's happened
recently, and I reckon a clever old Greek like this
will take a long time dying.'*

*'Long as you like, Captain,' said the Greek. 'I'm
in no hurry whatsoever. I'll*

'Shit,' said Ellie Pascoe.

Through the open window of the boxroom which

she refused to dignify with the name study she had heard a car turning into their short drive.

She finished reading, *take as long as ever you like.'*, pressed *Save* to preserve her corrections and went to the window.

A man and a woman were getting out of the car and heading for the front door.

'Hello,' called Ellie.

This voice from above made them start like guilty things surprised, and the woman dropped her car keys.

Perhaps they think it's the voice of God, thought Ellie.

Or perhaps (one thought leading to another) they think they *are* the voice of God.

'If you're Witnesses,' she called, 'I think I should tell you we're all communist satanists here. I'll be happy to send you some of *our* literature.'

'Mrs Pascoe?' said the woman. 'Mrs Ellie Pascoe?'

She didn't look like a Witness. And Witnesses didn't drive big BMWs.

A pair of assertions as unsupported as a Hottentot's tits (she plucked the phrase from her collection of Andy Dalziel memorabilia), but evidence is what we look for when intuition fails (one of her constabulary-baiting own).

'Hang on. I'll come down,' she said.

By the time she got downstairs and opened the front door, the couple had recovered their composure. Now they just looked concerned.

'Mrs Pascoe?' said the man, who was slim, thirtyish, not bad-looking and wearing a rather nice Prince of Wales check suit which looked like it had been cut in Savile Row. Would look even nicer on Peter. 'You are Mrs Pascoe?'

'I thought we'd established that.'

'My name's Jim Westcombe. I'm with the council's Education Welfare Department. It's about your daughter, Rose. She's at Edengrove Junior, isn't she?'

'Yes, but not today. I mean, it's their end-of-term trip to Tegley Hall Theme Park . . . look, what's this about?' Ellie demanded.

The man and woman looked at each other, then the man went on, 'Honestly, there's nothing to worry about, she's fine, you're not to worry, really . . .'

'*What*?'

There are few things more worrying to a mother than being told not to worry, especially a mother who a few short weeks ago was sitting by a hospital bed, not knowing if her child was going to recover from meningitis or not.

The woman gave her a look which combined empathy of her feelings and exasperation at her companion's heavy-handedness.

'Jim, shut up,' she said. 'Mrs Pascoe, the coach taking the children to Tegley has broken down. There's a replacement coach on the way, but it seems your little girl wasn't feeling too well and the head teacher thought it best to make arrangements to get her home, only when he tried to ring you he couldn't get through . . .'

Ellie turned and grabbed the hall phone. It was dead. In the mirror hanging above the phone, she saw an unrecognizably pale face whose pallor shone through her summer tan like a corpse-light through muslin. This was it. This was the punishment she deserved. She had brought it on herself . . . worse . . . on Rosie . . . on Peter . . .

'. . . so he tried your husband but he wasn't available, so then he rang into the Education office and as Jim and I were coming out this way and would be passing your road end, we said we'd call and check if you were in.'

'Oh God,' said Ellie.

I'm confused, she thought. I'm not hearing properly.

She leaned against the door frame to steady herself and the woman reached forward to rest her hand on Ellie's arm and said, 'Really, it's OK, Mrs Pascoe. You know how it is, end of term, kids getting excited, rushing around like mad. I've got two myself, I know how they can keep us frightened, believe me. It's just a matter of getting out there to pick the little girl up. Have you got your car here? Jim can go with you, he knows where the breakdown happened. I can't come myself, I'm afraid. I've got an urgent appointment, but Jim can spare a couple of hours, can't you, Jim? He'll even drive if you don't feel up to it.'

'Surely,' said the man. 'No problem at all. Let's

get started, shall we? Sooner we're on the way, sooner you can get your little girl home.'

Ellie took a deep breath. It wasn't enough. She took another. It was like squirting oil onto a piece of rusty machinery. She could almost hear the gears of her mind starting to grate against each other as she reviewed everything that had been said to her.

She said, 'Sorry. This has knocked me out. I'm not usually so slow. It was just a bit of a shock. I thought you were trying to tell me there's been an accident . . .'

'Nothing like that,' said the woman. 'Really.'

'And did you talk to Mr Johnson, the head, yourself? You're sure he said it was nothing to worry about?'

'Yes, I spoke direct with Mr Johnson,' said the woman firmly. 'Just a tummy bug, he reckoned. But she really wants to be home rather than bumping around on a bus all day.'

'And if it was anything more serious, the sooner we get out there, the better, eh?' said the man heartily.

'Jim, please!' said the woman reprimandingly.

'No, it's OK,' said Ellie, stepping forward and smiling at the man. 'It's always best to be ready for the worst. Are you ready, Mr Westcombe?'

Then she brought her knee up as hard as she could between his legs.

It was good to see his face drain pale as her own.

Now she swung her right arm round hard at the woman's neck. The blow would probably have felled her, but she was quick and ducked low, though not low enough to avoid all contact. Ellie's hand caught her on the temple just above the right eye with enough force to send her reeling back into the *Climbing Pompon de Paris* growing up the pillar to the left of the front porch.

When Ellie had bought it, Peter had grumbled that nowadays it was surely possible to get a less prickly, more user-friendly rose, but she'd been unrepentant. The tiny pink pompom blossoms had been her father's favourite before Alzheimer's robbed him of even that. And now, as she heard the woman scream, Ellie knew she'd always love the thorns too.

She retreated over her threshold and slammed the door shut. Ramming the bolts home, she became aware of pain in her right wrist, and as she slid to the floor with her back against the door, in her right knee too. She sat there, breathing deep, as if she'd just run a hundred metres up a steep hill. Outside she heard car doors shut and an engine start up and reverse away.

She sat there till there was nothing to hear but her own harsh breathing, and when that too finally faded, she rose and went to an upstairs window and looked down at the empty driveway.

Whatever had happened was over. So why did she feel it had just begun?

41

iii

memories are made of this

'And you kneed him in the balls?' said Detective Superintendent Andy Dalziel gleefully. 'Well done, lass.'

'Sure. Except they must have been made of brass,' said Ellie, who was sitting sideways on a sofa with a large pack of frozen oven chips draped over her knee and a smaller pack of fish fingers pressed against her wrist. Having a non-gourmet kid sometimes came in useful. 'Have they got hold of Peter yet?'

This was aimed at Detective Sergeant Edgar Wield who'd just entered the room, carrying a mobile phone.

'No, but they're still there, they've located the coach. I've sent Seymour down there. He'll spot them eventually, but Tegley Hall Theme Park's a big place. And you said you didn't want him paged over the speakers.'

'No,' said Ellie firmly. 'Softly, softly. I don't want him getting the kind of shock I had.'

The two detectives exchanged glances, then Dalziel said, 'Talking of which, lass, as you won't let us take you to the quackery, I've got Wieldy here to organize the quack to come to you. And afore you start sounding off again, I reckon you could do with a bit more than fish and chips for them joints of yours. Also, I don't like your colour.'

'And I bet you've arrested people for less than that. Sorry, Andy. That was stupid. I'm still feeling so angry. As for my colour, you should have seen me half an hour ago. I was grey. Not as grey as that bastard, though, after I'd kneed him.'

'Aye, that's where we'd got to, wasn't it?'

'Second time round!'

'Aye, well. You were a bit excitable, first time.'

'Hysterical, you mean?'

'Nay, lass. You know me, if I'd meant hysterical, I'd have said it. Wieldy, you're lurking. Summat else?'

'Checked with the Education Department. No one there called Westcombe or fitting the descriptions.'

'Christ, you're checking up on me!' exclaimed Ellie angrily. 'You think maybe I just lose it when I'm confronted by stupid officials? Well, you could be about to find out you're right.'

Wield went on as if she hadn't spoken. 'The car's number. How sure are you you got it right?'

'As sure as I could be considering it was going through my mind these two wanted to abduct me in order to do God knows what to me. So if I got a figure wrong, it wouldn't be surprising, would it? But it was definitely a dark-blue BMW, one of the big ones. Look, why're you wasting time grilling me like this? I scribbled everything I could remember down soon as I could. Christ, I haven't been married to the Force all these years without picking up some of your nasty habits. Why aren't you out there looking for these people?'

'You'd be surprised how often I get asked that question and I've not worked out a smart answer yet,' said Dalziel. 'Can't even say it's raining. Why're you asking about the car, Wieldy?'

'Did a check, sir. And according to Swansea, what Ellie gave us isn't a number in use.'

'False plates then,' said Dalziel. 'But try the obvious variations just in case.'

'Yes, sir. By the way, phone wire was shorted with a pin where it goes into the hall window. Pull it out, it should be OK, but we won't touch it till Forensic's finished out there. Oh, and Novello's here.'

'Ivor? Good. Send her in.'

'Hang about,' said Ellie. 'If you're thinking I need a friendly female copper to unburden my heart to . . .'

'Nay. I brought her for the strip search but I'll do it if you like,' said Dalziel.

Wield made for the door.

Ellie said, 'Wieldy, sorry I snapped at you. I think I may still be a bit . . . excitable.'

The sergeant's generally inscrutable features

which, in Dalziel's words, were knobbly enough to make a pineapple look like a pippin, smoothed momentarily into a warm smile, and he said, 'I'll let you know soon as we get a hold of Pete.'

'By God,' said Dalziel after the sergeant had gone. 'Was that a smile, or has he got toothache? Nearest yon bugger ever came to cracking his face at me was the time I fell into the swimming pool at the mayor's reception. Oh aye. I see you remember that too.'

A smile had touched Ellie's lips, and she forced it to broaden as she saw the Fat Man observing her closely. Anything was better than having a womanly weep in front of Andy Dalziel. And even more, in front of Detective Constable Shirley Novello, who had just slipped into the room. Five-four, sturdy frame, minimum make-up, dark-brown hair neat but nothing fancy, baggy sweatshirt and matching slacks, she should have been two steps from invisible, which was presumably her intention. Down-dressing did not deceive Ellie Pascoe's expert eye, however. She'd heard her husband talk a little too appreciatively of the girl's professional qualities, and she saw the way even Fat Andy's spirits perked up a notch or two at her entry. This was definitely one to watch.

'You going to make an old man happy, lass?' said Dalziel.

'Don't think so, sir. Just a first take on house-to-house. We've got two people who noticed the BMW. Confirmation of colour, but nothing extra on the numberplate. One of them thought it had an unusually long aerial compared with her husband's car, which is the same model.'

'Well-heeled neighbours you've got, Ellie,' said the Fat Man. 'Mebbe we're paying Pete too much. That it, Ivor?'

'Except for an old lady lives at the corner, towards town, that is, says she looked out to see what all the fuss was when she heard the sirens and saw a car doing a three-point turn and going back the way it came. Metallic-blue, sounds like a Golf. Driver looked swarthy and sinister, she says.'

'Watch a lot of telly, does she? Ivor, it's what happened before we came that I'm interested in. Afterwards, any poor sod driving along and see-ing the street full of flashing fuzz is going to find another route, specially if he's had a swift snort or two at a business meeting.'

The notion was suggestive. Ellie looked long-ingly at the bottle of Scotch which the Fat Man had dug out as soon as he arrived. At the time it had seemed virtuously sensible to quote what her first aid course said about avoiding alcohol in cases of shock, but now it seemed merely prig-gish.

She said, 'OK, Andy. Let's do it one more time. Then I don't care if it brings on complete amnesia, I'm going to have that drink you prescribed.'

'I'm feeling better already,' said Dalziel. 'No, Ivor, don't sneak off. Got your short stubby pencil ready? I want you taking notes. Everything, not just what you think's important, OK?'

'Sir,' said Novello.

Her eyes met Ellie Pascoe's and she gave a little smile. All she got in return was a small frown. Confirming what she'd felt on their previous few meetings, that La Pascoe didn't much like her. Couldn't blame her, the WDC thought complacently. When I'm her age, I've no intention of liking good-looking women ten years my junior who work with my husband. Not that her own husband, if she ever bothered, would be anything like Chief Inspector Pascoe. It would probably be a comfort to Ellie Pascoe to know that her fantasies featured chunky, hairy men on surf-pounded beaches, not slim, nice-mannered introverts who would feel it necessary to buy you a decent French meal before checking into a good four-star hotel. But it was not a comfort she was about to offer.

The Great God Dalziel was speaking.

'Right, lass. One more time. You were really taken in at first?'

'Damn right I was. All I could think was, not again, oh God, it's not all happening again. You know, Rosie in hospital, me camping out there, all the fears . . .'

The memory of that time was still so powerful, it had the therapeutic effect of reducing her present aftershock to manageable size, and she went on more strongly, 'She'd only gone back to school for this final week before the summer hols . . . she insisted, and you know Rosie, when she makes up her mind . . .'

'Can't think who she takes after,' said Dalziel. 'Wanted to see all her mates, did she? And not miss this end-of-term outing.'

'Both of those. Also to get out from under me, I suspect.'

'Eh?'

Ellie said, 'Andy, I'm ready for that drink now. Please.'

She took the proffered tumbler and said scornfully, 'That wouldn't drown a tall gnat. Cheers.'

It went down in one. Dalziel, who'd poured himself a good three inches, poured her another millimetre.

'God Almighty, man! And it's not even your whisky,' she said.

'Not my stomach either,' said Dalziel. 'You said something about Rosie getting out from under you. Never had you down as the clinging-mother type.'

'No? Perhaps not.'

She brooded on this for a moment, glanced at Novello, then, with an effort at matter-of-factness, went on, 'Since we got her back, after the meningitis, I've hardly been able to bear letting her out of my sight. She goes in the garden to play and two minutes later I have a panic attack. I think in the end I just began to get on her nerves, so school seemed a desirable alternative.'

'Nay, you know what kids are like about missing things . . .'

'The trip to Tegley Hall, you mean? Well, there's another thing. They invite any parents who feel like giving a hand to go along. It's a big responsibility, ferrying that number of kids around somewhere like that. I was going to go, but last night Rosie suddenly said, "Why can't Daddy go? Miss Martindale says it doesn't just have to be mummies." Peter, bless his heart, said, why not? He'd like nothing better than a day in the company of his daughter and a hundred other kids. And he rang you and you kindly said that considering how hard you'd been working him for the past hundred years or so, he was long overdue a bit of time off . . .'

'Don't recollect them as my exact words,' said Dalziel.

'Peter is one of nature's paraphrasers. So, nothing for me to do but say, "Great. It'll give me the chance to get on with some work," and smile through my tears.'

'So you worried?'

'Of course I worried. I worried about what kind of mother I was. And I worried about them out there in the big wide world without me to look after them. And I worried about myself for worrying about them!'

Plus the other worries she wasn't about to air in front of Novello. Or Dalziel either, for that matter. Or indeed herself if she could help it. Worries like damp patches on a kitchen wall, that you could

49

stand a chair in front of, or hang a wallchart over, or even just ignore, but you knew that sometime you were going to have to deal with them.

'So I went upstairs, switched my laptop on and started working,' she concluded.

'That help with worries, does it?' He sipped his Scotch and looked at her doubtfully.

Something else she wasn't going to lay out in present company.

'The poet Cowper managed to keep religious mania at bay for several decades by dint of writing,' she said spiritedly.

'God moves in a mysterious way His wonders to perform,' said Dalziel, whose capacity to surprise should have ceased to surprise her. 'Then the doorbell rang?'

'No. I heard their car and spoke to them out of the window. Then I went downstairs and opened the door.'

'Oh aye, you said. No print on the bellpush then. Pity.'

'I'm sorry. I should have thought on.'

He smiled at her sarcasm, then said seriously, 'When they mentioned Rosie, it must have been right bad.'

'Bad? It felt like the bottom had fallen out of the universe. It was like getting the worst news you could imagine, and knowing it was all your own fault.'

She spoke with a vehemence which came close to being excessive.

'All your fault? Nay, luv, can't see how you could ever think that,' he said, viewing her closely.

If Dalziel had been by himself, she might have stumbled into an explanation.

Maybe something like, *I felt so relieved that morning not to be going with Rosie, to know she was in Peter's care, to have a day at last when I could stop worrying about her. But not just for her sake, and not even because I could probably do with the rest myself, but because when we nearly lost her, I knew then what I must have known before but never had occasion to look straight in the eye, that my single-handed sailing days were over forever, that I'd been pressed as part of a three-man crew on a lifelong voyage over what were hopefully oceans of absolute love. Except if it's so absolute, how come there's a little part of me somewhere which, like Achilles's heel, didn't get submerged? Forgive me muddling my metaphors, it's probably this story I'm writing. But that's another story. No, what I'm trying to say is, no matter how I try to hide it from myself, there's something in me that sometimes yearns to be free, that gets nostalgic for the long-lost days of free choice, that comes close to seeing this love I feel not as a gift but as a burden, not as a privilege but a responsibility. Perhaps I'm simply a selfish person who knows now she can never be selfish again. Does anyone else feel like this? Am I a monster? That's why I was so ready to believe them, that's why I felt so guilty. It was like God had decided I hadn't got the message loud and clear last time and I needed another dose of the same to get me straight.*

Something like that, maybe. But probably not,

even if Novello and her little notebook hadn't been there.

'Just a figure of speech, Andy,' she said.

'So you'd have gone with this pair?' asked the Fat Man.

'Anywhere they wanted. If they'd kept it vague I'd have got in that car and . . . and *what*, Andy? What did they want with me?'

'That's for them to know and us to find out,' said Dalziel. 'So what put you onto them?'

'I've told you!'

'Aye, but telling's like peeing to a man with a swollen prostate, you think you've got it all out but there's often a bit more to come.'

'Who speaks so well should never speak in vain,' said Ellie. 'OK. At first I couldn't think of anything except Rosie being ill again. Then when they said about trying to contact Peter and being told he wasn't available, I nearly said, of course he wasn't available because he's on the coach!'

'But you didn't? Why not?'

'I don't know. I reckon to start with it was just a case of being too shocked to speak, and that gave me time to think, I suppose. And suddenly it was like fireworks going off in my brain. I found myself thinking, it's not just Jehovah's Witnesses that don't drive thirty thousand pound BMWs. I mean, I know the council tax has gone up, but surely the Education Department doesn't kit its employees out like this? Sorry. It makes sense to me, I assure you. At the same time I registered that two or three times they said *he* when they were talking about the head at Edengrove. Now, one thing anyone in our local Ed Department will know is that the head of Edengrove is Miss Martindale. Not to know her argues yourself braindead. So I thought I'd just give them a little test. I made up a Mr Johnson as head teacher. And when they didn't respond to that, I knew something very funny was going on.'

'So you decided to assault them?'

'No. I thought of challenging them, but there were two of them and only one of me and if their purpose was as nefarious as I was beginning to imagine, I didn't like the odds. Time to retreat and lock the door, I thought.'

'So what brought out the beast in you?' asked Dalziel.

'It was the man. The woman was trying to play it cool, very reassuring, nothing to worry about. She could probably see that I was already sick to guts with worry. But he decided that the more worried I got, the less trouble I'd be, and he said something about getting a move on just in case it turned out to be more serious than they thought. God, that really got to me. I thought, you callous bastard! The woman tried to calm things down, but it was too late. I was so angry that I must have been the best advert for gun control you ever saw. Because if I'd had one, I would have shot him, no problem.'

'Not then,' said Dalziel. 'Might have had one

now, but. On the other hand, we'd have had a body to work on. Nowt like a body when you're short of a lead.'

'Are you saying you'd rather I'd killed one of them?'

He considered.

'No,' he said finally. 'Gets boring interrogating corpses. Serious wound, but, now that would have been nice. Something that would need hospital treatment. How hard did you say you kneed him?'

'I shouldn't think he'll be troubling his wife for a few nights, but I doubt if he'd go for treatment.'

'Wife? You reckon he was married?' said Dalziel casually.

'Well, he wore a big gold ring on his wedding finger . . . Andy, that was clever. I'd forgotten that. I mean, I didn't think I'd noticed that.'

'Not all rubber-truncheon work down the nick. Anything else come to mind, apart from what you scribbled down?'

He looked at the piece of paper Ellie had scribbled her notes on.

'*Man was six feet,*' he read. '*About thirty – slim build – light-brown hair – bushy – needed a cut – left-hand parting – brown eyes, I think – not blue – squarish face – open honest expression – God the bastards were good!* . . .'

He looked enquiringly at Ellie.

'Yeah, sorry about that.'

'Nay, it's useful what you felt. By *good*, you mean . . . ?'

'Saying they were with the Education Welfare Service. That's the council department that helps deal with problems like absenteeism, truancy, bullying, parental complaint, anything that a school finds it can't cope with internally. But what I mean is, at first they came over perfect for it. Nice, caring, positive people . . .'

'Bumbling do-gooders, you mean? Sorry. Just trying to put it in terms my lads would understand. *Clothing – suit – Prince of Wales check – light-blue shirt – blue and yellow diagonal striped tie – could have been Old Boys or a club – on his feet dark-brown sandals . . .'*

'Did I put that? No, he was wearing a sort of soft leather moccasin, no laces, dark-tan, casual but elegant, in fact, they looked rather expensive, come to think of it. Which is what you've made me do, you cunning sod. I never mentioned sandals!'

Dalziel grinned.

'No. You put nowt. But shoes are important. Change everything else, but you want your feet to stay comfy.'

'So if he changes into something else because he's worried that I can describe him, he might keep the same shoes on?'

'Aye, but don't get excited. Not the kind of info we pass on to Interpol. *Voice – light-baritone range – Irish accent . . .'*

'No, that one's not going to work, Andy,' said Ellie firmly. 'I said no distinguishable accent, and that's what I mean.'

'So not a Yorkshireman.'

'Not like you, no.'

'Not deep and musical then. But there's all sorts of Yorkshire voices. There's that high squeaky one, like yon journalist fellow who used to shovel shit for Maggie Thatcher. And there's that one like a circular saw –'

'No, not northern at all,' interrupted Ellie.

'So, not northern and not Irish. We're getting somewhere. Scottish? Welsh? Cockney? The Queen? Michael Caine? Maurice Chevalier?'

'You're getting silly. No, he didn't have any accent at all, really. Like an announcer on Radio Four.'

'You think Radio Four announcers don't have accents?' said Dalziel. 'No, hang about, I think I'm with you. It's *you* you think doesn't have an accent! What you mean is this guy spoke the same way you do? Middle-class posh, but not so much it gets up your nose.'

Ellie, faced as so often with a choice between laughing at Andy Dalziel or thumping him, decided she'd been involved in enough violence for the day and laughed.

'Yes, I suppose that is what I do mean,' she said.

'Grand. Now the woman. How's she for injury, by the way?'

'She might have a black eye, and a few scratches,' said Ellie, thinking affectionately of the *Pompon de Paris*. 'Hey, and there could be a few threads from her dress hooked on the rose bush by the front door.'

'We'll check. So. *Age thirties – five-eight or -nine – dark eyes – long face – not bad-looking – expensive make-up* – what's the difference between expensive and not so expensive?'

'The more you pay, the less you see.'

'Like sending your kids to public school. *Hair black – natural – short – classy stylist* – I won't ask – *build slim – good figure* – there's that *good* again. Know what I mean by good, but what's it signify to you?'

Ellie threw an exasperated glance at Shirley Novello who returned it blankly.

'Well, I'm sure that to you, Andy, a good figure suggests something like two footballs in a gunny bag, but what I mean is something you can see's there but all in proportion, back, front, and middle, OK?'

'Like you, you mean?' said Dalziel, looking at her appreciatively. 'In fact, sounds a lot like you, except mebbe for the expensive make-up. Joke. Now, *clothing – olive-green cotton dress – sleeveless – leather shoulder bag – no stockings – pale-green sling-back shoes*. Was she married?'

Ellie thought then said, 'Yes, she was wearing a wedding ring. And she had a ring on her right-hand middle finger too. Green stone. Plus a wristwatch.

Expanding bracelet, gold, I think. Sorry, I should have put that down.'

'You're doing fine. The watch on the same hand as the ring?'

'Yes. The right. Hey, that means . . .'

'She could be left-handed. That's summat. *Voice husky – accent Midlandish.* Birmingham? Wolverhampton? Black Country?'

'Any. It was just a patina, so to speak, not a full-blown accent.'

'Might have made it to Radio Four, eh? Hello, here comes Smiler again.'

Wield had re-entered the room.

He said, 'We've got Peter,' and handed Ellie the mobile phone, then looked at Dalziel and jerked his head doorwards, suggesting they leave.

The Fat Man yawned, scratched his nose and poured himself another Scotch.

'Peter! Yes, yes, I'm fine, really . . . And you two . . . that's great, I knew you would be, but I just wanted to hear it from your own lips . . . Wieldy's told you all about it, I'm sure . . . honestly, no harm done . . . Well, you'll guess I was a bit shook up at first, but once I realized it was just a stupid jape . . . what else could it be? . . . No, no, don't do that. I don't want Rosie worried. Just carry on, enjoy the rest of the day . . . I'm fine, really . . . no, I won't be on my own, and you're not due back late . . . give my love to Rose . . . and you too . . . yes, I will, I do . . . yes, he's here. 'Bye, darling.'

She handed the phone to Dalziel, then bowed

her head and let out a deep breath as she relaxed from the effort of keeping her feelings in check. The temptation to let it all flood out as soon as she heard Peter's voice had been very strong, which was probably why the fat bastard had stayed in the room. She looked up to find Wield watching her, and jerked her head at him in a mirror image of his own gesture, then led him outside.

'Well, that's a relief,' she said in the hall.

Novello had followed them out. Dalziel must have dismissed her. All right for her to hear me spilling my guts, but not to eavesdrop on his conversation with Peter, thought Ellie.

'You're looking a lot better,' said Wield.

'Yes? Well, I suppose a lot of that's down to Andy, though I hate to say it. He's . . .'

'Good?' offered Wield.

'Let's not go overboard. He's subtler than I imagined. In a very unsubtle way, of course. So what happens now, Wieldy? You all go away and start to wonder if maybe it wasn't just an over-reaction by a hysterical woman after all?'

'No. We go away and don't rest till we find out what's been going on here.'

'Any ideas in the pipeline?'

She saw Novello's brow crinkle as if she might have something to say, but before she could speak, if that were her intention, Wield said very firmly, 'No.'

Ellie looked into that violently contoured face in which nothing was readable except the affection in his eyes and wondered if the *No* was a lie or the truth.

And which of them would she find more comfort in?

iv

spelt from Sibyl's leaves

Edgar Wield . . .
Edgar Wield . . .
biking through the glen . . .

Poof.
Perve.
Shirtlifter.
Arse bandit.
All these and more figured in Gaw Sempernel's
brief remarks when he dropped by in person to tell
me to add Sergeant Wield to his current operational
folder which, with what he probably sees as subtle
wit, he has christened *Sibyl's Leaves.*

It's not often Gaw and I meet face to face these
days.

Well, not face to face exactly, he towering, I
at wheelchair level, his eyes never meeting mine
direct, mine looking straight at his immaculately
tailored crotch.

If I reached out and touched him, how would he react?

Not, I suspect, as once I could make him react just by smiling and moistening my lips at him across a crowded committee room.

'Reasons for inclusion?' I asked him.

Because I say so, hovered in the air between us.

Then the famous Sempernel diplomacy clicked in and he said, 'Close associate of Dalziel and Pascoe, very friendly with Eleanor Pascoe, lives with Edwin Digweed, former solicitor, struck off shortly after qualifying when he was convicted of committing an act of gross indecency with a gentleman whose voice is now listened to with great attention when he speaks from, appropriately enough, the cross-benches in the Upper Chamber. It was theorized at the time by our masters that, had not the case become public, it might have been a prelude to long-term political blackmail.'

'Grounds?' I asked, fingers poised.

'Irrelevant now,' he said dismissively. 'Point is, here we have a policeman whose private life makes him vulnerable. The only way he's been able to survive is with the protection of his superiors, and we would be wise, I'm sure you'll agree, to ask ourselves why that has been given.'

'You're not suggesting that Superintendent Dalziel and DCI Pascoe are gay?' I exclaimed.

'If they were, that would make things simple,' he said pompously. 'It is the fact that they probably are not that I find sinister.'

You find friendship sinister, I thought. *Oh, Gaw!*

'In any case, the sergeant's sexual orientation is no longer a matter of law,' I said.

'Sexual orientation?' he mocked. 'You have been too long immersed in the obliquities of Sibylline utterance. Let us call a spade a spade.'

And then came out the long list of mocking insults.

Oh Gaw, I thought. *What indignities did you suffer at that school of yours to make you so vehement? Or perhaps the question should be, what ecstasies did you experience which make you feel so guilty?*

But nothing I said.

Mine is not to reason why, or at least not to be seen reasoning why.

Mine is merely to obey orders and collect here all those whom Gaw Sempernel sees fit to designate as leaves on his tree.

Edgar Wield . . .
Edgar Wield . . .
Most inscrutable of men . . .

Working-class background. Can't have been easy growing up feeling as you did in a Yorkshire mining village, son of a lurcher-loving, pigeon-fancying father, with the pit gaping at your feet and the only traditional ways out university for the very bright or professional Rugby League for the very brawny.

You were neither, Edgar, but you found a third

63

way which, though it attracted the contumely of your peers, diverted their suspicion from the truth of you.

The police.

Were you perhaps still trying to convince yourself that it was, as they used to say, only a phase? That given the right environment you'd wake up one day and say to yourself, what I really fancy is finding a willing lass and giving her a right good shagging?

Or were you looking for a job where most people see only the uniform, never the man?

You were good at the job.

Not ivory tower university bright perhaps, but sharply focused with a phenomenal memory and a huge capacity for marshalling intricate detail, you took all the police exams in your stride, you won commendations for bravery, your annual reviews were undiluted paeans, you looked set to rise high. But once you became sergeant in the CID, you remained fixed.

Not for you the exposure of high rank.

You enjoy what you are doing. You are good at it. And your association with those other two who have also come fluttering down into Sempernel's *leaves*, Dalziel and Pascoe, has given you confidence enough to live your life more freely, not to flaunt who you are but not to hide it either.

And still Gaw Sempernel suspects you.

Or at least feels he might at some point be able to use you.

From what I know of you, lying here in my little casket, Sergeant, this may not be the least of his errors.

loved by his friends . . .
refusing to yield . . .
Edgar Wield . . .
Edgar Wield . . .

v

revenge and retribution

Every age has its own defining philosophical speculations, often best expressed in terms which may at a glance appear over-personalized and tainted with self-interest.

It was, for example, in relation to her prospects of professional advancement that Shirley Novello first asked herself the question, was being treated like a man a form of sexual discrimination?

Things had seemed pretty straightforward the first time she had attended a CID gathering in the Black Bull with the Holy Trinity and found she was expected to go to the bar and collect the drinks no matter who was actually buying the round. She was disappointed without being surprised, as this chimed perfectly with the expectation at all levels in the Force that if tea or coffee were to be fetched, any woman present would be the fetcher. Novello had worked out various non-confrontational strategems to avoid doing this, but she had not been afraid to fall back on confrontation.

Confrontation with Andy Dalziel, however, felt as futile as confrontation with Uranus. (Or any planet, but Uranus somehow seemed most fitting.) Hit it hard as you could, you weren't going to jolt it out of its orbit.

The other two, however, gave the impression that they might in their better moments be susceptible to the nudge of right reason.

But before she could nerve herself to put this to the test, she had discovered by distant observation that if the group consisted of the Trinity alone, it was usually Wield who did the fetching and carrying, while if the three became a pair, it was Pascoe.

So now right reason asked, if a male sergeant and a male chief inspector could accept this as the natural order of things, was it reasonable for a female constable to cry discrimination?

Or, to put it another way, what should a woman do who fought for equal treatment and then found that the equal treatment she fought for was in fact unequal?

These were the speculations thronging her mind as she returned from the bar at eleven o'clock on the morning after the attempted kidnapping of Ellie Pascoe, bearing a tray loaded with a pint of best, a half of the same, a fizzy mineral water and a Coke.

Pascoe's request for the mineral water had emboldened her to buy the Coke.

They were in the Black Bull to discuss possible ramifications of yesterday's events. The chief inspector had arrived late at the station, having spent the morning ensuring that his house and Edengrove School were being watched over to his satisfaction. He looked worn out, and it was this wanness which the Fat Man had used as an excuse to retire instantly to the pub where, he averred, he had his best thoughts, and they would be free from interruption. Novello's inclusion had had all the appearance of a throwaway afterthought, coming as Dalziel led the trio out of the CID room. But Novello had long since concluded that most of the Fat Man's apparent afterthoughts were carefully planned. The wise thing was to be neither flattered by his attention nor offended by the lack of it.

She placed the tray on the table, noting with some satisfaction that she'd managed to slop a little beer over Dalziel's change (the seriousness of the occasion was marked by the fact that Dalziel had actually bought a round), and then put all personal and philosophical considerations out of her mind to focus on the debate in progress.

The on-the-table theory was that the attempted abduction had something to do with Pascoe's work.

'Wieldy, you were trawling that mind of thine for folk Pete's put away who were nutty enough to take it personally.'

Dalziel's natural Luddism was expressed in his boast, 'Who needs great ugly lumps of hi-tech equipment cluttering the place when we've got Wieldy who's twice as efficient and three times as ugly?' but Novello had noticed that the sergeant's computer skills were state of the art.

Whatever its source, the list of perps who'd gone down threatening the DCI with personal injury was impressively long. For a nice quiet guy, Pascoe seemed to have got up a lot of criminal noses.

But Wield's conclusion was that in most cases the threats had just been empty, if over-heated, air.

'You need a special kind of twist to nurse a grievance and plan revenge,' said Wield.

'Is that right, Sigmund?' said Dalziel. 'So what you're saying is, you've dug deep and ended up with nowt but an empty hole?'

'No,' said Wield. 'In fact, I struck a root. Franny Roote.'

Dalziel looked blank for a moment, then let his jaw drop in the mock-amazement he had taken to affecting if Wield essayed a joke.

'You mean that weird student at yon college? My memory serves me right, we couldn't do him for owt but being an accessory.'

'That's right,' said Wield. 'But after listening to what had gone on there, the judge ordered a psycho-evaluation before sentencing. And after getting an earful of that, he decided best place for Roote was a secure hospital. To start with the lad refused all treatment, and during this period he seems to have fixed on the DCI, or sergeant as he was then, as the man responsible for putting him there. He seemed to think you had something personal against him.'

'I know it's silly, but I do tend to feel strongly about people who try to kill me,' said Pascoe. 'I recall I got a weird letter from him while he was waiting trial. I passed it on to the court, so in a way he was right about me helping to get him certified. But there's been nothing since. I haven't thought about him for years.'

'Doesn't mean he's not been thinking about you,' said Dalziel. 'Wieldy, I take it there's summat else.'

'Only that he finally accepted the treatment and settled down to being a model patient-cum-prisoner. Did an OU degree in English Literature, and went on to start a research course for a Ph.D. or some such thing. Finally he convinced them he wasn't a menace to society any more and got himself discharged. Last month.'

There was a moment's silence, then the Fat Man said, 'That it?'

'Except . . .'

'What?'

'He'd know Ellie, she was teaching at the college then, wasn't she? When you met her.'

Pascoe nodded.

'So?' said Dalziel.

'Nothing. Just a connection,' said Wield. 'Also, probably means nowt, but this research he's doing. His topic is, I made a note of it, aye, here it is . . . *Revenge and Retribution in English Drama*.'

Another silence, then Dalziel said, 'Beats sewing mailbags and breaking rocks, I suppose. Got an address?'

'Aye. Sheffield.'

'Not so far, then. Set up liaison with South Yorkshire, then pop down there in the morning and check him out.'

'Can't do it tomorrow, sir. Day off.'

'Oh aye? And what are you doing that's more important than finding out who's threatening your colleague's family, Sergeant?' demanded Dalziel in that tone of high moral dudgeon he saved for underlings who dared suggest they had a private life.

Wield glanced at Pascoe, who said, 'Actually, Wieldy is very kindly entertaining that same colleague's family. He's invited Ellie and Rosie out to Enscombe to look round the Children's Zoo at the Hall.'

'Oh,' said Dalziel, slightly flummoxed. 'Right. That's fine. Only don't try putting it down as overtime. Best go to check Roote out yourself then, Pete. If you feel up to it.'

'It'll be a pleasure,' said Pascoe. 'I'm in court with Kelly Cornelius at twelve, but that should give me plenty of time.'

Shirley Novello listened and learned. These three had a pretty cosy relationship, she thought. Though perhaps *cosy* was not a word that fitted well on anything to do with Andy Dalziel. But they meshed easily together, like well-oiled cog wheels. It was a piece of machinery she'd like to get herself linked up with, but she recognized the dangers in trying to poke yourself too brutally among moving cogs.

She'd noted with interest the reference to Ellie Pascoe's job way back in the dark ages when they'd met. A college lecturer. Queen of the kids in never-never land. That figured.

'Right,' said Dalziel. 'That's revenge took care of. Let's move on. Cases in progress where your involvement in the prosecution could make it seem worthwhile to some no-brain wanker to get you by the goolies. How's that look?'

Pascoe winced at the language, then sent an irritatingly apologetic glance to Novello, who winced, less obviously, in her turn. Hadn't marriage to the Nutcracker Fairy taught him *anything*?

Wield shrugged and said, 'Nothing obvious. Any road, I'd have thought they saved threats for civilians. Cops they'd offer a bung.'

'Yeah, you and me, mebbe, Wieldy. But every sod knows fancy pants here's incorruptible. So, tell us, Mother Teresa, is there owt you're working on that gives you that funny feeling you're famous for?'

Pascoe, with more than his customary diffidence, said, 'Well, it is just a feeling, but for some reason I keep on thinking Kelly Cornelius.'

'*Her!*' cried Dalziel in derision. 'She's a lass, not to mention a sodding accountant. You've got more chance of getting aggro from a Siamese waitress.'

Putting aside this touchstone of timidity for

future deconstruction, Pascoe said, 'She is actually being charged with assault on a police officer, don't forget.'

'Oh aye, but that were Hector, and usually they give you a medal for thumping him,' said Dalziel. 'Any road, why should she want to frighten you off? You're just keeping her on ice on this assault charge while the Fraud boys get their act together, isn't that the arrangement? They're the ones who are going to send her down for ten years when they finally get their fingers out. What's going off there, anyway, Pete? I don't mind helping out, but won't tomorrow be the third time you've had to go along and ask for a further remand in custody? And what's Desperate Dan know that we don't?'

Desperate Dan was Dan Trimble, Mid-Yorkshire's Chief Constable, who in Dalziel's eyes didn't need to know anything other than how to pour single malt without missing the glass whenever the Head of CID graced him with his presence.

'If I knew that, then he wouldn't,' said Pascoe. 'OK, I'm just concerned with the assault charge, but that's what's keeping her remanded in custody. Two possibilities. One, some accomplice wants her loose so that she can do a runner. Someone at the bank, maybe, who's afraid if this goes on much longer, she's going to start pointing the finger.'

'Someone like who?'

'Well, I gather Fraud are looking very closely at her immediate boss, George Ollershaw. They've got nothing definite yet, but you can tell they're sniffing the air.'

'Ollershaw? Him? Nay, he's a right banker, and like most on 'em can probably play a fair tune on the fiddle, but I can't see him getting mixed up with owt violent.'

'Know him, do you, sir?'

'I've seen him down the Gents. And heard him too, sounding off to his mates. Big I Am, but a long way off Mr Big, I'd say.'

The Gents, as Novello had learned after an embarrassing misunderstanding, wasn't a lavatorial reference but a popular shortening of the Borough Club for Professional Gentlemen, the Athenaeum of the North, an exclusive social and dining club, men only, of course, which made Novello think that perhaps her misunderstanding wasn't. When she'd wondered to Wield why someone as anarchically unclubbable as Dalziel should have joined such an organization, the sergeant had replied, ''Cos they didn't want him, of course.'

'All the same, I think they've still got him in the frame,' said Pascoe. 'But there's another possibility. One way of looking at it, the prime target for intimidation is Kelly herself. Until the Fraud Squad get a line on the Nortrust Bank money, it's floating around somewhere in cyberspace, and she may be the only one who can get at it. So maybe someone wants her out so they can use methods that even Fraud draw the line at to get her to tell where it is.'

It seemed to Novello that the DCI was putting forward his Cornelius hypotheses with more stubbornness than conviction.

Dalziel clearly thought so too. He said, 'Doesn't make sense. Anyone serious could easily get to her in the remand centre, bend her over a table and threaten to shove a broken bottle up her jacksie, happens all the time.'

'That's fine if what you want to find out is where the swag's buried, but it's not like that here,' insisted Pascoe. 'OK, it's easy enough to get some prison hardcase to do the job for a couple of rocks, but what's Kelly going to tell her? Nothing that makes any sense, I'd bet. No, it could be the only way to get at this loot is to sit Kelly down in front of a state-of-the-art computer and make her an offer she can't refuse. To do that, you want her out of custody. All they'd need from me is to make our opposition to her reapplication for bail tomorrow a bit feeble.'

Dalziel snorted doubt and provoked Wield into a display of loyalty.

'Makes sense to me,' he said. 'Twisting Pete's arm to perjure himself is one thing. Bloody hard to do, and harder to get away with 'cos everyone in the job would sit up and take notice if suddenly his evidence changed. But subtly getting up some magistrate's nose so as he grants bail just to show who's in charge of the courts here, that would be dead easy. And not such a strain on the conscience either.'

'Oh aye? You'd do it, would you, if that antique bookie of thine were threatened?' said Dalziel.

Antiquarian book dealer, corrected Novello mentally, watching with the keenness of an ambitious student to see how Wield would react to this reference to his partner.

'Straight choice between Edwin and a crook, no problem,' said Wield without hesitation, looking the Fat Man right in the eye.

'Well, bugger me,' said Dalziel. 'Thank God there's thee and me left with some moral fibre, Ivor, and I'm not so sure about thee. You're keeping very quiet for a lass. Didn't your trip to the wishing well get you any ideas?'

'Wishing well?' echoed Novello uncertainly.

'Aye, I take it that's where tha tossed my change,' said Dalziel, poking at the wet coins with his forefinger. 'Only, when I were young, you had to leave it there to get any results.'

'I can take it back and get some more drink if you like, sir,' said Novello sweetly.

'Nay, it's some other bugger's shout,' said Dalziel, closing his fingers round the money, shaking it dry, and thrusting it into his pocket. 'And while we're waiting for Mr and Mrs Alzheimer here to remember the way to their wallets, why don't you give us the benefit of female intuition, Ivor? Or are you only here for the beer?'

You tell me, fatso! thought Novello. But even as she fought the impulse to tip the remnants of her Coke over his great grizzled head, the answer came

76

to her in that curious admixture of gratification and indignation which was her frequent response to Dalziel.

She was here not because he fancied her or wanted someone to fetch the beer; she was here because he simply reckoned she could make a useful contribution.

She looked around. Like Mrs Robinson, all she could see were sympathetic eyes. Well, four anyway. The Fat Man's expression was one of confident expectation, like a ringmaster watching a performing pig. Bastard.

She said, 'Well, there was one thing that did occur to me about what happened yesterday . . .'

'Spit it out, lass, afore I die of thirst.'

'What if you, that is we, are all barking up the wrong tree? What if it's got nothing whatsoever to do with the DCI and the people he's put away or is trying to put away? What if in fact it's all to do with Ellie, Mrs Pascoe, herself?'

Silence fell and the three men looked at each other with a wild surmise, though Novello feared it had more to do with her sanity than her insight.

Then the phone behind the bar rang and Jack Mahoney, the landlord, after listening a moment, called, 'Are you buggers here?'

Dalziel said, 'How many times do you need telling to put your mitt over the mouthpiece first, you thick sod? Ivor.'

For once Novello felt nothing but relief at being appointed gofer.

She went to the phone, identified herself, and listened.

Then she looked towards the waiting men.

'Well?' said Dalziel. 'Have I won the lottery, or wha'?'

But it was to Pascoe that Novello addressed herself, trying and failing to sound neutrally official.

'Sir,' she said. 'It's Seymour. It's lousy reception, but there's been more trouble at your house. I'm sorry, but I think he said he's following an ambulance to the hospital.'

vi

citizen's arrest

Ellie Pascoe hadn't realized just how shaken up she still was until the doorbell startled her so much she knocked a fortunately almost empty cup of coffee over her computer.

Get back to normal, she'd told herself, and then recalled that this was also what she'd told herself after Rosie's illness and had soon come to an understanding that normal wasn't just a sequence of repeated activities, but a condition like virginity which could never be regained.

But she'd followed the pattern of her normal day, retreating (a nice religious word for what sometimes felt like a nice religious activity) to the boxroom which she refused to call a study. Real writers had studies and you weren't a real writer till you got something published. Well, she had hopes. The rejection of her third attempt at a novel might have driven her to despair had it not come at the time of Rosie's illness when despair wasn't a place she had any desire to visit, and certainly

79

not for the sake of anything as unimportant as a sodding book!

As Rosie started to recover, Ellie had started to write again, but just as her daughter seemed in her play to have turned away from the games of imagination which had once been her favourite territory, so the mother now found herself toying with characters and situations from long ago rather than the snapshot here-and-now realism she'd hitherto thought of as her forte.

. She'd pursued this new line without questioning, even after she realized that it wasn't likely to lead to anything she could submit for publication. But it was . . . fun? Yes, it was certainly that. But, like the fun of children, like child's play, it was learning also. Here was something important to her at that time in those circumstances, but also in other times and future circumstance maybe. During her previous existence as a lecturer, a colleague who ran a Creative Writing course had moaned to her that he spent far too much time dealing with the hang-ups of students who clearly regarded narrative fiction as a branch of therapy rather than a branch of art. Now she knew what he meant. Therapy you kept to yourself. Art took you, trembling, in front of the footlights.

She brought this perspective to bear on her rejected third novel. Suddenly she found herself asking paragraph by paragraph the two essential questions. *Is this really so important to me I've got to say it? Is this potentially so interesting to readers, they'll have to read it?*

And for a whole week without saying anything to Peter or anyone else, she had launched a savage attack upon her holy script, like Moses going at the tablets with a sledgehammer. The result had been . . . she had no idea what the result had been, except that before, the book had read clever and now it felt like it read true. *A deep distress has humanized my soul . . . ?* Well, maybe. Three days ago she'd sent it off to the publisher who'd rejected its previous manifestation. Her accompanying note said, *Last time you said it showed promise but . . . So tell me what it shows now. Only this time I'd appreciate it if you told me quick!*

And then she'd returned to the therapy of her tale of old, parodic, far-off things and battles long ago. Self-indulgence is the novelist's greatest sin, but here she could indulge herself to her heart's, and her head's, content. Here she could mock, mimic, talk dirty, wax sentimental, be anarchic, anachronistic, anything she wanted. Here she had power without responsibility, for she was writing solely for herself. No one else was going to read this. She ruled alone in this world, its normalities were whatever she made them. Or, to put it rather less grandiloquently, this was her comfort blanket she could pick up and chew whenever her fragile sensibilities felt the need. So that's what she called it in her computer. *Comfort Blanket.* It was still unfinished but so what? The real pleasure was being able to go back over it again and again, changing things, trying new things out.

Nice if life were like that, she thought as she switched on her laptop. Call it up, click on *Edit*, and cut, copy, find, replace, delete . . .

Her words suddenly came from nowhere to fill the screen. She smiled. To her essentially non-technological mind, it was still magic.

Now where had she got up to in her revision? Oh yes. There it was.

Chapter 2

As they came down from the headland, the storm died, not a belly-wound death, but quick as an arrow through the heart. One moment the wind off the sea threatened to whirl them along with the racing tatters of low grey cloud, the next the air was still and balmy and the full moon, riding in a star-studded sky, lit the camp site below like a thousand lanterns.

Hadn't she used that simile before? So what? Homer used his stock images over and over. Get obsessed with novelty and you ended up with a wardrobe full of lovely clothes you could never wear again.

Here, those so tired that they'd slept despite the howling wind were now aroused by the sudden silence. Men began to busy themselves drying off the weapons and armour which had got soaked in the storm, while the women started building up the tiny fires which were all they'd dared kindle in face of the gale. But all activity stopped as they became aware of the approaching procession.

The Greek came first, his hands bound behind his back and the guard commander's sword resting lightly against his neck. For all that, he managed to look like a returning traveller greeting old friends, head held high, teeth showing bright through the tangle of beard as he smiled this way and that, nose wrinkling appreciatively at the smell of cooking already arising from one or two fires.

But his eyes were never still, drinking in every detail of the camp.

Bringing up the rear was the wounded guard. He gripped his bleeding left wrist tightly with his right hand and his face showed white as moonlight beneath the weather-beaten skin.

'What's up, mate?' called someone.

'Bloody Greek spy. Nearly took my fucking hand off. Bastard!'

'That right? Don't worry, we'll chop more than his hand off before we're finished.'

The guard commander said mildly, 'Glad to see you're so keen for action, soldier. You can take over up the headland. Go on, don't hang about. Could be there's a whole army of Greeks landing there already.'

The word Greeks buzzed quickly through the camp, and soon the way ahead was blocked by a crowd of men, many with their weapons out. Unperturbed, the prisoner advanced at the same steady pace, forcing them to retreat before him, till someone at the rear set up a cry of, 'The Prince! The Prince!' and the men moved to either side, leaving a path clear.

Two men had emerged from the sole substantial shelter in the camp, a small pavilion erected in the lee of a huge boulder which had shielded it from the worst of the storm. One was grey-bearded and bent with the weight of years, the other young, slim, upright, with still, watchful eyes set in a narrow clean-shaven face.

Suddenly the fat man sank to his knees and prostrated himself with his face pressed against the young man's sandals.

'Have mercy, great Prince,' his muffled voice pleaded. 'Like the gods you are clearly descended from, take pity on this poor miserable wretch whose only hope for life and succour lies in your infinite generosity.'

The young man didn't look impressed.

'What's this you've brought us, Achates?' he asked.

Succinctly the guard commander told his story.

'So, a Greek, you say? And probably a spy?'

A cry of protest rose from the recumbent man, cut off sharply as Achates pressed the point of his sword into his neck.

'Could be. Shall I set him on a griddle over a slow fire for half an hour till he's ready to tell us?'

A murmur of approval went up from the listening men, but the Prince said gravely, 'This is not how our religion has taught us to treat the wayworn traveller who comes as a guest in our midst. Let food and dry clothing be brought, and when he is refreshed, I shall talk to him to discover what manner of man he is and his purpose in coming here.'

The fat man began to gabble fulsome thanks, but the Prince silenced him with a sharp movement of his foot and went on, 'Nevertheless, heat up the griddle in case I am not satisfied.'

The Prince disengaged his foot and Achates prodded the Greek upright with his sword. Two young women came forward, one with some clothing, the other with a bronze platter piled high with steaming food.

'That smells grand. I'm right grateful, lord. Only I need a hand to eat with.'

'Only one?' said Achates, raising his weapon. 'Which would you like to keep?'

'Nay, not so hasty,' said the Greek, starting back. 'Hang about.'

He flexed his broad shoulders, took a deep breath, bowed forward, his body hunched, and with a single convulsive movement, he snapped the length of cloth which bound his wrists.

At this moment the doorbell rang and Ellie, dragged back from the dangerous world of her imagination to the equally dangerous world of her life, knocked over the cup.

'Fuck!' she said, jumping up and shaking the coffee from the keyboard.

Amazingly, when she finished, the screen still displayed her story but for safety's sake she saved and switched off.

The doorbell was ringing again.

Even the knowledge that Detective Constable Dennis Seymour was sitting in his car right opposite the house didn't prevent her from checking on the bellringer from behind the curtains like any suburban housewife in a sitcom.

It was her friend, Daphne Aldermann, full of eager curiosity after having been intercepted and checked out by the watching policeman. After a short hiatus to pour herself and her guest a nerve-soothing Scotch – once you got on Dr Dalziel's books, you followed his prescriptions to the bitter end – she had launched into the narrative with mock-heroic gusto, and thence to the calmer pleasures of self-analysis. As a long-time opponent of all forms of violent action, she felt it necessary to explain in detail to Daphne, who had no objection whatsoever to a bit of violence in a good cause, what had provoked her to physical assault.

'It was using Rosie that did it,' she said. 'It was my own guilt feelings that really exploded, I suppose.'

'*Your* guilt feelings?'

Daphne wasn't Dalziel and she certainly wasn't that nebby infant, Novello.

She gave her a version of the confession she'd rehearsed when talking to the Fat Man, ending with, 'So you see what a mixed-up cow I've turned into. I feel like that base Indian – in *Hamlet*, is it? – who threw away the pearl richer than all his tribe. Only I got it back.'

'*Othello*, I think. And the point was he had no idea that what he'd got had any value at all. And you didn't throw Rosie away anyway,' said Daphne Aldermann sensibly. 'And you've always been a mixed-up cow, so no change there.'

It was, she felt, in her relationship with Ellie Pascoe, her avocation to be sensible. In upbringing, outlook and circumstance, the two women were light years apart. But the mad scientist of chance had chosen to set their opposing particles on a collision course some years earlier, and while a great deal of energy had been released, it had been through fusion rather than fission.

Ellie looked ready to meet her head-on in battle, but in the end diverted to a minor skirmish.

'You sure it's *Othello*?' she said truculently. 'I thought the nearest you privately educated lot got to literature was carrying the *Collected Works* on your head during deportment lessons.'

'You're forgetting. They made us learn a classic each morning between the cross-country run and the first cold shower,' said Daphne. 'So OK, something bad happens to our kids, we feel responsible. Mothers are programmed that way. Or conditioned – let's not get into that argument.'

'I know that. But knowing doesn't stop you feeling. And being shocked how much you feel. Why ever I did it, I still can't believe I actually assaulted those people.'

'Oh, come on,' said Daphne, with all the ease of a natural supporter of corporal and capital punishment. 'They had it coming. God knows what they were going to do with you, but if they get caught, probably they'll get off with writing a hundred lines and probation. At least as he smiles at you out of the dock, you'll be able to think, I left my mark on you, mate!'

Ellie laughed and refilled their glasses. It had been one of the mad scientist's better ideas to have Daphne call round that morning. As soon as she saw her, Ellie realized that of all her friends, here was the one best suited to the circumstances. With Daphne she could get serious without getting heavy, and her different world view provided a stimulating, if sometimes infuriating, change of perspective.

They drank and Daphne said, 'So, how's Rosie? Did she get a whiff of all the excitement?'

'We tried to keep it from her, but you never know what they pick up, do you? I was tempted to keep her off school today, but that would have confirmed there was something going on. Anyway, the holidays start tomorrow, and she made such a fuss about getting back after her illness, she'd have been brokenhearted to miss the fun of the last day.'

'Children's hearts are made of one of the least frangible materials known to man,' said Daphne with a mother-of-two's certainty. 'Especially girls'. I seem to recall breaking mine on an almost daily basis but somehow surviving without resort to Dr Christian Barnard. You too, I bet.'

'Perhaps. I never lost my best friend when I was Rosie's age, but,' said Ellie.

There'd been two girls stricken by the meningitis bug. The other, Rosie's classmate and best friend, Zandra, had died.

Daphne grimaced and said, 'I was forgetting that. Sorry. It's funny, a child's grief, unless you've experienced it yourself, you don't think about it much . . . but she was keen to get back to Edengrove, you say? I'd have thought . . .'

'Me too. We've talked about Zandra, naturally. Or rather I've talked. Rosie listens. But she doesn't say much beyond, the nix got her. You remember the nix? The water-imp in that book she used to be crazy about, whose hobby was abducting young girls? The educational psych, who looks about fifteen and has a stutter, says I shouldn't worry, in fact I should be pleased Rosie's found a formula which enables her to deal with her loss. Like she's bottling it up, you mean? I said. Like she's dealing with it, says this adolescent expert firmly. She'll talk when she wants to talk, just leave the channels open. Just try to let things settle back to what they were before. Routines are more than comfortable, they are essential. Christ,

I reckon she must have majored on *The Little Book of Psycho-pap* or some such thing!'

'You didn't actually say that, did you?'

Ellie laughed and said, 'No. I'm getting soft. In fact, I came home and dug out *Nina and the Nix* from where I'd hidden it, then I had a drink and a think, and then I went and hid it again. In other words, I've no idea how to cope. So I decided to go with the flow and when Rosie wanted to go back to school, I said, OK, why not?'

'That sounds sensible.'

'Yeah, except I did start wondering if it was just a way of getting out from under this madwoman who'd turned from a straightforward modern *laissez-faire* mum to an overbearing, over-anxious, ever-present earth mother. OK. No need to say it. That's me all over. Self-centred. Everything comes back to me.'

'You said it. But everything includes all the pain and worry too, so don't whip yourself too hard with them scorpions.'

'My, we are full of literature this morning. *Othello* again?'

'The Bible. My father *was* an archdeacon, remember, so you can hardly feel threatened by that.'

Daphne gave as good as she got, thought Ellie, which was one of the reasons she liked her.

She said, 'Listen, can you stay for lunch? I'd really like to talk. Or we could go out and get a sandwich at the pub.'

'Sorry, I'm on my way to the Mossy Bank Garden

Centre, would you believe? It's the other side of the bypass and as I was going to be so close, I couldn't resist dropping in to see how you were. Patrick and I are lunching in their caff, God help us. He's been advising them on roses and I think he feels the sight of his expensive wife will help prepare them for the sight of his expensive bill. I'd suggest you came but I think your Save the Peatbogs T-shirt might be counterproductive. I could manage a drink this evening though.'

'Shit. I've got my Liberata group coming round.'

'What's that? Plastic kitchenware or one of those sexy undies groups?'

'No, the Liberata Trust's a human rights organization, sort of Amnesty with feminist attitude . . . oh, ha ha.'

She saw from her friend's face that she was being sent up.

Daphne said, 'Oh well, if you'd rather save the world than have a drink with your friend . . .'

'Yeah, yeah. Truth is, the world's had to look after itself over the past couple of months. I've been feeling guilty – yes, I know; there I go again – so when Feenie rang about the next meeting, I said why not have it round here?'

'Feenie? You don't mean Serafina Macallum, the mad bag lady?'

'That's right. Our founder, chair and driving force. How on earth do you know her?'

'She sold us the bothy. Or at least her lawyer did. We never met her during the negotiations, but

I've come close to being run down by her several times, both in that clapped-out Land Rover she drives, and on that ancient bike. You'd think she had something against me.'

Ellie concealed the thought that this was probably truer than Daphne guessed. She knew that what Feenie Macallum resented about the break up of her family estate wasn't losing bits of property but the kind of people she had to lose them to.

Her own ignorance of the details of the Aldermanns' purchase of a country cottage lay in her knee-jerk disapproval when Daphne had mentioned it a couple of years earlier.

'Patrick loves to see the kids and their friends enjoying themselves but he does go white when he sees them turning the garden into a football pitch or a badminton court, so I said, Why don't we buy a chunk of unspoilt countryside which they can then spoil to their hearts' content,' she'd said.

And Ellie hadn't been able to bite back the caustic comment that helping put the price of rural housing out of the reach of other people's children hardly seemed a proportionate solution to Patrick's concern for his precious roses.

The cottage hadn't been much mentioned between them thereafter, and when it was, Ellie hadn't been able to decide if Daphne's insistence on calling it *the bothy* was diplomatic understatement or provocative meiosis. Nor was she really sure whether her own attitude was pure social indignation or part dog-in-the-manger envy.

Now she wished she hadn't been so quick to make it a no-go area, both conversationally and geographically, as her certainty that Feenie Macallum would have soaked the purchasers for as much as she could get, then put the money to some very good use, would have allowed her to have her cake and eat it.

'Anyway,' continued Daphne, 'she doesn't look as if she knows what day of the week it is. Ring her up, tell her she's got it wrong.'

'Feenie is as sharp as a butcher's knife,' retorted Ellie. 'And there are others concerned and I've mucked them about once already. The meeting should have been yesterday, but when I thought I was going to be riding herd on the school outing, I had to ring round everybody and rearrange. Oh God. I forgot to remind Peter they were coming.'

'Never mind,' said Daphne. 'What pleasanter surprise can there be for a hard-working bobby than to come home and find his house full of anarchist do-gooders? So let's see if we can find a window in your crowded calendar. Lunch sometime later this week? Patrick's going to some horticultural conference in Holland in the morning, Diana's down at her cousin's in Dorset and David's at the bothy with some sixth-form chums. God, you are lucky to be in the State system. Costs you nothing and they spend most of their time at school, while we pay a fortune and ours are hardly ever there!'

Ellie smiled, but didn't rise. A wise avenger picks

her own payback time. Lunch at Rosemont, which invariably consisted of Marks and Sparks goodies tarted up to look home-made, should provide a good launch pad.

'That sounds great,' she said. 'Any day but tomorrow. We're going out to Enscombe. They've got some kind of menagerie at the Hall. Ed Wield, who lives in the village, was foolish enough to mention it to Rosie and she didn't leave him alone till he promised to show her round.'

'Wield? That's the ugly sergeant, isn't it? Didn't you say he was a bit . . . ?'

Daphne made a rocking gesture with her hand.

'Gay?' said Ellie. 'That's right. Except not a bit. All of him. And despite anything you learned at Sunday School, it doesn't mean he lies in wait for small children.'

'Never thought it did,' said Daphne. 'He struck me as a very nice man. And I recall Daddy saying that he preferred his curates gay, as it was easier to look after the choir when the curate was around than it was to look after the curate with the Mothers' Union in full cry. Now I must whizz off and earn my keep. A garden centre caff! The mind boggles.'

'Regards to Patrick,' said Ellie. 'And watch out for greenfly.'

She waved her friend goodbye, noting with self-mocking envy that since last they met she'd changed her car again for a sporty Audi, gave another wave to DC Dennis Seymour, and went back inside.

Mention of her Liberata meeting reminded her that she'd promised herself to do a bit of preparation. She'd completely neglected this and most other commitments during the past few weeks, but when Feenie Macallum asked questions, a wise acolyte had answers. She went back upstairs and switched on the laptop. There were no visible aftereffects of the coffee and she clicked on Liberata in her *Documents* and studied the names that came up. These were the women Feenie had allocated to her to be in correspondence with. Most were in prison. All were in trouble. Few were able to reply, so writing to them was often an act of faith. But as Feenie said, even if the letter is intercepted, it tells someone out there that we know these women exist and are victims, and that might make the difference between life and death.

She selected the first on her list, Bruna Cubillas, the first alphabetically but also the first in Ellie's affections. There'd been replies from Bruna, enough for a real relationship to be established, and written with an intensity of feeling that took Ellie by surprise. She'd mentioned this to Feenie, who'd said, 'If someone offers you a helping hand when you're drowning, you grip tight.'

She began to write.

Dear Bruna,

How are you? I am sorry I have not written to you for so long but my life was turned upside down a little while ago.

She paused and tried to think how *turned upside down* could be rendered in Spanish. She usually made some attempt to translate the more idiomatic bits of her letters, though perhaps by now it wasn't necessary. Bruna had said she was keen to build on her smattering of English, and asked for some books to help her. Ellie had sent off a boxful, ranging from *The House at Pooh Corner* to a complete Shakespeare, but what progress she might have made Ellie had no idea. A hasty postscript to Bruna's last letter had offered a *gracias* for 'the book', meaning presumably the suspicious and repressive prison regime had allowed only one of her boxful through. That was, she worked it out, almost a year ago. Ellie had written several letters since, but her last had been several weeks before Rosie's illness. She thought ruefully of how flimsy a thing her concern for this poor imprisoned and probably tortured woman thousands of miles away had proved in the presence of immediate and personal pain, but she couldn't feel guilty. Once, perhaps, but not now. *Am I growing more or less selfish?*

She returned her attention to the letter.

How much of her recent trauma should she lay out here? Feenie's words came back to her. 'Tell them everything about yourself,' she commanded. 'However trite, however tragic. That way they'll know you really care, you're not just dishing up nourishing broth for the peasants. What you're doing is letting them know there is a real world

96

still going on beyond their prison walls, there are real people still living their lives beyond the blank faces of their guards and torturers.'

But when Ellie had asked for information about Bruna, Feenie had shaken her head.

'Best you don't know,' she said. 'These women live under regimes and in circumstances you can't imagine. Sometimes they are totally innocent, but sometimes they may have done things which you in your ignorance could find hard to understand or justify. All you need to know is that they are suffering cruel and unnatural treatment. It is your task to give them hope. What they give you in return is up to them.'

Ellie began typing again.

My little girl Rosie was taken ill . . .

The phone rang.

Irritated, she went next door into the bedroom and picked up the receiver.

'What?' she bellowed.

'Charming. I wish I hadn't bothered.'

'Daphne, is that you? What's up? You forget something?'

'Only how brusque you can be. Listen, I just thought I'd ring you to tell you you're being watched.'

'Yes, I know. Dennis Seymour. I thought you said he spoke to you . . .'

'Don't be so *dim*, Ellie. I don't mean him. You know those plane trees on that little triangle of no-man's-land at the corner of your road? Well,

I noticed this fellow hanging about there when I drove past earlier. Only then, not knowing anything about yesterday's punch-up at the Pascoe corral, I didn't pay much heed. But when I passed the trees just now and saw he was still there, still looking towards your house, I thought, Hello-Hello-Hello, this looks like one for a citizen's arrest.'

'Daphne, don't you dare! Don't do anything. I'll get the guy on watch to deal.'

'So what are you going to do? Run out of the house and point this way? No, listen, untwist your knickers. Count up to a hundred. All I'm going to do is get out of the car and stroll back towards him and distract him with brilliant conversation. When you get to a hundred, *then* head out to your guardian angel and send him winging this way as quick as he likes. And if chummy here tries to do a runner, I'll stick my leg out and send him sprawling, a tactic for which I was once renowned in Mid-Yorkshire girls' hockey circles.'

'No,' insisted Ellie. 'Do nothing. I'll –'

'Start counting. One, two, three . . .'

The phone went dead.

Ellie didn't hesitate. She went sprinting down the stairs, out of the house, down the drive, waving and calling to the watching Seymour. He spotted her and started to get out of the car.

'No!' she screamed. 'Stay there! Start up!'

He was, God be thanked, quick-witted enough to obey.

'Turn, turn, turn! Go, go, go!' commanded Ellie,

scrambling into the passenger seat.

'Where are we going?' he asked calmly as he accelerated through a U-turn, getting the car up to sixty in about nine seconds.

'We're there!' she yelled. 'Stop. Oh, sweet Jesus.'

The car snaked to a halt alongside the plane trees.

A figure slumped against one of them, head thrown back to show a face which was a mask of blood.

'Call an ambulance,' cried Ellie, leaping from the car and rushing towards her friend. 'Daphne, are you all right?'

The woman made a gasping noise which may or may not have been an answer, but at least her eyes were open and she was moving and breathing.

'Why didn't you wait?' Ellie couldn't stop herself from asking as she knelt to examine the damage. 'Oh Jesus. What a mess. Is it just your face or are you hurt anywhere else?'

'. . . aar . . .' gasped Daphne.

'What? Where?'

'Car. Bastard took my car. Oh God. Look at the state of this blouse.'

vii

a pint of Guinness

'That's two days in succession our street's been full of police cars,' said Ellie. 'The neighbours are going to start complaining about you bringing your work home.'

'They should think themselves lucky I'm not a rock star,' said Pascoe.

'We should all think ourselves lucky for that,' said Ellie.

They were at the hospital, to which Ellie had accompanied Daphne in the ambulance. Pascoe had arrived almost simultaneously. He could see she was seriously stressed, but coping by dint of having someone else to look after. Activity had always been her way of dealing with life's ambushes.

She'd told him what little she knew. Daphne had gasped out her car number and the policeman on watch had put out an alert. Apart from that, she had on Ellie's insistence concentrated on using her mouth for breathing.

'Peter, how're you doing? You here for Mrs Aldermann?'

Dr John Sowden was an old acquaintance, almost an old friend, of Pascoe's. They had first met at the intersection of a police and medical case and perhaps because that had marked out so clearly the parameters of their areas of common ground, their friendship had somehow only flourished in miniature, like a bonsai tree.

'That's right. How is she?'

'Fine, considering someone's given her a fair bang on the nose. Broken but I think we'll get away without surgery.'

'Any other injuries?'

'No. Some shock from the assault and the loss of blood, but nothing that a good night's rest won't put right. I've got a nurse cleaning her up now, then she'll be ready to go home. What is it? Your friendly neighbourhood mugging? Were you with her when it happened, Ellie? Can check you out as well, if you like.'

He was looking at the blood on her T-shirt.

'No, thanks,' said Ellie. 'This is Daphne's. I got there later. I'm fine.'

It wasn't a complete lie. She consulted her body and mind and found that she felt a lot better than she thought she ought to. Perhaps like a vampire I need blood to feed on, she thought, watching as Pascoe, with an apologetic smile in her direction, drew Sowden a little way along the corridor and spoke to him in a low voice.

When he rejoined her she said, 'So?'

'So you heard it all. He wasn't keeping anything back for my ears only.'

'Well, I'm pleased about that, else this new, violent doppelgänger of mine might have been tempted to break his nose too.'

But she smiled as she said it. She liked John Sowden. He was pretty sound on issues like abortion and euthanasia and he had a mouth to die for.

A few moments later they were allowed into the treatment room where they found Daphne sitting on the edge of a bed, drinking tea.

She said, 'Ellie, have you seen the state of me? I shall have to go into purdah for a month at least.'

'No, you look fine, honestly. You'll have those English-rose looks back in no time.'

'An English rose I don't mind but not when I'm wearing it bang in the middle of my face. Oh God, has anyone been in touch with Patrick? No way I can go to the garden centre like this. They'd probably spray me with an anti-black-spot mixture.'

'I tried your home number on my mobile,' said Pascoe. 'No reply. Give us the name of this garden centre and I'll make sure he gets a message to come here and collect you.'

'No, please. Just say I can't make it to lunch, I'll see him at home later,' said Daphne firmly. 'It's called Mossy Bank. Thank you, Peter, you're a darling.'

Pascoe stepped aside to make the call and Ellie

sat on the bed next to her friend and put her arm around her.

'Watch out for blood,' said Daphne. 'This blouse is ruined.'

'It'll come out,' said Ellie. 'And I'm well spattered already.'

'Are you? Let me see. Oh, I'm sorry. I hope it's not one of your best.'

Ellie, knowing well Daphne's view that baggy T-shirts, especially those printed with subversive messages, were the nadir of style and taste, laughed out loud and said, 'I'll insist that you personally buy me an exact replacement in the market. So, my girl, what the hell did you think you were playing at, provoking this hoodlum? He might have had a knife or a gun or anything.'

'Didn't see why you should have all the fun. But why is it when a snotty-nosed Trot like you mixes with the lowlife, you get to kick them in the balls, while a respectable Tory lady like me ends up in hospital?'

Before Ellie could answer, Pascoe rejoined them, saying, 'That's done. Daphne, I hope you haven't been telling Ellie your tale because you're just going to have to tell it to me again.'

'She was just going to start,' said Ellie.

'I was just going to tell you it was all your fault, actually,' said Daphne. 'I had it all sorted. I was going to stroll up to this fellow and distract his attention. Then while he had his back turned on your house (after the count of one hundred, remember?), you were going to get your guardian angel to come scooting along to make an arrest. Except that just as I got to him, you came belting out of your driveway, waving your arms and screaming at that poor policeman in the car. Naturally my man realized something was up and turned to make his getaway. Equally naturally, I attempted to grapple with him and keep him there. Upon which he nutted me, I think is the phrase. It's something I've often seen on the telly and I've always assumed its effect was a touch exaggerated, like people in Westerns being hurled backwards when someone shoots them. Now I know better. It's a funny thing how much closer I've got to the realities of lowlife since I met you, Ellie.'

'It's another funny thing,' said Ellie, 'that now you can't talk down your nose, you sound almost normal.'

'Daphne,' said Pascoe quickly. 'This man, can you describe him?'

'Well, he was furtive, you know. Perhaps not so much furtive as simply loitering. That's what made me notice him, though, as I told Ellie. I wouldn't really have paid any attention if she hadn't told me about her dreadful experience of yesterday . . .'

As Daphne Aldermann got older, she sounded more and more like an archdeacon's daughter, thought Pascoe. Or rather the way you expected an archdeacon's daughter to sound in an old black and white play, circumlocutory and slightly prissy, with audible inverted commas appearing round any modernism. She should have been a judge. Or at least a magistrate. Yes, she was precisely the type of woman who, despite valiant efforts to broaden the selectorate, still dominated on the magisterial bench. Not that she'd ever shown the slightest ambition in the direction so far as he knew. And while she might make *bath* sound like an American novelist, she could pronounce the shibboleth which got you admitted to Ellie's friendship so there had to be more to her than met the eye. Which was probably true of her husband also. A quiet, charming man who lived for roses, he had been in the frame for not one but several apparently accidental deaths. Nothing was ever proved, and in his company Pascoe blushed to recall his suspicions. And yet . . . and yet . . .

'Could you describe him, please, Daphne?' he said.

'Yes, of course. Sorry, I'm jabbering a bit, aren't I? First time I've been assaulted, you see. Comes as a shock, especially when the motive isn't sexual. No, that's a stupid thing to say, it would obviously have been a much greater shock if he'd then gone on to rape me. What I mean is, he just nutted me as if . . . well, as if I were a man.'

'Not an English gentleman then?' murmured Pascoe, winning a Medusa glare from Ellie. 'Sorry.'

'No. You're right. I mean, I'm not saying he wasn't English, or British anyway. As Ellie keeps on telling me, we're a rainbow society now. But he certainly wasn't Anglo-Saxon. He was dark, not negroid, just well-grilled, like Ellie. I wish I tanned like that but with my colouring all you get's a splotchy pink. Still, they say nowadays it's bad for you, too much sun, gives you skin cancer . . . not that I'm suggesting for one moment, dear, that you're in danger of *that*. No, I'm sure in your case it's all down to natural pigmentation . . .'

'Putting aside the interesting question of Ellie's ethnic origins,' said Pascoe, 'you're saying this fellow was well-tanned? Hair?'

'Yes, of course. Sorry, I mean it was black, cut short, I don't mean shaven, not like those – do they still call them bovver boys?'

'The term is, I believe, a trifle passé,' said Pascoe. 'So, short hair. Moustache? Beard?'

'Yes, now I come to think of it, he did have a moustache,' said Daphne. 'Not a big one. Short too. Like his hair. In fact, he was very neat generally, almost dapper. He would have made a very good head waiter at a decent restaurant.'

Was she taking the piss? He glanced at Ellie, who gave him her sardonic smile. She had once advised him, not much point in mocking Daphne when she's so much better at it herself. But it was hard to resist the temptation. And she seemed to enjoy it in a harmlessly flirty kind of way. Harmless because there wasn't the slightest sign he turned her on, and he himself had never gone overboard on English roses, who, in a metamorphosis which might have been of interest to Ovid, often seemed to age into English horses.

Whatever, the technique finally got him a pretty good description. Not very big, five-six, five-seven maybe, slim build, thin face, sharp-nosed, wearing a dark-blue lightweight jacket of good cut (Daphne had an eye for clothes), well-pressed light-grey slacks without turn-ups, wine-coloured loafers (this with a *moue* of distaste), an open-necked powder-blue shirt, and a gold chain with some sort of medallion round his neck.

'Excellent,' said Pascoe. 'Hang on.'

He raised Control on his mobile and passed on the description. In return he was told that the Audi had been found.

'That's quick,' said Pascoe.

'Didn't get far. Leyburn Road. A shopping parade. You know it, sir?'

'Know it? I owe money there.'

It was five minutes' drive from his house, ten minutes' walk via the recreation ground.

'Who's there?' he asked.

'Sergeant Wield.'

That was good. Everything would be in smooth running order.

'Pass him the description,' said Pascoe, unnecessarily, he was sure, but he said it anyway. Ellie, who'd picked up the gist, was hissing something at him.

'What?'

'The car, is it OK?'

For a second the words *who the hell cares about the sodding car?* formed in his mind. But the answer was too obvious for them to get near his lips. Ellie cared. Not about the car, but about the fact that her friend had been hurt acting, albeit unasked, on her behalf. Her concern about the car was, literally, a damage-limitation exercise.

'Is the Audi OK?' he asked.

'Far as we know, no problem. Just neatly parked.'

'Thanks.' He switched off and said, 'The Audi's parked in Leyburn Road. It looks fine.'

'That's something, isn't it, Daph?'

Daphne managed a smile at her friend and said, 'Yes, that's something.'

She doesn't give a damn either, thought Pascoe. But she understands what Ellie's on about.

He said, 'OK if we move on? This guy, did he speak at all?'

'Not a word. What in the circumstances do you think he might have found to say?'

'Well, something like, *Take that, you bitch*, when he hit you.'

'*Take that, you bitch*? Really, Peter, you're so old-fashioned sometimes. No, he said nothing, or nothing I heard. What I did hear was my Audi revving up and I thought, the bastard's stealing my car.'

'You'd left the key in the ignition?'

'Yes, and my mobile phone on the dash. Is that still there, by the way? No, of course you won't know. Stupid of me, now I come to think of it. If

I'd got chummy to the car, he'd have been dead suspicious soon as he realized I could have rung for help, wouldn't he?'

'Not as suspicious as he'd have been when he turned the key and the engine started first time,' smiled Pascoe. 'I'll check out the phone. There'll be a car waiting to take you home soon as you're ready.'

He left Daphne in Ellie's care and went out. Dennis Seymour was waiting for him in the corridor, looking anxious. Reason told him his watching brief hadn't extended to covering all Mrs Pascoe's friends and acquaintance, but he knew from personal experience that in the matter of a man's family, reason did not always apply. But Pascoe was not in the accusing mood.

He said, 'So, Dennis. You been racking your brains for me?'

'Yes, sir. Sorry. Nothing more than what I told you. Like I said, I took a note of every vehicle that went along the street while I was on watch. Nothing acting suspiciously. Control's checked the numbers. Nothing dodgy. All good citizens, nothing known.'

'OK. Try this for size.'

Pascoe repeated Daphne's description of her assailant.

Seymour said, 'No. Didn't see anyone like that in any of the cars. As for on foot, I saw nobody except the postman. I'm really sorry.'

'Don't be. It takes up space in your mind and I

want every iota of your attention focused on Mrs Pascoe. In your sights at all times, OK?'

'Yes, sir.'

'Right. I'm on my way to Leyburn Road.'

Seymour watched Pascoe go with relief. No bollocking, no attempt to suggest he was at fault. But sometimes Pascoe being quiet and reasonable could be as intimidating as Fat Andy Dalziel on the rampage.

In Leyburn Road he found Wield watching the Audi getting a preliminary going-over by a white-overalled technician. There was a mobile phone on the dash.

'How's Mrs Aldermann?' asked the sergeant.

'Stiff upper lip, literally,' said Pascoe. 'Nose broken, some shock, but still talking. And making sense. What's happening here?'

'I've got a couple of lads checking the shops to see if anyone noticed the car arriving or anyone fitting your description. Also, they're asking if the shopkeepers can remember any of their customers in the last hour in case they can come up with something.'

That was good thinking, but Pascoe didn't say so. Wield would merely be puzzled at being complimented on doing the basics of his job.

Pascoe looked around. The car was parked by the roadside in front of the little shopping complex – grocer, greengrocer, butcher, baker, newsagent, hardware store – which people in the area used conscientiously, aware that letting themselves be lured by the cheaper prices of the superstore only ten minutes' drive away would soon unleash a drowning shower of rain on the Leyburn Road parade. But the shops were rarely so busy that the assistants wouldn't have time to glance outside occasionally.

The technician backed carefully out of the Audi and straightened up with a groan of relief.

Pascoe said, 'Anything?'

The man shook his head and said, 'Sorry. Looks like he was careful. Everything wiped clean.'

'Thanks, anyway,' said Wield. 'What now, Pete? I'm out of ideas.'

Pascoe smiled as if at an absurdity and said, 'OK, let's suppose this guy left his own car here and walked round to watch my house because he felt he'd draw less attention on foot. He steals Daphne's car because he needs to get back here quick, but he isn't panicking. He still takes time to wipe his prints. If he's as cool as that, he wouldn't park next to his own car because that's the kind of thing that draws attention, a man jumping out of one car and getting straight into another. So he parks, gets out, and walks.'

As if doing a reconstruction, Pascoe set off at a brisk pace with Wield in close pursuit.

'Doesn't help us unless we get a witness saw him walking,' panted the sergeant.

'I know. But listen, parking's bad around here. Not a lot of room.'

Wield could see he was right, but not what he was getting at. In front of the shops there was kerbside parking space for only half a dozen cars. In one direction Leyburn Road curved into a double-yellow-line bend and in the other it ran into the busy ring road via a roundabout, beside which stood a pseudo-Victorian shiny-tiles-and-leaded-lights pub, the Gateway.

It was the pub Pascoe was heading for.

As he walked he explained, 'When it's busy here, shoppers often use the pub car park. Billy Soames, the landlord, wants to avoid getting into dispute with the shopkeepers, so he's put up a sign at the entrance: *No charge to shoppers, but it helps if you at least buy a packet of crisps in the bar!* Could be that's where chummy parked his own car. Let's ask Billy if he noticed a small suntanned man with a moustache using his facilities this morning.'

'Why not?' said Wield.

His mobile rang. He put it to his ear and listened. When he switched off, Pascoe, who, like an astronomer after a lifetime's study of the pocked and pitted surface of the moon, had learned to interpret a few of the sergeant's expressions, said, 'You look pleased.'

'Something I recalled from house-to-house yesterday. One of your neighbours, Mrs Cavendish, noticed a car stopping at the end of the street then turning back when all the troops had turned up. Didn't seem important then. But it popped into my mind just now when we got Mrs Aldermann's description of the man who attacked her, so I checked it out.'

'And?'

'Her words were, the man was swarthy, moustachioed and sinister.'

'That sounds like old Mrs C.,' said Pascoe. 'And the car?'

'Metallic-blue. Sounds like a Golf. Could be owt or nowt but the description fits, sort of. She half remembered a bit of the number too, so if it turns out there was a blue Golf in the pub car park . . .'

'Anyone ever tell you you're a treasure?' said Pascoe.

'Not since breakfast. By the by, that guy we talked about this morning, the student, Franny Roote. I never saw him. This sound anything like?'

'Not like the way he was back then. Size might fit, but he was blond.'

'Perhaps prison's turned him black.'

'Perhaps. I'll find out tomorrow. Somehow I doubt he's got anything to do with this, but if he has, could be the sight of me will make a good gloat irresistible.'

'You still fancy Cornelius, do you?'

'Don't know. Maybe. There's something odd going on there. You know that they found this message on her computer at the bank? It just said, TIME TO GO. And there was another on her e-mail at her apartment. STILL HERE? OH DEAR. Unsourced, but dated the day she took off. So there's someone in the background.'

'Ollershaw, you think? Trying to scare her into making a run for it? But he didn't want her caught and talking, so now he wants to pressure you to get her out?'

Wield's tone was dubious.

'Doesn't sound likely, does it?' said Pascoe. 'And I tend to agree with Andy about Ollershaw. Slippery but not physical. Anyway, I'm back in court with her tomorrow, so if someone really is trying to twist my arm to go easy opposing the bail application, then they'll need to get in touch soon.'

They had reached the pub.

The landlord greeted them with the wariness all landlords exhibit on spotting the fuzz on the premises, but soon relaxed when he understood the nature of their enquiries. Inured by long experience to disappointment or at best ambiguity, Pascoe was almost taken aback when Billy Soames said instantly, 'Yeah. Sure. I remember them.'

'Them?'

'That's right. I saw them arrive, two of them got out of the car, the little dark one set off down the road and the other one came in and ordered a pint of Guinness and a bag of crisps. First customer of the day. He sat there reading his paper for maybe three-quarters of an hour, then his mate looked through the door and sort of beckoned like he was in a hurry. And the pop-eyed one got up straightaway and went out.'

'Pop-eyed? What do you mean?'

'He had these sort of bulging eyes. Light-coloured

hair going a bit thin. About forty. Big scar, newish-looking, along the left side of his head. Pasty complexion, didn't look like he spent much time in the sun.'

'And the car? Did you spot the make, Billy?'

'Merc sports. White.'

'Oh. Not a blue Golf,' said Pascoe stupidly.

The landlord gave Pascoe a long-suffering look and said judiciously, 'Well, it wasn't blue, it was white, and it wasn't a Golf, it was a Merc, so I'd have to say no, Peter, unless I'm deceived, it wasn't a blue Golf. Sorry to be such a disappointment.'

'You've done great,' Pascoe assured him.

Wield said, 'Where was he sitting?'

'Over there. By the window.'

Wield wandered across and picked up a news-paper from the windowsill.

'Was this the paper he was reading?'

'Probably.'

Carefully Wield fitted the paper into an evi-dence bag.

'Which way did the car go?' asked Pascoe.

'Out onto the bypass,' said the landlord. 'All this any help to you?'

'Oh yes,' said Pascoe, knowing the value of friendly eyes and ears in public houses. 'Tremen-dous. Billy, you are a prince among publicans.'

'I'll remember that next time I'm being hassled about after-hours drinking.'

'Anything else you can tell us about the man you served?'

'Popeye? Not really. Didn't have much of a crack, got a delivery just after I served him. Except the way he spoke, that is.'

'And how was that?'

'Well, drinking the Guinness it didn't surprise me. He was Irish.'

viii

spelt from Sibyl's leaves

I'm Popeye the pop-up man . . .

So called because he's harder to keep down than
Bounce-back Bill Clinton.

Started way back on Bloody Sunday when eleven-
year-old schoolboy Patrick Ducannon, uninvolved
son of uninvolved parents got shot by the paras.

Registered d.o.a. at Belfast Infirmary, but sat
up and asked for his mammy when the priest
dropped some hot candle wax on him. (Well,
that's the crack, and why not? No reason the
devil and Gaw Sempernel should have all the
good stories.)

After that, of course he was involved.

And very unlucky or very lucky depending on
how close to him you were standing.

Age twenty: dragged out of an exploded bomb
factory in Derry covered with burnt flesh and
bleeding offal, most of which turned out to belong
to his two fellow ham-fisted bombardiers who in

death proved so inseparable they had to be buried in the same grave.

Age twenty-four: shot as he drove a stolen car through a checkpoint. Car crashed through a wall and rolled down a railway embankment. Three passengers killed instantaneously. Popeye crawled out of the wreckage and ran down a tunnel from which he emerged a few moments later pursued by a train. Three days in hospital, three years in jail.

Age twenty-nine: shot, stabbed and beaten by a unit of the UVF as he lay in his bed with his girlfriend. She died four days later. He went to her funeral.

Age thirty-three: retired from active service with the IRA, perhaps because of his reputation for out-living everyone he worked closely with. Became a quartermaster, specializing in the acquisition of cutting-edge weaponry which was put in deep storage against the long promised day of total insurrection.

Kept out of trouble for a while till one winter's night in Liverpool docks he turned up in the cab of a truck carrying a consignment of arms which we knew had been landed somewhere on the east coast during the previous forty-eight hours.

Straightforward search-and-detain operation went haywire when one of the Provos suddenly reached into his jacket pocket. By the time it was estab-lished he was suffering an anxiety asthma attack and was pulling out his inhaler, he was dead, as were two of his companions and even Popeye, naturally the sole survivor, was seriously injured. Worse still (in the Great Gaw's eyes at least, for he was in charge of the operation), the truck turned out to be carrying only a small part-load of ammo and a few rifles, not the large consignment of state-of-the-art weaponry Gaw had expected.

It must have been cached en route and there was only you left, Pop-up Popeye, who had any idea where.

That got you off the NHS waiting list and into Gaw's own favourite hospital where you got better care than a royal who was a fully paid up member of BUPA. But it was still a close-run thing. Intensive care for two months, convalescent for another six, offered a deal which you refused so reluctantly that it was hard not to believe your medically supported claim that your injuries had left you seriously amnesiac.

The court, however, was unimpressed by this as a defence against the long list of charges prepared against you.

Sentenced to twelve years.

So Popeye the pop-up man, it looked like the system had done what its trained shooters couldn't and buried you.

But . . .

I'm Popeye the pop-up man
Let them hit me as hard as they can
I'll be here at the finish . . .

Came the peace process.

Age thirty-seven: released from jail after serving less than two years.

Maybe it was enough.

You and I have a lot in common, Popeye. Members of ruthless and dangerous organizations, we have both had to learn to survive any which way we could.

And we both have unfinished business with Gawain Sempernel. Or rather, I have unfinished business with him while he has unfinished business with you.

He's going soon. He thinks no one beneath him knows it but you cannot keep a Sibyl and a secret at the same time.

And you, Popeye, are his farewell finger to the envious gods who he believes cannot bear such rival effulgence near their throne. Six months from now he hopes to be clasped to the bosom of our common alma mater, in the holy shrine of a Master's Lodge, where he will sit with one buttock firmly on the faces of those poor dons whose careers are in his gift, and the other discreetly offered for former colleagues to kiss when they beat a path to his door in search of that advice and expertise only his lost omniscience can offer.

The poor sod has overdosed on Deighton and Le Carré!

So there you are, Popeye. We have both been screwed by Gaw Sempernel.

In fact, you could say that, thanks to him, in

our different ways we both know what it is to exist locked up in a cell.

And now, though I am officially the turnkey, we find ourselves cheek by jowl in this cell within a cell that the great comedian Gaw calls *Sibyl's Leaves*.

Imprisonment changes people. It gives them time to think.

I think a lot.

Popeye too. What he thought was probably something like – it's coming to an end. Maybe I can finally get a life which doesn't involve my old body being full of bullets and surrounded by corpses. I've survived the war, surely it can't be all that hard to survive the peace?

It was going to be harder than you could have dreamt, Popeye.

You found a movement split and splintering under pressure of internal debate as to how to proceed in face of the new situation.

Worse, despite your continuing claims of amnesia, you found yourself courted by the most extreme groups for your knowledge of where the arms were hidden.

There must have been lots of heated debate.

There were certainly hairy moments when you were threatened with having the information tortured out of you by men who thought that Amnesia was a popular Far Eastern sexual tourism centre.

Still, a man who has survived being interrogated by Gaw Sempernel can survive anything.

But something had to give.

Finally, confused as to whether you were victor or victim, unable to understand whether you'd got what you'd been fighting for or not, you decided like many a thwarted philosopher before you that it was time to cultivate your own garden.

Maybe it was now your memory came back. Maybe it had never gone.

And if it brought you peril, it might as well bring you profit too.

Uniting for safety with a small group of fellow disenchanted releasees who thought that being applauded onto the platform at a Republican meeting was little enough reward for what they'd been through, you advertised for customers. And when you found your former colleagues less than keen to pay for what they regarded as already their own, you looked further afield.

A couple of minor but lucrative European and near-East deals followed. But your ace-in-the hole, the 'biggie' which was going to make your retirement fortune was the cache of state-of-the-art guns and missiles you'd left buried somewhere deep in enemy country during that cross country trip which ended in the Liverpool fiasco.

We know now (and as usual with Popeye, we've got the bodies to prove it) that the chosen site was a remote and inaccessible spur of Kielder Forest on the English/Scottish border.

For this cache you wanted a customer with serious money.

What you found was PAL, the smallest but most

extreme of the Colombian guerilla groups, fallen on hard times not so much because of the activities of the official counter-insurgency forces, but because its immodestly, though not altogether inaccurately, self-styled 'legendary' leader, Fidel Chiquillo, had managed to get up the noses of high command in both Farc and ELN, the two most powerful rebel organizations.

They set about squeezing PAL out of existence by drying up its source of arms in the Americas. Word was spread; you sell to PAL, you don't sell to us.

So here we have Chiquillo, desperate to re-establish himself on the Colombian scene, ready to go anywhere to do a deal. He has a contact in Europe, his negotiator, who sniffs out the deal with Popeye.

But even so far afield, deals are not easy for Chiquillo to make.

To get himself safe to the UK, to do the deal securely, then to get the shipment intact to South America, he needs allies powerful enough to ignore Farc, ELN, the drug barons and even the elected government itself.

So he turns to the *los Cojos*, that is *el Consejo Juridico*, the national security group whose operations are so clandestine they make the official secret police look like Dixon of Dock Green. Their *jefe supremo*, Colonel Gonzalo Solis (who lost a foot in a bomb attack in 1981, hence the nickname *cojo*, the lame one), knows where all the bodies are buried, which is not surprising as he has buried so many of them himself. Colombian politicians need to be nimble-footed indeed to satisfy the conflicting demands of such rapidly changing partners as the guerilla groups, the drug lords, the United Nations and their own electorate, and over many years, El Cojo has come to call the steps. He is the only man powerful enough to guarantee the deal, but even he hesitates before going up against the loose anti-PAL alliance which applies in the Americas.

But in the end the offer of a commission to be paid in Colombia's favourite currency, pure cocaine, equal to the amount required by Popeye for his weapons proves impossible to resist.

The PAL embargo back home, he decrees, does not apply to deals done in Europe.

And to those in both high and low places who are ready to protest against his decision, he offers a private reassurance that there is no risk of a PAL resurgence. Indeed, quite the contrary. Chiquillo must come personally to close the deal as El Cojo's guarantee of safe conduct applies only to the guerilla leader himself, not his negotiator. And once the deal is done, the Cojos' European chief, Jorge Casaravilla, a man so ruthlessly violent that the colonel likes to keep him several thousand miles of blue water away, has instructions to scoop up everything and everyone with extreme prejudice.

Chiquillo agrees to the terms and makes his payment to El Cojo. His negotiator makes the final arrangements, and at last, by ways and means undetectable even by the eagle eye of soaring Gaw and the strange magic of his Sibyl, Chiquillo arrives in the UK and goes with his two Cojos escorts to the rendezvous in Kielder.

Anyone familiar with Popeye Ducannon's track record might have forecast what happened next.

As always, chaos, catastrophe, corpses, and blood on the forest floor.

And, equally as always, when the gunsmoke settles, Popeye pops up out of the forest with nothing worse than a couple of flesh wounds, a crease along the side of his skull, and a bad headache.

All this and more he tells his one surviving colleague, Jimmy Amis, known as Amity James because of the friendly way he has with him when blowing off your kneecaps.

And all this and more Amity tells us when we pick him up and shake several credit cards under several names out of his pockets and point out that having qualified for early release under the Good Friday Agreement does not disqualify him from early return under the common law.

The *more* he tells us is that Popeye heard Chiquillo, the other survivor, telling someone on his mobile that he'd be with them at somewhere called the CP in two to three hours.

If he made it, that was. For according to Popeye, Chiquillo had taken a hit.

More importantly to Popeye, he'd taken both the weaponry and the bagful of coke which was payment for it.

Having worked all his life in a twilight world of

deceit and betrayal, Popeye isn't much bothered by the whys and wherefores. All he wants is what he regards as his pension fund back. The only clue he has is what he knows about Chiquillo's negotiator. This, together with what the Cojos know about Chiquillo himself, might well lead them to both the man and the arms.

Alliances with Jorge Casaravilla are notoriously dangerous.

But so are alliances with Popeye Ducannon!

The last thing he said to Amity James was, 'I'm just off to see a man about a dog. Or maybe it's a dog about a man. Mind the shop while I'm gone, will you?'

Since then, absolute silence.

Except in our work as in nature there is no such thing.

Have you heard that silence where the birds are dead, yet something pipeth like a bird?

There's always something piping.

And here I sit, Sibyl in her lonely cave, recording and replaying till finally I recognize the tune.

Piper, pipe that song again!

They're still here, that's what my sensors tell me and that's what Gaw wants to hear, those arms and the man who stole them, and the drug fortune he didn't pay for them, all still here hidden away somewhere connected with something contracted to CP. What does my *Word Search* give me?

Canadian Pacific? It's a long way round to Colombia!
Cape Province? As above only more so.

Central Park? Worth checking which northern cities have a Central Park.

C.P. Snow? Does anyone still read him, I wonder.

Chelsea pensioner? At least it's vaguely military.

Command post? So's this. Right place for arms, I suppose.

Common prostitute? Hardly.

Communist Party? An office? Do they still have offices since *glasnost*?

Perhaps it was *sea* followed by something beginning with P?

Or maybe it was Spanish. *Si pez*? Yes fish. *Si pie*? Yes foot.

You're getting silly, girl.

Face it, you're not expected to work things out, just sit here and feed things in.

While the great giant Gaw is striding around out there, making sure he doesn't tell anyone, including me, more than they need to know.

Oh, there are things you need to know, Gaw, and one day soon I look forward to telling you them. Then perhaps you'll realize that walking over people is not a vocation for a true man, or even a grotesque imitation of one.

I'm Popeye the pop-up man
Let them hit me as hard as they can
I'll be here at the finish
'Cos I eat up my spinach
I'm Popeye, the pop-up man!

ix

bag lady on a bike

Shirley Novello lay back in the front seat of her Fiat Uno.

Well, maybe *lay back* was stretching it a bit, which was more than even a medium-sized woman like herself could comfortably manage in such a small car. At least she could drive it comfortably, which longer legs would have made difficult. Mind you, a bit of discomfort would have been a cheap price to pay for longer legs. She looked down at hers with a critical eye. Even with ninety-five per cent of them visible as they emerged from a leather skirt hardly broader than a lumberjack's belt, they couldn't be termed long. What they could be termed was muscular. And what the hell was wrong with muscular? Muscularity was a quality she greatly admired in men. She found it a turn-on, and saw no reason to bother with people who didn't return the compliment. Anyway, above the waist she could compete with anyone, she thought complacently, raising her eyes to the straining buttons of her sun top. Not many of those in a kilo ho ho, as the wet wankers in the canteen would say if they ever got wind of the battened-down bounty lurking beneath the sack-like muddy-brown T-shirts she favoured at work. These, plus a matching selection of baggy trousers, had dampened down awareness of her as a woman to the point where the sexist cracks were conventional rather than focused. A cop-out? Not really. A cop-in, more like it; meaning you sussed out the best way to permit yourself to function most efficiently as a cop. Like Sergeant Wield. There were still plenty of mutt-headed myopes around the station who didn't realize he was gay, and were ready to give you an argument about it. *How could anyone who looked like him and talked like him and put the fear of God into you like him be gay? Stands to reason.* Wankers!

It was because of Wield that she was here on duty now, dressed in play gear rather than her workaday drabs. She'd been clocking off at four when he'd grabbed her.

'Shirley, I need a body to spell Seymour watching Mrs Pascoe. Any chance?'

At least he framed it as a question.

She said, 'Sarge, I've got plans for tonight that it'll cost hearts to break. I can give you till eight if that's any good.'

'That'll do fine. Thanks,' he'd said.

So he was grateful which was nice. But was he trustworthy? She was due to meet a new boyfriend at a new club, both of which she had high hopes of, at eight thirty. Thirty minutes wasn't much to get home and changed in even if her relief turned up on time. So, working on the principle that she wasn't going to be under the gaze of the station neanderthals, she'd come on duty dressed for partying.

Privately she thought this watch on the Pascoe house was overkill. Chummy, who was probably this lad Roote, wasn't likely to come back for a third go. She'd dug up the case file and he sounded a real nut. It had been back when Pascoe was still an unmarried sergeant and La Pascoe was teaching at a college where the Principal had been topped. Roote had evidently assaulted both Pascoe and the Fat Man, breaking a bottle of Scotch over the latter's head. Just went to show there was good even in the worst of us! So, bang him up and fix for a patrol car to crawl past *maison Pascoe* every couple of hours!

Still, overtime was overtime. She turned on Radio One full blast and settled back to fantasize about the muscular young man who was her escort that night.

Then, just before seven, she saw the bag lady.

She was on a bicycle, but she was undoubtedly a bag lady. There were three plastic carriers dangling from the handlebars and another two either side of the saddle. The woman herself was something the far side of seventy, maybe the far side of eighty, with a round leathery face like an under-inflated football and wispy white hair escaping from beneath an unravelling straw hat whose brim looked like a horse had dined on it. Her ample body was draped in several layers of clothing that it would have taken an archaeologist to date. The bike itself was coeval with its rider, or perhaps a little older, its flaking khaki paint suggesting it might have seen service in the Great War.

Novello watched with mild amusement as this figure creaked towards her, then with heightened interest as the machine scraped to a halt, and finally with active alarm as the dismounted woman began to open the Pascoes' gate.

It was hard to leave the car with dignity, but practise had enabled her to emerge from it with speed. The woman saw her coming and paused by the open gate. It occurred to Novello that if any, or all, of the carriers contained a deadly weapon, she was presenting a pretty unmissable target. A low ornamental wall to her right offered the only real cover and she flinched towards it as the old woman dipped her hand into one of the bags. But all she came out with was a large magnifying glass which she raised to her eyes, the better to study the approaching DC.

'Excuse me, madam,' said Novello, pulling out her ID. 'Detective Constable Novello, Mid-Yorkshire CID. Do you mind telling me who you are and what you're doing here?'

'If you experience difficulty in answering these questions yourself, then perhaps you have strayed into the wrong employment, my girl,' said the woman, in a voice rich with the kind of orotundity Novello only ever heard when she chanced on some ancient actress being interviewed on the telly.

She'll probably turn out to be the DCI's gran, she thought, but she persisted. 'Please, madam. If you could just answer the question.'

'Very well. I am Serafina Macallum, founder and life president of the Liberata Trust, and I am here to attend, nay, to chair, a meeting of our local group. For the record, and I assume we are being recorded though where the necessary apparatus might be concealed in such a deshabille as yours I cannot imagine, I would like to say that though long resigned to having my phone tapped and my mail interfered with, I had not thought that this so-called democracy of ours had degenerated to such open interference with the free move-ment of its citizens twice in the space of fifteen minutes.'

'Twice?' wondered Novello.

'When I left my vehicle in the car park of the Gateway public house, I was accosted by a child in uniform under the pretext that he wished to know if I had been there earlier in the day.'

That figured. She'd heard that the landlord of the Gateway had spotted a white Mercedes parked there about midday with a driver fitting Daphne Aldermann's description of the perp. Wield would have made sure someone went back there to check if any of this evening's customers had been there at lunchtime and seen or heard anything.

'And were you?' asked Novello.

'Certainly not. You think I do not have better things to do with my time than frequent public houses?'

'But you're parked there now,' said Novello reasonably. 'Incidentally, why didn't you just keep on driving and park in the street here?'

'I drive, reluctantly, on the main highways and some rural byways. But when I reach the environs of the town, I prefer the greater freedom of pedal power, and in addition I do not care to pollute other people's living space.'

Stark staring, thought Novello. But that doesn't stop her being the DCI's gran. In fact, it might be a necessary qualification.

On the other hand, she didn't have La Pascoe down as being religious which was all that Liberata suggested to her. Still, these days you never could tell.

'This Liberata thing, that's as in St Wilgefortis?' she enquired.

The old woman looked at her sharply, then said, 'It is good to see how thoroughly your masters brief you.'

'Not masters. Mistresses. I went to a convent school. For a while anyway. The nuns were very keen to hammer home the important things like the lives of the saints. I've still got the broken knuckles to prove it.'

Why am I telling this old bat the story of my schooldays? she wondered. I'll be telling her why I got thrown out next.

She said abruptly, 'So Mrs Pascoe's expecting you?'

'Of course she is, though no doubt to maximize the harassment, you will wish to go through the motions of ascertaining that for yourself.'

She was right there, thought Novello, following the bicycle up the drive.

She rang the bell while Miss Macallum disengaged her bags from her bike. They were full of cardboard files, clipboards, sheets of newspaper, and other varieties of stationery. Novello noted with amusement that supermarket names printed on the bags had been scored over with a black marker pen.

Catching her gaze, Miss Macallum said, 'I see no reason why the moguls of Mammon should make me the instrument of their aggrandizement.'

The door opened and Ellie Pascoe appeared.

Her expression gave Novello the information she required without need of question, and more besides.

Yes, Miss Macallum was telling the truth about the meeting, but Ellie Pascoe had forgotten all about it and found the prospect as appealing as a day-old hard-fried egg, an image which came to Novello's mind as this was the only edible substance she'd found in her flat that morning when she started to prepare breakfast.

She risked a wry sympathetic smile and wished she hadn't bothered. La P. gave her the cold cut, then her face blossomed into a welcoming smile as she said, 'Feenie, good to see you. Come on in. Let me help you with your bags.'

Novello waited till the door was closing before saying, 'Will there be many others, Mrs Pascoe?'

'Three, maybe four. All women. And I'd prefer it if you didn't march them all up to the door.'

'I need to check them out,' said Novello. 'Maybe you could give a little signal before you let them in, just to confirm you know them?'

'A signal?' said Ellie, with an intonation normally reserved for *A handbag?* 'What had you in mind?'

'Nothing complicated. Just a little wave maybe.'

Ellie nodded and closed the door.

'You do know how to wave, don't you, Mrs Pascoe?' said Novello to the woodwork.

Over the next ten minutes four more women arrived, all looking disappointingly normal after Feenie Macallum. The first three were admitted with a perfunctorily dismissive gesture of La P.'s hand. Only with the fourth was there a hesitation. Then the bag lady appeared behind La P. and spoke, the hand fluttered, the newcomer stepped inside and the door closed.

Novello settled down to pass the remainder of her stag with dreams of her stag to come, but about twenty minutes later she saw the DCI's car turn into the drive. Pascoe got out and came back through the gateway towards her and she slid out of the Uno once more.

She saw him clocking her legs and the gear, but guessed he'd be too politically correct, or at least too polite, to comment.

'Hi, Shirley,' he said. 'Anything happening?'

'Yeah. Some kind of prayer meeting, I think.'

She told him about the Liberata Trust. He smiled as if she'd said something funny, but she also saw him repress the cold-fried-egg reaction. Not in front of the servants.

He said, 'How long have you been here?'

'Took over from Dennis at four.'

'Good. I appreciate it.'

He gave her the Pascoe smile. Does he think we won't be claiming the overtime? she wondered. But then he rubbed his hand across his face and suddenly looked very tired, very vulnerable, and Novello felt a pang of sympathy, but recalling his wife's dusty response, she didn't let it show.

'Any development on the car spotted in the Gateway car park?' she asked.

'Not on the car, but one of the two men, the one in the pub, we got a print off his newspaper.'

'That's good. Known, sir?'

He hesitated. Wondering whether he wants to share this with underlings, thought Novello resentfully. But when he did reply, her resentment quickly faded.

'Yes. Patrick Ducannon. He's IRA, got a twelve-year stretch but out in two after the Good Friday

Agreement. Word is he's given up the cause. Certainly he's blotted his copybook in Republican circles.'

'Jesus,' said Novello. 'This is serious stuff. And the other guy . . . ?'

'Nothing. Doesn't fit any known associate, at least not on our books.'

Meaning it might on somebody else's? Like the security services whom all regular cops regarded as anal-retentive gits.

'So this guy parks at the pub because he doesn't want to be spotted sitting in his car, watching your house, and takes a stroll, thinking he's safe, only Mrs Aldermann spots him . . .'

'That's how it looks,' said Pascoe, suddenly impatient. 'OK, Shirley, you can clock off now.'

'Sir? I mean, I'm on till eight, then Seymour . . .'

'I've cancelled Dennis already,' said Pascoe firmly. 'When I'm home, I'll take care of things.'

Things being your wife and daughter, thought Novello. Then told herself, Stop that, Shirley! Why do you find it so hard to be nice to one of the few guys in the Force who's gone out of his way to see you get an even break?

Answer: because anyone who has to think about treating you equally is treating you differently.

In other words, I'll only accept help from people who don't offer it. Which makes me nana of the month!

She said hesitantly, 'Maybe I should check that out, sir.'

He said, 'I don't think so,' very pleasantly, but with a finality that brooked no denial.

Please yourself, she thought, getting back into her car. Means I can get to the club all that earlier and stop anyone else trying to put a brand on my hunk of beef.

But best to play it safe, and as she drove away, she called Control and put it on record that she was abandoning her watch in response to a direct order from the DCI.

And finally, because she was a good cop as well as an ambitious one, she made a mental note to check out if possible what made the old bag lady so unsurprised to find herself, as she imagined, under surveillance. Probably a waste of time. What could someone as comically decrepit as Feenie Macallum have to do with the real world that a smart young cop lived in? But she'd noticed the DCI's flicker of amusement when she'd talked about a prayer meeting, and certainly she couldn't see religion playing a large part in La Pascoe's profile.

Then she closed her mental notebook, hit the accelerator, and as the tiny engine shook and roared, she gave herself entirely to a matching anticipation of the delights which lay ahead.

X

spelt from Sibyl's leaves

Feenie Macallum . . .

A blast from the past. Dear old Feenie, whose first entry was probably made with a quill pen on parchment. Box file, card index, microfiche, this Serafina has flown through the lot and here she is, wings neatly folded, sleeping in my casket waiting for the kiss of Sir Gawain to awaken her.

fighting the world with a protest that no one
   will heed . . .
except those in need . . .

What does Daddy think as he looks down upon, or perhaps up at, his beloved daughter? Mungo Macallum, whose Celtic beginnings not even my little electronic moles have been able to dig up. The working classes of the nineteenth century still offered that option which all classes of the twenty-first century would give their eye teeth for – impenetrable obscurity.

But there he was, an exile in Yorkshire at the turn of the century, already a man of brass, busy turning himself into a man of steel.

But not knives and forks and spoons for Mungo. Oh no. He didn't let himself be dazzled by the bright dawn of this new Edwardian age, he looked beyond that last long garden party of privilege and class, he saw the approaching darkness and knew that this was to be the century of the gun.

Mungo Macallum, the armaments king.

There are some who say that you were the model for Undershaft in *Major Barbara*, Mungo. Great wealth from a morally dubious source, yet not without your own moral concerns. Poverty you saw as a cause of evil, not an effect. You paid, by the standards of the time, fair wages, and you underwrote the establishment of a savings bank to encourage providence among your workers, and a building society to give those who desired it the chance of buying their own homes.

And you led by example, showing the world how money wisely invested was the basis of prosperity.

In 1914 you were already rich. By 1918 you had wealth beyond computation.

> *In Flanders fields the poppies blow*
> *Between the crosses, row on row,*
> *While westward eighty miles or so,*
> *In England's fields the profits grow.*

And in a Yorkshire field, in that remote and peaceful wedge of coastal land called Axness, you found Granary House, a bat-infested, rat-infested ruin of a mansion looking out across the sea, far far away from the glow of the furnaces and the dust of the spoilheaps. Not that you were ever ashamed of the source of your wealth. And when you heard as you rebuilt and refurbished Granary House that your mocking friends were referring to it as *Gunnery* House, that's what you officially renamed it.

Here at Gunnery you hoped to found a dynasty in a world which your own weaponry had made safe for your descendants. Lord Macallum of Axness. Oh, your title was all chosen, your coat of arms prepared. Cleverly you forbore to stoop for the windfalls the dying storm of war shook from the many branches of the new and Most Excellent Order of the British Empire. The golden fruit you wanted was not to be scabbed with war-profiteering sneers. Through the twenties you paved the way with charitable deeds. But you could not forbear to make assurance doubly sure by crossing the palms of those who claimed to be able to tell your noble future with gold and silver, and all your hopes died in the Honours for Sale scandal of 1933.

One plan had failed. Another looked like to fail. Three wives (by death, not divorce) had left you with a single child. But not the son you needed to lead off your dynasty.

Yet a man may do something, may do much, with a biddable daughter.

Alas, poor Mungo, what you had was not a biddable daughter.

What you had was Serafina, born as one war ended to come of age as another began.

Serafina, the passionate one.

And, for a while, Serafina, one of us.

For they were all ours for a while, those brave boys and girls who played their merry games in the enemy's own yard. So many going, so few returning. But for that few, such a bright future, such a world of profit and delight lay ahead in those years after the shooting stopped and the real war, our kind of war, began.

But by that time you, Serafina, had been too long away, had caught a foreign infection, had gone native.

What you saw was not a world in the glorious turmoil of necessary re-creation, with populations shifting, new battle lines being drawn up, new alliances formed, a glorious opportunity to play a part in the last and greatest crusade. No, what you saw was individuals suffering pain and deprivation and loss and injustice. Instead of population patterns, you saw refugees. Instead of demographic trends, you saw orphaned children. Instead of the forest, you saw the trees.

Oh, here it all is, Serafina, in your little casket. The charities, the agencies, the foundations, the movements, the causes, and hardly a one of them, to start with, whose strings were not being pulled by us. Or someone somewhere very like us.

look at her spending . . .

And Mungo, as he saw his hopes in you fade, began to nurse new hopes of ennoblement after the Restoration of '51, till your cries of outrage over our failure to intervene in Hungary and our ill-fated intervention in Suez set heads a-shaking. How could our dear Queen be asked to ennoble a man who could not control the behaviour of his own child? Furious, he gave you the ultimatum. Hold your tongue or lose your inheritance to charity. Furious, you told him by all means to leave his tainted wealth to the poor and the needy, which is what you intended doing with it anyway. His charitable donations, his paternalistic care for his workers through savings schemes and building society loans, meant nothing to you. These were the indulgence fees that sinners in peril of their immortal souls paid to pardoners, and worth just as much.

Who Mungo would have left his wealth to, we shall never know. His lawyer's car was pulling up at the front door when he suffered the stroke which was to kill him. Several efforts he made in the next few days to speak, but nothing came out that even the most partial of auditors could interpret as an instruction. An approach was made via us to the lawyer with a view to drafting a will along the lines he would most probably have chosen, with a signature to be provided by our finest calligrapher, but the lawyer proved too conventional to corrupt, too rich to bribe, and too upright to blackmail. And when you finally arrived, dear Serafina, from some distant part of the globe, Mungo took one look at you and died.

So let's see how the money has gone.

It's amazing how hard it is to dissipate the fortune of a clever man who has invested cunningly, setting his wealth to beget more wealth, which in its turn will beget still more until the fourth and the fifth generation thereof.

But you have tried, Serafina. For more than forty years you have tried.

> *pouring her pelf into bottomless pits of*
>   *despair . . .*
> *why does she care?*

Till at last you saw the beginnings of the end, not of your compulsion but of your cash, and so, though Mungo missed out on ennoblement, you at least came to that last infirmity of a noble bankrupt and started selling your land and property.

Mungo's country estate which he had established out at Axness as authentication of his wished-for title and which you had tried to turn into a kind of communistic Arcadia, all those farms and fields and copses and cottages where horny-handed peasants cut corn with a sickle, all have gone under the hammer. But not Gunnery House, not that refuge for the fast-talking fugitive, not that sump for all the dross and dregs of modern life – though most of them have fled now, most of them have voted with their fear – this you left too long, this you cannot sell or lease or mortgage, for it is held in fee by a force more greedy, grasping, and unrelenting than even a high street bank. The sea.

So this is how it ends, Serafina. Without your wealth, what will you become? A figure of fun, an object of ridicule, yesterday's activist, listened to kindly by those in the aid game who remember your glorious past, listened to gloatingly by those whom you elbowed aside in your certainty of rectitude, but paid heed to by no one except those few belonging to the Liberata Trust, who can hardly ignore you, its sole founder and financer.

Oh, Serafina, with my strange magic, I resurrect you as you were when you were still one of us. So young, so fresh, so full of joy and sparkle. I could fall in love with you just looking at my screen.

What a loss we suffered when we lost you, Serafina. All that energy, all that passion. How much you might have achieved with us, how far you might have gone.

Then I touch the keys again and see you as you are now.

Oh, the sad change.

And yet . . . and yet . . .

With us, you must have long since been retired, laden with gifts and reputation perhaps; perhaps even with some version of that honour poor Mungo so coveted; but definitely and irrevocably retired.

By yourself, with your bicycle and your bags, so far gone down that wrong road you can probably not recall the moment you took the wrong turning, you may be ridiculous, yet for a while, for a final innings, you are still a player, else Gaw would not have instructed me to fold you up in *Sibyl's Leaves*.

Why they want you, what they have in store for you, is, of course, not for me to know. I am merely the instrument of the gods.

But you cannot give a child toys, Uncle Gaw, and not expect her to play. And I am beginning to put things together, to see something . . . a speck, a mist, a shape, I wist! Oh yes, Gaw, you will know me again as a player before these leaves of mine all fall!

Now once again I look at you as you were, poor sad, mad Feenie Macallum, and I wish you well.

All these looney people, where do they all
   come from?
All these looney people, where do they all
   belong?

xi

a game of hearts

In the house, Pascoe found Rosie in the lounge watching television.

'Hello, darling,' he said, picking her up and giving her a hug and a kiss. She responded briefly then struggled free and refocused her eyes on the screen.

'All by yourself, dear?' he said.

'The house is full of *people*,' she said in her long-suffering voice, which made *people* sound like termites. 'Mum said we'd have a game of Black Bitch after tea, then all these *people* came.'

For some reason, as she recovered from her illness, Rosie had turned her back on the make-believe world which had been her favourite recreational territory hitherto. Storybooks, dolls, even computer games, had all been put aside in favour of playing cards. Ellie theorized that she wanted to give her imagination a rest as there were things there which were a trouble to her. Whatever, she devoured every new card game greedily, and was not deterred by limitation of numbers. Black Bitch or Hearts, her current favourite, was not really a two-handed game, but Rosie got round this by dealing three hands and playing two of them herself. She would even, at a pinch, play it solo.

'Never mind,' said Pascoe. 'I'll just get myself a bite to eat, then I'll have a game with you before you go to bed.'

'You're not as good as Mum,' she said, meaning she saw through Pascoe's amateurish attempts to let her win, whereas Ellie, who understood her daughter's needs better, kept up a front of solid competitiveness. 'Anyway, the holidays have started.'

'So?'

'So you always say I've got to go to bed because I've got to get up for school in the morning. Well, now I don't.'

Pascoe tickled her stomach and said in his Jimmy Cagney voice, 'Nobody loves a smartass, kid,' a combination which rendered her a giggling wreck.

'Well, I'm glad someone's having fun,' said Ellie from the doorway.

Pascoe kissed her and said hopefully, 'Prayer meeting over?'

'What?'

He explained Novello's error. In anyone else she might have found it amusing. Or, the way she was feeling, perhaps not.

'The only prayer being said in there is me praying for Feenie to get a move on,' she said. 'I'm on my way to make coffee. Sorry about this, but I'd forgotten all about them what with everything else. I'd made us a salad to go with that salmon pâté, it's in the fridge, so you just go ahead.'

'You mean you haven't had anything?'

'I was waiting for you, wasn't I? And I could hardly sit down and have my supper while the meeting was going on, especially as we're talking about people being starved in jail.'

'Well, I'll wait for you,' said Pascoe firmly. 'If you like I'll make a lot of noise and rattle dishes at the door. Or Rosie could go in and faint.'

Rosie looked up hopefully at the prospect.

'Rosie can start thinking about going to bed,' said Ellie. 'Yes, I know it's not time yet, but if you start thinking about it now, perhaps it won't be the usual devastating shock when it is time. Shall I make you a coffee?'

'Please.'

He followed her into the kitchen and said, 'You OK?'

'Fine. Just I could have done with a quiet night. Funny. I only suggested they came round here to show myself we were back to normal after, you know, Rosie. Maybe if you marry a cop, this is normal, people trying to kidnap you and beating up your friends.'

'Happens all the time. Can I have one of those biscuits, or are you sending them all to Somalia?'

'This is Liberata, not Oxfam.'

'I'll take that as a yes,' said Pascoe, helping himself to a biscuit.

Ellie busied herself making coffee. Instant, he noticed, not cafetiere, always a sign that she would be glad to see the back of her guests.

'So, are the mighty brains of Mid-Yorkshire's Finest any closer to an arrest?'

'Oh yes. By definition, every hour that passes takes us an hour closer to what is yet to pass.'

'Seriously.'

'We have a fingerprint. We have a make and colour of car with perhaps two numbers and possibly one letter. We have a description. All this to add to what you were able to give us yesterday. So I'd say we were making progress.'

'Well now, that's a comfort. Peter, over the years I've got used to you bringing the job home with you. But now it seems the job's coming home without you, and I'm not sure I want to get used to that. Could you get the door for me?'

He held open the kitchen door to let her pass with her trayful of coffee mugs, then overtook her to open the dining room door.

'You'll take care of Rosie?' she said as she passed through.

'Of both of you,' he said to the closing door.

In the dining room, Serafina Macallum was giving a precis of a documentary on Nicaragua some of the others had managed to miss. She was one of the most single-minded women Ellie had ever met, mind-blastingly so in Pascoe's eyes, but Ellie felt that a bit of tedium was a small price to pay for the assurance that any cause Feenie got her teeth into would be fought over to the death. It did occur to her now that with almost any other group of women she worked with, a coffee break would have been the signal to relax into an exchange of gossip and personal news, might even have given her the opportunity to share some of the traumas of the past two days. But she wasn't on that kind of footing with these people, or rather the group didn't offer that kind of closeness. This too was down to Feenie who'd insisted from its foundation that the only way Liberata could perform its function of helping endangered women all over the world was if its members left their own concerns and problems, large and small, at home.

So with these women with whom she shared a common cause, Ellie had very little social relationship. Whereas Daphne, who regarded most foreign aid work as unwarranted intrusion into the private affairs of other countries ('just like those Euro-nerds trying to tell us Brits what to do!'), had somehow wriggled into her heart.

Tonight, she thought, as Feenie guided them briskly through the rest of the agenda, even the glue of common interest was pretty weak.

'Right,' said Feenie. 'Correspondence.'

Like a kid who hasn't done her homework, Ellie tried to avoid catching the woman's eye.

One of the others began to talk. The usual thing, she'd written, no one had replied. It was like sending radio messages into space, Ellie thought dispiritedly. Feenie gave the usual pep talk, insisting that it was worthwhile reminding the authorities that this particular prisoner wasn't forgotten. No one likes being watched, tyrants and torturers least of all, she said.

And if feeling there might be someone out there watching them troubles the oppressors half as much as it terrifies me, she's dead right, thought Ellie.

Was *terrifies* too strong a word? She consulted her feelings. Yesterday after the adrenalin rush of her assault on the invaders and their undignified retreat, she had settled into a sense of threatening unease, balanced by her recollection of utter triumph. But now, after the incident with Daphne . . .

No, it wasn't too strong. Not with Rosie in the house . . .

'*Ellie?*'

Feenie was studying her through the magnifying glass she used instead of reading glasses, a preference she explained by saying, 'Spectacles mark a weakness, but a magnifying glass is a weapon.'

'What? Sorry. Oh yes . . . I mean, no . . .'

She'd drifted away, missed what the others had to say, and now it was her turn. Feenie said with impatient emphasis, 'Have you heard from any of your girls?'

Girls might have been a point of issue with anyone else, but not with Feenie.

'No, nothing.'

'Not even Bruna?'

'No, I'm sorry, nothing, not since before . . .'

Before Rosie had been taken ill. Time now tended to be divided as before or after Rosie's illness. She must stop doing that.

'. . . since I last saw you.'

She thought that was true. During the critical time of the illness she had had no energy to spare for anything else. She still occasionally came across references to events which meant nothing to her, and knew they must have occurred during those crisis days. Could be that somewhere in the house there was a card from Bruna that had got set aside for future reference then slipped out of sight. Only the other day she'd had a letter threatening to turn off the gas supply as she'd seen fit to ignore their last Final Notice. She'd sent them a cheque, and a letter pointing out that as they'd now sent her another Final Notice, their previous Final Notice was not in fact their last Final Notice but their penultimate Final Notice, or perhaps simply their Penultimate Notice, as *finality*, like *uniqueness*, was not a quality readily susceptible to qualification. So far she had had no reply.

Feenie said, 'I had thought . . .' then changed her mind about what she'd thought and continued briskly, 'So, no reply to your last. When was that?'

She was talking about Bruna, of course, not the gas company.

'Well, I'm writing to her just now actually,' she said evasively.

Feenie was giving her that cold, turn-you-transparent stare which came as a shock to those who didn't know her, like a shaft of laser light out of a damped-down fire.

Ellie found herself wondering, does she know about Rosie's illness? Surely someone must have told her. But would it have registered?

She certainly wasn't going to say anything now, she thought resentfully, meeting Feenie's gaze head-on.

It was the older woman who broke off.

'Fine,' she said, draining her coffee mug noisily and setting it down with an emphasis which said clearly that she wouldn't be averse to some more. 'Now, let's see what's been going on round this crazy world of ours, shall we?'

She reached for her cuttings bag. Every day she trawled through all the British papers and any foreign ones which came her way in search of relevant detail which she felt it her duty to interpret and share. Around the world with Serafina Macallum might not take eighty days, but it sometimes felt like it. It was, however, a voyage which even someone as packed with moral fibre as Ellie found it hard to curtail.

But tonight help was nigh, and from an unpromising source. The last woman to arrive, who had joined the group during the period of Ellie's neglect (hence the slight hiatus in giving Novello the OK wave), hadn't struck her as a very forceful personality. In her thirties, with wispy blonde hair, a pale anxious face, and that habit of constant hand-wringing which Ellie always found so irritating, she had made only a minimal contribution to the discussion, and that in a voice so low as to be almost inaudible. Ellie, never scared of rushing to judgement, had instantly categorized her as the kind of woman whose heart is in the right place but the rest of whose body might as well be somewhere else for all the use she was. Even her name, Wendy Woolley, seemed peculiarly apt.

But as Ellie was always finding out, snap judgements, like snapshots, often went well wide of their target. Earlier Helen Gough, the group's secretary, had reminded them apologetically that this was her last meeting with the group as her husband's job was taking him down to London. This too had happened during the period of Ellie's non-participation, but she guessed that Feenie had treated the news as she did most things she didn't want to hear by completely ignoring it. Now she looked at the secretary as if this was the first she'd heard of this treachery and said in a tone of uncomprehending astonishment, 'Well, if you are adamant about accompanying him, then I suppose we must appoint a successor,' upon which most of those present, recalling their departing colleague's frequent complaints that what Feenie Macallum expected was a full time PA-cum-troubleshooter-cum-secretary, found something very interesting in their laps to occupy their attention.

Then, amazingly, Wendy Woolley had whispered that if it wasn't too presumptuous of her as the newest member, she would be very happy to take on the job.

'Splendid,' said Feenie. 'I suggest you start taking notes now. No doubt Helen will be far too busy packing to write up the minutes. And then we must fix up a day for you to come down to Axness and get acquainted with the files. Tomorrow, shall we say?'

Wendy Woolley had again surprised everyone by shaking her head and whispering that tomorrow might be difficult.

'The day after then,' said Feenie irritably. 'We'll speak on the phone to confirm it.'

Mrs Woolley had subsided, and Ellie had guessed that this first show of resistance was likely to be her last, but now, as Feenie Macallum levelled the magnifying glass at the first cutting, she firmly closed the pad on which she had been making notes, clicked shut her fountain pen, stood up and said clearly, 'I'm sorry, but I really have to go.'

It was like the first chord of the National Anthem at a Tory Conference. The other three rose instantly, with Ellie close behind. Only Feenie remained seated, her disbelief unconcealed.

In the hallway, the others said their thank yous and good nights and headed out into the still balmy evening. Wendy Woolley was last and when she said, 'Thank you for the coffee,' Ellie replied, 'No. Thank *you*.'

The woman didn't pretend not to understand, but smiled faintly and said, 'I thought you looked rather, well, weary. Sorry. None of my business . . .'

'Believe me, I'm glad you made it so,' said Ellie, smiling back. 'See you again soon, I hope.'

She went back into the dining room. To her relief, Feenie Macallum was slowly assembling her bags.

'A good meeting,' said Ellie brightly.

'You think so? A pity we had to finish so precipitately. Knowledge is power and unless we use every means at our disposal to find out what is going on in the world, we will end up impotent. When Mrs Woolley has been with us a little longer I am sure she will understand this and make her arrangements accordingly.'

Ellie said firmly, 'I'm sure that Wendy had excellent reasons for wanting to get away. And it's great that she's got the commitment to take over as secretary.'

'Yes, there's that,' said Feenie grudgingly. 'Ellie, before I go, I wanted to say how pleased I was to learn that your child has recovered from her illness. I have been rather preoccupied with one thing and another during the past few weeks, but I should have contacted you earlier. I'm sorry.'

Apologies from Feenie were as rare as resignations from cabinet ministers. Rarer since New Labour had got in.

'That's OK. Yes, she's fine now. Still getting over it inside, though. Me too. But it's going to be OK.'

Feenie smiled.

'Knowing you, I'm sure it is. Now, about Bruna . . .'

Oh God, thought Ellie. Am I *still* going to get the reproof?

'Look, really, I'm writing,' she said.

'No, it's not that. But two or three weeks ago I heard from one of my contacts that she had been released. I thought in view of the close relationship you seemed to be establishing, she might have contacted you.'

'That's great news,' said Ellie. 'I'm really pleased. But she certainly hasn't been in touch, not for some time, in fact. Some considerable time. I thought the Colombian authorities must have tightened up on their censorship. Maybe if she had some notion she was going to get out in the next few months, she thought it best not to be provocative by writing to someone like me. And of course, the letters that she managed to get smuggled out for someone outside to post, she'd want to be very careful not to risk rocking the boat by getting caught doing that. Or maybe knowing she was going to get out, she just wanted to back away from our relationship.'

She was being over-loquacious in her search for reasons because the truth was she felt a little bit hurt, which was absurd. This kind of correspondence was never about herself, it had always to be about the imprisoned woman. Except, of course, in another sense it was all about herself, and you couldn't go on pouring yourself out in front of a stranger without in your mind turning that stranger into a friend.

'Don't feel hurt if you don't hear anything more,' said Feenie, with that startling incisiveness. 'She may have very good reasons for avoiding all contact with the outside world. Now she's free I can tell you that Bruna is the sister of one of the most wanted guerilla leaders in the country. That was why she got picked up in the first place, in the hope of being able to use her to flush him out. All they got for their efforts was a wave of violence. Now they might be hoping she will lead them to her brother, which is very good reason for her to keep her head down. I know we don't do what little we do for thanks, but don't give up on her.'

'Thanks, Feenie,' said Ellie. 'I'm glad you told me that.'

They had moved through the hallway as they spoke and were now standing on the front doorstep. On impulse, Ellie kissed the old woman's cheek, a liberty she had never dared take before, and got the laser look again but this time accompanied by the flicker of a smile.

As she cycled through the gateway, Feenie looked up and down the road, then called over her shoulder, 'I see our spy has flown. Once spotted, they're quickly replaced. Security is a hydra, my dear, a veritable hydra.'

And glaring at one of Ellie's neighbours out walking his dog as if she suspected both of being undercover Special Branch officers, she took her serpentine way down the street.

With a long sigh of relief Ellie closed the door and went into the lounge, where Pascoe was pouring a large Scotch which she downed in one.

'Bad as that?' he said.

'I'm a fraud,' she said. 'First hint of personal danger and the rest of the world can take a hike.'

'The rest of the world wants you safe,' said Pascoe. 'Otherwise who's going to take care of it?'

'And am I safe, Peter? I've been thinking about it. Best bet seems to be that someone wants to get at you through your family, right? But is it so they can twist your arm to do something they want? Or is it just to hurt you? In other words, intimidation or lunacy. I know which I prefer.'

'Probably the former,' said Pascoe lightly. 'In which case, having tried and failed, they'll go away.'

'But they didn't, did they?' said Ellie. 'They were still here today and we've got Daphne's nose to prove it.'

'Look, if they were just after hurting me by hurting you, some twisted kind of revenge, they had their chance when you opened the door, didn't they?' argued Pascoe.

'Bucket of acid in the face, you mean? This is really cheering me up.'

'But it didn't happen,' insisted Pascoe. 'So the odds are on some idiot looking for a bit of leverage in the hope of keeping himself or his nearest and dearest out of jail. Of course, there's a third possibility . . .'

'*Candid Camera*?' she said.

'No. This could have nothing at all to do with the job. It could quite simply be you for your own sake they're interested in.'

He offered this merely as a distraction and it seemed to work.

She looked at him, mock-gobsmacked.

'Little old me?' she said. 'Important for my own sake? Surely there's got to be a mistake?'

'You never know. It was Novello who suggested it, actually.'

'Shirley sodding Temple? Then it must be right. Girl who wears her skirts so short she air-conditions her brain-stem can't be wrong, can she?'

'Pity you aren't Jewish,' he said. 'Then you could be anti-Semitic also.'

She said, 'Don't go subtle on me. I'm beyond the reach of subtlety. Rosie OK?'

'Upstairs in bed. But she is not going to sleep till she gets that game of cards you promised her.'

'That girl. Who the hell does she take after?'

Pascoe grinned.

'Well, her favourite game is Black Bitch,' he said.

'I'll see you pay for that,' said Ellie over her shoulder as she headed for the stairs.

'Oh, I do hope so,' said Pascoe.

xii

doppelgänger

Ellie Pascoe leaned out of the open window and shouted and the woman below looked up in surprise and dropped her car keys, and Ellie in her turn was so surprised that she dropped the keys she was holding in her hand.

Ellie turned over in bed. But a moment later she was up again and leaning out of the open window and the woman below was looking up in surprise and dropping her car keys, and Ellie was dropping her keys too.

After she woke from the dream a third time, she really did get up. Peter was enjoying the sleep of the just or the completely knackered. He was a very still sleeper and repose rubbed the lining years off his face so he lay there like the monumental effigy of a child, or perhaps a childe, who'd died young.

She went into Rose's room. Her daughter had pushed the duvet back and lay curled like a stranded sea horse on the sand-coloured mattress.

Ellie covered her up. The heat of the day had

not seeped into the night. Or maybe she was still carrying the chill of her dream with her.

She knew that for the time being at least sleep was impossible. All that awaited her in the bedroom was that sense of being adrift on a storm-tossed sea with ravening birds screeching overhead and the drowned faces of everyone she loved staring up at her from beneath the water.

She headed into the boxroom which she refused to call a study. Not too long ago she'd have sneered at anyone nerdish enough to claim to have a relationship with a boxful of electronics, but now her laptop was waiting for her like a friend.

Time for her Comfort Blanket.

She switched on, brought up the story and scrolled through Chapter 2 till she reached the point where Daphne's arrival had interrupted her.

He flexed his broad shoulders, took a deep breath, bowed forward, his body hunched, and with a single convulsive movement, he snapped the length of cloth which bound his wrists.

The watching men gasped in admiration and at the same time brought their weapons to bear. The Greek smiled benevolently on them as he stretched his arms to restore the circulation. Then he removed the sack still hanging round his neck and dropped it to the ground, followed by the rest of his ragged robe. For a moment he stood naked before them, and they viewed his body which was as lined and cratered as the moon which lit it. Here was carved the history of a life of violence, with stabbing scars, and slashing scars, and scars which marked the bite of savage fangs and scars which recorded the impact of heavy clubs. Awe touched the onlookers and a sense of menace. Then he straddled a small cooking fire and with a deep groan of pleasure, began to massage his genitals dry. One of the young attendants put her hand to her mouth and giggled, and instantly he became a fat old Greek castaway again.

He reached out, pulled a woollen robe from her arms and draped it round him.

'Thanks, luv,' he said. 'Here, fancy a clam?'

He shook the remaining shellfish out of his discarded rags.

'You can eat 'em raw, but they're better baked with a drop of vinegar. Just thinking on it makes me hungry.'

And without more ado, he took the steaming platter from the other attendant, squatted down in front of the fire, and began to eat.

The Prince watched him for a moment, then said, 'Achates, now that the storm has abated, it may be that our guest has friends who will be anxious for his wellbeing and come looking for him. It might be well to double the guard.'

'No need of that,' said the Greek out of a full mouth. 'All on my lonesome, that's me.'

But Achates moved away and started disposing his men.

The platter was soon empty and at a nod from the Prince, the attendant took it and piled it up once again.

'Ee, I'd give my old gran to a one-legged sailor for a drink,' said the Greek.

Another nod. A jugful of wine was produced and a cup which the Greek ignored. He took the jug, poured a small (a very small) libation onto the ground, then raised the vessel high and with unerring accuracy directed the xanthic linn down his gullet till the last drops fell.

Ellie paused and considered. *Xanthic linn*. How to justify such an oddity? You could point out that it was Greek, from *xanthos*, meaning yellow. Also Xanthos was Homer's alternative name for the Scamander, the great river which Achilles fought and would have been overcome by if the fire god hadn't come in on his side. But a carper might retort that it sat very uneasily with Scots *linn*, meaning waterfall. In any case, while euphuism as comic euphemism was fine, and *xanthic linn* to describe a stream of piss might raise a smile, wasn't this just wilful preciosity? Also, did they have both white and red wine way back then? Red seemed more likely, though she couldn't say why. Because it was rougher, more basic maybe, though they'd give her an argument about that in Bordeaux. Still, that was what the French were made for, to give the English arguments.

Her fingers ran over the keys.

directed the red jet down his gullet till the last drops fell.

Now he returned his attention to the food and cleared the second platter as fast as the first.

Finished, he handed the dish to the female attendant.

'That were grand,' he said. 'Thanks, lass.'

And he let out a huge appreciative belch which set the watching men laughing, except for the Prince, who said, 'I am pleased you are pleased, stranger. But now we have satisfied your natural hunger for food and drink, it is your turn, I think, to satisfy our equally natural hunger for information and news.'

'Ask away, lord. I'm just a simple man, with little about me to interest a great leader like yourself, but owt that I can tell you I'll be glad to.'

'I thank you, stranger.'

The Prince seated himself on a stool on the far side of the fire, Achates crouched at his side, and the men squatted on the ground in three or four circles around the central group, while the women went about their business beyond the circles, but with eyes and ears attentive to what was going on at their centre. The old man after a word in the Prince's ear retired within the shelter against the big boulder.

'Now, stranger, before we enquire of your name and history, satisfy my curiosity in this. How was it that you threw yourself at my feet when you arrived, begging for mercy and assistance, and not

at the old man, my father's? From my little knowledge of Greek society, you are as accustomed to defer to the dignity and wisdom of age as we are.'

'As you are? You mean you're not Greeks?' said the stranger, his great face wrinkling in surprise.

'I should have thought our garments and our speech told you that.'

'Nay, but there's all sorts and conditions of Greeks. They come from all over. I met a lad from Crete once, all dressed in blue, he were, like some daft tart going to a party. And the way he spoke. I could hardly make head or tail of it. Made you sound no worse than my cousin with the cleft palate. So I thought you must just belong to this island, which I don't know the name of but am mighty glad to be cast ashore on, believe me. So if you're not Greeks, what might you be then?'

'Have a guess,' said the Prince with gentle irony.

'Phoenicians? No, not dark enough. Egyptians? The same. Medes? Aye, that's it. You could be Medes. Am I right?'

'I'm afraid not. We are Trojans. And I am Prince Aeneas of Troy.'

Pious Aeneas. Who fled from the fall of Troy bearing his father on his shoulders and leading his son by the hand with his wife following behind (perhaps with her old cock linnet?), till she lost her way, and ultimately her life. Pious Aeneas, obeying the command of the gods and following his star north from Carthage to found the Roman Empire, while behind him Dido lit the southern sky with her own terrible light.

Not the cleverest of moves to be a woman trailing in the wake of Pious Aeneas!

Dido, of course, came later, which was a pity. Would have been nice to take a look at him with that on his conscience! Ah well, nothing's easy, pity then the writer more than other women when she's got to stick to the facts, even though the facts are pure fiction. As she'd once heard a Booker winner say at a signing, pour out your soul and the world will probably react with silence; get something wrong and smartasses from five continents will e-mail you to tell you about it. Though why this should bother her when she had no intention of letting anyone else see her Comfort Blanket she didn't know.

Back to Pious Aeneas.

He regarded the stranger's face earnestly for a moment then went on, 'You don't look alarmed.'

'Why should I? I mean, you're not cannibals or owt like that, are you?'

'No, nor owt like that, as you say. But I did think it might have come to your notice that forces representing just about every corner of Greek territory, under King Agamemnon of Mycenae, were at war with Troy, a war which lasted ten years, time enough for news to spread to most places, I should have thought?'

The Greek's face screwed up in the effort of recollection.

'Now you mention it, it does ring a bell. Yes, I'm pretty sure someone did say something about it in the taverna one night. Something about a tart, was it? Aye, that's it, I recall now. We couldn't credit it. I mean, fighting over land, or fish, or cattle, that I can understand. But grown men fighting a war over a flighty tart, that's plain daft. You're not telling me it's right, are you? Bloody hell, I do believe you are. Well, well. Nowt so queer as folk, eh? So, this war, which of you won it then?'

Prince Aeneas regarded him quizzically.

'Your compatriots. Not by force of arms, where we matched them; nor by nobility of action and moral desert, where we excelled them; but by low trickery and animal cunning, in which areas they predominated, one man above all others being a master of lies, deceits and treachery. The wily serpent Odysseus.'

Odysseus, gross, untrustworthy, wheeling, dealing Odysseus, always ready with a fluent lie, often complicated beyond the needs of plausibility out of simple delight in the very act of invention. At least it wasn't any highfaluting sense of duty or destiny which drove *him* on. In the end what made him give up a life of endless bliss on Calypso's enchanted island was simply his unquenchable longing to get back home to his wife and family.

She and Peter had both been pious Aeneas's in their way. It had taken Rosie's skirmish with death to bring their questing ships together. Which, time and tide being what they are, didn't mean they would sail in convoy for evermore, but now they both knew up front what before they had only assumed subliminally, that no matter what wild waters might seem to separate them, they were bound together as intrinsically as the hulls on a catamaran.

Jesus, all this nautical metaphor from someone whose longest voyage had been on the old ferry to Skye!

Where was I? Oh yes.

Odysseus.

At the name, a groan of mingled pain and hatred went up from the watching men and they rattled their weapons in anger.

The stranger, who was listening with the rapt expression of a child hearing a fascinating adult tale which he only half understands, shook his head and said, 'Odysseus, you say? Now him I have heard of. Right slippery customer from all accounts. Buy a used boat off him and you'd soon have a wet arse. Well, it takes all sorts to

Was that a noise outside?

She rose and went to the window, the same window she'd leaned out of twice in her dream.

It was a fine moonlit night, just like the one she'd described in her story. No camp fires here, though. Just an empty driveway. Gate slightly ajar; Peter must have forgotten to close it. Deserted street. Some parked cars, but there always were, the over-spill of neighbours whose kids had gone through this western rite of passage but couldn't leave the evidence on the drive as Dad's chariot still had pride of place in the garage and he needed to be out first in the morning. Nothing moved, not even a cat.

Then a little way up the street a car began to move forward, sidelights on, at kerb-crawling pace. Short-sighted punter perhaps? It was going left to right so she could see the driver, or at least the oval of a face as he looked towards the Pascoe house, a thin sallow face with a pencil moustache and staring eyes whose gaze locked momentarily with hers in the brief moment of passage.

Or was she imagining it, deceived by moonlight and shadows, and seeing darkly through the glass of the window, and the distorting glass of her own imagination?

'Mummy.'

Anyone else's voice might have startled her but she was still too close to the time when she'd half accepted she might never hear her daughter's voice again for joy not to swamp all other reactions.

'What are you doing up, my girl?' she said. 'Come here.'

Rosie came into the room and her mother swept her into her arms.

'I heard a noise and I was coming to your room, then I saw the computer light. Are you working?'

Ellie in Great English Novelist mode had once been a no-go area.

'No, darling. And it wouldn't matter anyway.'

The girl looked at her doubtfully. Christ, I must really have hammered home that sacred muse crap, thought Ellie guiltily.

'This a private party?' yawned Pascoe from the doorway.

'No. Couldn't sleep. Didn't mean to raise the house.'

'No problem. Too hot to sleep anyway.'

He spoke lightly but his eyes were asking questions.

She thought of telling him about the passing car. But what was to tell? He was worried enough.

She said, 'That's probably it. Here, take Rosie. I'm sure she's putting on weight. Too much ice cream and burgers. I hope Wieldy doesn't overdo the hospitality tomorrow.'

The child had fallen asleep in her arms. Pascoe took her and carried her carefully back to her bed.

When he returned, Ellie was still standing by the window.

He said, 'Look, if you'd rather she didn't go to Eendale . . .'

'No. I didn't mean that. Let's keep things normal as possible for her sake, right? It's important, normality. I was just getting used to the idea of it myself when all this . . .'

As she spoke, she continued to stare fixedly out of the window. Pascoe moved to her side and peered out too. Nothing. Just the garden, the drive, the road.

He said, 'What is it?'

She said, 'Something, I don't know, maybe nothing. I kept on dreaming about seeing that woman, you know, the one who said they were from Ed Welfare, and she got out of the car and I called from the window and she was so surprised she dropped her car keys. And in my dream, I'm so surprised by this that I drop my keys too . . .'

'Which keys?'

'Don't know. House keys, I presume. Not much of a nightmare, is it? Not when you think what the old subconscious could be having a go at. The lies about the bus breaking down, me cracking his nuts, poor Daphne getting her nose broken . . .'

'Even your subconscious is determined not to be intimidated,' said Pascoe. 'Now how about we try for some sleep?'

He drew her away from the window, but she broke free from him after a couple of steps and headed back.

He could tell from her face that something had happened, one of those illuminations of memory which make the previous darkness seem attractive.

'Oh shit, Peter. Shit,' she said.

'For Christ's sake, what's the matter?' he demanded with the aggression of fear.

She stared out of the window then slowly turned to face him.

'That woman. She was so surprised she dropped her car keys. That's what I told you, isn't it? Only she wasn't driving. She got out of the passenger door. So what was she doing with keys in her hand? Not car keys, that's for sure. He was the driver.'

'Then what?' he snapped, demanding an answer he already had. 'What?'

She hesitated before answering, and when she did it was in a controlled, almost resigned voice.

'Peter,' she said. 'I think she had a key to the house. Why else would she be heading towards our front door with a bunch of keys? She was planning to unlock the front door and walk into our house. As if she owned it. And that was why I was so shocked in my dream I dropped my own keys. It was like a mirror image, Peter. When she looked up at me in my dream, I saw myself.'

They stood stock-still, staring at each other like two actors in a freeze frame at the end of a movie. Except it wasn't over yet, not by a long way.

Pascoe broke the freeze, saying lightly, 'If there's another you wandering around, I want my money back. Listen, love, it's probably nothing but we'll take no chances. I'll get the locks changed tomorrow.'

'I'd like that. You did bolt up?'

'Of course. But I'll check. You get back to bed.'

'I'll just look in on Rosie.'

This was getting to her, he thought as he went downstairs. Day out at Enscombe would do her good tomorrow, but it would be better if somehow he could contrive to spirit her and Rosie right out of town till things got sorted.

The bolts were all in place as he knew they would be. But there was something which hadn't been there when he came to bed.

A folded sheet of paper lay on the hall mat.

He picked it up and opened it.

Fair Mistress Pascoe, though thou art watched, yet am I near, unseen. Our very eyes are sometimes like our judgements blind. I am long past fearing the frown o' the great but still must fear the tyrant's stroke, so though faithful still, I still must take care to know you true, which if disproved, then all goodseeming shall be thought put on for villainy.

This was the oddest stuff. It rang some bells. Elizabethan? Jacobean?

Hadn't Wield said that Franny Roote was writing a thesis on Revenge Drama?

Christ! The man, or *a* man, had been here, tonight . . . up the path to the very doorway . . .

Why the hell had he been so arrogant to believe that while he was at home, he didn't need any guard on his house to protect his family?

He checked up the stairs. Distantly he heard Ellie coming out of Rosie's room and going into the bathroom. He went into the lounge, picked up the phone and rang South Yorkshire. Happily, despite the hour, he got hold of Stanley Rose, the CID sergeant he'd spoken to earlier when he'd called to register his proposed visit to check out Roote.

'Stan,' he said. 'Peter Pascoe again. Listen, something's happened.'

He explained briefly, concluding, 'Could you get someone to call round now, check if he's there? If he's not, pull him when he comes back in. If he is, get him to account for his movements earlier tonight and tell him not to go out in the morning as he's going to have a visitor. Yes, by all means tell him who. I don't mind if he runs. I'd be almost glad if he did.'

He put the letter in a plastic bag and slipped it into the pocket of his jacket hanging in the cloakroom. He didn't like keeping things from Ellie but she was stressed out enough with that crazy nightmare.

Leaving all the lights on downstairs, he went back to bed.

xiii

the death of Marat

The next morning Pascoe got up very early and phoned South Yorkshire again.

DS Rose had called personally and found Roote in bed.

'He said he was on shift at the hospital till midnight – you know he's got a job as a porter there? – and he got home about one. Long time, I said. The hospital's not far. It is if you don't have a car and can't afford taxis, he said.'

When told of Pascoe's proposed visit Roote had replied, 'How kind of him to remember me. I must make sure I've got the place nice and tidy for him the way he'd want to find it. Didn't I hear he'd married someone from the college staff, Miss Soper, I think it was? Tell him I look forward very much to having a chat about the good old days when we were both footloose and fancy-free.'

'Didn't show any curiosity about why I was coming then?' said Pascoe.

'No, but I told him, yes, Mr Pascoe was married,

and he got seriously pissed off if he thought anyone wasn't treating his family with respect, and so did all his friends. Seriously pissed off. I think he got the message.'

Pascoe didn't doubt it, though he would have preferred it hadn't been given. From his recollection of Roote, old-fashioned threats were not a helpful option. Way back then, he'd been into mind games, and that was where you had to beat him, not in a back alley with rubber truncheons.

He said, 'Thanks, Stan.'

'Pleasure. Give us a call if you need a hand.'

'Don't you ever go to bed?'

'Of course not. Don't have a nice old pussycat like Fat Andy to tuck us in down here. Take care now.'

'You too. And thanks.'

He put the phone down as Ellie came into the room, looking sexily sleepy in her dressing gown.

'Business or pleasure?' she said.

'You inviting or asking?'

'I'm too knackered even to fake it, love,' she yawned. 'Why so early?'

'Need to be on my way soon as DC Bowler shows.'

'Bowler? Oh, that good-looking new boy? Make a change from Miss World of Leather, anyway. So where are you off to?'

Moment of truth?

Except what was the truth? That he was going to descend on Sheffield like an avenging angel? Or that he was simply pursuing another routine enquiry?

More the latter, it had to be. And it was. There was nothing of substance to tie Roote into this business more than anyone else. So it really was routine. Like every cop, he knew that detection was ninety-nine parts elimination to one part inspiration, but he knew that to an outsider (meaning anyone, no matter how close, who wasn't actually a cop) this often looked simply like an admission of defeat, activity for the sake of not looking idle.

He imagined saying, 'You remember Franny Roote, the young man I put away some years ago for the killing of a former principal of the college you taught at? I'm going to see him.'

'Really, dear? Why?'

'Because he is known to be writing a thesis on Revenge Drama. And because someone dropped you a note last night couched in a sort of Elizabethan English. I need to eliminate him.'

'Kill him, you mean?'

'No, just cross him off my list.'

'Oh yes. And then?'

'Then I'm appearing at the magistrates' court to oppose bail in the case of Kelly Cornelius.'

'Has that anything to do with protecting your family?'

'Well, there's a vague chance that some seriously nasty people would prefer her to be out on bail where they could get their hands on her.'

'Perhaps the people who are threatening me and Rosie?'

'Perhaps.'

'And you are *opposing* bail?'

No, it didn't make much sense even to an insider. So he replied vaguely, 'Nowhere nice as you. Hope you have a great day in Arcadia.'

'Yes. Though I thought I might leave Rosie in Wieldy's tender care for a couple of hours and pop off to see how Daphne is.'

Pascoe thought, shit! Dalziel wouldn't like this. Pascoe had assured him that Bowler would be free after escorting Ellie and Rosie to Enscombe where protection duties would be handed over to the off-duty Edgar Wield.

'Unpaid overtime,' Fat Andy had said gleefully. 'Owt for nowt, eh? We'll make a Tyke of you yet.'

But now the escort would be needed to stick with Ellie on her visit to Rosemont, stretching the CID's currently rather thin resources and Dalziel's always rather thin patience even more.

'That'll be fine,' he said. 'Give Daphne my love. I think that's Bowler now.'

He went outside and told the young DC about the plan modification.

'You stick with Mrs Pascoe, the sergeant will take care of Rosie.'

'No sweat, sir,' said the cheerful young man. 'I'll see they come back in one piece.'

Oh, the certainties of youth, thought Pascoe.

He went back inside. Rosie had appeared at the kitchen table.

He gave her a kiss and said, 'Have a nice day.

And don't get too friendly with that mad monkey of Uncle Edgar's.'

'Yeah, yeah,' said the child, absorbed in a game of clock patience which surrounded her cereal bowl.

'Never thought I'd feel nostalgic for Nina,' he said to Ellie as he kissed her goodbye.

Driving south, he reviewed what he'd dug up about Roote. There'd been some concern about his mental state during the early part of his sentence and for a while he'd undergone treatment at a medical secure unit. Judged fit to return to the main system, he had served thereafter as a model prisoner, and there'd been little question about releasing him as soon as he became eligible for parole. He'd observed the conditions meticulously and through one of the rehabilitation groups had obtained a job in Sheffield as a hospital porter, opting for unpopular night-shifts so that he could spend his free time in research for his postgraduate degree when the libraries were open.

So, from the penal point of view, a success story; a boat floating peacefully in a placid sea which Roote's Scottish parole officer hoped, rather aggressively, DCI Pascoe's visit would not turn gurly.

Rush-hour traffic was so heavy that what should have been a forty-five-minute run to the northern suburb where Roote had his flat turned into an hour and a quarter. If this proved a long-drawn-out interview it was going to be tight for Pascoe to get back to oppose Kelly Cornelius's bail at midday.

On the other hand, if the reason for delay was that he found out Roote really was the man responsible, who gave a toss about Kelly Cornelius?

There'd been a recent photo in the material faxed through from Sheffield. Pascoe had set it alongside his own memory of Roote at twenty-three, a fair young man always dressed in white or cream, a languid cat-like mover with something of a cat's reserve and watchfulness behind the easy smiling manner; a charmer when he wanted to be with women of all sorts and conditions, and with men too an effortless leader.

The man in the photo looked very different, difficult to age between thirty and fifty, gaunt of face and figure, with hair cropped just this side of shavenness.

Only the controlled watchfulness of the eyes remained.

'I'd not have recognized him,' Dalziel had said.

'Oh, I would,' said Pascoe.

You didn't forget people who'd tried to kill you with their bare hands.

The flat was on the top floor of a converted terrace in an area which, by morning light at least, gave an impression of being, if not well-to-do, well-ordered and well-maintained.

He rang the bell. Waited. Rang again. Then knocked hard.

A woman came out of the other flat on this landing.

'He'll be asleep,' she said. 'He works late. Won't

it keep till later? Seems a shame to wake him.'

She was in her fifties, maternally defensive. The Roote charm obviously still worked.

'No, it's urgent,' said Pascoe, resuming his knocking, then shouting, 'Mr Roote? It's Peter Pascoe. Could you open the door? Mr Roote? Can you hear me?'

'They can probably hear you in Rotherham, you're making enough noise to wake the dead,' said the woman.

Pascoe looked at her and saw the awareness of what she'd said register in her eyes.

'Does anyone have a spare key,' he asked.

'Well, yeah. As a matter of fact, I do. I sometimes pop in and tidy up for him.' She blushed faintly as she spoke and Pascoe emended his previous *maternally*.

'Could you get it, please?' he said. And when she still looked doubtful he pulled out his ID and said, 'I'm a police officer.'

The door opened onto a small living room. Armchair, table, dining room chair, crowded bookshelf, all very neat and tidy. There were three closed doors.

Pascoe opened one of them. Kitchen. Sink. Draining board, cup and saucer recently washed. Kettle on a small gas stove. He touched it. Still warm.

The woman had opened another door. Bedroom. Bed made up, unslept in.

She turned to the third door.

'No, let me,' said Pascoe.

He pushed it open. Bathroom. Steam. An old chipped enamel bath, filled with water the colour of cherryade. And, sitting up at one end, with an open book on the soap rack in front of him and half leaning sideways as if posing for the Death of Marat, was Franny Roote.

Blood dripped from the wrist of the hand trailed along the floor. The other was beneath the ever darkening water.

His eyes were closed.

The woman started to shriek.

Pascoe said, 'Shut up!', pulled out his mobile and hit 999.

The eyes opened, blinked, focused on him.

'You're late,' said Franny Roote.

xiv

a man's best friend

'A child?' said Edwin Digweed. 'We are going to have a child?'

'Not as such,' said Edgar Wield.

'Not as *such*? As *what*, then? As an entrée at supper, fricasseed à la Swift? As a parthenogenetic earnest of Jehovah's good intentions? As an early entry to some new Dotheboys Hall you are planning to found here in Enscombe to finance your dotage? Or is this infant in fact a Mafia dwarf turned Queen's Evidence for whom you are caring under the Witness Protection Programme?'

Wield, accustomed to his partner's blasts of invective fancy, bowed his head meekly before the storm.

When it abated, he said, 'Pete Pascoe's lass, Rosie. I promised I'd show her the menagerie.'

'With a view to joining it, perhaps?'

'Eh?'

'Edgar, since we set up house together, I have put the interests of domestic harmony above my

186

professional calling and pandered to your biblio-phobia by making this cottage to all intents and purposes a book-free zone. And what have you brought into our life by way of return? I shall tell you what. First an aerobatic ape. Then a possibly rabid dog. And now a female child. What more need I say? I am speechless. I rest my case.'

It was a long time since a scandalous episode in Digweed's youth had obliged him to give up the law, but he could still sound very forensic. Books, however, were now his livelihood and his life. When Wield first met him he was living in a flat above his antiquarian bookshop in the village High Street, fighting a doomed rearguard action against the relentless advance of dusty old volumes up the stairs. Forewarned is forearmed, and when they agreed to set up house together in Corpse Cottage by the churchyard, Wield had made it a condition of cohabitation that only books for personal use should be admitted to the premises, his own con-tribution being limited to *Moriarty's Police Law* and the complete works of H. Rider Haggard.

The price of keeping Digweed to his side of the bargain was eternal vigilance. Returning late from a book-buying foray, it seemed perfectly reason-able for him to deposit a couple of cardboard boxes on the kitchen floor with the assurance that he'd move them down to the shop first thing in the morning. And perfectly reasonable too for him to start unpacking some of the books in order to share his delight in his trove with Wield. But reasonability ended two or three days later when the boxes were still there and the sergeant had to eat his cornflakes standing up because all the chairs were occupied by incunabula.

But Wield's strong moral position had been considerably weakened by what Digweed referred to as the menagerie. First there'd been Monte, not the great ape of Edwin's fancy, but a marmoset which Wield had 'rescued' from a pharmaceutical research lab. That problem had been solved by the intervention of Girlie Guillemard, the chatelaine of Enscombe Old Hall, who had just added a Children's Animal Park to the visitor attractions of her ancestral home. Monte had first joined the other more tender inmates of the Park in their winter quarters, a heated old barn. But when spring came, he moved out to a treehouse from which he was easily lured by promise of food, and more easily still by the presence of his beloved rescuer, Edgar Wield.

The dog was more problematical. Tig, a mongrel terrier, had belonged to seven-year-old Lorraine Dacre, whose death while out walking her pet had triggered off one of Mid-Yorkshire's most disturbing cases. The animal's noisy entry into the Dacre house had always presaged Lorraine's return home, and now the family found its bark unbearable. Wield had undertaken to take care of it, on a temporary basis, he averred, but it soon became clear that there was no way the Dacres would ever take the beast back. Relocation wasn't going to be easy. The RSPCA rescue centre said they would try, but they couldn't keep the animal indefinitely if a new owner couldn't be found, and Tig's aggressive demeanour towards everyone except Wield, who was just about tolerated, didn't make this likely. Digweed in particular it thoroughly disliked, and the price of his continued tolerance was a proliferation of book boxes in unexpected corners.

That very morning Wield had found some in the bath. They'll be in the bed next if I let him get away with turning Rosie's visit into a major incident, he thought.

He said, 'I mean I'm taking her up to Girlie's animal park. And I would have told you, only you were supposed to be off to York today, so I thought what the mind doesn't know, the heart won't fret over.'

'Sneaking her in behind my back, eh?' sneered Digweed. 'A real CID undercover job.'

Their gazes locked, the bookseller's patrician face wreathed in a haughty sneer, his eyes flashing a challenge. But it was Childe Roland before the Dark Tower. Like shadowed windows in a blank wall, Wield's eyes gave no hint of what lay within.

Finally Digweed passed his hand over his face, erasing hauteur and shaping rue.

'I can't believe I said that. Sorry. It was stupid.'

'Aye,' said Wield. 'That'll be them now. If you want to hide . . .'

A car had drawn up outside.

Digweed strode to the door and flung it open.

'Mrs Pascoe. Ellie,' he cried. 'Welcome to our humble cot. And this must be Rose whose beauty doth outshine report. Step in, my dears, step in.'

Ellie and Rosie came in, the woman mildly amused by the hype of Digweed's welcome, the girl peering up at the tall silver-topped figure with wide-eyed curiosity.

'Coffee, Ellie? Will you have some coffee? *Real* coffee, not Edgar's revolting ersatz.'

Ellie said, 'No, thanks.'

'What about you, Rose? Would you like a glass of barley water? Or perhaps a fizzy drink? Edgar here occasionally smuggles some cans of cola into the fridge to abrade the few remaining flakes of enamel clinging to his teeth.'

Rosie glanced at her mother, who nodded.

'Yes, please,' said the girl. 'A Coke.'

'Of course. Do help yourself. You'll find the fridge through there, first left.'

Rosie went out.

Wield said, 'How do, Ellie. You OK?'

'Yes, thanks.'

'By yourself?' The question casual.

'Except for some Mad Max in a beat-up sports car I can't seem to shake off.'

Wield smiled.

'That'll be DC Bowler. Not long with us. Should have introduced himself.'

'Oh, he did,' said Ellie laughing. 'Nice polite boy. I told him Mid-Yorkshire would soon knock that out of him. Quite a dish too, or haven't you noticed?'

'Happen we'll knock that out of him as well,' said Wield gravely.

Digweed gave him a sharp glance, but before he could follow it with a matching remark there was an outburst of excited barking from somewhere close.

'Oh, God. I forgot the hound from hell was loose in the kitchen,' exclaimed Digweed.

He moved towards the door but Wield was quicker, with Ellie close behind. When the sergeant came to a sudden halt on the kitchen threshold, she tried to push past, but his broad right arm prevented her. Leaning over it like a pop fan at a crush barrier, she saw Rosie on her knees in front of the fridge with her arms around a small brown and white dog which had its forepaws on the girl's shoulders. For a terrible moment, she thought the position was defensive. Then she realized that far from assault, the dog seemed to be trying to lick Rosie's face off, while at the other end its stubby tail was signalling spasms of delight.

'You OK, Rosie?' said Wield lightly.

'Oh yes. Isn't he lovely? What's his name? Is he yours, Wieldy?'

Before Wield could reply, Digweed, demonstrating that his mind as well as his tongue still retained a legal sharpness, said, 'Actually, he's no one's, dear. We're just looking after him till we can find him a good home, aren't we, Edgar? A lovely beast, but we can't keep him here forever. Such a shame if he had to be . . . let go.'

He wouldn't have balked at *put down*, but Wield had turned to look at him, no Dark Tower blankness in his gaze this time, but a volley of arrows.

Rose's face had twisted in alarm, and hope.

'We've got a good home. Could we have him, Mummy? He wouldn't be any bother. I'd take care of him. Please.'

Before Ellie could respond, Wield advanced into the kitchen and said gently, 'We need to do what's best for Tig, luv. He's got a good home here already, you see, and you'd always be welcome to come and play with him. Now, how about that Coke?'

But Ellie could see that the sergeant's placations were falling on stony ground. Her daughter's hands had locked about the dog's spine like a Cumberland wrestler taking hold and her mouth was set in a stubborn line which Ellie had seen before. In her mirror. Across her mind a pack of questions hunted. *Do I want a dog around the house? Does Peter want a dog around the house?* And, leading them all, *Do we want* this *dog around the house?*

For she knew Tig's background, knew that every time they saw him, she and Peter would think of little Lorraine Dacre walking off along Ligg Beck that sunny Sunday morning, and her parents' growing anxiety, and the fear of uncertainty slowly changing to the horror of knowledge . . . Could she bear to think of this every time she saw Rosie and Tig together?

But she was seeing something else too, something she hadn't seen since that day they gently revealed to their recovering daughter that her friend, Zandra, stricken with the same meningitis bug, had not recovered. It was a loving brightness in Rosie's eyes as she hugged the little dog. A barrier which had come down as she took in the news of her friend's death, a barrier which had made her turn away from Ellie's or anyone's offers of unstinted love, had been raised a little, and that had to be worth almost anything.

She said, 'Let's see how you two get on together, shall we? There's more to having a dog than just playing with it, you know. Dogs are like children, no use to anyone unless they do what they're told.'

In her mind she heard Daphne ironically applauding this fine old traditionalist viewpoint. *Daphne*. She must get round to see her.

Rosie stood up, said firmly, 'Tig. Stay!' and took the can of Coke which Wield had fetched from the fridge. Then she moved over to the kitchen table, sat down, and started drinking. The dog remained where it was, but its eyes never left her.

'Knows how to make a telling point, that child,' said Digweed. 'She ought to think of becoming a lawyer.'

'She is inclined in the other direction, I think,' said Ellie. 'Wieldy, can I have a word?'

She went back into the living room.

Wield, anticipating rebuke, started apologizing as soon as he came through the door.

'Ellie, I'm sorry. Don't know what Edwin was thinking of. I mean, yes, I do, and I'll be giving him a good talking-to afore the day's out . . .'

'It's OK, Wieldy,' she said smiling. 'All he was doing was taking the tide. Rosie was three-quarters gone already.'

Wield considered this then said neutrally, 'So you think there's a chance maybe . . .'

'A chance maybe, very maybe,' said Ellie firmly. 'I'd need to talk to Peter, who will take some persuading, I imagine, as word around the factory seems to be that Tig's turned into a ravening monster.'

'Well, he did have a go at the super . . .'

'Is that right? Now that's a very good selling point. Seriously, if there's any chance of the animal turning nasty . . .'

Wield said, 'He's just a bit nervous round strange men. Not surprising after what happened. Doesn't seem to mind me too much, but Edwin and him can't get on. You saw how he was with Rosie, but. Another little girl, what he's used to. I can see how that might be a problem, for you, I mean.'

One of the many things Ellie liked about Wield was that, like Andy Dalziel, he didn't mince words, though, unlike his great master, he usually peppered them with kindness.

'My problems are in the grain, Rosie's can still be smoothed away, and if Tig's what it takes . . . sorry,

Wieldy, not your problem, though your concern's much appreciated. Listen, what I wanted to ask is, do you mind if I bunk off? I want to go and see Daphne. After what happened, well, I feel responsible. Rosie won't mind. Black Bitch apart, I seem pretty dispensable these days. So if it wouldn't be too much bother . . .'

'Not for me. It'll bother Pete, though, if he finds out you're traipsing about without an escort.'

'I warned him and I think he had a word with DC Bowler.'

'Fine. I'll just have another word to make sure he's quite clear.'

He went outside. The detective constable had parked opposite the cottage and was leaning back against the bonnet of his MG, studying through binoculars the famous leaning tower of St Hilda and St Margaret, just visible over the high stone wall against which Corpse Cottage was built.

'Hi, Sarge,' he said, lowering the glasses. 'Anyone told you your church is falling down?'

His eyes ran up and down Wield's form as he spoke. Not, the sergeant guessed, in admiration of my magnificent body, but because he wants to check out the rumours that I wear a tutu and nipple rings when I'm at home off duty.

Wield had been 'out' for some little while now, but had never thought that explaining yourself to the prurient or even making things easy for the embarrassed was an essential ingredient of 'outness'. He knew there was a wide range of rumours about his rural retreat. Some his own extremely sharp ears had caught floating round the station, others had been retailed to him by Peter Pascoe who for a while had been one of the embarrassed but only because, despite being as close to Wield as anyone in the Force, he hadn't taken in what had been clear to both Ellie and Dalziel from the outset. Since then he compensated, perhaps over-compensated, by keeping his friend abreast of in-house speculation, ranging from those who dismissed talk of the sergeant's gayness with confident assertion that Digweed was merely his landlord, or (they liked this one) that he had gone sexually undercover to help break up a vice ring, to those who claimed that his true residence in Enscombe was in fact a house called Scarletts, a Morris design in pink brick and turquoise slates with hipped gables and battered chimney breasts, in which he and his partner organized S and M weekends for many of the great and good of Mid-Yorkshire.

Bowler, the most recent addition to Mid-Yorks CID on transfer from the Midlands, would be naturally curious to check out the rumours of northern naughtiness.

Wield said, 'See anything you fancy?'

That dropped his jaw a good three inches.

'Sorry, Sarge?'

'Birds. You're a twitcher, aren't you?'

Jerk him around a bit, then let him see that while he might still be speculating about you, you already knew all about him.

'Yeah, that's right, but I never said . . .'

Never said anything to anybody at the station. A new member of a CID team was under close examination till you saw how he shaped up, and some things you kept quiet about, like that your hobby was bird-watching, which while not as nerdish as train-spotting, was certainly a very large peg for the would-be wags to hang their wit on.

'Aye, and I wouldn't. So, did you see owt interesting?'

'No birds, but I thought there was something moving up there . . . and there was this funny little gargoyle, but then I lost it . . .'

Wield smiled inwardly, though if he'd smiled outwardly, Bowler probably wouldn't have noticed. Funny little gargoyles on St H. and M.'s tower tended to be Monte the marmoset, one of whose favourite perches this was.

'That's something else to keep quiet about, losing gargoyles,' he said.

'Yeah. So is Mrs Pascoe staying here or am I still playing escort.'

'Playing?' said Wield reflectively. 'If you mean, is Mrs Pascoe going off to see her friend, Mrs Aldermann, and are you going with her to ensure her safety, the answer is yes. I'm sorry if you feel baby-sitting the DCI's family's a bit beneath you. Mebbe you'll feel different when you've followed far enough in Mr Pascoe's footsteps to have made some enemies of your own.'

Bowler, like Peter Pascoe, was a graduate-entry

recruit, with good prospects for rapid promotion if he shaped up right. One of the reasons for his transfer north had been to widen his experience.

He was physically not unlike Pascoe, slim, tallish, with a long narrow face and deep watchful eyes. Sensitive, too, like Pascoe. Wield's reproof had made him flush. Ellie's type, clearly. Hadn't she called him a dish? Strawberry ice, perhaps, with that interesting flush suffusing his rather pale cheeks.

'No, I didn't mean . . . except maybe it's more a job for uniformed . . .'

'No way,' said Wield. 'When it's hard getting trained CID men who should know better to take the job seriously, just imagine how easy it 'ud be for some plod whingeing about special treatment for CID brass to take his eye off the ball. If an attempted abduction and an assault isn't enough to catch your interest, maybe you should specialize in traffic.'

It was heavy talk, but if Bowler was going to survive the kind of remedial education Andy Dalziel liked to offer what he called the educationally disadvantaged, he was going to need strong shoulders and a very thick skin.

'Yes, Sarge. I see that. Sorry. Don't worry. I'll stick closer to Mrs Pascoe than . . .'

He hesitated. Was going to say *shit to a blanket*, thought Wield, but suddenly it didn't seem appropriate.

'Closer than that,' said Wield. 'She can be a very elusive lady if she takes the fancy.'

The elusive lady came out of the cottage and walked towards them.

She said, 'I'd get back in there quick, Wieldy. Edwin seems to be expiating some strange guilt feelings by force-feeding Rosie all kinds of exotic goodies from his larder.'

Very sharp lady too, thought Wield.

'Leave you in good hands then,' he said.

'I hope so,' said Ellie, smiling at the young DC. 'What do I call you, by the way?'

'Bowler, ma'am,' he said.

'Yes, I know that, but what do you get called? I presume you've got a first name?'

'Yeah, well, my friends all call me Hat. You know. Bowler . . .'

'Yes, got it, I think,' laughed Ellie. 'So, Hat it is.'

'You don't get Bert then?' enquired Wield gravely.

It wasn't a cruelty, just another degree in the don't-mess-with-me learning curve, to let the youngster know that Wield's omniscience included the fact that Bowler's parents, under the influence of history and/or alcohol, had christened him Ethelbert.

Life in CID for a bird-watching graduate called Ethelbert could very easily be hell.

'No, Sarge. Just Hat.'

'In that case, Hat, you use them bins of yours for watching Mrs Pascoe here, nowt else. OK?'

'OK, Sarge.'

He stepped gracefully into his open sports car.

'This car, bit showy, isn't it? For the job, I mean,' said Wield.

'Well, I wouldn't use it for a stake-out on a wet winter's night on a run-down council estate,' said Bowler pertly. 'But I don't anticipate Mrs Pascoe going down many mean streets.'

'I may surprise you,' said Ellie. 'Wieldy, thanks a lot. I'll ring. Or you ring if there's any problem. I've left my mobile number with Rosie. See you later. Come on, Hat. Wagons roll!'

She gave Wield a kiss on the lips, climbed into her car, started up and set off down the slope to the High Street with a smiling Bowler in hot pursuit.

Wield watched them go. Young Bowler seemed OK, he thought. Though you couldn't really tell, not till a man was tested. But he hoped the test wouldn't come while he was baby-sitting Ellie Pascoe. All the Pascoes were special to Wield. But Ellie was special special. The kind of woman who made an old queen wish sometimes that he was a lesbian.

Smiling to himself at the old joke, Wield went back into the cottage.

The phone was ringing.

Pascoe, he guessed as he picked it up, ringing to check that his womenfolk had turned up safe.

He was wrong about the caller, but right about the call.

It was Fat Andy Dalziel, pretending to be checking whether Bowler was going to be needed all day.

'Yes, sir. They got here safe and sound . . . Ellie's just headed off to see her friend . . . yes Bowler's gone with her . . . I think he'll be fine, sir . . . and I'll take good care of the little lass . . . no need to worry, sir . . . cheers . . .'

He put the phone down.

No need to worry, he'd said.

Except if Andy Dalziel was worried enough to call, mebbe there was more need to worry than anyone was letting on.

The Fat Man claimed to be able to sense trouble in his piles and Wield for one believed him.

Or maybe he was just going soft in his old age.

Andy Dalziel going soft?

Aye, when Gibraltar turned into a mound of pink blancmange!

Grinning at the notion, he went through into the kitchen to rescue Rosie from Edwin's compensatory force-feeding.

XV

spelt from Sibyl's leaves

Ol' man Dalziel
that ol' man Dalziel
he has to know something . . .

Indeed he does, else he wouldn't be sleeping here in his little casket waiting for the trumpet to sound his reveille.

Let it blow! Let these electronic bones reassemble and put on flesh. Let's take a look at him in glorious technicolour.

Good Lord!

Is this the face that . . . ? Here's a big genie to keep in such a little bottle. Once out, in bulk as large as whom the fables name of monstrous size, Titanian . . .

But why has the archpriest commanded that this monster should be poured out of his bottle into the *Leaves* folder?

Let's have a look and see why the Great Gaw took an interest in him in the first place.

Not apparently for the excesses of his mad youth, whose indiscretions seem to have been of quite another kind . . . no, here it is . . . sweet mystery of life at last I've found thee . . . now it all comes back. He got his clodhoppers tangled in the weedy depths of the Mickledore affair . . . twice . . . once at its beginning and again when it was recalled to life all those years later . . .

This was Gawain Sempernel's finest hour. With the scandals of the Profumo affair waiting to be resurrected . . . the royal connection . . . the American link . . . he was a man walking through a minefield while juggling flasks of nitro.

And he emerged at the other end with not a hair out of place, everything under wraps, the dogs of the Press happily chewing their drugged titbits, the wolves of Westminster howling at nothing closer than the moon, which at that time looked like Gaw's for the asking. But there's many a slip . . .

Oh yes, he has cause for resentment. But so have we all.

Back to the Fat Man.

He stirred things up, no doubt about that. He displayed a touching loyalty to a dead colleague upon whom Gaw found it convenient to tip any residual blame for miscarriages of justice, etc.

But in the end, Gaw saw to it that Mr Dalziel came nowhere near the real truth . . .

Or if he did he was clever enough to keep it to himself.

Could a man who looked so brutish be so bright? Perhaps. After all, are not these electronic urns a memorial more lasting than monumental marble to man's protean soul?

And Gaw Sempernel has added an ambiguous footnote. *Should not be under-estimated . . . perhaps.* Of course, it's rumoured among the young ones that old Gaw spends an hour each morning looking in the mirror till he's convinced he really is himself.

Oh, I could tell them a thing or two about how Gaw once liked to disport himself in the morning . . .

No more of that.

But an analysis of what actually happened over in the States when the Mickledore business blew up again does suggest that our plump Innocent Abroad was more manipulator than manipulated.

So, one to watch. One who is close to DCI Pascoe who 'accidentally' encountered Kelly Cornelius on the Snake Pass and whose wife is an acolyte of Feenie Macallum's.

All very vague.

The only positive reason for Mr Dalziel's presence in *Leaves* seems to be that Gaw who likes to cover all contingencies is not totally convinced that the *cordon sanitaire* he has thrown around Kelly Cornelius will keep the unsavoury superintendent from sticking his nose in.

Forewarned is forearmed.

But that works both ways.

Clever cool calculating Sir Gawain has thought to give an extra twist to the stopper that keeps this fat genie in his bottle.

What fun it might be to simply crack the bottle and let him out!

And more than fun. A new way to pay old debts.

But how to approach this monster?

Let's see . . . no home computer, no fax, not even an answer machine!

Ned Lud, thou shouldst be living at this hour!

But though he shakes the earth with his dinosaur tread, yet his police force with quiet but unrelenting step marches on into the new millennium.

Think of it as ancient magic, ol' man Dalziel. Think of it as Sibyl's leaves fluttering down onto your desk. And then just be yourself . . .

He just keeps strolling . . .
just keeps on strolling . . .
along . . .

xvi

oats for St Uncumber

Andy Dalziel pretended to believe that e-mail was what they called a transvestite in Lancashire, so it was with some trepidation that Sergeant Harmony from the computer room entered the great man's office.

'E-mail for you, sir. For your eyes only,' he said.

'Oh aye? What's it say?'

'Don't know, sir, I've not looked at it,' said Harmony, scenting a trap.

'How do you know it's for me then?'

'Looked as far as your name, sir. Didn't read any more.'

'Bollocks,' said Dalziel, taking the print-out. 'How's that lovely missus of thine?'

'Fine, sir.'

'Tell her I want a tango with her at the next knees-up.'

'I surely will, sir,' said Harmony retreating, grateful to have escaped so lightly.

The Fat Man read his e-mail twice, sat back in deep thought, read it again, then leaned back in his chair and bellowed, 'SHOP!' And waited. But only the echoes came.

After a while he rose, flung open his door and went striding through the CID offices like Uranus through his starry halls, and like Uranus he found them empty.

There was no escaping the fact. Mid-Yorkshire CID was short-staffed.

A couple of its members were on leave. Not that this meant anything to Andy Dalziel who lumped holidays, meals and sleep together as privileges granted by his personal benevolence and which could be curtailed or cancelled at his personal whim. So the wise detective headed for faraway places and left no forwarding address, and these two were very wise detectives.

Of those who remained, one was in hospital recovering from a broken leg, a couple were out on enquiries, Pascoe was pissing about in Sheffield talking to yon looney, Roote, DC Bowler was standing watch over Ellie Pascoe, and Sergeant Wield was entertaining Rosie Pascoe at Enscombe.

Sometimes he thought Mid-Yorks CID should be retitled Pascoe's Private Army.

But there should have been someone here.

God-like, his thoughts were commands.

The door opened and Shirley Novello came in.

'Where the hell have you been?' he demanded.

'I just popped down to the washroom, sir,' she said.

'Oh aye? What's up? Spotted a crack in tha make-up, didst'a?'

Provoked by her awareness that at work her face was practically a cosmetic-free zone, Novello said briskly, 'No, sir. Actually, I needed a piss.'

Dalziel looked at her in amazement and said, 'Nay, lass, don't shatter an old man's illusions. What are you working on?'

He didn't wait for an answer but rustled through the papers on her desk.

'Feenie Macallum? Yon batty old do-gooder? What in God's name are you bothering yourself with her for?'

'Just covering all the angles, sir,' said Novello, with what she hoped was an air of brisk efficiency. 'She turned up at the DCI's house yesterday evening, and for some reason she seemed to think our surveillance had something to do with her, and I thought, with everyone so worried about Mrs Pascoe and everything, I'd better check out what the meeting was about.'

In fact, it hadn't been any kind of concern for Ellie that had sent her down to Records, it had been mere vulgar curiosity, plus a dislike of making a fool of herself.

'Waste of time,' said the Fat Man dismissively. 'It 'ud be in aid of Women with Headaches or Underage Welsh Refugees with Acne. What the hell's Wilgefortis? Something you rub on your chest?'

He was looking at her scribblings.

She thought of his likely reaction to her explanation, considered a selection of lies, then thought, what the hell?

'St Wilgefortis, sir. One of the Queen of Portugal's septuplets. She took a vow of virginity but her father wanted to marry her off to the King of Sicily. Virginity wasn't going to be part of the deal, so she prayed to God to make her too unattractive to marry.'

Dalziel said, 'Oh aye? I think I've met her sister. So what happened?'

'She grew a moustache and a beard, sir. The King of Sicily got the next boat home. And her dad was so pissed off, he crucified her.'

The Fat Man nodded as if this made good sense, then examined her upper lip and chin closely and said, 'You trying to tell me something, Ivor?'

'Just that she prayed while she was dying that women everywhere who felt sorry for her and acknowledged her pain should be freed from all trials and troubles and encumbrances.'

'And what the hell has this got to do with owt you're getting paid public money for?'

'She was known by various other names. One of them was Liberata. This is the name of Miss Macallum's organization which is a trust she set up to work on behalf of women who've been wrongly imprisoned and tortured and generally abused by repressive regimes.'

Dalziel shook his head and said, 'So this is how you spend your time? I'm all for freedom of religion, luv, but not in working hours. Specially not all this foreign crud.'

'English women were especially fond of her,' said Novello defensively. 'They called her St Uncumber and they used to lay offerings of oats under her statue and pray that she'd uncumber them of their menfolk.'

'You're joking? Bloody hell. My wife were always making porridge and I hated the stuff.'

This did not seem a profitable avenue to explore.

Novello said, 'Anyway, Miss Macallum is in our records. Mainly in connection with various protest groups. Obstruction. Abusive language. Breach of the peace. Plus one conviction for dangerous driving. Ran some guy off the road. Seems he knew her and was trying to avoid her and at first he wanted her done for attempted murder. Looks like she's a pretty physical lady when the mood takes her.'

'You're not looking at her for threatening Ellie, I hope?' said Dalziel.

'No, sir. Just being thorough.'

'Thorough's grand but not if it's wasting time. Listen, I need your help. A woman's touch. Who the hell's that?'

This in response to the shrill of a telephone.

Novello listened carefully then said, 'Sorry, sir. Don't recognize the voice.'

'God spare me from women comedians,' groaned Dalziel. 'Well, answer it, lass, if it's not against your religion. And if it's not mass murder or my knighthood, tell 'em to get stuffed.'

Novello picked up the phone and listened.

'The DCI, for you, sir,' she said.

Dalziel took the phone and bellowed, 'What's up? Got lost and ringing for directions?'

Then he listened for a while, and said, 'Jesus, Peter, nowt's ever simple with you, is it? Will he snuff it? . . . So no harm done . . . Yes, I've got the letter back. Covered with prints but none of 'em Roote's . . . Aye, you'd best hang around. Leave the scene and them buggers in South Yorkshire will likely fit you up for attempted murder . . . Yes, I know you should be back for Cornelius, but don't worry. I'll sort it out. Keep in touch.'

He banged the phone down and stood there scratching his great head as if in search of something he'd buried there.

'Something happened, sir?' ventured Novello.

'You could say. That nut Roote the DCI went to check out in Sheffield, well, he's found him with his wrists slashed in a bath. I never asked, but I bet the daft bugger pulled him out.'

Novello considered the alternatives and said, 'But if he was alive, sir . . .'

'What? Oh aye, see what you're getting at. Question is, which is worse, a looney on your conscience or blood on your trousers? I've been there, and believe me, lass, you never get it out.'

Uncertain which stain he was referring to, Novello said, 'If this guy's tried to top himself, along with the letter that looks pretty much like an admission, doesn't it, sir?'

Dalziel smiled sadly at her and said, 'Nice to be young, is it? Aye, I can remember when I used to go jumping to conclusions like a newborn lamb. Now I'd not believe the Pope if he came to me with a signed confession. Didn't you hear me say there's nowt to connect the letter to Roote?'

'What about the language, sir? I thought the DCI reckoned it were in some sort of cod old-fashioned English.'

'Like what Shakespeare wrote, tha means? I hope you're not turning out to be another of them arty-farty types, Ivor.'

'No, sir. Bored me to tears at school . . .'

Except there had been a drama teacher at the comp, after she'd been chucked out of the convent school, shoulders like a draught horse, black hair bubbling out of the neck of his shirt and promising to cascade all the way down to his crotch . . .

She shook the memory loose and went on, '. . . but if it is like this revenge stuff Roote's studying . . . ?'

'Studying Enid Blyton doesn't make you Noddy,' he said impatiently. 'Or mebbe it does. Any road, like I said, I need your help. I bet you did secretarial studies like all the girls, eh? Means you ought to know your way around filing systems. I need the DCI's notes on Kelly Cornelius and he's always moaning I leave his room a mess.'

It took him thirty seconds to get impatient and join in the hunt, and when Novello saw the chaos he managed to create in the further half-minute it took her to unearth the file, she resolved that in the unlikely event he ever wanted something from her handbag, she'd defend it like her honour. Or maybe even harder.

She said, 'I think this is it, sir,' opening the file just to make sure.

'Oh aye? Give us it here then.'

But something had caught Novello's eye.

'Sir, what's a red tab with CCR mean?'

'It means it's nowt for gabby little girls to be sticking their nebs into,' said Dalziel, grabbing the file.

Even from Dalziel, this was intolerable. Perhaps fortunately there was a moment of mental debate between the response verbal and the response physical, each equally violent, which she used to turn away and smother both.

Her back must have been eloquent, however, for he said, 'Nay, lass, don't take on. If it's any comfort to you, it means hands off to nebby detective supers too. CCR. Chief Constable Refers. Means there's things going off that are reckoned too important for us poor bloody infantry to mess with.'

Novello had never hitherto thought of herself as being united with the Fat Man in the ranks, but she wasn't so braindead as not to accept this apology for an apology.

She turned back and said, 'Don't know much about this case, sir, but I got the impression yesterday you weren't too happy with the way Fraud was leaving Mr Pascoe to deal with it.'

'Did you, now? Well, sharp ears, sharp eyes

and a sharp nose. That's what makes rattons and detectives.'

He gave her a nod that was both approving and assessing.

He's debating whether to say more, she thought. Treat me like one of the boys. No, that was unfair. She'd got the same treatment as everyone else, i.e. bad. Labelling Dalziel with *isms* was like calling the wind sexist 'cos it blew your skirt over your head.

He said, 'The DCI's sharp too, lass. Don't let his poncy manners fool you. Sharpest nose in the place, me excepted. That's how he got on to Cornelius. He were driving back from Manchester over the Snake one morning couple of weeks back when he came across an accident. Lorry coming down our side had had a blow-out and jackknifed, hit a taxi coming up the other way. Not much damage. Dented the front, driver OK but passenger not wearing seat belt got a bloody nose. That was Kelly Cornelius. Off to Corfu, she says, and right upset at the delay. Peter took a paternal interest, or maybe more. I've not seen this lass in the flesh but from all accounts she's a looker and the DCI goes all balmy-eyed when he talks about her.'

Balmy or barmy? wondered Novello.

She didn't ask, but said, 'I'll watch out for it, sir.'

Dalziel said, 'Nay, lass, tha's not his type,' in a kindly voice. 'Any road, he starts wondering about her when the taxi driver lets slip he's booked for the domestic terminal, and when he sees her flight bag luggage, his nose begins to twitch.'

'Why was that, sir?' asked Novello.

'Well, she's a lass going on holiday. Women normally need a cabin trunk for a long weekend. Flight bag didn't seem much, not even for a place where next to nowt looks over-dressed.'

'Spend a lot of time on Corfu, do you, sir?' enquired Novello.

'Never away since I saw *Shirley Valentine*,' said Dalziel. 'Any road, Pete starts ringing around, finds there's no Cornelius booked on a flight to Greece, but there is one booked on the shuttle to Heathrow with a tight connect to Quito. That's in Ecuador. That's in South America. That's south of North America.'

'I'll make a note,' said Novello.

'You do that. Oh, and the booking's first class, one way. With just a flight bag. Looks like she's left in a real hurry. What she's left, among other things, is a job as Technical Assistant to the Director of Investment Services at the Nortrust Bank, where they think she's at home with a touch of summer flu.'

'So Mr Pascoe starts thinking fraud?' said Novello.

'No! Not the DCI. Me, I always think the worst. He's more the Pollyanna school of investigation. Sees good in everyone. That's his only failing. Also, like I said, he seems to have taken a shine to Miss Cornelius.'

Novello said primly, 'I can't see the DCI letting that affect his judgement.'

'You reckon?' He gave her a cynical leer. 'Best check it out in your little red feminist rule book, luv. About the only thing they've got right – it affects *all* men's judgements. Except mine. And mebbe Sergeant Wield's.'

He suddenly grinned and said, 'Hey, you don't think the sergeant's dad wanted him to marry the Queen of Sicily, do you?'

A Wield ugly *and* gay joke all in one. Was this some sort of stamp of approval?

She said, 'But Mr Pascoe did start making enquiries, didn't he?'

'Aye. But likely only 'cos he felt guilty about fancying the lass. That's another thing that sorts out the good cops from the traffic cones. Doesn't matter what hang-ups you've got so long as they lead you to the right conclusions. Like you. If you were an in-your-face beads-and-incense left footer, you'd be no use to me. But from what Paddy Kerrigan says, you do more back-sliding than a trainee figure-skater, and that means your brain's covering a hell of a lot of ground.'

Perhaps she should have felt indignant at what was not the first hint that her own moral failings had been added to the common ground of rugby football and malt whisky on which Father Kerrigan, her parish priest, and the Fat Man met each other. Instead she was experiencing an upsurge of delight at the thought that being talked to like this had to confirm her approval was well and truly stamped.

But she was wise enough not to let it show.

'I'll say a novena for you, sir,' she said. 'So the DCI checks her out at work and discovers she's got her hand in the till.'

'Till? Get with it, lass. Bankers nowadays wouldn't recognize a till if they got their fingers caught in one. But, aye, he makes enquiries at Nortrust and gets told very snootily that Ms Cornelius hasn't been with them long, but in that time she's proved herself a hard-working and most trustworthy colleague. Also, she's a woman, so not bright enough to be on the fiddle.'

'They actually said that?' interrupted Novello.

'Nay,' said Dalziel grinning. 'But I'd lay odds some of 'em thought it. But a cop on the phone is bound to get them scared and I don't doubt they started counting the spoons straight off. Meanwhile Cornelius has gone home via a check-up at Casualty, and Peter finds that she's rearranged her flight for the next day. Comes the morning and Nortrust still can't give him anything to hold her on. If she'd been ugly as sin, Pete would likely have given up by now, but because he's determined to show the world he's not susceptible to his hormones, he sends a couple of uniformed round to her place, checking a few points on her statement, but really taking any chance they get for a look around. Burton and Noble, he asks for. Bright lasses. Only Noble gets held up on another case and the duty sergeant, not realizing that brightness is of the essence, assigns Hector.'

'Hector.'

If into every life a little rain must fall, Hector was Mid-Yorkshire's monsoon. Shortly after his arrival at HQ and before the full extent of his mental and physical uncoordination was understood, he had been told to take a visiting councillor to the custody area. The man had been locked up for thirty minutes before he managed to attract attention. Thereafter Hector stories proliferated like the *Arabian Nights Entertainments*, and like the *Arabian Nights Entertainments*, their eerie fascination often saved their progenitor from violent death.

'Aye, Hector,' said Dalziel. 'Burton talks to Cornelius, Hector wanders off. There's a lot of noise from the bedroom and in the end Cornelius goes through to see what's happening. Her wardrobe's open, there's clothes and stuff everywhere, plus Hector has broken into her flight bag, taken out a pair of panties, and is sitting on the bed, chewing on them.'

'Chewing?'

'Aye. Says he'd read an article about drug smugglers soaking clothes in a solution of coke, letting them dry, then washing the stuff out when they got it through Customs. He claims he were just testing for taste.'

'You believe him, sir?'

'Oh aye. Sexual perversion's too complicated for Hector. But sight of him with her knickers hanging out of his gob were too much for Cornelius. She hit him with a straight right. Pushed his nose back into the space where his brain should have been. The lass should have got a medal. Instead she got arrested for assaulting a police officer. Next thing we know is a super from Fraud turns up, has half an hour with the Chief, and Pete gets told off to stand up in court and get a remand in custody on the assault charge pending further enquiries. Did the same last week. Today will be the third time.'

'Bit low-key for the DCI, isn't it?' said Novello. 'Simple assault charge. Unless Fraud want her on ice while they have a good scratch around. How are they doing anyway?'

'Bit of a bad smell hanging around her boss, George Ollershaw, it seems, but nowt on her. But they did find some sort of warning messages on her computer at work and another at home. TIME TO GO, summat like that, which could explain why she decided to do a runner.'

'But it doesn't necessarily mean there's fraud involved,' said Novello. 'And why tie someone like the DCI up in court when anyone could have taken care of it?'

The Fat Man scratched his nose as if he wanted to remove it.

'That's what I wondered,' he said. 'But when I did a bit of prodding, all I kept on hitting was yon red tab.'

'Suppose Fraud could just want someone with

enough clout to impress the magistrate,' suggested Novello doubtfully.

'Mebbe. Well, let's see how they like a real heavyweight, eh? Look after the shop, Ivor. I'm off down the courts. Mustn't be late. Or at least not very late.'

He showed his teeth in a Jurassic grin.

What's the old sod up to? she wondered as he lumbered away, all buttocks and thighs. It was like standing behind a rhinoceros. What would it be like to have sex with him? This was a topic with which the female officers of the Mid-Yorks force often teased their fantasies in social hours. Speculation usually ended in hysterical laughter as impossibility piled on impossibility. Yet it was well known he was still active, his current inamorata being a woman called 'Cap' Marvell who, though far from his match, was built on the same generous lines. Must be like the battle of the mastodons in *The Lost World*, she thought. The image made her giggle. But it also, she admitted, turned her on just a little. Christ, she'd better watch it. Time to offer a few oats to St Uncumber, maybe.

Unaware, and uncaring if he had been aware, that he was an object of such prurient speculation, Andy Dalziel made his slow way to the magistrates' court. He wasn't technically late, but sufficiently on the cusp of lateness to have provoked the irritation of uncertainty. And not just in the magistrate's clerk, whose thin lips pursed like a tomcat's arse-hole as Dalziel humbly explained that Mr Pascoe had been unavoidably delayed, but in a couple of sombre-suited gents, one stocky, one thin, seated at the back of the court, who exchanged a relieved word at his appearance, then settled into blank-faced attentiveness.

The presiding magistrate was Mrs Nora Broomhill, a woman of indeterminate age but very determinate opinions, one of which was that any police force which numbered men like Andrew Dalziel amongst its senior officers was an Augean stable in need of intensive cleansing.

The Fat Man gave her a nod and a smile with just a hint of a rueful wink in it. She gave him a glare which would have gone well with a black cap, and instructed the clerk to begin.

As the rigmarole was gone through, Dalziel looked towards the dock where Kelly Cornelius sat. Hitherto he'd only known her from her picture in the file, which had been taken while her nose was still swollen in the aftermath of the accident. Now she was almost back to normal and he could see what a striking young woman she was. Not beautiful, or rather not possessed of that particular concatenation of feature which men of his generation were conditioned to regard as beauty, her long rather sallow face with its big dark eyes and angled cheekbones nevertheless caught and held his attention. Even in repose, there was something vibrant about her, like a landscape trembling under heat. He suddenly understood what it was that Peter Pascoe had felt he needed to show the world, and himself, he wasn't affected by. Usually when the Fat Man looked at a slim (meaning skinny when translated into Yorkspeak) woman, he thought in terms of force-feeding with Yorkshire pudding and plum duff. This one instead made him think of doing the tango on a moonlit dancefloor with the orchestra invisible and the scent of bougainvillea filling the warm night air . . .

Watch it, Hamish! he said to himself, full of amazement, particularly as he doubted if he could have picked out bougainvillea from bog myrtle. Tha must be on the turn!

'Mr Dalziel!'

Nora Broomhill's tone made it clear she had addressed him once already.

'Oh aye. Yes,' he said.

Cornelius's eyes rose to meet his now, either attracted by the intensity of his gaze or merely directed by the magistrate's steely focus.

'I understand that the police wish to make an application for a further remand in custody in the case of Ms Cornelius?'

'That's right, ma'am.'

'Perhaps you would care to share with us the grounds for this application.'

'Oh aye. Well . . .' He reached into the inner pocket of his jacket, produced some dog-eared papers, examined them with a look of faint perplexity while his upper teeth nibbled his lower lip like a hungry dog sampling a discarded tyre, then went on '. . . well, I expect they're much the same as before.'

Mrs Broomhill's eyebrows rose into a Norman arch.

'*The same as before*?' she echoed.

'Aye. I expect you'll have it written down somewhere, ma'am,' said Dalziel, with a confidential smile.

'I expect we will, Superintendent. But this court is not a rubber stamp. Each new application is distinct and separate from any previous application. Arguments need to be repeated and where necessary reinforced. It is a citizen's liberty we are dealing with here, Mr Dalziel, a citizen who enjoys that right under the law of being regarded as innocent until proven guilty. So let me hear your arguments.'

'Well, she thumped one of our lads, broke his nose . . .'

'I understand it is so *alleged*,' said Mrs Broomhill coldly. 'Am I to understand you are saying members of the police force would feel at risk if Miss Cornelius were set at liberty?'

'No! Don't be daft. Oo, sorry, ma'am . . . didn't mean . . . what I'm saying is there's other serious charges against her being investigated and we're feart she might flit.'

'Leave the country, you mean? But I understand Miss Cornelius has voluntarily handed over her passport. Miss Dancer?'

The young woman solicitor acting for Kelly

223

Cornelius who had been listening to the exchange with growing delight popped up and said, 'That is correct, ma'am.'

'And what stage has been reached in the investigation of these other possible offences, Mr Dalziel? Is there an end in sight.'

Dalziel looked round appealingly at the two suits at the back of the court. They studiously avoided his eyes.

'Couldn't say, ma'am,' he said helplessly. 'Sorry. But I thought someone 'ud have had a private word with you . . . mebbe . . .'

The arch of the magistrate's eyebrows went from Norman to Perpendicular.

'Have you finished, Superintendent?' she said coldly. 'Miss Dancer?'

The solicitor rose and said demurely, 'If it pleases you, ma'am, my client has now been held in custody for nearly three weeks on a charge which, if proven, and without trying to preempt the court's judgement, is unlikely to result in a custodial sentence of such duration. These alleged other offences have not resulted in any further charge, nor, from what the superintendent says, does there seem any likelihood of their doing so in the foreseeable future. Continued detention in such circumstances would seem to be manifestly unjust and unjustifiable. I would therefore ask that the application be denied.'

Mrs Broomhill consulted briefly with her clerk and then announced, 'I agree, Miss Dancer. The application is denied. In its place I will make an order requiring Miss Cornelius to report daily to her local police station. Failure to do so will result in a further warrant for her arrest. Do you understand this, Miss Cornelius?'

The defendant stood up.

'Yes, ma'am,' she said in a low musical voice.

Then she turned her head towards Andy Dalziel and gave him a heart-stoppingly grateful smile, and he found he was grinning back like an idiot.

Outside the court, Dalziel saw the two suits in close confabulation. He went up to them and said to the thinner of the pair, 'It's Barney Hubbard, isn't it? We met at that conference in Derby. Is it your lads checking out how deep Cornelius has had her hand in the till?'

His voice boomed round the crowded vestibule.

'Yes, Mr Dalziel,' said Hubbard at a much lower level. 'And we would have preferred the woman to continue a little longer in custody. What the devil were you playing at in there? Where's DCI Pascoe?'

'Got held up so I had to step into the breach last minute. Sorry if I weren't up to speed on things, but finding out what's going on here's like trying to find out who really shot Kennedy. Here, don't I know your friend?'

The stouter suit had stepped away from the conversation. Now, under Dalziel's benign smile, he said, 'No, I don't think we've met. Hubbard, I think we should be on our way.'

The thin suit gave Dalziel a glance at once accusatory and promissory and the pair began to move away.

The Fat Man let them go two or three paces then he called, 'I remember. Didn't you used to hang about with yon funny bugger, Pimpernel, sorry, I mean Sempernel? Aye, that's it. Didn't recognize you without your cloak and dagger. How is old Gawain? Still sifting through wastebins to keep us all safe for democracy, eh?'

The suits slowed momentarily then increased their pace without looking round.

'Well, give him my regards anyway,' called Dalziel as they went through the door.

Then he smiled benevolently round the listening room like a medieval pope after a good burning, and said, 'Nice to meet old friends, isn't it? But I can't stay here all day enjoying myself when there's work to be done,' and headed out into the sunshine and towards the Black Bull.

xvii

the juice of strawberries

Rosemont was a house for all seasons, but at summer's height the extensive gardens were a green canvas on which an artist had painted heaven with a palette of roses. From the purity of *Iceberg* and *Virgo*, through the faint flush of *Félicité et Perpétue* and *Escapade* to the clear-pink of *Dandy Dick*, the lilac-pink of *Yesterday* and the salmon-pink of *Evensong*, the shades ran ever darkening down the red blush of *Perfecta*, the bright flame of *Wilhelm*, the dried blood of *Kassel*, the velvet burgundy of *Roseraie de l'Haÿ*, ending in the depths of midnight-purple in the robes of *Cardinal de Richelieu*.

A seeker after sensation could voyage long hours across this ocean of colour and scent, uncaring because unknowing whether his fate was directing him to *Sweet Repose* and *Penelope* or *Clytemnestra* and *Crimson Shower*. As Ellie's car emerged from the tunnel of over-arching hollies which stood sentinel about the main gate, her heart sang at this sense of bursting into a new and golden land. It wasn't true, of course, but somehow it seemed that the sun always shone at Rosemont, as indeed it had seemed to shine always upon the life of its owner, Patrick Aldermann.

Ellie was no rose expert but she could identify the long-stemmed sweet-smelling blooms in deep gold, opening to a scarlet flush, which had pride of place in the beds flanking the front door. These were the fruits of Patrick's own breeding and he'd named them after his wife, who was standing alongside them on the doorstep as Ellie drew up.

Today, however, the resemblance between bloom and eponym was not as clear as it had once been, though there was presumably some sort of scarlet flush beneath the white gauze taped across her nose.

'Ellie, it's lovely to see you,' said Daphne. 'I hoped you would come.'

'You mean you've been lurking in the porch all morning on the off chance?' said Ellie.

'Don't be silly. The noise that wreck of yours makes is identifiable five miles off. Careful!'

This in response to the kiss Ellie offered to plant on her cheek.

'It's all right. The danger zone's pretty well signposted. How are you? I'd have brought some flowers only it seemed sort of coals to Newcastle.'

'Belgian chocolates or exotic fruits didn't cross your mind then? Let's sit outside. Patrick's just making some coffee, or is your alcoholism so advanced you'd prefer a gin?'

'Coffee's fine. Patrick . . . ? I thought he was on his way to Amsterdam or somewhere?'

'He should be, but he's come over all macho and says he can't possibly go. I'm working on him.'

They sat at a handsome round table in delicately scrolled wrought iron. The chairs looked to be made from the same material but proved to be gently yielding and very comfortable. Patrick Aldermann was not inclined to let anything get in the way of his creature comforts.

'So, how are you feeling today?' asked Daphne.

'Aren't you getting your script wrong? It's you who's got the cauliflower nose, remember?'

'Because I got in the way, not because I personally am being terrorized,' she said firmly. 'You're the one who matters here, Ellie.'

This was one of the things that made Daphne special, thought Ellie. After an audition as violent as hers, few people could have resisted the temptation to be prima donna, if only for a couple of scenes, in someone else's opera.

'It's the kind of distinction I could do without,' said Ellie glumly. 'Anyway, I came to say I'm really sorry. And I am.'

'Darling, it wasn't your fault. Not at all. Or not unless there's something you're not telling me.'

'Don't be stupid. Why do you say that?'

'Because, being a bleeding-heart liberal and a product of the let-it-all-hang-out state educational system, you are little skilled in the arts of social

229

hypocrisy. What's bugging you? I use the phrase horticulturally, of course.'

'Nothing. I mean, everything. Oh, what the hell. It's stupid, but it does feel like it's all my fault. Sort of, I mean.'

'Such clarity, such brevity,' murmured Daphne. 'But perhaps you could expand just a little.'

Ellie said, 'Before Rosie was taken ill, I was feeling, you know, a bit sort of down. Self-analytical. Looking at my life and asking what it really added up to. I know, I know, in terms of what I'd got, nice home, by my plebeian standards anyway, nice husband, good sex, lovely kid, a fridge full of exotic grub and Australian chardonnay, a decent circle of friends, present company excepted, in terms of all this I was doing OK. And I couldn't moan on about giving up my career, because any time I wanted I could pick up some lecturing work, and if I really got the bug, I could even go back full time, Peter would have fallen over backwards to be supportive. Only I thought about it and realized that attending for a check, or even a cheque, was exactly what I didn't want! So, no complaints there.'

'Ellie, my dear, I hope this isn't leading up to a confession that you've been screwing the milkman?' said Daphne.

'Our milkman is a milk*woman* who, rumour has it, is fully occupied realizing the randy-squire-and-young-dairymaid fantasies of Mr James, the merry widower at number seventeen. No, I flung my fling, or came close, a few years back. But that was in another country and besides, the boy is dead. So, been there, done that, have no desire to pay another visit. I love Peter, and when he's not absolutely knackered running around after the Fat Controller, he can make the earth move and the welkin ring for me like we used to read about in mucky books.'

'Our educational systems did have some overlap then,' said Daphne. 'So that's sex, love, maternalism, and creature comforts all sorted out. What's your problem, dear?'

'I just feel that I haven't really done anything,' said Ellie helplessly. 'Not anything that matters.'

'Come on! When I first met you, you were waving a banner and chanting abuse even though you had a papoose basket strapped on your back. For years you were to protests like Kate Adie is to civil wars, they couldn't really start till you got there.'

'Oh yes, I marched and made speeches and wrote letters and joined pickets, I did all that. But I never got shot at, or beaten up, or tortured like the people I was protesting for. I never even had to go hungry because I was on strike like the people whose pickets I joined. But it wasn't just social-conscience stuff. I've never lived abroad, I've never bummed my way along the Golden Road to Samarkand. I've never sailed round the world single-handed, I've never been close when something really interesting has happened, like an earthquake or a revolution or a film star getting into a fight in a restaurant. I sometimes read the author blurbs on novels and think that if ever by some miracle I get published, they'll have to have a blank!'

'Wow,' said Daphne. 'Is this perhaps why you started writing? I don't mean to fill the author blurb blank, of course. Or perhaps I do.'

Ellie laughed and said, 'I don't care what your therapist says about you, I think you're pretty sharp. Yes, possibly. It's a way of getting a life, isn't it? In fact, an infinity of lives. Plus, if it comes off, you're Ellie Pascoe the novelist instead of just Ellie Pascoe, the policeman's wife. But there's more to it than that, I think. I hope. Anyway, my laboured point is that when Rosie nearly died, suddenly all this crap dwindled away to nothing. There was me, there was Rosie, there was Pete. That was it. Holy Trinity. I even prayed to that other Trinity, the one I don't believe in. And I made promises. Like if we got through this, I'd never be dissatisfied again.'

'Do promises to something you don't believe in count, I wonder?'

'More than any other, I'd say. Never cheat something that can't cheat back. Anyway, to cut a marathon story down to ten thousand metres, all that stuff I thought had dwindled down to nothing, well, it's like stuff on your computer screen, it goes out of sight but it's really still there. I can feel it. I think I got the first reminder when I got rung up about that Liberata meeting I told you about. Part of me said, I'm finished with this stuff, from now on it's cultivate your own garden, girl. Then guilt clicked in. But worse than guilt. I found myself thinking about old Feenie Macallum. Her life, you couldn't get it on the back of a dust jacket, you'd need a whole thick volume. You see what I'm saying, Daphne? I know I've been changed by what happened, what nearly happened to us. I look at Rosie and Pete and I know that they're so important to me, I'd die for them. And yet I can still feel deep down inside of me the old seeds of dissatisfaction! Lovely character, ain't I?'

'And you think that this Trinity you don't believe in, having tried to set you right earlier this year by nearly killing your daughter, has decided to give you another lesson by having you persecuted by a bunch of loonies? Come on!'

Daphne laughed, not a forced superior bray but a bubbling gurgle of real amusement which left you no option but to join in.

As if at a signal, which indeed perhaps it was, Patrick Aldermann appeared carrying a tray which he placed on the table, then stooped to peck Ellie's cheek.

'How nice to find you both in such high spirits,' he said. 'I thought you might have come to blows over who should bear most responsibility for yesterday's fiasco.'

'Patrick, please!' said Daphne. 'We've got that sorted.'

'Oh yes? And?'

Ellie said, 'I freely accept complete responsibility, despite the fact that what actually happened to Daphne was her own silly fault.'

Aldermann considered this as he poured the coffee.

As he handed a cup to Ellie, he smiled. It was a good smile. His normal expression was an unexpressive blank, brown eyes observing you neutrally from an oval face whose complete regularity of feature enhanced the sense of a mask. Another kind of man, realizing how attractive and juvenating his smile was, might have used it more often and more calculatingly, but Aldermann was the least self-conscious man Ellie knew. She wasn't sure how much she liked him, not because she knew anything about him to dislike, but simply because he gave so little away. People with something to conceal often reveal themselves negatively through the way they wish to be seen, but Patrick was simply . . . Patrick. A man for whom life had seemed to arrange itself with the natural beauty and perfect proportions of this garden. Except, of course, that this garden owed most of its beauty and lay-out to the working brain and working hand of its owner. Which made you wonder about his life . . .

'You're right, of course,' he said. 'She has this fond belief that danger can't touch her, or that if it does, the gods will protect her by turning her into a bush.'

'Well, you've turned her into a flower,' said Ellie.

'Pity you weren't around yesterday to spray some sense into her.'

It was a light-hearted joke at Daphne's expense but her husband seemed to take it seriously.

'Yes. A pity. But I'm around now.'

'Which you shouldn't be,' said Daphne. 'You should be on your way to Amsterdam. For heaven's sake, I'm not under threat. It was, as you two moral philosophers keep banging on, my own stupid fault that I put myself in the way of this thug who, having got me out his way, can't have any more interest in me, can he?'

'He may still have an interest in Ellie,' said Aldermann. 'At least I assume Peter thinks so from the presence of that young man lurking behind the *Zéphirine Drouhin*.'

Ellie followed his gaze down the garden to an eight-foot-high pillar covered with carmine-pink blooms, through which the shape of DC Bowler was just discernible.

'Shall I ask him up for a cup of coffee?' said Daphne.

'No!' said Ellie, irritated. 'I'll tell him to sod off.'

'Why not let him be?' said Aldermann. 'He's doing no harm and can come to none. *Zéphirine* has a glorious scent and no thorns. So what does Peter think is going on, Ellie?'

'I can't go into details,' said Ellie virtuously. 'Except he thinks the danger's probably over now. My minder down there in the rose bush is more for Peter's peace of mind than my protection.'

'Exactly the reason you're hanging around here, Patrick,' said Daphne. 'It's a typical male control thing. *Your* feelings masquerading as *our* fault.'

'Bravo,' laughed Ellie. 'You've been reading one of those books I loaned you.'

'Don't be silly. You lot think you invented female insight the way kids think they invented sex. It's been around a lot longer than Germaine Greer, if that's possible. Ellie, help me get it into his head that just because I got a bang on the nose doesn't mean I have ceased to be able to stay in my own house by myself.'

'Well,' said Ellie. 'I can see how you might be concerned, Patrick. Frankly I don't know how you can bear to let anyone so completely headstrong and so totally unreliable out of your sight for a moment. But isn't the solution obvious? Take her to the conference with you.'

'Oh, he's tried that,' said Daphne. 'And I'd go if it was anywhere but Holland! I feel so depressed there, mentally and geographically. Only fish and crustaceans were created to exist below sea level. The thought that only some small child's finger is preventing a tidal wave from the North Sea gushing all over me is more than I can bear. But wait. I feel an idea coming on. There is a Plan B. This involves me going away to stay somewhere safe with someone sound. Patrick's preferred candidate is my cousin Joyce in Harrogate. I would prefer the bed of the North Sea to the company of my cousin Joyce in Harrogate. On the other hand, Ellie, you are someone sound whose company I *could* bear, for a little while at least. As for somewhere safe, David and his chums are abandoning the comforts of the bothy today for the more character-building terrain of a camp site in the Trossachs. Why don't we head out there for a few days, Rosie too, of course, and solve both our husbands' problems by looking after each other?'

So, thought Ellie, must Marie Antoinette have sounded as she put forward her solution to the bread-shortage crisis. And so looked too, probably, except maybe for the nose bandage; but certainly the same shining eyes, the same delighted smile, the same exudation of exultation, which probably made the feyer members of the French court a little warm under the collar, were on show here.

She left it to Patrick to point out the major flaw in the proposition, viz, that when stung by a wasp, you do not achieve safety by running away with the jam-pot. When he didn't speak, she put it down to natural spousal reluctance to hurl the first stone and said, 'Daph, that's great, except for one thing. It's me these lunatics are interested in, not you. Safest thing for you is to keep as far away from me as possible.'

'There you go again,' said Daphne. 'Me, me, me all the time.'

Ellie looked at Patrick for the delayed support.

Instead, after another long moment's reflection, he said, 'Nosebleed, as you know, is about fifty miles away on the coast.'

'Nosebleed?' echoed Ellie, trying to interpret this as an obscure and untypically discourteous reference to Daphne's injury.

'Yes. Our cottage. Nosebleed Cottage. That's its name.'

'Good Lord. Charming.'

Patrick smiled and said, 'Don't let it put you off. It's a local name for the common yarrow, *Achillea millefolium*.'

'*Achillea*? As in Achilles?' said Ellie, suddenly thinking of her story.

'That's right. Yarrow is a potent medicinal plant and has magical properties too, though the distinction is often blurred. Hang on a moment.'

He went through the window into the house.

Daphne said, 'Haven't you learnt never to express an interest in any form of vegetation when Patrick's around, not even if you're eating it?'

'Shut up. I am interested.'

Patrick returned, bearing tomes of various size and antiquity. He leafed through what looked the most ancient.

'Here we are. Gerard's *Herball*, 1597. "The plant *Achillea* is thought to be the very same wherewith Achilles cured the wounds of his soldiers." And Grigson in his *Englishman's Flora* cites Apuleius Platonicus's *Herbarium*. "It is said that Achilles the chieftain found it and he with this same wort healed them who were stricken and wounded with iron." So, a kind of Homeric Savlon.'

'As Achilles seemed to spend the best part of

his life running around, wounding people, I imagine he had plenty of opportunity to try it out,' said Ellie. 'That's medicine. You mentioned magic before too.'

'Oh yes. Powerful for or against evil, says Grigson. And he quotes from Hurlstone Jackson's *Celtic Miscellany* a translation of a Gaelic incantation to accompany the plucking of yarrow. I have Jackson's slightly modified 1971 version here. You read it, Ellie. It's for a woman.'

He handed her a Penguin paperback with his finger laid against the passage.

Ellie read, hesitantly at first, but in a strengthening voice as the words caught her imagination.

'I will pick the smooth yarrow that my figure may be more elegant, that my lips may be warmer, that my voice may be more cheerful; may my voice be like a sunbeam, may my lips be like the juice of the strawberries. May I be an island in the sea, may I be a hill on the land, may I be a star when the moon wanes, may I be a staff to the weak one: I shall wound every man, no man shall wound me.'

The air seemed to grow heavier and warmer and more richly scented in the silence after she spoke and she felt close to fainting till Daphne broke the spell by saying, 'That was really beautiful, Ellie. Patrick, why isn't our garden full of yarrow?'

'Because here it would be a weed,' said Aldermann firmly.

'But there's a lot of it at Nosebleed, is there?' said Ellie, recovering.

'Indeed. But there's a lot of it on most uncultivated ground. I expect the cottage got its name originally because some early occupant was a healer. Or a witch.'

'Yes, but why call it Nosebleed – the plant, I mean?' asked Ellie.

'Grigson says if you put the leaves up your nose, they can make it bleed, which is a way of finding out if your love is true. *Yarroway, yarroway, bear a white blow. If my love love me, my nose will bleed now.*'

Ellie thought, well, I shan't need to try that, and smiled.

Patrick smiled back, but made no irritating enquiry as to the source of her amusement. He was good at that, not at all pushy, content to let people – and things – come to him.

Daphne said, 'Nose-bleeding is a rather insensitive subject for you two to be going on about in view of my condition, don't you think?'

'Sorry,' said Ellie. 'But clearly I was never going to get any of this fascinating information from you. Thank you, Patrick.'

Patrick said, 'My pleasure. I don't know why, but I assumed you would know all about the cottage, perhaps even have visited it.'

Ellie said, 'No, I know nothing about it, except that Daphne refers to it as the bothy, which makes it sound like some rural slum. I didn't even realize till yesterday that in fact you bought it off my good friend, Feenie Macallum.'

She said this to preempt any snidery about Feenie, though to the best of her recollection, she'd never heard Patrick Aldermann say anything unpleasant about anyone.

Daphne snorted at the name and winced as her nose reacted badly.

'Weren't you about to make some point about the cottage before you got diverted, dear?' she said.

'Was I? Oh yes. I was going to say that, despite its distance, I believe the Axness area falls within the purlieu of the Mid-Yorkshire Force? In other words, if you did spend some time there, it would be no problem for Peter to maintain a supervisory programme?'

'You mean, set someone to watch over me? Well, yes, I suppose so. But, Patrick, this is silly . . .'

'Why?' he said. 'In view of what's happened over the past two days, I'd be surprised if Peter hadn't already considered the possibility of removing you and Rosie to a place of safety.'

'Well, yes, he did say something, but –'

'There you are then,' said Aldermann who, despite his quiet and unassertive manner, was somehow very good at inserting his words into the apparently unbroken speech flows of other people. 'And the fact that you've never been there before would make it even less likely that anyone could get a lead on where you'd gone, in the unlikely event that anyone should attempt to get such a lead, I mean.'

'Perhaps, but I think you're missing the point. Like I just said, it's having me around that could be dangerous to Daphne.'

'Forgive me, Ellie; not having you around Daphne is one thing – though I should point out it was your choice to visit us this morning –'

He smiled the smile at her, but it didn't take away the faint sting.

'– but not having Daphne around you is quite another matter. I know you may find it surprising that in some matters I know my wife rather better than you know your friend, but what is preventing me from catching my plane today isn't any suspicion that as soon as I leave, kamikaze terrorists will come spilling across the lawn, it's the certainty that Daphne would be heading to your side as fast as she could, frightened you might enjoy the next episode of your adventure without her company.'

He looked from Daphne to Ellie and back again. They were silent, whether from amazement or indignation they hadn't yet made up their minds.

'Therefore if I am to go to my conference, and I don't disguise that missing it would be a blow, I should feel happier if the pair of you were safely stowed somewhere these people couldn't possibly know about, under the aegis of a police escort, than I would be relying on any assurance my wife or indeed your good self might offer of avoiding each other's company.'

This was more packed with insults than a philanthropist's Christmas pudding with silver threepennies.

Ellie opened her mouth to spit out retaliation, but Daphne was quicker.

'Oh good. That's settled then,' she said brightly. 'Nosebleed, here we come. Ellie, darling, when can you be ready?'

xviii

the flowers that bloom in the spring, tra-la!

Kelly Cornelius lay in her hot foaming bath and closed her eyes.

Through the open door she could hear her Gilbert and Sullivan compilation disc pulsing full blast out of the hi-fi. It had been playing almost continuously since she got home but so far none of her neighbours had complained. Possibly even the macho dickhead who occupied the flat above had been given pause by his awareness that she'd been accused of assaulting a police officer.

'Taken from the county jail,' she sang along. 'By a set of curious chances . . .'

As a precocious kid she'd used to mock her Hispanic/Hibernian father for his love of something so English as the Savoy Operas, but at times of stress this was the music which she could rely on to bring back his lean, smiling face and her sun-filled, love-filled childhood.

'. . . liberated then on bail, on my own recognizances . . .'

A musical bath had been the second most important thing on her mind when she got back to her flat after her unexpected release. The first had been to check that the hollow wooden light pull in her bathroom had not been touched, unscrew it, and do a couple of lines of the coke hidden there. She'd been pleased to discover how well she managed in custody without it. Not that it would have been hard to score in the remand centre where most things were on offer, but she'd been advised by experts, or at least by one expert, that your weaknesses were what both the screws and your fellow prisoners were looking for, so keep them hidden as long as you could. It had been a comfort to be able to confirm what she'd often asserted to herself, that she was still a long way from being an addict.

But, Christ! it had been good to feel the jolt once more.

Then straight into the bath to get the smell of the place off her. She topped it up with boiling hot water for the third time. She'd have to watch it or her skin would be going all puffy!

She raised one arm out of the water and examined it for puffiness. No signs yet. She reached out her hand to the glass which stood on the stool beside the bath.

'So bumpers – aye ever so many – And then if you will, many more! This wine doesn't cost us a penny, Tho' it's Pommery seventy-four!'

She emptied her glass and looked contemplatively at the bottle resting in the bidet. Just one more glass . . . ? Better not. Coke high got you clear and sharp, but bubbly, delicious though it was, just got you pissed. Shame to waste it though.

She stood up in the bath, picked up the bottle, pressed her thumb over the top and shook it violently. Then, pointing it at her crotch, she removed her thumb and shrieked as the icy bubbling jet played on her hot pink flesh.

Jesus! she thought. I should patent this!

She squatted in the water for a moment to wash away the wine, then got out and walked out of the bathroom draped in a huge white towel. God knows what kind of surveillance they'd set up, but she saw no reason to give them a show.

Dried and dressed, she put a large floppy sun hat on her head and went out of the flat, leaving the music blaring behind her.

'The flowers that bloom in the Spring, tra-la,' she sang as she ran down the stairs and out into the sunlight. 'Breathe promise of merry sunshine . . .'

On the steps she paused as if drinking in the fresh air of freedom. Which indeed she was, except she wasn't sure if she was enjoying it with the compliments of that pair of suits who always turned up at her court hearings or whether that barrel of lard who'd rolled in instead of nice lean Mr Pascoe really was as incompetent as he appeared.

Never mind. Calculation or cock-up, they were going to regret it.

She headed for the town centre on a route which took her through Charter Park, the great expanse of open green space which was the city's main lung. As she turned into the gate, the car which had been following her slowed down to permit its passenger to get out. He strolled through the gate after her while the car continued on its slow crawl around the one way system which circumscribed the park. She paused from time to time, to call encouragement to some children playing cricket, to exchange a few laughing words with an old lady feeding ducks on the canal, to sniff at the roses in the municipal flower beds. She was still singing '. . . we welcome the hope that they bring, tra-la, Of a summer of roses and wine . . .' as she emerged at the other side of the park, stepping out onto the pavement almost coincidentally with the arrival of the kerb-crawling car.

She spent the next hour wandering round the department stores, buying first of all a small haversack and then various odds and ends of clothing and make-up which she shoved into it. Finally she bought herself a huge ice cream cone with chocolate sauce, and with her long pink tongue burrowing into it like an aardvark at a termite tower, she retraced her steps into the park.

The man on foot followed while the car continued on its long one way circle, moving even more slowly now that the late afternoon traffic was building up.

A couple of hundred yards into the park on a slight raise and partially concealed by a small grove of trees was a public lavatory. Dumping the remnants of her cone into a wastebin, Kelly Cornelius went into the ladies. As she disappeared she was humming, 'When constabulary duty's to be done, to be done . . .' The man found a bench to sit on from which he could observe the path leading up to the conveniences.

He'd only been sitting thirty seconds or so when she reappeared.

'Oh shit,' he said.

She was riding a bicycle.

She came swooping down the track towards him, then did a wide loop across the hard baked grass to avoid getting too close. He began to run in an effort to cut her off but even though the bike looked pretty ancient and heavy, it moved fast downhill under the thrust of those elegant young legs, and his outstretched arm came nowhere near her, though he was close enough to hear her voice raised in song as she shot by.

'. . . the policeman's lot is not a happy one – happy one!'

He pulled out a mobile phone and punched in numbers but she was out of the gate and weaving away along the pavement against the traffic flow long before the phone began to ring in the crawling car which was now a quarter of a mile away, bogged down in traffic and facing the wrong direction.

'. . . the flowers that bloom in the Spring, tra-la, Breathe promise of merry sunshine . . .'

xix

pooh on the patio

Ellie Pascoe had brought her laptop down from the room she refused to call a study to the kitchen. This was so that she could keep one eye on a gently simmering pan of ratatouille and the other on Rosie who was playing in the back garden.

Ratatouille hardly needed an eye upon it, except that Ellie knew from experience that she was quite capable of forgetting all about it and redefining chargrilled vegetables. Rosie hardly needed an eye either, being totally absorbed with her two play-mates, one (slightly worryingly) invisible, the other (very worryingly) not.

Despite these demands on her attention and her care, she was able to let some sort of third eye which might have been the bliss of solitude if that was a condition enjoyable by those with ratatouille and children to worry about, check the scrolling screen for the point she'd reached in her revisions.

There it was. First mention of Odysseus. She

began to read and was instantly geminated, one of her personae experientially present in her imagined universe, the other peering into it god-like through the window of her computer. This second was a right carping cow, always finding something new to worry about. Literally, something new in this case. How could she justify putting expressions with a modern ring in the mouth of an ancient Greek, except of course as an easy route to a cheap laugh? Here for instance in the stranger's reaction . . .

'Odysseus, you say. Now him I have heard of. Right slippery customer from all accounts. Buy a used boat off him and you'd soon have a wet arse. Well, it takes all sorts to make a world, eh? So your lot lost this war then? That's always the way, there's got to be losers and winners. But I'm right glad you and your old father and these good-looking lads here all managed to come off safe and sound.'

That bit about buying a used boat bothered her slightly, with its clear reference forward to modern car salesmen. Did this make it unusably anachronistic? On the whole she thought not. The phrase might ring modern, but it wasn't really anachronistic either in content or in concept. The notion of sharp practice was as old as Homer himself. Wasn't there a bit in the *Iliad* where a Greek warrior spares one of the Trojans he recognizes as a distant relative, then as token of their kinship offers

251

to exchange armour with him, a noble-seeming gesture until the poet wryly points out that the Greek's gear is a right load of old tin while the gullible Trojan's is all bronze and gold?

As to the objection that this didn't sound like the way an ancient Greek would speak, well, of course it didn't! For a start he'd be speaking in ancient Greek. And why that should have to be presented in some version of eighteenth-century poetic diction she couldn't see. It struck her as being as daft as those movies where foreigners allegedly speaking in their own tongue are made to speak English with a foreign accent.

Convinced by her own reasoning, she carried on.

'Thank you for your concern,' said Aeneas. 'But you still have not answered my first question. Why did you address your supplications to me and not to my father?'

The stranger leaned forward and spoke confidentially, as if he and the Prince were all alone.

'Well, lord, of course, you're dead right. In the normal way of things I'd have gone for the old gent. But in this case, he looked ... if you'll pardon me for saying it, lord, but you did ask ... he looked so frail and weighed down, like he's been through a lot of bad stuff and it's all getting to be too much for him, and it didn't seem fair to add to his burden.'

'That was very considerate of you,' said Aeneas.

'Aye, mebbe it was. But I'll be honest, there were a bit of self-interest there too. What I mean is, it seemed to me that while a word from you might be enough to stop any of these good-looking lads of yours from skewering me, I wasn't so sure that they'd pay the same heed to your dad, not in the heat of the moment, I mean.'

Aeneas said softly, 'Be assured, any who didn't would rapidly suffer an equal fate.'

'Mebbe so. But a lot of good that would do me, lying there all stuck with spikes, like a hedgehog that's been hit by a chariot.'

The Prince nodded, as if accepting the argument.

'Now tell me your name and degree, of what family and fortune you come, from what region so remote that news of the great war at Troy hardly seems to have troubled you, and whether it is the vagaries of uncaring fortune or the just wrath of one of the great Olympians which have driven you in such a state of nakedness onto this inhospitable shore.'

The Greek took a deep breath, then he smiled and slowly opened his arms wide like a patriarch inviting a troop of grandchildren to his embrace, and where before he had spoken as if he and Aeneas were all alone, now his tone and manner included everyone present in his audience.

'Lord, my name is Nikos, and I was born on an island so small and out of the way nobody's heard of it save them as lives there, and they call it Orkhis because of its shape. My family are fishermen, not poor, not rich, 'cos them things are relative and as we're all fishermen on Orkhis and we take care of our own, poor or rich don't come into it.'

'No overlord then?' interposed Aeneas.

'Not on the island. Nowt there to warrant some great man like your lordship's self building a stronghold and creating a fiefdom. Yet it's hard in these troubled times to get by without the protection of belonging to someone or other, and we have long paid what humble tribute we can afford to Ithaca. Now here's an interesting thing, lord. According to our rude historians, King Laertes once visited the island himself many years ago, and our ruder gossips say that on that visit he took a real shine to my ma who was a right bonny lass by all accounts, and a bit of a flirt, and the next year after his visit, she gave my father a manchild, me, which is why though I'm named Nikos after my old dad, my mates down the taverna usually call me Nothos, signifying bastard.'

A ripple of amusement ran round the listeners.

'You do not mind this signification?' said Aeneas.

'Nay, lord, why should a man mind being told he's got noble blood in him? And besides, a lot of them as called me bastard have found out the hard way they were only telling the truth.'

Now the ripple of amusement turned into a wave of laughter.

Even Aeneas smiled as he said, 'So, Nothos, now we know who you are, and what you are, pray tell us how you come to be here?'

The fat man rolled his eyes piously upwards and said, 'By heavenly grace and your lordship's equally divine mercy. Three days past, I set out with my fellows to fish, but the buggers weren't running, and my mates soon headed off home, saying they might as well be sitting around playing with their wives by their own hearths as playing with themselves out here on the rocking sea. Me, though, I don't give up so easy. If the fish weren't here, they had to be elsewhere, so I let the wind and current take me further and further from our usual fishing grounds. Then it started getting dark, and the sea got right gurly, and I thought, Nothos, my lad, it's time you were home. Only which way was home? And any road, it made no matter, 'cos I didn't have choice of which way I would go. For there was a storm blowing up and no ordinary storm either. No, this was one of them storms the gods send when they've really got it in for some poor sod. Well, I knew it weren't me. I mean, what business would the gods have with a poor fisherman? No, it had to be someone a lot more important. Here, come to think of it, lord, could it have been you? You haven't been getting up old Poseidon's nose, have you? Or one of your followers, mebbe?'

'We try to give all the gods their due worship,' said Aeneas coldly. 'You, on the other hand, *according to Captain Achates, were uttering fearsome blasphemies against the lord of the sea after you were cast up on the beach.'*

Nothos looked abashed.

'Aye, well, mebbe I did get a bit carried away. But not without cause, lord. There was I, a poor fisherman going about my trade, and suddenly I'm in the middle of someone else's storm, being driven along God knows where, for the best part of three days, I reckon. Then finally my boat hits a rock and down it goes, and that's my living gone with it, you understand, just about everything I own in the world. Down deep, I went, so deep I thought I'd be bound to run into the old bugger, and if I had, I tell you, I'd have been tempted to do more than shake a fist at him! But you're right, no use fighting with the gods, eh? And I must have done something to please one of them at least, for I didn't drown, but up I came again, and managed to stay afloat I can't tell how long, till finally I got cast up here on this land. For which I give thanks, and especially for falling into the hands of such a generous and noble lord as your good self, followed, as you'd expect, by such a splendid bunch of fighting men.'

He finished and lowered his gaze, his body sagging as if with fatigue, but under his bushy eyebrows his keen eyes were regarding the Trojan shrewdly to see what effect his story had had.

'So,' said Aeneas. 'You have said much to make us pity you. On the other hand, though low and

ignorant, there's no denying that you are one of our sworn foes.'

'Nay, lord, I'll admit to low and ignorant, but as for the other, here's one who'll deny it. I've sworn to nowt about you lot. I've never heard owt about you but good, nor do I wish you any harm, and I'll swear to that here and now, if you like. Great lords like yourself decide what lowly folk like me do and are. You say I'm your foe and that's got to be true. But if you say I'm your friend, why, that's just as true, isn't it?'

'It is not for me alone to judge you, fellow,' said Aeneas sternly. 'Where the fate of all is involved, a leader must also be a democrat. You know the word? It is one of yours.'

'Aye, I know it,' said Nothos unenthusiastically. 'Comes between horse thief and sheep-shagger back home.'

'Indeed? Such a primitive society yours must be. So, men, what do you say? Shall we show mercy here, or shall we make this one Greek pay for the crimes of all his fellows?'

'I say, let's take him back up the headland and toss him back into the sea,' said Achates. 'There's something about him I don't like the look of.'

There was a loud murmur of agreement among the listening men which did not bode well for a democratic vote.

'Hey, come on,' protested the Greek to the captain.

'If you're going to start chucking folk off cliffs just for the way they look, I reckon I'll get a soft landing 'cos I'll be landing on thee!'

Some of the men laughed at this till Achates turned his craggy, unreadable face towards them.

'One for death,' said Aeneas. 'Anyone else? Palinurus?'

A slim young man stepped forward and said, 'Lord, even though I can now see the moon and the stars, I cannot look at my charts and tell exactly where we are. If this Greek has any knowledge of this island's location and of its waters, their reefs and rocks and channels and shallows, he could be of use to us.'

'Well, fisherman?'

Nothos scratched his chin through the tangles of his beard, producing a sound like saw teeth digging into a forest oak.

'I won't lie to you,' he said. 'I've not been to this place afore, but if it's where I think it is, I've heard tell of it from some of the old men back home, and you know how these old buggers go over the same thing again and again till you could just about join in with them. So yes, I reckon I could navigate you safe back to Orkhis or wherever you're bound for. If you've got ships safely harboured, that is?'

'That is for us to know,' said Aeneas before Palinurus could reply. 'Right, Greek, for the time being, we'll spare you . . . Why do you smile?'

'Nothing, lord. Except I were thinking, if I'd

258

known this is how democracy works, I'd mebbe have joined long since.'

Their gazes met for a moment, then the Greek lowered his modestly and Aeneas continued, 'If you prove useful to us in this matter, then we will land you somewhere as close to this island of yours as our voyage takes us. If not, then perhaps we'll take another look at democracy. Now come with me. You must be in need of sleep after all your excitements.'

He stood up and led the way to the shelter by the boulder.

'Keep guard by the exit, Achates,' he said. 'And if he shows his head without permission, chop it off.'

Inside the pavilion, a pair of oil lamps burned and by their amber light, the Greek saw that the shelter was bigger than appeared from outside, as the huge boulder was hollow to a depth of ten or twelve feet. The furthermost part of it had been turned into a separate chamber by a curtain of heavy bearskin, which was drawn aside now to let the old man, Anchises, come out.

Before the curtain fell again, Nothos glimpsed a figure lying on a makeshift bed with a woman sitting beside him, bathing his head with water from a silver bowl.

'How is he?' asked Aeneas.

The old man shrugged. His tongue said nothing but his face showed despair.

'Go outside, Father,' urged the Prince gently. 'Take some food. I will join you shortly.'

With a glance of hatred at the Greek, Anchises obeyed.

'Don't think your old dad cares for me,' said Nothos.

'He has little reason to like Greeks,' said Aeneas. 'None of us has.'

'Just as well I didn't apply to him for mercy then, wasn't it?' said the Greek.

'Indeed. What he might have replied I cannot imagine,' said the Prince. 'It's a leader's job to dwell in the world of reality, and leave imaginings to other men. That way, when the gods speak, he may hear with a pure ear. You on the other hand seem particularly blessed in that department.'

'Ears, you mean?'

'Imagination,' said Aeneas. 'In fact, you might like to try a little test. Would you object to a little test of your imagination, Nothos?'

'Nay, I dearly love a game of riddles to pass the time after supper, lord. Ask away.'

'Thank you,' said Aeneas.

He paused a moment, his narrow, fine-featured face still and serious in the amber lamplight, whose flickering flames made his deep-set eyes bright and shadowy by turn.

Then he leaned forward till his face was close to the other man's and said earnestly, 'Tell me then, what do you imagine the men out there would do to *you if I went out and told them that I'd discovered you were the man they hated most in the whole world? If I told them that you were the treacherous and cunning bastard who gave Troy the gift of the wooden horse, what do you imagine they'd give to you, Odysseus?'*

For a moment the big fat Greek's face was as unreadable as the Carpathian bear who on a mountain track surprised by, and surprising, a Magyar hunter, rears his great bulk high and stands quite still with only his small questing eyes betraying the inner debate between flight and attack.

Then he leaned forward and said confidentially to the waiting prince, 'I don't suppose the answer's a big wet kiss, is it?'

God-like, Ellie smiled at her own joke. Castaway Ellie smiled too as she looked into and out of Odysseus's eyes on that remote island. Then the sound of a key turning in the front door reunited both Ellies and made all smiles stop together.

Her reason reminded her that the lock had been changed first thing that morning but somehow its reassurance couldn't reach her stomach.

Then Pascoe's voice called, 'I'm home.'

Rosie heard it too and came rushing in from the garden, building up sufficient speed to take off and hit her father at solar plexus level as he came into the kitchen.

'Jesus,' he gasped, swinging her up high. 'You

keep tackling like that, I'll get you a trial for the Bradford Bulls . . . what the hell is that?'

That was a noise like a rowing boat grounding on a shingle beach. It came from the small dog standing in the garden doorway, viewing Pascoe with the unmistakable message in its eyes, *I can't make up my mind which part of you to bite first.*

'This is Tig,' said Rosie, sliding to the floor. 'He's come to live with us. Come and meet him. He's a bit shy.'

She took her father's hand and drew him towards the dog.

'Tig, this is my dad. He lives here too only he has to be out a lot.'

The dog stopped growling, advanced a step, sniffed at Pascoe's shoe, then turned to cock his leg. Ellie moved swiftly, scooping the animal up and dropping it over the threshold.

'He's really quite well house-trained,' she said.

'You mean like he's really shy?' said Pascoe, looking out at the dog which was still glowering at him.

'He'll be all right now he knows your smell,' said Rosie confidently.

'He's good at recognizing the hot sweat of terror, is he?' said Pascoe. 'Talking of smells . . .'

He sniffed.

Ellie said, 'Shit,' and dived for the cooker.

'Ah well,' she said. 'Chargrilled veg is all the thing. I'll pour us a drink.'

'Big ones. Tell me, is that beast what I think it is?'

Ellie nodded, signalling with her eyes that this might be a topic best left till Rosie went to bed.

But the girl said, 'Wieldy was looking after him but he couldn't keep him forever because Edwin doesn't really like dogs and anyway, Wieldy's like you, he's got to be away from home such a lot it wouldn't be fair. He used to belong to a little girl who had to go away like Zandra but Nina says she'd like me to help take care of him now.'

Zandra was her dead friend, Nina was her imaginary friend. Neither had been mentioned since the day they'd told her of Zandra's death.

Pascoe said carefully, 'Nina's come back, has she?'

Rosie sighed the exasperated sigh of one required to state the obvious and said, 'Yes, she had to come back to make sure that Tig was being taken care of, didn't she?'

'Of course. Sorry. Well, if Nina wants you to help take care of Tig, that's the end of the matter. Tig, you're most welcome.'

The dog regarded him with an expression an optimistic pacifist might have classified as neutral. Then Rosie ran past him down the garden and Tig went in pursuit, barking excitedly.

'Don't say anything till you've had your drink,' said Ellie, handing him a glass.

He downed it in one and said, 'So, do I need to murder Wield or buy him a bunch of flowers?'

'If you mean, were we ambushed?, the answer's no. The dog did the choosing and when Wieldy saw the way the wind was blowing, he was as usual impeccable. No pressure, very sensitive to all aspects of the situation. Edwin, however, I would rate in this regard as extremely peccable. And as I ducked out early on to visit Daphne, I wasn't around to interpose my own body. So I suppose if anyone's pecced, it's me. Sorry.'

Pascoe poured himself another drink which he approached more decorously.

Then he sat down at the kitchen table and laughed.

'What?'

'First time I've come home in ages and not been dragged into a game of Black Bitch. That's a big plus. And she's more like she used to be than she has been since . . . she used to be it. If it takes a dog and the return of Nina, it's a small price to pay. So, it's been a good day?'

'Yes, it has. Rosie had a great time. Me too, I think. Something else though . . .'

She told him about her visit to Rosemont and Daphne's proposal.

'So what do you think?'

Pascoe said, 'What do *you* think?'

'Well, great for Rosie and the dog. Nice to spend some time with Daph. Also I feel I owe her.'

'Wouldn't she drive you mad, ideologically speaking, I mean?'

'There is that, but we're both very long-suffering.

Also I'd have an antidote on my doorstep. Feenie Macallum. Did you know the Aldermanns bought their cottage off her?'

'No.' Suddenly Pascoe looked alarmed. 'Hey, this place isn't about to fall into the sea, is it?'

'Relax. It's about a quarter-mile inland. It's Gunnery House that's in trouble, and that's probably been exaggerated anyway. So, what is your considered judgement, dear husband? I shall be guided completely by your wise head in this. Do you think it would be all right for me to go?'

'Ellie, why are we having this conversation out of Trollope?' said Pascoe.

'Enjoy it while you can. But I'm not asking permission. I'm thinking of what's safe for Rosie, and Daphne, and me, in that order. If you say this would be a crazy thing to do in the circs, that's it. I totally reserve the right to make any decisions I like affecting just myself, but not my family and friends.'

'Good Lord. This smacks dangerously of democracy. What's so funny?'

'Nothing. Just something I was working on. So, what's the verdict?'

'Let me tell you about my day first,' said Pascoe.

She listened without interruption, then she said, 'He's going to be all right, Roote?'

'Oh yes. Fine. It was all stage management. Only me being late let it go as far as it did. And he had the failsafe of his neighbour bringing his breakfast in if I didn't turn up at all.'

'But why?'

'Stark bonkers. Always was. That's my partial, prejudiced and non-expert view. What he certainly was, and still is, is the great manipulator. I left him sitting up in bed talking to the press and giving the impression, without actually saying anything specific, of a poor sensitive soul who's paid his debt to society being hounded to despair by an insensitive and uncaring police force. Mrs Driffield and Miss Mackie, that's his parole officer, are a very telling supporting chorus. And from the way I got treated in the hospital, it's clear he is regarded less as a porter and more as a cross between St Francis and Mother Teresa.'

'Peter, why are you sounding guilty?'

'Am I?' He rubbed his face wearily. 'Could be because I feel ... well, not exactly guilty, but responsible anyway. OK, he's a nut, but he's a nut who's served his time and has got a job and isn't doing anything that's a threat to society, then because of me he starts feeling hassled ...'

'And decides to give you a lesson by slashing his wrists in the bath? Listen, love, if that's the way his mind works, then you've done him a favour by putting him in the professionals' hands. Anyway, what's to say that he isn't our man and the reason he decided to top himself was because he realized the implacable sleuth Pascoe was on his tail and the game of terrify-the-little-woman was up?'

'I'd really like to believe it,' said Pascoe. 'But

there was nothing in his flat to suggest a connection. Except he had a book open on the soap rack in the bath, like he was reading himself to sleep. It was Empson's *Seven Types of Ambiguity*, ha ha. That's just his kind of joke.'

'So he's still down as a maybe. Fine. Got any other *maybes* you haven't bothered to tell me about, Peter? It would be nice to know just how many more lunatic clients of yours are running around out there looking to get even.'

'No other strong candidates for vengeance,' he assured her. 'And my own preferred choice for simply putting pressure on me has been taken out of the frame.'

He told her about Dalziel's debacle at the Kelly Cornelius hearing. But he didn't tell her about the weird letter. He was still making up his mind about that, and this was reassurance time.

'You know, I've got this suspicion Andy cocked things up on purpose,' he concluded. 'Partly because he reckons the Fraud boys are mucking us about, but also because if all this has got anything to do with Cornelius, cutting her loose should put an end to it.'

'So perhaps he did it for you. Because he knew you wouldn't do it for yourself,' said Ellie, observing him gravely.

'Who knows?' said Pascoe.

'Whatever, it sounds to me like your front runners have both been scratched. So can we assume the danger's over? I should tell Daphne yes?'

Pascoe hesitated then said, 'Look, let me have another word with Fat Andy. He's got a nose for these things.'

He went out to use the hall telephone. A couple of minutes later he returned looking pensive.

'Problem?'

'Not really. Andy says he's pretty sure nothing else will happen, either because we've sorted the trouble or failing that because whoever it is knows now we're on to them. But he agrees we ought to stay on full alert.'

'Meaning he thinks a trip to the seaside would be a bad idea?'

'On the contrary, he reckons that Daphne's cottage sounds an ideal safe house, so long as you're accompanied by a minder.'

'Like dishy young Hat? Yes, please. So why the worried face?'

'He just sounded a bit preoccupied, that's all.'

'You rang him at home? Maybe he was just about to scale the mountainous Miss Marvell.'

'Why am I not allowed to make jokes like that? Well, maybe. Anyway, it's on. And there's one big plus. It will allow that ravening beast you picked up at Enscombe to demonstrate just how house-trained he is on someone else's carpets.'

He studied his wife's expression, then said, 'You have told Daphne about Tig, haven't you?'

'I didn't know about him till I got back to Enscombe and found the deal had been done,' said Ellie defiantly.

'Never mind. Nice upper-class English girls are practically suckled by dogs, aren't they? It'll be a pleasant surprise. Work going well?'

He leaned over to squint at the laptop screen but Ellie half closed the lid.

'I've told you, I can't seem to get down to anything, not while I'm waiting for word on the Great English Novel. This is just my comforter, something for me to keep sucking at till I grow out of it.'

'Is it the thing you started at the hospital? I'd love to see it sometime.'

She smiled and said, 'No, you wouldn't. It's for my eyes only. It's a course of therapy I need to complete. No, that's too heavy. Let's call it a *jeu d'esprit* for one player.'

'And you'll know it's over when the good news from the publisher comes thudding onto the hall mat?'

'Oh no. Haven't you learned anything, Peter?' said Ellie. 'A thud means a returned script. Gloom, doom, rejection. What I want will come floating through the letterbox light as a feather shed from the snow-white plumage of the sweet bird of success who nests on the topmost slopes of Parnassus.'

'Eh?'

'A letter,' said Ellie. 'A long, eloquent, enthusiastic, and accepting letter.'

'Talking of letters.'

He'd made up his mind. He'd taken a photocopy of the weird letter that morning as he dropped the

269

original off for examination. Dalziel had asked how Ellie had reacted and when he'd heard she hadn't had the chance to react, his great shoulders had shrugged and he'd said, 'She's your missus.'

Ellie read the few lines quickly and said, 'Why didn't you say anything last night?'

'I thought you'd had enough to be going on with.'

'And now?'

'I think I was wrong. I mean, I think I was wrong to think I could protect you by keeping you in the dark.'

She said, 'I don't know whether to thump you or give you a big gluey kiss. Listen, there was a car last night. It sort of crawled by. I thought the driver stared up at me. I didn't say anything because I was starting to think that I was turning everything I saw into something sinister and significant.'

Pascoe shook his head and said, 'I don't know whether to give *you* a big gluey kiss or thump you. What did he look like? What kind of car?'

'Smallish, with a moustache, I think. But the car wasn't a white Merc. No, it was a hatchback, possibly a Golf. And darkish. Blue, I think.'

Pascoe recalled the neighbour's sighting of a metallic-blue Golf turning round and driving away on the day of the attempted abduction. He hadn't mentioned it to Ellie then. He mentioned it now.

'Anything else I should know?' she said.

'There are fingerprints on the letter, not Roote's,

not on record,' he said. 'So, does it mean anything to you.'

She read the text again, frowned and said, 'Sort of cod Elizabethan. Some of the phrases sound familiar . . . hang on.'

She went and got her one-volume Shakespeare and thumbed through it.

'Here it is, that bit about the frown o' the great and the tyrant's stroke, it's from *Cymbeline*.'

'Missed that one,' said Pascoe. 'What's it about?'

'Explaining the plot takes longer than seeing the play,' said Ellie. 'Basically about this guy, Posthumus, who lets himself be conned into thinking his wife's been unfaithful by an Italian called Iachimo, which is a diminutive of Iago, ha ha.'

'Another stab at *Othello* then?'

'Not really. It all ends happily. But dramatically it creaks along, full of unconvincing coincidences and anonymous gents having a chat to keep you up to speed with the plot, which has got the lot: princes kidnapped at birth, mistaken identities, poisons which don't work, transsexual disguises, and history dodgier than a TV documentary. The verse is odd too, sometimes very lyrical, sometimes positively rough and bizarre.'

'Sounds like the old Swan was getting low in the water,' said Pascoe, happy to go along with Ellie's apparent preoccupation with the source of the letter's language as long as it kept her from brooding on its underlying threat.

'I don't think so,' she said. 'It's like he's saying,

this one isn't for the wits, crits and media twits, this one's for the folk who live and work at the sharp end. Let's take a look at this arty-farty drama business and see how it really works. OK, I've done slick, I've done elegant, I've done well-constructed, you know I can do them standing on my head. But why should I bother with that stuff when real stories and real feelings will always shine through muddle anyway, like they do in real life? And like in life, poetry's usually accidental and comes in brief flashes rather than in great elegant preordained chunks. As for the happy ending, tragedy's easy 'cos tragedy's the norm. It's happy-ever-after that sorts out the men from the boys. He would of course be sexist.'

Pascoe began to feel that going along had gone along far enough.

'Specifically,' he said. 'The letter.'

'It's from a song that's sung over Fidele's body, only he's not really dead, and he's not really *he* either, but Imogen, or more properly Innogen, the wrongly accused wife who has disguised herself as a boy and called herself Fidele, which even you can see means faithful, but is also an anagram of *defile* which is what the wicked Iti claims to have done to her.'

'I'm glad it all ends happily so long as it ends,' said Pascoe. 'But what's its significance here?'

'Look, I've done the exegesis, it's you who gets paid to do the detection. I don't know what it means, except that it means I'll be even gladder to get Rosie away safe to Nosebleed Cottage in the morning. I'll go and ring Daphne now.'

'Aren't you forgetting something?'

'What?'

'You were making up your mind between thumping me and giving me a big gluey kiss.'

'So were you.'

'OK. On three. One . . . two . . .'

They were still glued together when a polite cough drew their attention to their daughter, who was patiently spectating.

Seeing she had their attention she said, 'Mummy, Tig's done a big pooh in the middle of the patio. What shall I do with it?'

XX

the last of the cobblers

Ellie Pascoe's guess had been partially right. Cap
Marvell was in Dalziel's house when Pascoe phoned,
but they weren't about to do anything more inti-
mate than share a pot of tea.

And Ellie's epithet was hardly even partially
accurate. Well-built the woman was, but her curves
were more Cotswold than Caucasus and a long way
short of the Himalayan heights offered by a supine
Dalziel.

They had a relationship which both realized
might not survive complete honesty, but which
both recognized would certainly wither without
it.

So when Dalziel came back from the phone in
his entrance hall and said, 'Pop upstairs for a couple
of minutes, luv. There's someone calling you don't
want to meet,' Cap did not demur, but picked up
her cup and went quietly up the stairs, confident
that all would be explained later.

The doorbell rang.

Dalziel checked that Cap Marvell had left no sign of her presence, then went to answer it.

On the doorstep stood the tall, thin, silver-haired man whose approach, observed through the one clear pane in the coloured glass panel in the door, had made him cut short his conversation with Pascoe.

'Mr Dalziel, how pleasant to see you again,' said the man. 'Gawain Sempernel. We met . . .'

'Aye, I recall. You've not changed much. How're you keeping?'

They shook hands gently, neither trying to turn it into a competition.

'I'm well. No need to ask you. I can see you're blooming.'

'You'd best come in before the neighbours clock us holding hands. I were just having a pot of tea. Or if you'd like a drop of summat stronger . . . ?'

'Stronger than Yorkshire tea? Does such a liquor exist? No, tea will suit me very well. What a charming little place you have here. Charming. Reminds me of my niece's mews cottage in Chelsea, except that her place seems to me to have had all the character modernized out of it. I'm so pleased to see you've had the good taste not to tinker.'

Dalziel looked round the small square sitting room he'd led the way into. It was true, he hadn't tinkered. In fact, it had changed very little from the way it had looked when he and his wife moved in all those years ago, and not at all from the way it looked when she moved out a few years later. But it was tidy and clean, what more could a man ask?

'Aye, bags of character here if that's what you're looking for,' he said, filling the cup he'd plucked from the dresser. 'Thinking of making me an offer? I'd expect Chelsea prices.'

'Ah, the gap between expectation and achievement is filled with the screams of good men, still falling,' said Sempernel. 'Except in the case of Yorkshire tea which exceeds all report.'

He put down the cup from which he'd taken a cautious sip and regarded quizzically the plateful of Eccles cakes Dalziel was offering him.

'Thank you, no,' he said. 'A clear head requires a clear stomach. First things first, Mr Dalziel. I shall come straight to the point, as you are famed as a man who approves direct speaking. Indeed, outside the court this morning you spoke directly to a colleague of mine and made a passing reference to myself. I am intrigued to know how you came to make a connection between myself and the gentleman you were addressing?'

'Lucky guess,' said Dalziel off-handedly. 'I can spot a funny bugger two miles off. Must be the way they walk. You ought to do summat about that. As for you, well, yours is the only name I know, isn't it? For all I knew you might be retired to Eastbourne, or pushing up the daisies. So, lucky guess.'

'Lucky indeed,' said Sempernel dryly. 'Let me know if you start selling racing tips. So you have flushed me out. I too have flushed you out of our record system. Your file made interesting reading as I flew up this afternoon. I see that I expressed some doubts as to whether you were in fact quite so intellectually limited as you were at pains to appear last time we met. I am both pleased and disappointed to have my percipience confirmed. Though your performance in court hardly gave the impression of a fine mind at full stretch.'

'Just badly prepared, and yon cow on the bench had a few old scores to pay.'

Sempernel shook his head, smiling.

'No, I don't think so, Mr Dalziel. I think you set out to get the application for a further remand in custody refused. And having succeeded in that, you threw away any chance of persuading me that it was simple inadvertence by going out of your way to embarrass my observer in the court vestibule. Now why did you do this, Mr Dalziel? What is your peculiar interest in Ms Cornelius?'

'Me, I've got none,' said the Fat Man. 'But you lot must have. Stood out a mile something odd were going on. Tying up my DCI in court on a simple assault charge, banging restrictions on the file. I thought at first it were just Fraud playing funny buggers. They like a bit of cloak and dagger, that lot. Then I got to thinking.'

'Thinking, eh? You really are the most surprising fellow, Mr Dalziel,' said Sempernel, trying his tea again. 'And where did your thinking lead you?'

'Led me to wonder, what if the real funny

buggers were involved? What if when Cornelius took off, you lot were on her case, watching to see where she'd lead you. Then she got involved in the accident, and my DCI happened to be on the spot, and he's so sharp he's forever cutting himself, and suddenly she's under arrest for assault and under investigation for fraud and you don't know what the hell to do. So you decide, let's keep her under wraps on the assault charge while you make up your mind what to do next. How'm I doing?'

'Well. You are doing well. But I still do not understand why you decided to take such an active part in the affair?'

Dalziel inserted a whole Eccles cake into his mouth, chewed twice and swallowed.

'Impulse,' he said. 'My DCI got tied up, couldn't make it to court this morning. I thought I'd go along myself, see what was what. And when I saw what had to be one of your lads sitting alongside Barney Hubbard at the back, I thought, bugger this for a lark, let's piss into the junction box and see what happens.'

Sempernel shook his head impatiently.

'Won't do, Mr Dalziel. For you to draw attention to yourself in this way – and you must be aware that people who piss into junction boxes often get nasty shocks – you must have had some motive stronger than a sudden urge to make mischief.'

'All right, I'll tell you,' said Dalziel. 'My DCI and his family have been through a lot lately. A right bad time. They survived. Now, a couple of days back, someone starts throwing a different kind of shit at them. I've been looking to see where it might be coming from. There's various possibilities, but this case looks to be up there with the strong contenders. So just on the off chance I'm right, I wanted to take it out of his lap and give notice to anyone who cares to hear that I'll not have folk I'm fond of mucked about. OK?'

Sempernel pursed his lips in puzzlement, like a maiden aunt being offered a good deal on a vibrator.

'So just on the off chance, as you put it, you interfere recklessly with what you suspect might be a case of much greater import than appears on the surface? You must be very fond indeed of Mr Pascoe and his family. Indeed, in the eyes of some people, you may appear fond in the older sense of the word.'

'Aye, mebbe. You come to have me sectioned, have you? Or do you reckon I'm a suitable case for Care in the Community?'

'That would depend on how much I cared *for* the community in question, I think, Mr Dalziel.'

'Oh aye? And how much is that?'

'More perhaps than you, when you consider the reckless abandon with which you release criminals into it.'

'Criminal? Don't recollect owt about a conviction. Any road, what's the problem? She's got to check in with us on a daily basis and I don't doubt you've got your spooks haunting her wherever she goes . . . hang about though. I'm getting a funny feeling in my piles . . . she's slipped the leash, hasn't she? Come twelve noon tomorrow, clocking-in time, she's not going to show. That's why you're here, isn't it?'

Sempernel put his hands together in a soundless clap and said, 'Perhaps after all I will have one of those curious sweetmeats. They obviously do wonders for the intellect.'

He took an Eccles cake and sank his teeth into it.

'Charming,' he said. 'Flaky on the outside, succulent within, an experience almost Greek in its intensity. Let us assume you are right, Mr Dalziel. Let us assume that Ms Cornelius went for a stroll in the park and somehow contrived to evade the surveillance of one of my operatives, who is now looking forward to a prolonged stint of duty in our Falklands Office. What then do you imagine the true purpose of my visit is? Apart from the obvious one of spelling out your punishment for such unwarranted interference in matters of state far beyond your brief or competence?'

Dalziel pondered a while then said tentatively, 'Help? You could reckon that when it comes to tracking down a missing person in Mid-Yorkshire, a fat old cop with a bit of local knowledge might be worth half a dozen funny buggers with microphones up their jacksies. Also, by telling me now, you get me on the job twelve hours or so before I'd have found out officially there was a job to be on.'

He looked expectantly at his visitor, who nodded approvingly and said, 'With what is in terms of my trade a very slight adjustment, you are completely right, Mr Dalziel. The slight adjustment is to stand everything you've said on its head. I have come to tell you that tomorrow morning when you learn officially of Cornelius's disappearance, I would appreciate it if you did nothing. Go through whatever motions are necessary to keep you right with the formidable Mrs Broomhill, but if you or your operatives come within sniffing distance of Cornelius's spoor, you are to turn and gallop off in quite the opposite direction. Do I make myself clear?'

'Nay, you can make yourself clear as a prossie's price list, but I take my orders from Mr Trimble.'

'Your Chief Constable?' Sempernel began to laugh. 'I am sure he would be delighted to learn of this change of heart. Mr Trimble has, of course, been put in the picture and will no doubt speak with you in the morning. But it is my reading of your relationship with him that brings me here this evening. You may find ways of doing more or less what you will within the elastic confines of your constabular hierarchy, but in this matter you will be stepping outside your league, and after our little talk tonight, you can no longer offer a plea of inadvertence. Consider yourself warned off, Superintendent. Any further attempt to interfere in this business can only result in the direst consequences for yourself as well as for your what-did-you-call-them? Your friends. A cobbler should stick to his last, Mr Dalziel. Kelly Cornelius is not part of your mystery. I use the word in its medieval sense, of course.'

He stood up.

'You off then?' said Dalziel. 'You've not finished your tea.'

'Busy, busy,' said Sempernel.

He went out into the tiny entrance hall and opened the front door.

On the step he said, 'I take it we understand each other, Mr Dalziel.'

'Stick to my last. Got it,' said Dalziel reassuringly.

'Excellent. Do apologize to Ms Marvell if I have spoiled her evening. Good day to you.'

Dalziel closed the door gently after him as Cap came down the stairs.

'Sounds like I might as well have stayed to meet him after all,' she said.

'No, you might have caught something,' said Dalziel.

They went back into the sitting room.

'So, are you going to tell me about him?'

'Rather listen to the wireless.'

He switched on an old wooden-cased radio, spun the dial till he found some pop music and turned the volume up high.

'Good Lord,' said Cap. 'Are we being bugged? How exciting.'

'No point taking chances,' said Dalziel. 'Shall I make some more tea?'

'No, just tell me what's going on.'

'You tell me how much you earwigged first.'

She smiled, and he said, 'As much as that? Who needs to plant bugs? Well, you'll have got the gist.'

'So tell me, what exactly is this man, Sempernel?'

'You're too young to understand the words. Officially I expect he's got a title like Assistant Director Department 55A (Intelligence). I met him a few years back. There was a case involving . . . well, least said, soonest mended, but it were pretty murky and I were glad to come out of it without too much damage.'

'Damage? You mean, physical?'

'That too. But there's more ways of breaking bones than tickling your ribs with an iron bar. There was a public version, and an official version, and the truth. I let on I went along with the official version.'

'You mean you let them think you weren't really bright enough to get near the truth?'

'More or less.'

'But now they'll begin to wonder, won't they? I mean, the way you got onto them. Incidentally, Andy, I didn't find your explanation all that convincing. All that stuff about getting to thinking and lucky guesses and spotting a funny bugger a mile off. I'm your greatest admirer but that's a load of crap, isn't it?'

'You've been keeping bad company,' admonished the Fat Man. 'But you're right. I got this message over the computer. All about Kelly Cornelius. All about how her job's laundering money for South American subversives. No indication of where it came from, but it mentioned my old chum, Pimpernel, and that made it sound like the horse's mouth.'

'Couldn't have been Sempernel himself, could it?' said Cap, frowning.

'Don't see what's in it for him, but it's true he's so devious, he probably pees through his ears. Or maybe he's got another kind of leak.'

'In which case, won't he have spotted that you were being a bit economical with the actualité? And won't that get him seriously worried?'

'Doubt it,' said Dalziel confidently. 'I've got one big advantage over sods like old Pimpernel. He's like you. Born with a silver spoon up his jacksie, went to the best schools, all that stuff, and he's clever enough to suss out that mebbe an uncouth slob like me may be brighter than appearances suggest. But he's got a built-in genetic governor which stops him from ever admitting that even a very good cobbler could possibly run the shoe shop.'

'I thought I heard you promise to stick to your last.'

'Oh aye. And I meant it. Have you ever seen my last?'

'Not for a little while.'

'Lot of hammering involved.'

'Is that so? Tell you what, why don't we let those poor chaps out there hear a craftsman at his work?'

She stood up, switched the radio off and began to undo her skirt.

'Hang on,' said Dalziel reaching for another Eccles cake. 'I think I'm going to need to keep my strength up.'

BOOK TWO

What seas what shores what grey rocks and
   what islands
What water lapping the bow
And scent of pine and the woodthrush singing
   through the fog
What images return
O my daughter.

T.S. ELIOT: *Marina*

i

strange encounter

'I don't believe it,' fumed Ellie. 'He's just doing it to annoy me.'

'Peter? Of course, you know your husband better than I do, dear, but that doesn't sound his style. And while not denying the attraction of having some handsome young fellow dancing attendance, another female living cheek by jowl with us in the bothy will attract less comment.'

Ellie, who always preferred a present to an absent foe, turned her irritation on Daphne and said, 'If this bothy of yours is so cramped I can't imagine why you said you could put her up anyway.'

'Well, we are a tad isolated and we can hardly expect the poor child to keep watch on us from up a tree and sleep at nights in her car, can we?' said Daphne. 'I must say that she's no slouch behind the wheel.'

This was apropos a glance in her driving mirror. Daphne drove with what she called aplomb and what her friends called abandon, but the Fiat Uno of Shirley Novello had shown no sign of losing contact along the winding minor roads leading out to Axness.

Ellie glanced back, smiled at Rosie in the rear seat with Tig sleeping on a travelling rug by her side, then let the smile fade as she refocused on the supermini.

Why she should feel so antagonistic towards Novello she didn't know. Or maybe it was a case of didn't want to know. She was fairly sure sexual jealousy didn't come into it. If Peter found himself turned on by the woman, he never showed it, which a neurotically jealous wife might have found significant in itself. She, of course, was neither neurotic nor jealous, but sometimes wondered if there weren't worse conditions, worse that is as grounds for personal antagonism. They'd met for the first time only recently when Ellie had called in at the station to thank everybody for all their messages and gifts during Rosie's illness. Novello, Pascoe had told her, had lit a candle in her parish church for the little girl. Ellie, though she hoped she'd have the courage of her lack of conviction never to use God as a last gasp insurance on her own behalf, had no such compunctions when it came to her daughter, and had thanked the young woman warmly. Then, as was natural to her, she'd tried to deformalize the boss's wife/junior officer relationship by suggesting they slipped into first names. She'd seen something shift behind the DC's eyes, and for the rest of the visit, the young woman hadn't called her anything. When next they met, it had been back to Mrs Pascoe.

Now, it would have been OK to think that here was an ambitious young female officer who was being careful not to look as if she hoped to cut corners by chumming up with the DCI's missus. Ellie could have accepted, even applauded, such caution. The rising unto place is even more laborious for females than for fellows. And it's by a whole lot of indignities that policewomen with a bit of luck and a lot of care might one day come to dignities.

But Ellie couldn't rid herself of the feeling that there was more to it than that, or rather, *less* to it than that. What she half suspected she had seen in Novello's eyes was the kind of half-scornful pity she could recall experiencing herself in her younger days when confronted with some middle-aged middle-class woman who'd tried to come on too friendly too quick; not so much a reaction against being patronized as against the poor old sod's assumption that her fixed and finished life had something in common with, or superior to, the empowered, liberated existence of the new generation of females.

'For Christ's sake, I'm not much more than ten years older than her!'

'Sorry?' said Daphne.

Ellie realized she had spoken her thought out loud.

'I was just saying that she looks older than her age, wouldn't you say?' she recovered.

Daphne considered then said, 'No. I'd say . . .'

'What?'

'I'd say she has that extremely rare kind of face which doesn't remind you of anyone else you know. What in particular do you have against the girl, dear?'

'Nothing,' said Ellie, facing the front once more. 'Daphne, has it ever occurred to you that other vehicles, not to mention flocks of cows and herds of sheep, are also permitted to use these narrow country roads?'

Criticizing her friend's driving was an excellent diversionary tactic. Ellie was willing to share much with Daphne, but not the possible selfish triviality of her reasons for disliking Shirley Novello, which she wasn't even willing to share with herself.

'Really, Ellie. What is it you would like me to do?'

'Well, how about slow down for a start?'

'And if as a result of slowing down, I collide with a cow which would not have been there if I'd continued at my preferred speed, how will you feel then?'

This was, like many of Daphne's arguments, unanswerable, unless you had the time, energy, and intellectual resources to attack the assumptions which underpinned it, and as the principle of these seemed to be an assurance of vehicular invulnerability which only a fatal accident could contradict, a QED seemed unreachable, in this life anyway.

In fact, as it now occurred to Ellie, Daphne in driving resembled her husband in life, in possessing a certainty that all would be well so powerful it seemed to be self-fulfilling. Whatever, they reached Axness a good hour before their ETA of noon without even a sniff of danger.

Or perhaps, thought Ellie, it was more accurate to say they *achieved* Axness, for as a reachable place it hardly seemed to exist. She had remarked on this on her only previous visit some three years earlier when Feenie Macallum had hosted a Liberata meeting at Gunnery House. There was no boundary sign, no village green, no pub, no church, very little sign of human habitation at all; even the fields seemed accidental, marked off not so much by hedgerows as by little lines of sportive wood run wild, with the beasts that grazed them looking like members of one long herd stretching for miles as they migrated waterwards under the burning sun.

But it had an identity which you could certainly feel. Ellie had forgotten how strange that feeling was, as if when you came away, some mnemonic censor lowered a curtain between the world you were heading back to and the world you were leaving. But now on return, the recollection of that previous visit came flooding back. It had been a chilly day of late winter beneath a lowering sky, grey and cracked like an old plaster ceiling, very different from this dome of Wedgwood-blue soaring to the golden boss of the sun. But that same sense of a changed dimension had been there, that impression of a neutral emptiness waiting to be filled momentarily by whatever you brought to it, but leaving no doubt in your mind that whatever it was, it would drain away ineluctably as soon as you departed.

A large part of this feeling derived from the subtle change in the light ahead which marked the end of land and the start of sea. Long before the first glimpse of water, the sky was preparing you for the change which always comes when humans are reminded what a tenuous grip on existence they have, scratching a living on the spoilheaps the gods threw up when they dug out the oceans . . .

Ellie shook her head to dislodge these irritatingly irrational thoughts. I've been spending too much time with that fat old sod, Odysseus, she told herself. But as the car reached the crest of a ridge and she saw half a mile ahead the blue and silver savannah of the sea, she shuddered. Even on a windless day under a summer sun, there was no mistaking its power and menace. No wonder the Greeks nicknamed Poseidon *the Earth-Shaker*.

'Lovely, isn't it?' said Daphne. 'That's one childhood memory you never forget, your first sight of the sea.'

'I've seen it before,' chimed Rosie from the rear, taking this personally. 'Often.'

'Yes, of course you have, dear,' said Daphne. 'But I bet you can still remember the first time.'

Rosie screwed up her eyes in an effort of recollection, then said triumphantly, 'Yes, there were lots of seagulls and some donkeys and a whole lot of sand and Mum and Dad took their clothes off and wrestled on it.'

Daphne shrieked with laughter and Ellie said, 'Jesus. She was nine months old. And we thought she was asleep.'

'I hope at least you didn't frighten the donkeys,' said Daphne. 'Nearly there. And all in one piece, you'll have noticed.'

She paid immediately for her overmod when she turned at speed off the narrow country road into an even narrower high-hedged lane and came into confrontation with an ancient rusty dusty Land Rover. The Audi skidded to a stop only a foot from the other vehicle's bumper. The seat-belted humans lurched forward against their restraints, but the sleeping dog shot off the back seat, hit the floor, and set up a frenzied barking.

'Oops,' said Daphne. 'You OK, folks?'

Ellie had already turned to check on Rosie who was only concerned for Tig.

'Don't touch him till he's calmed down,' urged Ellie anxiously.

'Oh God, do you see who it is? Ellie, would you care to mollify your giant?' murmured Daphne.

For a second Ellie thought she was referring to the yapping dog. Then she turned her head to see Serafina Macallum climbing out of the Land Rover and approaching the Audi with grave displeasure printed on her face.

She leaned to the open driver's window and said sternly, 'This is not a race track but a public highway . . .' then her monitory gaze widened to take in the passenger seat and she said in a doubtful tone, 'Ellie, can that be you?'

'Hi, Feenie. This is my friend, Daphne Aldermann.'

'Hello, Miss Macallum. We met briefly I think when my husband and I were negotiating for Nosebleed Cottage.'

'Did we? Clearly your driving skills were not a factor in the negotiation. Child, could you ask your dog to bark a little more softly?'

Rosie said anxiously, 'He fell off the seat. I think he might have hurt himself.'

'I don't think so. That doesn't sound like a hurt bark to me. Let me see.'

Feenie went to the rear door, opened it, and picked up Tig who fell silent instantly. She held him up, looked into his eyes, prodded him, then said, 'No, he's fine. I expect he needs a pee after the shock.'

She put him down where he immediately proved her right by cocking his leg against the wheel.

'You should make sure that he is strapped in too,' said Feenie to Rosie. 'His safety is your responsibility, remember that.'

'Yes, I'm sorry,' said Rosie meekly.

'Don't worry, Rosie,' said Daphne. 'My fault, really. I should have thought . . .'

'No,' said Feenie sternly. 'Your responsibility is for the passage of your vehicle along the highway in a manner which does not endanger the health of other road-users. Your passengers clearly travel with you at their own risk, which I should guess is considerable. Rosie is her mother's responsibility, and the dog is Rosie's. I would advise a safety harness for the beast in future.'

'Yours doesn't have a safety harness,' said Rosie, looking towards the Land Rover.

A black and white collie had scrambled from the rear of the vehicle over the front seat and was now hanging out of the open window, viewing Tig with great interest.

'Mine is a highly educated animal,' said Feenie. 'Carla, down!'

Carla yawned widely, then having established her independence, retreated.

Feenie's attention was now attracted to the entrance to the lane.

'Ellie, is not that the young woman who was on watch outside your house? Did you know you were being followed? My God, I do believe she is armed!'

Ellie got out of the car and looked back to see Shirley Novello standing at the lane entrance, watching them. Feenie's reaction was understandable. Novello, back to her work 'uniform' of baggy brown T-shirt and baggy combats, wore a broad leather belt with a mobile phone clipped to one side and a leather pouch to the other. It did have something of the look of a holster but in fact, as Ellie knew from observation, contained nothing more offensive than the necessaries of a young woman's existence.

'It's all right. She's with us,' said Ellie.

'Indeed.' Feenie looked from Novello to Daphne and back to Ellie, teetered on the edge of some irony about the perils of bad company, but said instead, 'So you intend staying at Nosebleed? I noticed the rather rowdy young men who were there for the past week have moved out.'

Daphne, who had also got out of the car, said coldly, 'That was my son and his friends. Yes, we will be in residence for a few days.'

'Are you going to be around, Feenie?' asked Ellie. 'Maybe I'll wander over later with Rosie and say hello.'

The old woman needed to consider this prospect longer than was perhaps courteous, almost long enough indeed to appear calculating. But her conclusion was hospitable enough.

'Come for supper tonight,' she said. 'Six thirty sharp.'

'All of us?' said Ellie.

Feenie gave a little smile. There were times when you felt she was on another planet, and others when she seemed smarter than Miss Marple.

'Of course,' she said. 'It will be a pleasure to

have you all under my . . .' She hesitated, as if considering *eye*, but concluded, '. . . roof. Come away, child. You can make Carla's acquaintance this evening.'

Rosie had been drifting towards the Land Rover, but Feenie's peremptory tone fetched her up short.

I'll have to learn that, thought Ellie.

She said, 'Come here, dear. Get a hold of Tig and get back in the car.'

Pouting, the girl obeyed.

Feenie said, 'Right, now I'll get out of your way. Till tonight.'

Daphne began to say, 'No, it will be easier for me to back up . . .' but Feenie was already back in her Land Rover and reversing at speed down the lane.

Daphne said, 'Silly woman. She'll have to go all the way to the bothy. Still, if that's what she wants . . .'

She slid back behind the wheel.

'She live round here then?' said Novello, who had come up behind Ellie quietly enough to startle her.

'Yes,' she said irritably. 'Incidentally, shouldn't you have come running, brandishing your truncheon or something, when you saw our way was blocked?'

'I was thinking about it till I saw who it was,' said Novello. 'Talking of security though, these are very narrow roads to be driving round at Mach three.'

'Really? Well, let me tell you, it's not long since

299

Serafina Macallum drove a ten-ton truck full of relief supplies all the way from Yorkshire to Bosnia, and despite the problems of negotiating mountain roads in winter, not to mention the attendant dangers from gunfire, land mines, assault and arrest, she got there and back without a scratch.'

'Yeah? Well, that's great, Mrs Pascoe. Only I wasn't talking about the old girl, I was talking about your friend, Mrs Aldermann. I mean, a couple of times, if I'd been in Traffic, I'd have belled her down and given her a ticket. Maybe you could have a word? It 'ud be a bit embarrassing if one of our cars did pull her over. Hope you don't mind me saying.'

To which of course the only reasonable reply was an abashed, 'Not at all, my dear. You are only doing your job, and in fact you're quite right. She does drive far too quickly.'

Ellie said, 'Oh, but I do, Constable Novello. I have been married to a policeman all these years without ever feeling the need, nor indeed ever being asked, to act like one. If you wish to report Daphne for a road traffic offence, that's both your privilege and your job. Now let's get on, shall we?'

Back in the car, Daphne said, 'What was all that about?'

'Parameters,' said Ellie.

'Oh dear. With you and Modesty Blaise at loggerheads, and old Meg Merrilies clearly planning to slip deadly nightshade into my cup of acorn coffee, this could be a very fraught few days. We may have done better to stay in town and run the risk of the Black Hand Gang. Where on earth has she disappeared to?'

They'd turned a slight bend in the lane and could see straight ahead to where it ended in a gate with a building behind it.

'I think she's taking the short cut,' said Ellie. 'Or perhaps she's hunting dinner.'

The Land Rover had reversed into a field and was now bucketing across it through a bow wave of sheep.

A few moments later, the Audi reached the lane end and halted before the gate which bore in flaking black paint the legend *Nosebleed Cottage, beware –*

'Of what?' enquired Ellie.

'Bull? Feenie Macallum? I don't know, it had faded away when we bought the place, but for the next few days it had better be Tig. Rosie, dear, would you like to open the gate?'

Rosie hopped out and pushed the gate open and Ellie turned her attention to the cottage itself.

It was certainly, as she had expected, a bit more substantial than a bothy, but her imagination had widened the litotic gap to such an extent that the square-built, lichen-stained, grey-pebble-dashed building she saw was a bit of a disappointment. For some reason she had expected finely pointed York stone, louvred green shutters, blooming window boxes, a rose-arbour porch, a kidney-shaped swimming pool . . . no, the swimming pool she admitted had always been a fantasy, but just as physical self-depreciation was only acceptable from a truly hunkish fellow, it seemed to her that Daphne's playing down of Nosebleed ought to have been based on something a little more des-res-ish than this.

'So what do you think?' asked Daphne as they got their bags out of the car.

'Fine. I mean, lovely. Very rustic.'

'Yes, we decided against prettification. Much more honest to stay true to your roots, that kind of thing. I thought you'd approve.'

Ellie smiled bravely, but suddenly she was recalling from the lessons of her reading just how spartanly the upper middle classes embraced their pleasures. For them, back to nature meant really *back* to nature. Oil lamps, washing under the pump in the yard, cooking on an open fire, sleeping on boards under a scratchy wool blanket, up at dawn and off on long walks during which you refreshed yourself with berries from the hedgerows and draughts of spring water so porridgy, you couldn't spot the liver flukes . . .

There, she was overdoing it again, like she was trying to prove to herself she was a real imaginative writer, but being hyperbolical didn't mean you were wrong.

Upside was that Rosie and Tig obviously thought it was great, rushing round the cobbled forecourt, scrambling over the broken-down, nettle-festooned walls, the dog jumping up at a knotted rope dangling from a branch of a tall oak tree, the child pulling at the arm of a metal pump over a stone trough . . . oh God, the dreaded pump! Ellie's heart sank. Then she registered that the fearful engine was encrusted with rust and the arm wasn't moving. At the same moment Daphne unlocked the unwelcomingly solid front door which looked as if successive generations of Heathcliff had tried to kick their way through it and said, 'Come on in then. It's not much but it's home.'

And Ellie stepped out of the eighteenth century into the kind of interior you could safely be interviewed in for *Hello!* magazine. Whitewashed walls hung with old samplers, a rustic dresser lined with Delft, stone-flagged floor scattered with woven rugs, a huge fireplace occupied by a brass scuttle filled with flowers and foliage, a wide-screen TV and a hi-fi system with Quad speakers, lovingly polished antique furniture – even the radiators had an old oak finish.

'Central heating,' said Ellie stupidly. 'You've got central heating?'

'Oh yes. I know how much you'll disapprove but with walls this thick it really gets cool in here even in the warmest weather. Kitchen through here.'

There was, of course, an Aga (oil-fired), and a table so large it must have been built within the kitchen as it didn't seem possible it could have come through any of the doors or windows. But

Ellie was distracted from the logistics of its construction by the sight of a hobgoblin seated at its head, bloodily dismembering a small mammal with a cleaver.

'Hello, Mrs Stonelady. You got my message all right? Oh lovely, you're doing us one of your stews.'

The creature's face, in colour and contour very like a walnut kernel, with a mole on her upper lip from which sprouted three black hairs, gave no sign of acknowledgement, but Daphne, after standing there for a moment, smiling as if at an exchange of pleasantries, said, 'That will be lovely, Mrs Stonelady. We'll talk again later. Ellie, let me show you the bedrooms.'

'You didn't tell me the medieval healer Patrick talked about was a sitting tenant,' whispered Ellie, once out of the kitchen.

'She is rather quaint, isn't she? That is Mrs Stonelady who does for us. She has a son, Donald, who is two leeks short of a harvest supper, but is excellent for heavy work around the garden, so she's a double treasure.'

'And does she speak? I mean, when you said, you got my message, you were talking telepathy, I presume?'

'Don't be silly, Ellie. She lives a couple of miles away and she doesn't have a phone, so I leave messages on the answerphone here and when she comes in to see everything's OK, she always checks it out.'

'You mean, she's into modern technology?'

'Really, Ellie, for a tie-dyed Trot, you're sometimes so elitist. By now I'd have thought that, having decided the role you would like to play in the world, at least you would have learned your lines properly.'

These words were the surface manifestation of something faintly sardonic in Daphne's manner since their arrival and it occurred to Ellie now that neither her disappointment at the prospect of unspoilt rusticity nor her relief in finding that after all she was not to be a guest at Cold Comfort Farm had been as well-concealed as she believed. Daphne was jerking her about.

'Bitch,' she said.

'I'm sorry?'

'You know what I mean. OK, where's my bedroom? I hope I'm *en suite* with the jacuzzi.'

'But of course. Shirley, there you are. Everything OK?'

Novello, who'd presumably been checking for booby traps, said, 'Fine, Mrs Aldermann.'

Daphne said, 'Daphne. I hope you don't mind, but in the cottage at least you will be Shirley to me and I shall be Daphne to you. What the regulations say about modes of address between constables and the wives of senior officers I do not know, but they will not apply in these confined spaces. Ellie, Shirley; Shirley, Ellie. Now let's go upstairs.'

She was right about confined spaces, as far as the

stairs went at least. They were narrow, dark and steep. But the bathroom, though jacuzzi-less, was sparklingly modern and the bedrooms, a double and two singles, were a reasonable size. There was also a narrow boxroom with bunk beds.

'I thought Rosie might like this, but I'll give you the double just in case it's a bit much for her being alone in a strange place and she wants to snuggle in with you,' said Daphne. 'Shirley, you're in here. You'll find the window covers the front approaches with a good arc of fire.'

Novello, Ellie was pleased to see, was still in the early stages of working out whether she was dealing with a genuine upper-class twit or an accomplished deadpan comedienne.

Then she made up her mind and said, 'That's fine. Is it OK to boil my oil on the Aga?'

'Of course, as long as you understand damage from spillages must be paid for.'

The two women exchanged a smile and Ellie dealt quickly with what might have been a pang of jealousy if she hadn't suppressed it.

Rosie was delighted with her bunk beds, declaring that she would sleep in the upper one and Tig could occupy the lower. When Ellie demurred and a crisis threatened, Daphne quickly moved in with the assurance that this would be fine as long as Tig slept on his own travel rug, adding with a severity that would have pleased Feenie Macallum, 'And of course, if there are any accidents, you will be solely responsible for cleaning them up. Mrs Stonelady has had enough to do clearing up after my son and his sociopath friends. Animal waste products do not fall within the terms of her contract. So, any messes, and it's down to you, Rosie. Do you think you can manage that?'

Ellie watched her daughter make a solemn undertaking, her face lit by the religious glow of a Pre-Raphaelite knight pledging himself to the quest for the Holy Grail, and she sighed a deep, cynical sigh.

Beside her, Novello said, 'I shouldn't worry. Looks to me like she means it.'

'You reckon? Perhaps that's because she hasn't yet had the pleasure of dealing with shit on a blanket,' said Ellie with more asperity than she intended.

She looked for words to soften the effect but already the young policewoman was moving away.

Oh dear, thought Ellie, returning to her room to unpack. I've got to find a way of dealing with this, else this is going to be a really bumpy ride!

She opened a drawer to put her underwear in and saw that someone else had had the same idea and had left behind a pair of flowered briefs so skimpy that Ellie couldn't recall a time when she'd have got into them.

So much for young David Aldermann's all-lads-together action holiday. Country sports clearly covered more than walking, climbing and swimming!

Mention it to Daphne?

Hell, no!

Probably all she'd get in reply was a raise of those exquisitely plucked eyebrows and some crack about growing into a Mrs Grundy.

She put the briefs back in the drawer and added her own. Then she went to the window and looked out.

The room faced eastwards. Fields, hedgerows, small clumps of trees, then perhaps a quarter of a mile away, that exuberance of light where the land met the sea.

Suddenly she felt very happy. Here whatever had happened back in town had no presence, no meaning. This was the realm of earth and air and ocean. She was no pantheist, but nature, heartless witless nature, she felt she could deal with. It was man who came after you red in tooth and claw, and here if anywhere there was a No Admittance sign at the entrance.

She resumed her unpacking, whistling, rather off key, 'In A Mountain Greenery'.

ii

drudgery divine

Philosophy rarely survived Andy Dalziel's presence for long without cheerfulness breaking in or wind breaking out.

This morning, however, when on a summons which lacked much of its customary force, being audible no more than half a furlong, Pascoe and Wield attended their prince's matutinal levee, they found him apparently as subdued in spirit as he was in voice, chins on his chest, eyes hooded, and in a curiously contemplative frame of mind.

'Kelly Cornelius,' he said in an incantatory tone, like a Buddhist priest, or in profile Buddha himself, proclaiming the morning's mantra.

Pascoe, fresh from seeing Ellie and Rosie off to Axness under the, to him, reassuring tutelage of Shirley Novello, flashed a grin at Wield, and echoed with a mocking sonority, 'Kelly Cornelius.'

'That's right,' said the Fat Man, nodding slowly as if the DCI had made some profound observation.

'It's all in the way you look at things. Seeing what's really there.'

'A man that looks on glass,' said Pascoe, 'on it may stay his eye, or if he pleaseth, through it pass, and then the heav'n espie.'

The eyes unhooded and moved round to rest on him, balefully.

'You going religious, or wha'?'

'Just trying to demonstrate how, as so often, you are in accord with other fine minds of the past.'

'Well, don't bother. And that's not what I meant anyway. Not see *through* summat, but see what it really is even though it doesn't change.'

'Hope till hope creates from its own wreck the thing it contemplates?'

The eyes closed again and the Fat Man sighed deeply.

'Can you cover its cage, Wieldy?'

'What you mean is, know what ought to be there and look till you see it?' said Wield.

'No. Not that either. That's just the same as see-ing what you want to see, and that's the road to all kinds of trouble. Like marriage, for instance. No, I mean, knowing what has to be there, and going on as if you can see it even though you can't.'

'Like walking across an invisible bridge?' suggested Wield.

Dalziel considered this then his eyelids flicked up like the headlight covers on a sports car and the great face lit up.

'That's more like it. Aye. Though mebbe not

completely invisible, mebbe what you can see is like a thread of cotton, and you've got to say to yourself, it's a bridge, and step out on it.'

'And if you're wrong?' said Pascoe.

'You're in the clag but at least that's a soft landing,' said Dalziel. 'Now what I see here is, Kelly Cornelius has got summat to do with what's been going off with your missus.'

'Well, maybe,' said Pascoe, surprised. 'As you know, I always had it down as a possibility, though I seem to recollect you weren't all that convinced . . .'

'You're missing the point, lad. You're seeing what's there, or at best what you'd like to be there; that someone's trying to frighten you into letting Cornelius out on bail. But no one ever tried to suggest you should do this, did they?'

'No, but she's out, isn't she?'

'Aye, because of me, not you. And no bugger tried to twist my arm either.'

'That's right, sir,' said Pascoe, accepting this as a clear admission of what he'd suspected, that the Fat Man's cock-up had been deliberate. 'So why did you do it, sir?'

'I did it because of you, lad. Nay, don't go all gooey-eyed, I don't mean 'cos I thought it 'ud get Ellie off the hook. I mean, because when all this crap started happening, the Cornelius case came out top of your list of possible connections. Why?'

'Sorry? We've just been through all this . . .'

'Aye, but ask yourself – all this stuff about some-one out there wanting Kelly loose so's they could have a pop at her, how convincing does it really sound to you?'

'Not very, maybe, but a long way from impossible,' said Pascoe defensively.

'Oh aye? Listen to yourself. You'd not convince a barman you were old enough to serve shandy, sounding like that. But the fact remains, you still had this notion that the Cornelius case figured here somehow. So I got to thinking, mebbe there's more to it than you're saying. No, don't start pursing your lips, I don't mean you're deliberately holding summat back. It's just that you've always been a bit inclined to go wandering off in a world of thy own, and sometimes I've had to nudge you back onto the straight and narrow, and it could be I've nudged so hard in the past that this time you started making up the kind of reasons you thought I'd want to hear.'

Pascoe regarded Dalziel doubtfully. Introspection on this scale unprefaced by a skinful (which in the case of this skin was at least two gallons of bitter beer) was rare if not unique. And as their morning confab was taking place in Dalziel's office rather than the Black Bull, unless the Fat Man was pouring whisky on his cornflakes, he was stone-cold sober.

Only thing to do was take him seriously. There were men staring vacantly at whitewashed walls because they had not taken Dalziel seriously.

Also, he got the impression that the Fat Man knew more than he was saying. This didn't bother him. Dalziel was his own interpreter and he would make things plain when it suited him. That was how it had always been and always would be, world without end, amen.

He said, 'Give us a moment.'

He thought about Kelly Cornelius from the time of their first encounter at the accident on the Snake. He was gifted with great clarity of recall, and when someone made a strong impression on him, the recollected image could be eidetic in its intensity. Cornelius had certainly made that kind of impression. It wasn't just sex, though sexuality definitely had a part in it. It was an emanation of vitality, a sense of her feeling her life in every limb. She was the kind of woman who could light up a morgue, the kind of person it felt good to be around. This quality, plus her evident top-grade computer skills, must surely have given her an entrée to the most glitzy and glamorous circles of high finance, and he wondered now as he'd wondered before how she'd ended up working in a relatively small-scale operation like Nortrust, having to bob and curtsey to provincial plonkers like George Ollershaw.

He set the thought aside as irrelevant to present purposes and ran on fast-forward through his subsequent encounters with the woman, up to and including the last time he'd opposed bail in court. When the magistrate had rejected the application, he'd looked across to the dock and she'd given him a thousand-watt don't-worry-about-it smile and he'd realized he was giving her a hey-I'm-really-sorry-about-it grimace.

He smiled now at the recollection and Dalziel said, 'Summat?'

'Sorry.'

And there wasn't likely to be any *summat*, he thought. Looked like the Fat Man had over-reached himself, and in the weirdest direction for a man whose usual attitude to psychology was to hate it as an unfilled can.

One more try before he told the silly old bugger he was slipping.

He turned down the brightness on Kelly Cornelius's image and ran the sequence once again.

And then, as when a man dazzled by the full moon turns his gaze aside and in the corner of his eye glimpses what was always there though unregarded, a star, and has to blink and quarter the sky several times before he finds it again, so now he saw a *summat* and looked again and saw it again, and still had to look a third time before he could acknowledge what he was looking at.

'What?' said Dalziel.

'When you were in court yesterday, you say you saw Superintendent Hubbard from Fraud?'

'Aye,' said Dalziel with retrospective relish. 'Saw him and spoke to him.'

'And was there someone with him?'

'Aye.'

'What did he look like?'

'Stocky. Dark hair, thinning. Mouth like a rusty

hinge, take a crowbar to open it. Grey suit, good worsted, nice cut, but he stuffed his pockets like a greedy poacher.'

'So, not thirtyish, fair-haired, nice smile, Prince of Wales check and expensive dark-tan moccasins?'

'Not unless he'd had a nasty shock since you saw him . . . hey, but, hang about!' The Fat Man riffled through the papers on his desk. 'That's Ellie's description of the guy who tried to snatch her! Are you saying . . . ?'

'Last time I was at court it was also the description of the man sitting with Hubbard,' said Pascoe. 'And I saw them outside, getting into a BMW. Shit! You're right, sir. I must have made a sort of subliminal connection. But it wasn't just wanting to please teacher that made me look for better reasons for picking on the Cornelius case. I mean, for God's sake, even now I think you may be right, I still can't see that it makes any kind of sense.'

'Just coincidence, you think?'

'Why not? It happens. Unless you know something we don't,' said Pascoe.

'Day when I don't, I'll resign,' said the Fat Man. 'What's the time?'

'Quarter to one,' said Wield.

'Past Kelly Cornelius's check-in time, only she won't have shown and she's not going to show,' said Dalziel.

'Oh? And how do you know that?'

'She skipped yesterday. Jumped her keeper.'

'Her keeper?' said Pascoe. 'You were having her watched?'

'Not me.'

'Fraud, then?'

The great grey head shook ponderously.

'Who, then?'

'You recall a few years back coming to meet me at Heathrow and us ending up supping very old malt in some fancy VIP room with a long streak of evasiveness called Sempernel? Well, he came to see me last night.'

Pascoe said disbelievingly, 'But I thought he was Intelligence?'

'He'd not disagree.'

'You saying there's some kind of security angle here?' cried Pascoe, now thoroughly alarmed. 'Jesus! I thought it was just decent old-fashioned thugs we had to be worried about!'

'Oh, I don't think our Kelly need worry about old-fashioned thugs. Take a look at this. One of them e-mail things, came for me yesterday.'

He tossed Pascoe the print-out. He read it with Wield looking over his shoulder.

When he finished he said urgently, 'What the hell's going on, Andy? What's all this got to do with Ellie?'

'Wish I knew, lad. Wasn't dead sure it had anything till you made the connection with Hubbard's buttie in court.'

'But if Sempernel came to see you . . . ? What did he want?'

'Find out what I were up to fucking about with the Cornelius case. Plus he wanted to let me know in advance she'd flown the coop.'

'So that you could help to get her back?'

'Just the opposite. He ended up putting down a very serious warning that from now on in, I should keep my neb out. Go through the motions, but keep my distance. I got the same message from Desperate Dan when I arrived this morning, only without the menaces.'

'Menaces?'

'Oh aye. Old Pimpernel talks polite, but he laid it on the line. Any interference and they'll chop off my legs. For starters.'

'So you're going to steer clear, are you?' said Pascoe disbelievingly.

'Think I should have a bit more bottle, do you, lad?' asked Dalziel. 'Mebbe before you start sounding the charge from the rear, you should know that Sempernel made it clear it weren't just my legs on the block. Friends and colleagues got the black spot too. You fancy mixing it with the Funny Buggers, do you?'

'I fancy finding out why they started mixing it with Ellie in the first place,' retorted Pascoe.

'That's reasonable. Wieldy, you got owt to say?'

The sergeant said, 'I'm just wondering why they've warned you off, sir. Don't make sense. All right, you stuck your neb in and she got bail then took the chance to do a runner. I can see how they'd be a bit pissed off with you, but I can't see why they wouldn't be glad of any local help they could get to track her down. That's cutting off your nose to spite your face.'

Dalziel looked at his sergeant and Pascoe read his thought. *In your case, lad, likely no bugger would notice.* But happily it remained unspoken.

Instead, the Fat Man said, 'Good point. I got to thinking about it last night.'

In fact, it was Cap Marvell who'd got to think about it, poking him in the middle of the night to at the same time make the point and offer a solution. Then, like the sensible lass she was, she'd suggested that with them both being awake they might as well improve the shining hour.

He smiled reminiscently, caught Pascoe's curious gaze, frowned and said, 'I think I did them a favour. I reckon Cornelius caught them on the hop when she did her first runner and headed off to the airport. It was you that sorted that out by getting suspicious after the accident. Past couple of weeks they've been rethinking the situation and wondering how to play it. Letting her think she'd got away from them again was one option, but she's bright enough to twig if they made it too obvious. So when I came along and did it for them they were probably chuffed to buggery. Which means they don't want our help in finding her because . . .'

He looked at them expectantly.

'. . . because they think they already know where she's heading,' said Pascoe.

'And they don't want us tracking her down and banging her up again with no possibility of bail this time,' added Wield.

The three men fell silent for a while, each turning the matter in his mind like a 3-D computer projection.

'So what do we do?' asked Pascoe finally.

'Well, me, I like to know what's what on my patch,' said the Fat Man. 'But no need for anyone else to risk getting their legs chopped off. What say you, Pete?'

'I won't be happy till I know that whatever links this business to what happened to Ellie and Daphne Aldermann is done and finished,' said Pascoe.

They both looked at Wield who shrugged and said, 'My legs were always my worst feature.'

'Thank God for long trousers,' said Dalziel fervently. 'OK, let's give it a go. But carefully, eh? Like we're just covering ourselves by going through the motions. So where do we start? Your call, Pete. It was you as got us into this mess to start with.'

Pascoe laughed aloud at the assertion. It was a sound that Wield realized he hadn't heard much for some little while.

'Well,' said the DCI, 'like you're always telling us, sir, only Chief Constables can vanish without trace. Don't suppose Sempernel gave any details of how or where she slipped the leash?'

'No. Except he did say something about the park. Charter Park, I think he meant.'

'Which is between her flat and the town centre. Right, Wieldy, you start there. See if anyone saw anything. Sir, one thing I wondered about a woman like Cornelius. With her abilities and personality, how come she ended up working for a small-scale set-up like Nortrust when the big financial world was her oyster? I didn't really get anywhere when I talked to people at the bank. It's like asking monks about their sex life, talking to bankers about fraud. You know everybody in this town, sir, including George Ollershaw. If he's seriously in the frame, maybe there's a personal connection there we don't know about. Anything you could prise loose could be helpful.'

'Oh aye. And what are you going to do?'

'I'll turn over her flat again. Plus, I've got details of all her credit cards and so forth. I'll check these out for activity since she got bail and follow up any leads. OK? It's tedious, I know, but like you're always telling us, sir, if you don't do the house-work, you can't have the vicar to tea.'

He sprang to his feet and strode rapidly out of the room.

'Did I really say that, Wieldy?'

'Think it was summat about, you can't expect the vicar's wife to put out on the kitchen floor, sir,' said Wield.

'Sounds more like it,' said Dalziel. 'But it makes a change to see the lad so full of bubbles. He's not been a bundle of fun recently. What's happened? Got a new supplier, has he?'

'Rosie's illness and the Beulah case really knotted him up,' said the sergeant. 'Then just as they're getting over it, along comes this business to knock him back. I know that this morning he was really chuffed to think he'd got Ellie and Rosie well out of harm's way.'

'Aye, well, I can understand that. Hostages to fortune, eh? Who said that?'

'I think it were you, sir,' said Wield.

'Think I were right to send Ivor with them, Wieldy? Mebbe Seymour or Bowler would have been better.'

'Novello's fine, sir,' Wield reassured him. 'Tough as either of them, and a lot less noticeable. Any road, they're well away from the action out at Axness. Makes Enscombe sound like Piccadilly Circus. Last time there was any excitement out there was when they heard about Mafeking.'

'Is that right? How did that turn out, anyway?'

'All right, I think, sir.'

'That's a relief,' said Andy Dalziel. 'Let's hope this one's got a happy ending too.'

iii

the pavilion by the sea

'Stupid bloody woman. Stupid bloody woman. Stupid bloody woman,' chanted Feenie Macallum in time with each impact as the Land Rover bounced over the field.

She kept up the mantra even when she reached the relative smoothness of the road, increasing the tempo as the vehicle hit the potholed gravel drive sweeping up to Gunnery House and bringing it to a climax as she drove through the doorway of a ramshackle barn.

'I hope,' said Kelly Cornelius, lying in the rear, 'you're not referring to me.'

'Of course not. That Aldermann woman turning up like that.'

'I thought you said it was her cottage?'

'What's ownership got to do with anything? Am I supposed to tell the sea I own this place? You stay here till I see what I can sort out.'

'*Here?*'

'There are worse places. As you should know.'

'Yes, I know, but I'm terrified of rats.'

'And there are worse things than rats. But have no fear. Most seem to have left. With the wisdom of their kind, they like to keep two steps ahead of the ocean. So just stay still.'

'Yes, but . . .'

'My dear, I am getting too old for this. *Bud' zticha*!'

Which was *belt up*! in Czech, but she didn't need to translate. The tone did it all for her.

Every language has its strengths, and access to so many gave Feenie Macallum a very wide choice of *mots justes*.

When she was eight years old, for example, she could tell her father to go to hell in six different languages, none of them English.

He'd had to hire a governess to teach her the language of her native country.

She had hated him, willing herself to believe that her mother was dying because she had come back to Gunnery, rather than that she had come back to Gunnery to die. But her mother's last words to her had been an instruction (in what language she couldn't recall) to love her father. And when the night before the funeral she had stolen into the room where the body lay and found Macallum weeping by the open coffin, obedience to this dying wish had seemed after all to be a possibility.

She had held his hand at the graveside, and that night when a loneliness more piercing than a Carpathian frost had gripped her heart, she had slipped out of bed and stolen into her father's room in search of warmth and comfort.

He was, she discovered, in no position to offer them. Indeed, as later (much later) reflection suggested to her, he was perhaps in search of them himself. But no such plea in mitigation rose in her mind as she watched him thrusting himself into the arched and eager body of the governess athwart the great double bed.

This set the pattern of their future relationship; reconciliations and armistices all ending sooner or later in new outbreaks of war.

The governess departed, to be replaced by a male tutor who presented a different kind of sexual problem. The arm around her shoulder as he sat by her side to help with her work could be put down to pedagogic familiarity. The hand sliding up her leg and the fingers trying to pry beneath her knicker elastic couldn't. She drove a fountain pen so hard into his forearm that she severed the radial artery.

He was taken to hospital and never returned. To her father's interrogation, Feenie only replied, 'Accidents happen.'

After that, he sent her to the local primary school. She was fluent in schoolyard English in a week and classroom English in a month.

And now all her memories were in English. As she grew older she was finding that the distant past projected itself on her mind with ever increasing clarity, but so far it still hit a barrier when it reached those non-English days before the return to Axness. There was something there, in fact a great deal, but all a blur of mingling colours and overlapping images. She looked forward to the time when her ageing memory eventually got these into focus, amusing herself with the thought that perhaps her dying words would be in a language unrecognizable to the attendant nurses. But until that breakthrough happened, even her image of her mother alive and well derived not from any firm recollection of those early years but from the portrait of Mr and Mrs Macallum at Home which hung above the fireplace in the Grand Hall of Gunnery House.

She paused before it now to gather her thoughts as she entered the house. It was the only painting left in the place. The rest were long gone to the salesrooms. Macallum, who had little time for art, had simply bought pictures of the size and style to fit the spaces on the walls of his newly acquired house. Some of the artists had, happily, come back into fashion and they'd brought a decent price.

The portrait was different. Macallum had enquired who was the best portrait painter around and on being told Augustus John, had pursued the artist with offers of a very large fee, though rumour had it that it was the exotic beauty of Feenie's mother that had made him accept the commission. It was probably worth more than most of the others put together, but Feenie had so far resisted the temptation to turn it into cash, justifying herself with the thought that at least its value was increasing. This justification she'd also applied to Macallum's well-stocked cellar, though in that case it had proven specious on account of the steady inroads she had made into it over the years, and some nights after a bottle or two, picked at random, she would stand before the painting, contemplating cutting it in half like an old photo and selling off her father while retaining her mother.

No such act of vandalism occupied her thoughts now, partly because sober she doubted if it would be financially very productive, but mainly because she knew the time was fast approaching (indeed, in the eyes of some had long past) when Gunnery House would be uninhabitable. She could camp out indefinitely in the back of her old Land Rover but it was no place for a full-length portrait.

'So it's the saleroom for you after all, my dears,' she said.

Her mother, whose high Slavic cheekbones and deep-grey expressive eyes had been splendidly caught by the artist, making it easy to believe she was the Russian aristocrat she claimed to be, looked out with the blasé indifference of one to whom the vulgarities of money meant nothing. Beside her, Macallum's expression of grim satisfaction, though doubtless inspired by the notion of a common old working man hiring a famous artist to record for posterity his wife's great beauty and his own matching success, could easily be imagined to derive from a posthumous awareness that the artist's fee had also been a very productive financial investment.

Not that he would take any satisfaction from the use it would be put to. But by now he ought to have grown accustomed to that.

'Thank you, *oteko*,' said Feenie, using the Slovak diminutive which so much irritated him.

A discreet cough made her start.

She turned to see Wendy Woolley standing in the doorway.

Feenie frowned. After a lifetime of making her presence felt, she found it hard to understand how anyone could be so self-effacing. It ought to mean the woman was too unobtrusive to be a nuisance, but in certain circumstances, such negativity was a positive danger. For instance, she was so forgettable that when things had started getting complicated yesterday, it hadn't occurred to Feenie to give her a ring and postpone her visit to familiarize herself with the inner workings of the Liberata Trust. And typically just as things got worse this morning, there'd been a clang from the old sepulchral doorbell, and there she'd been, smiling nervously on the doorstep. Worse, she'd had a battered suitcase with her and a recollection not shared by Feenie of having been invited to spend the night.

Time had had to be spent showing her the office and also a bedroom, both in a sufficient state of chaos to put off any but the most devout of acolytes.

Perhaps, thought Feenie, she's come to offer her resignation. It was not a serious hope. Her long sight might be failing but faces she could read, and all she saw on the Woolley features was the determined dutifulness of the weak.

'I'm sorry to interrupt,' said Wendy.

'Interrupt? I am alone, so interruption can hardly come into it,' said Feenie.

'Yes, I see that now. But I thought I heard you talking . . . are these your parents, Miss Macallum?'

'Why do you ask? Do you catch a resemblance, perhaps?' said Feenie with an unnecessarily savage irony.

Wendy Woolley didn't seem to notice. She looked closely from the portrait to her hostess and said, 'About the jaw perhaps . . .'

Feenie examined the delicate fine-boned sweep of her mother's jaw and snorted derisively.

'It's a long time since I looked like her, if I ever did,' she said.

'No, I meant the gentleman's,' said Wendy.

Feenie's gaze switched to Macallum's square prizefighter's jaw, then moved on to Mrs Woolley's face, where she saw nothing but an earnest desire to please.

'Yes, they're my parents,' she said abruptly. 'I'm sorry to have neglected you, but I had to go out. I ran into a woman who has one of my cottages. Ellie Pascoe was with her, you remember Mrs Pascoe whose house we had the meeting in the other night?'

'Yes, indeed. I look forward to meeting her again. A nice lady, I thought.'

'I doubt she would thank you for the description,' said Feenie. 'They're coming for supper tonight, so you'll be able to discuss the point with her yourself. Unless, of course, you get finished this afternoon, in which case don't feel you have to hang about just out of politeness.'

Even if the complexity of Liberata's affairs hadn't driven the woman to resignation, at least by now she'd have had the chance to see that overnighting at Gunnery was not for faint hearts in search of old-fashioned country-house-party luxuries, and with luck she might be eager to take the offered excuse and head straight back to the comforts of her suburban semi.

Luck was in short supply this morning.

'No, really, it's fine, I've nothing to get back to, and there really is so very much to get to grips with. I never realized how very widespread our work was. That's something I wanted to ask you about, Miss Macallum. I can find many references to the trust's funding, but I don't seem to have among the records passed on to me any balanced statement of the current state of our account. I'm sure you don't need reminding that as a registered charity, the trust is answerable publicly for the use that is made of its funds.'

'You are right, I do not need reminding,' said Feenie acidly. 'But perhaps I should remind you, Mrs Woolley, that your primary function is to deal with the trust's day-to-day running, the mail and minor expenses, that sort of thing. The trust's major financial dealings are naturally in the hands of my professional accountants. In any case, as I myself have long been the principal source of Trust funds, I hardly see that public accountability applies.'

When the previous secretary had hinted any uneasiness on this matter, the Macallum acidity had been quite enough to dissolve her to silence. But Wendy Woolley revealed an unexpected stubborn streak.

'No, Miss Macallum,' she said firmly. 'The money may have derived from you, but once paid into the trust, then it is the trust's, not yours, and subject to all the restrictions that that entails.'

Feenie muttered something in Serbo-Croat. It was a favourite maxim of her mother's, and roughly translated as, *A mouse in the dairy can be a bigger nuisance than a wolf in the forest.*

'I'll be sure to convey your concern to the accountants,' said Feenie. 'In fact, I'll ring them now. Might take some time, though, and I was going to pop along to Axness village. I can sort out the adult grub for this evening, I think, but we really ought to have some ice cream, soft drinks, choc biscuits, that sort of thing, available for Mrs Pascoe's child, and the shop closes early today. I don't suppose that you, my dear . . . ?'

'Of course, but where exactly is the village?'

'Turn right at the gates, then second left and

straight on for a mile and a half,' said Feenie. 'You can't miss it. I'm so grateful. You're very kind.'

The woman flushed, gave an embarrassed smile, and left.

Liar, said Feenie Macallum to herself. People who'd lived within the parish of Axness for fifty years still managed to miss the village. She still didn't like telling lies, but had come to accept over the years that a nit-picking honesty might earn you Brownie points in heaven but it didn't get much done down here on earth. The Liberata Trust was a case in point. It had seemed an excellent idea to register it as a charity with all the tax breaks provided by such status, and over the years it had seemed an easy and sensible policy to feed all her money into Liberata's funds so that it could enjoy the same advantages. But important though Liberata's work was, there were many other causes making financial demands upon her, and requiring that the trust's funds should only be used for the purposes specified in the original deed was like trying to bind God by His own precepts, she thought.

The Law was an ass. Each of her languages had its own version of that, but no other put it quite so forcefully and succinctly, perhaps because the law in England could be particularly asinine. It was pretty good on preventing people from being unjustly imprisoned, and excellent against torture and other cruel and unusual punishments, but when it came to defending the innocent and the ignorant against the financial depredations of the unscrupulous, it had more holes in it than an executed collaborator.

The image made her smile reminiscently, and also in anticipation of a great wrong soon to be righted. But only if she was able to get her mind working at something like its old level of efficiency. With age she had discovered that much could be got away with if you gave the impression of being a dotty old woman. But now she recalled the warning of an old and revered mentor during those wild mad war years – *The real danger of our line of work is not from bullets and betrayal, but that we might become what we pretend to be.*

She closed her eyes and thought wearily, perhaps I really am nothing now but a dotty old woman.

When she opened them she was glad to find it was the portrait of her parents she was still looking at and not her reflection in a mirror.

The grim satisfaction on Macallum's face seemed intensified.

She said, 'Sorry, *oteko*, but I'm not ready to lie down and die yet.'

All she had to do was find a new hiding place.

When Mrs Stonelady had told her yesterday that the young men were moving out, Nosebleed Cottage had seemed the perfect spot. The old woman had expressed no surprise or curiosity when told a friend of Miss Macallum would be staying there a few nights, but she'd had the wit to ring Feenie instantly that morning when she discovered Daphne Aldermann's message on the answer machine. The cow had said she'd be turning up sometime after midday, and even the complication of dealing with the forgotten arrival of woolly Wendy had seemed to leave plenty of time. So the shock of running into the Aldermann car, with Ellie Pascoe and child as passengers and a female cop in close attendance, at eleven o' clock, had been great.

Well, she'd dealt with that pretty neatly, and compared with situations she'd had to deal with in the distant, and not so distant, past, when the price of failure was a bullet in your back or a land mine under your lorry, this was pretty small beer.

She made a face at her father and went about her business. Ten minutes later she came out of the front door trailing a well-filled black bin liner and made for the barn.

She found Kelly Cornelius sitting disconsolately on the bumper of the Land Rover, in full view of anyone going by.

'Come on,' said Feenie. 'Got your knapsack? Let's get you settled in before the whole world sees you.'

'Oh good. I don't see why I didn't get to stay in the house in the first place,' said the woman, following her out of the rear of the barn.

'You're not going to stay in the house now,' said Feenie, striding ahead. 'As I explained before, when you don't report today, your picture will probably be in the papers. And while the house may seem like ultima Thule to you, there is a steady traffic of postmen, delivery men, petty officials from the council come to try and save me from falling into the sea, inquisitive rustics making inventories of what they might rescue from the imminent wreck, plus woolly Wendy, my new hon. sec. who shows signs of being both nosey and invisible. So we need a safe house for you.'

'Oh yes? And where do you suggest?'

'The Command Post.'

Kelly stopped dead.

'The Command Post? You want me stay there? No way!'

'My dear, it's perfectly safe. All right, the services are cut off but the weather is warm and in this bin liner you'll find a sleeping bag, bottled water, bread, cheese, apples, candles, some toilet paper and a copy of Gibbon's *Decline and Fall* considerably abridged. After a remand cell, I'm sure this must be the acme of comfort.'

'I prefer the cell. Or I'll take my chances back in the barn with the rats.'

Feenie was regarding her with a sharply speculative eye.

'But why? You're not normally spooked by a bit of solitude and discomfort. And you need to spend tonight somewhere safely out of sight.'

'That's it,' cried Kelly, as if seeing a lifeline. 'It's not safe, is it? I mean, it's so far beyond the council's Black Stump, it's almost into the sea.'

'What do those idiots at the council know?' said Feenie impatiently. 'My father had the ground properly surveyed and the theory is the pavilion's built on a stack of granite. Well, most of it. So it might list a bit, but I can't see it slipping into the sea till all the sandstone's been eaten away around it and that should take several more big storms, and the forecast is good for the next twenty-four hours, and we'll have you away from here tomorrow. So come on. Let's get you settled in before Mrs Woolley returns.'

She strode ahead again, with the younger woman trailing behind unhappily like a child being dragged around the shopping centre when it would rather be at home playing with its toys.

Mungo Macallum had seen fit to extend Gunnery House at the rear with an ornate terrace of white marble that looked like the bottom layer of a huge wedding cake. This gave out on an intricate formal garden, now sadly run to seed and decay, through which the path the two women were on meandered eastwards towards a rampant rhodo-dendron shrubbery. Just before they reached it, they had to duck beneath a broad fillet of fluores-cent red plastic stretched between a line of metal spikes running out of sight in both directions. Every fifth or sixth spike bore a sign consisting of a formalized skull and crossbones with beneath it in bold letters DANGER! and beneath that in smaller letters a warning from the Local Health and Safety Executive that it was strictly forbidden to pass beyond this point on account of the danger of landslip.

Ahead, beyond the rhododendrons, the garden came to an abrupt end where the sea, eating away at the soft sandstone cliffs, had left a scalloped edge over which shrubs and trees and at one point a trellised rose arbour still heavy with rich red blooms leaned drunkenly.

On the most extreme of the promontories thus formed stood a long low concrete building built like a Greek temple with its columns in the form of telamones consisting of military figures ranging from Greek warriors to tommies of the Great War. It should have been kitsch beyond mockery. Instead, occupying the narrow headland so completely that it seemed to be hanging in air, the effect was menacingly magical, as if anyone entering here would be stepping over the threshold of another world.

This was the Command Post, which had seemed a suitable sobriquet for a pleasure pavilion built by an armaments king so that his guests could enjoy nature at its most explosively sublime without relinquishing any of its or man's luxuries. Feenie could recall in her teens acting as a hostess to a couple of dozen of her father's friends enjoying an Epicurean dinner in the long viewing chamber while a spectacular storm lit the eastern sky, its thunders shaking the pavilion like an enemy bombardment. Back then the ground dipping away in front to the cliff edge had stretched for perhaps a furlong. Now the sea, whose storms had for so long been reduced to a spectator sport, was within a few feet of taking what the Greeks would certainly have regarded as its revenge.

Kelly stopped dead at the sight of it. The old woman turned and said impatiently, 'Stop looking so worried! It looks far worse than it is. And in any case the weather is set fair. Now let's get you inside. Remember, it's essential that you don't stray out of here this evening. I have invited those people who have ejected you from Nosebleed Cottage for supper . . .'

'That seems a bit unwise! Why not make it tomorrow when I'm gone?'

Feenie sighed and said, 'Do not teach your grand-mother to suck eggs, girl. By inviting them here this evening, I shall know exactly where they are. If I hadn't invited them, they might come wandering round at any time with all the risk which that would entail. Also, it will fix woolly Wendy in the house helping me prepare and inhibit her from idle perambulation.'

'She's your tweenie too?'

'She does not yet know it, but yes. So all you have to do is sit and admire the view out to sea for the rest of the day. Why I let myself be tempted by you in the first place I do not know. But having come so far, let us try not to end in fiasco. Come on, let's get you settled before woolly Wendy returns.'

She set off again.

Reluctantly, Kelly Cornelius followed.

But as they got within a few yards of the building it was the old woman who came to a sudden halt.

'Hello,' she said. 'Someone's been mucking around down here. That lock's been broken.'

She was looking down a flight of steps with a concrete chute on one side which led down to a basement doorway opening into the cellar where her father had stored the supplies of food and wine necessary to entertain his guests.

'And someone's been at this door too,' she went on, turning her attention to the main entrance. 'The council nailed a bar across it to deter visitors. Kids, I expect. They just do exactly what they want nowadays.'

Kelly laughed and said, 'That's rich coming from you!'

'Don't be cheeky,' Feenie reprimanded her. 'Let's look inside. I hope for your sake they haven't been using it as a public loo.'

'No, hang on,' said Kelly, her laughter dying.

'What now?'

The young woman sighed and took a deep breath.

'Before we go inside, there's something I need to tell you,' she said.

iv

spelt from Sibyl's leaves

Has anyone here seen Kelly? Kelly from . . .

And there's a curious thing.

Not where Kelly has gone. People are always going. Another name, another country, another life. But no one moves without a trace and late or soon, getting and spending, we work out their whither.

Not to know their whence, though, now that really is curious.

Four years you've been on my magic island, child, marooned here by that most princely of pirates, old Silvernob himself, Gaw Sempernel.

Low-level entry, basic details to start with. But not even the most basic checked out.

Kelly Cornelius.

Passport details:

Born London, April 4, 1972. (No confirmatory entry found in any registry of births and deaths.)

Passport issued January 23, 1994. (A Sunday.

339

Not normally a day for issuing passports, which is perhaps why the Passport Agency failed to find any record of it.)

Emergency contact names, to be informed in case of an accident. Only one given (and this made me laugh so much I almost fell out of my chair, which would have been unfortunate as I find it increasingly difficult to get back into it without assistance).

Gawain Sempernel, of this address.

She knows about you, Gawain.

With her command of cyber-space where we all track our spoors, how should she not know? And she knows that you know she knows. And she doesn't care.

I admire you, my Kelly. And I envy you. For you are young and I am old. You are lithe of limb and can make your escape on two wheels, while I can never escape, though permanently on four. And even out of our bodies and into our other dimension, I am only a cyber-sibyl, ordering my caskets in the confines of my magic island, while you are a cyber-queen of infinite space.

I know this because of what I do not know.

You appeared in England, and on my island, four years ago, a whizz in the world of financial technology, trailing clouds of praise from your previous employers, who have been for the most part financial institutions in the Americas. You'd been a busy bee for one so young, perhaps busier than anyone knew, for when we checked (uninvited, naturally) their personnel files, we found you there all right, but curiously incomplete, one job leading only back to another till suddenly we were back at the one we started with, impossible in real time of course, but someone had created a temporal Möbius strip which not all my best efforts could straighten out without destroying it.

And of course your real employers have been people whose records are not the common currency of the air, as ultimately everything reduced to electronic impulses must be, but word of mouth and cryptic scribbles on scraps of paper and nods and winks and all the old channels of communication inaccessible to such as me.

But we don't need them for we know what you have been doing. Your talent is turning dirty money into clean. You do this not by having your own set up which would be assailable and surveillable by the forces of law. You enter the world of international banking as a skilled and trusted employee and you use their systems with all their protections and connections and subtle interactions to move your masters' money around so quickly and quietly and untraceably that what might have been seizable as a drug baron's ill gotten billions ends up as clean and untouchable as a nun's pension fund. Nothing is illegal, nothing is stolen from the banks, in fact you do them sterling service and leave them better, or at least better off, than you find them. And you never stay long enough to become a fixture or an embarrassment.

And so it seemed would things carry on when you came back to Europe.

First you spent your time commuting between London and Switzerland, which is to dirty money what a privet hedge is to crisp packets. You straddled Europe like a whore up a back alley, with one foot planted firmly in Credit Apollyon de Zurich and the other in Arblasters, the kind of City merchant bank which has been making the rich richer, and the poor poorer, since Richard Arblaster of that Ilk sold his shares in the South Sea Company shortly before the bubble burst.

But next came a very strange move, away from the golden glow of the City to darkest Yorkshire, to take a dip in salary and status, social opportunity and cultural accessibility, by becoming an employee of Nortrust Bank plc, created five years ago out of a small and local demutualized building society.

What were you playing at, my Kelly from nowhere?

What impulse has turned you from a high-class laundry girl into a common embezzler putting you at last within reach of the long and predatory fingers of Uncle Gawain? Was this why you were suddenly upgraded from non-surveillance level to *Sibyl's Leaves*? Or was it just coincidental?

I don't yet know. All I know about you, officially, is all that Gawain wants to be known about you officially. That is Gawain's way. *Sibyl's Leaves* is full of such bits and pieces, shreds and patches, always just enough to cover his back in case our First Mover ever checks through the folder.

But once together in the dim light of my cave, all these individual spores and seeds of information take light and heat from each other and begin to germinate till finally, finally, the same god who binds his prophetess in darkness suddenly ravishes her with light!

I don't know where you've come from, my Kelly, not yet. But the way to find out where an animal comes from is to watch where it runs to.

Gawain, circling high in the sky, likes his prey to freeze on the ground so that he can descend on it like a thunderbolt when he feels the moment is ripe.

I, on the other hand, as fixed in my place as a convict in the electric chair, prefer to see the objects of my concern in movement.

Twice now I have flushed you out and set you running free, my Kelly. Once by a cryptic note on your computer screen, and this time by a little electronic billet-doux about you to that arch-mischief-maker, my twenty-stone Puck, ol' man Dalziel.

The game's afoot!

Has anyone here seen Kelly? Kelly from . . .

v

realms of gold

Edwin Digweed in an idly reflective post-coital moment had once asked Edgar Wield how much his choice of career had been influenced by the license it gave him to strike up conversations with strange men in parks.

The sergeant recalled the *facetia* (a word his partner had once used punningly, then had to explain in both its meanings, by which time the joke had fallen somewhat flat) as he traced Kelly Cornelius's probable route through Charter Park. In fact, on a day like this, being a cop was quite inessential as no one he approached showed the slightest concern even before he flashed his credentials (the kind of double entendre to which Edwin reacted as Wield had done to *facetia*), perhaps confirming Pascoe's theory that the English have been conditioned over centuries to regard bright warm sunshine as a rare gift from God under which no evil may flourish.

He struck gold instantly. The first person he

spoke to, a woman wheeling a pram which contained a chubby child who bore an uncanny resemblance to Andy Dalziel, had been in the park the previous afternoon. She needed only one glance at the photograph Wield showed her.

'Oh yes,' she said, her face lighting up. 'I remember seeing her. Lovely-looking girl. I remember thinking I used to have a figure like that before *he* came along.'

He looked up from the pram with a most Dalziel-esque curl of the lip.

It struck Wield, who was a connoisseur of intonation, that there was at least as much of admiration as of envy in the tone, a judgement confirmed when the woman went on, 'It did me good just to watch her, she were such a lovely mover.'

'You watched her?' said Wield. 'So which way was she heading?'

The woman indicated that Cornelius had been walking from the side of the park where her flat was located towards the town centre.

'Then she turned off the main path there and went down to the canal.'

Wield followed her pointing finger and asked, 'You see anyone else around?'

'Yes, well, there would be, it was a lovely day. Like today. People need to get out, enjoy it while you can.'

The Greenhouse Effect could turn England into a second Sahara and the natives would still be convinced each hour of sunshine was the last.

'So, anyone in particular?'

The woman thought then shook her head.

'No. Kids. People. But I remember her. Full of life, she were.'

This was strongly suggestive that the powerful impression Cornelius had clearly made on Pascoe and Dalziel was not merely sexual.

He said, 'Thanks a lot, luv. By the way, you don't know our Mr Dalziel, do you? Superintendent Dalziel?'

'No. Why do you ask?'

Wield looked once more at the baby, who bared his toothless gums in a mocking smile.

'No reason,' he said.

He made towards the canal, pausing to chat to a gang of pre-pubescent cricket players.

Several of them had been in the same spot the previous afternoon and had no difficulty in recalling Cornelius.

'She caught our ball and threw it back, proper, tha knows, not like a lass. Then she went down to the canal and watched the ducks.'

'Was there anyone else around by the canal?'

'No.'

'Yeah, there was that old tramp,' interjected one of the other boys.

'Oh yeah, but she don't count,' said the first speaker, unhappy at having his status as group spokesman challenged.

'Which old tramp?'

'Some old biddy, looks like she sleeps rough.'

'How old?'

'About a hundred,' said the boy without hyperbole.

'Did the young woman who can throw speak to the tramp at all?'

A moment's consultation, then a tentative affirmative.

'So, anything else you noticed.'

More consultation, then the spokesboy said, 'No. What's she done, mister?'

'Nothing. Just got lost,' said Wield. 'Thanks.'

As he turned away a voice said, 'She were on a bike.'

He turned back. The speaker, already looking like he was regretting it, was the smallest child there, slightly built, fair, almost white, hair, with a slack mouth and somewhat vacant expression.

'A bike?' said Wield. 'You saw her on a bike?'

The boy seemed to have exhausted his supply of words but he did give an almost imperceptible nod.

'Don't pay him no heed, mister,' said the spokesboy. 'He's a bit . . .'

He tapped the side of his head.

'Anyone else see a bike?' asked Wield.

A general shaking of heads. The fair-haired child looked close to tears.

'You sure it were her?' said Wield gently. 'The lady who threw the ball?'

The boy just hung his head and the others laughed, though more possessively than derisively.

'Well, thanks, anyway,' said Wield.

As he walked away the fair-haired child suddenly yelled, 'It were both of 'em on the bike!'

The laughter swelled behind him, and even Wield smiled at this extension into tandem.

But an hour later he had stopped smiling and was hurrying back towards the cricketers.

Peter Pascoe had developed many of the carapaces necessary to long-term survival in the police force. In fact, according to his wife he now had a shell thick enough to cause envious comment on the Galapagos Islands. But he had never been able to rid himself of the distaste he felt for searching other people's property.

He experienced it now as he went through Kelly Cornelius's apartment.

He'd been here before with a Fraud DI when the case had first broken. The Fraud man had removed the PC with the odd message and some disks but found nothing else of interest to him. Pascoe had done a general search, completing what PC Hector had begun with such devastating consequences.

'Looking for sackfuls of dosh, are you?' said the Fraud man derisively. 'If it's anywhere, it'll be in here, mate.' Waving a disk.

'Just getting a feel what she's like,' said Pascoe.

'From what I hear about her, I wouldn't mind a feel myself,' said the other.

Pascoe had said pleasantly, 'Do you think you

might have been too long with Fraud, Inspector? Perhaps you might consider a transfer to Vice?'

Conversation had died thereafter till the DI, ready to leave, found himself waiting while Pascoe carefully replaced on hangers and in drawers the clothing he'd been searching through.

'What's that in aid of?' he finally demanded.

'To stop it getting creased,' said Pascoe.

'Creased?' said the man incredulously. 'Je-sus!'

Now second time around Pascoe found the apartment much as he recalled leaving it. His excellent memory for detail plus the precise written notes he'd made at the time of the first search told him that Cornelius certainly hadn't come home and packed a case with clothes in anticipation of making a run for it. As far as he could make out, she must have come from the court after her release, opened a bottle of bubbly (empty on the bathroom floor), had a bath (damp towel and discarded clothing in the linen basket), got dressed and gone out. So nothing to indicate to Sempernel's watchers that she was on the point of doing a bunk.

There was a pile of unopened mail on a table. Circulars, bills, a DVLC reminder. Presumably she'd taken anything personal. If there'd been anything. They'd found precious little in the way of personal papers at the time of her arrest. The nearest he'd got to her past was via a thickish photograph album he'd found at the bottom of one of her cases, though even here the lack of names, dates, or places on or under the pictures meant he was left with only a vague undetailed impression of a life spent growing up in fairly exotic settings (Mediterranean? Caribbean? Asian?). He opened it again. At last an indication she didn't intend to hang around. There were now more gaps than photos.

As he was preparing to leave, his mobile rang. It was 'Hat' Bowler whom he'd delegated to check with Cornelius's credit card companies for details of transactions recorded in the last twenty-four hours.

There were several, all occurring the previous afternoon in town centre stores.

As he made a note, his gaze fell on the pile of mail. The DVLC envelope was at the top. He picked it up and opened it. It was a reminder that Cornelius needed to retax her car at the end of the month. The car was a metallic-blue Golf.

Pocketing the form, he went out into the sunshine.

He decided to walk to the centre, following Cornelius's probable route. They'd never even thought about her car. Of course it was likely she had one, but she'd been using a taxi to the airport, so it didn't come up. He checked the residents' parking spaces in the street. No sign of a blue Golf. He put it to the back of his mind and as he strolled along, thought with envy of Ellie and Rosie relaxing by the sea at Axness. Must be nice to have enough money to afford a holiday cottage. Must be even nicer to have enough time to make good use of it. He and Ellie had once run through a list of alternative careers during one of their quieter debates about the many disadvantages of the police force. In the end she had said with rueful affection, 'One thing's sure, whatever else you might have done, it probably wouldn't have affected the amount of spare time you have for your wife and family. You'd have always been banging away with Miss Whiplash.'

'What? Am I supposed to start like a guilty thing surprised?'

'Of course not. Far too controlled. Anyway, I'm not talking about your fancy woman but that other disciplinarian who turns you on, stern daughter of the voice of God, Duty. If you'd been a dustman, you'd have spent your weekends oiling wheelie-bins.'

Was she right? Was he work-obsessive? When Rosie was ill, he'd dropped everything and gone running. But there was little virtue in that. What father wouldn't? It hadn't been a matter of choice. And while it seemed to confirm his assertion, *I'll always be there when you need me*, even that (another of Ellie's obiter dicta) depended on your definition of need.

He was walking through Charter Park now without much recollection of how he'd got there. He paused to look around and there in the distance was Wield chatting to some kids playing cricket.

The Fat Man would probably have bellowed something like, 'Pay heed, lads! That's what comes of not wearing a face mask against fast bowlers.'

Is knowing the sort of things Dalziel would have said a step away from hearing me say them myself? he wondered.

He left the sergeant to his converse and made his way out of the park, across the busy road, into the town centre.

In the departmental stores he visited, his investigations proceeded at snail pace.

At till level, the assistants lived up to their reputation of being a timorous breed, herding together in shady recesses, and shying away nervously at the approach of a questing customer. When finally cornered, they expressed a positively Hectorian bewilderment at the notion that there might be a usable correlation between credit card transactions and till receipts, then picked up telephones and emitted whimpering pleas for assistance from the leader of the pack. This usually turned out to be a formidable lady wearing a westernized version of Kabuki make-up. She listened patiently (so far as one could read any emotion in that emulsioned face), asked the same questions three times, pronounced some oxymoronic mantra on the lines of *I don't know, I'm sure*, then declared, 'I'll need to have a word with Mr Earnshaw.' Mr Earnshaw (in Mid-Yorkshire, all deputy managers answer to Earnshaw), a callow youth who tried for gravitas by walking slightly stooped with his hands behind his back, as if in mourning for the passing of the frock coat, next invited Pascoe to follow him to Accounts. And here at last he was greeted with a smile and an acknowledgement that shops were for selling things, and technology was for facilitating that task, by a child of some twelve or thirteen years (apparently) who produced what he wanted in five seconds flat.

So finally he established that Kelly Cornelius had purchased various items of toiletry, lingerie, footwear and clothing, plus a small haversack into which she had presumably packed them.

Escape kit, he thought as he stepped from the cloying air of the inevitable supraliminal parfumerie department into the momentarily preferable stench of exhaust fumes, meaning she'd come out of her apartment not totally sure that she'd be doing her runner that same afternoon, though sufficiently aware the call might come at any time for her to stick the essential photos in her handbag. Then somewhere between the flat and the shops, she'd been given a signal, coolly spent the time she had left buying essential supplies, and then . . . vanished.

So, lad, he could hear Dalziel saying, you've established that she's gone? Grand! I always like having someone confirm what I've known for certain since yesterday evening!

It didn't worry him. This was his way. Drudgery divine, short but certain steps, all the time sweeping up information and gathering speed, till at last you reached the velocity necessary to take off into a flight of airy intuition.

While Dalziel . . . ?

He was probably spreading sweetness and light, or something, down at the head office of Nortrust. Pascoe recalled reading a short story once in which the hero, by refusing to believe in things, destroyed them. He ended up in Threadneedle Street turning his sceptical gaze on the mighty edifice of the Bank of England, which had begun to shake, when someone pushed him under a bus. After Fat Andy's little philosophical flight that morning with all that stuff about seeing what had to be there rather than what appeared to be there, Pascoe hoped that Nortrust had their premises well insured.

The thought made him smile as he made his way back towards the park, and people he didn't know or sometimes even notice smiled back at him.

In fact, Andy Dalziel wasn't in the offices of Nortrust. One thing he did see which the sharp eyes of neither Pascoe nor Wield could clearly discern was that the really important transactions of business life in Mid-Yorkshire weren't conducted on commercial premises but behind the imposing portals of the Gents.

Shortly after one o'clock he'd drifted with a cloud's slow motion into the long dining room which was set as always with small tables for those who wished to lunch *à deux*, or *trois* or even *quatre*, while at the far end where a huge bay window glowered down at the busy High Street stood the broad general table for members who came in alone.

Among those seated there was a white-haired man whose head would not have looked out of place on a marble plinth in Caesar Augustus's palace, which was not the most unpleasant place many would have paid good money to relocate it over the years.

This was Eden Thackeray of Thackeray, Amberson, Mellor, Huby and Thackeray, Solicitors, usually known as Messrs Thackeray, etc. Semi-retired now, he claimed modestly to have dropped from pole position as senior partner into the end slot formerly occupied by his nephew Dunstan who had leapt, by virtue of his name alone, into control of the firm, but no one who knew him doubted for a moment that Eden still called the important shots.

Over many years, he and Dalziel had often opposed, occasionally assisted, and always entertained each other.

The Fat Man plonked his bulk down onto the chair next to him which fortunately, like nearly everything else at the Gents, including the menu, subscribed to Victorian values.

'How do, Eden,' he said.

'Andy, my dear chap. We see you in here far too infrequently.'

'Oh aye? Been doing a poll, have you? Soup, steak and kid.'

This to the waiter who'd already written it down. The alternative never chosen by Dalziel would have been soup and boiled cod. There had once been a motion to include a light salad on the menu during summer months but it had been rejected by a heavy majority.

Thackeray, who was finishing his main course, deferred selection of pudding till Dalziel had caught him up. By the time they dead-heated on their final spoonfuls of Spotted Dick, they were the sole occupants of the common table.

'Coffee and malt. One Park, one Lag. Big 'uns,' said Dalziel to the waiter. 'We'll have it here. And put it on my tab.'

'Everything, or just the drinks, sir?'

The Fat Man looked assessingly at Thackeray.

'Everything,' he said.

Sipping his whisky appreciatively, Thackeray said, 'So, you've made a blind investment, Andy. I hope you find the return worth the risk.'

'Fees you lot earn, I'd not expect much back for a plate of grub and an ounce of mouthwash,' said Dalziel. 'Tell me about the Nortrust Bank.'

'Ah. Let me see. Would this have anything to do with the rumours of fraud circulating around the person of the delectable Ms Cornelius?'

'Know her well, do you?'

'I have been in the same room as her,' said Thackeray.

'Me too. Same courtroom,' said Dalziel.

'Then you'll know what I mean.'

The two men drank their malt in contemplative silence.

'The word is,' said Thackeray finally, 'that after Ms Cornelius had been interviewed for her job, George Ollershaw, chairman of the interviewing panel, declared, *We've got to have this woman. Preferably me first.*'

'Mucky sod,' said Dalziel censoriously.

'Indeed. I gather the lady director on the panel was greatly offended and expressed her offence by opposing Ms Cornelius's appointment.'

'So she didn't get a hundred per cent vote?'

'No. It was two-two, with the chairman using his casting vote. He was, of course, able to refute any accusation of undue hormonal influence by pointing to the evidence that from the technical point of view, Ms Cornelius was clearly superior to all other candidates. Of course, as it turned out, the bank might have done better if they had in fact appointed someone whose physical effulgence was not matched by hi-tech brilliance.'

'Eh? Oh, I'm with you. Big tits and no brains, gets her sums wrong but doesn't rip you off.'

'As ever your *reductio ad vernaculum* removes all ambiguity,' said Thackeray.

'That's what my old mam always used to tell me. So, did any of these dirty old bankers get any further than wishful thinking?'

'If they did, they were uniquely discreet. Tongues

have been observed hanging out, but none to my knowledge has ever made contact with any portion of Ms Cornelius's anatomy.'

This was good enough for Dalziel. In Mid-Yorkshire professional circles, Eden Thackeray's knowledge was like a London taxi driver's; as well as the broad and airy boulevards, he knew all the mean streets and dark ginnels.

'So, no sex,' said the Fat Man. 'Still, you can go partners with a lass without banging her, so they tell me. Anyone there with an appetite bigger than his income? George Ollershaw, for instance.'

Thackeray finished his drink, Dalziel crooked a finger and the watching waiter came with the prepared refills.

The lawyer said, 'I had heard that George was being examined by your people with more interest than a fan dancer's feathers at a police party. But personally I'd say you were urinating up the wrong tree there, Andy.'

'Oh aye? You know him well, do you?'

'Well enough. He trained as a lawyer, you know. Indeed, he worked with our firm for a while. A man of few scruples, but too clever to need to be criminal, I'd have thought.'

'You fire him or what?' said Dalziel hopefully.

'No. Amicable parting. He rapidly realized that for us poor solicitors, it is all a labour of love and we exist at mere subsistence level, so he rechannelled his talents into accountancy, moving into financial services during the eighties boom, and whatever benefits he may or may not have brought his clients, he certainly took his own advice to some good effect, emerging from the consequent recession with considerable wealth and property. When the old Nortrust Building Society demutualized five years ago, George was waiting for them. Now that's an interesting story –'

'Does it show him as a crook?' interrupted Dalziel. 'Or mebbe as someone owing big money to the Mafia?'

'Alas, no. Just a very sharp operator. And now he is a pillar of the community. No hint of financial problems, no reason to be helping anyone go scrumping round the Nortrust orchard when the golden fruit fall so freely and legitimately into his outstretched hand. He is of course seriously embarrassed by this investigation. Mud sticks, scrub you never so hard. And his mode of entrée into Nortrust's inner sanctum made him many enemies. I see from your polite yawn that I'm not telling you anything you find helpful, am I?'

'I liked the bit about hard-up solicitors.'

'I'm sorry. You will just have to look elsewhere.'

'Nay,' said Dalziel, shaking his huge head vigorously. 'I'll just have to look harder. There's got to be summat there at Nortrust. I feel it, like one of them planets the astronomers know must be there long afore they clock it, because of the way the others act.'

'Andy, that's almost poetic. Do be careful or you may be asked to leave the club. You know they don't permit poetry on the premises, not even between consenting adults.'

'How about history? Tell us about the Nortrust Building Society. Tell us how Ollershaw came to be such a fat cat on the board.'

'Andy, you put me down severely when I tried to do that just now. Are you so desperate?'

'Not desperate. I just know, like the man said, the truth's out there.'

'That would be Keats, would it? All right. Are you sitting comfortably, then I'll begin?'

And some time and several Parks and Lags later, Andy Dalziel at last began to feel like some watcher of the skies when a new planet swims into his ken.

vi

cheated by Protestants

Shirley Novello clung to a branch of the tree and ran her binoculars through an arc of three hundred degrees, the other sixty proving inaccessible without major surgery to her neck. Her mind reeled dizzily, not because she was sixty feet above the ground, nor even at the thought of that blue emptiness stretching eastward all the way to Holland (or maybe Denmark or perhaps even Norway – she'd usually bunked off geography lessons). No, it was the realization that the view west was just as empty. For God's sake, how many Irish miles was she from a takeaway pizza? A twenty-screen cinema? A hot nightclub? Or even a decent theme pub?

People raved about the countryside and came here for holidays – but what the hell did they actually *do*? The seaside wasn't so bad, when it was real seaside, with souvenir stalls, and burger stands, and ice cream vans, and she didn't even mind a tumble of dunes in easy walking distance where a young woman could take a young man with the body of a wrestler and show him a few holds he wouldn't learn at the gym . . .

But apart from a large building, presumably Gunnery House, about half a mile north-west, the land at the side of this sea showed little sign of human habitation till it stopped at the edge of a cliff. Maybe the beach below was packed with ice cream vendors and chunky young wrestlers, but she doubted it.

'What are you doing?'

The voice came from below, which was just as well as a voice from any other direction might have shocked her off her perch.

She looked down.

Looking up from the foot of the tree was the Pascoe brat. Cocking its leg against the tree was the Pascoe brat's pooch.

'Just having a look around,' called Novello.

'Can you see a long way?'

'Forever.'

'Forever,' echoed the child in a reverential tone. 'I'd like to see forever.'

To Novello's horror, the girl began to reach up to the lower branches of the tree. Child-minding was not in her job description, but she had a mental image of Ellie Pascoe emerging from the cottage to discover her daughter splattered over the grass with herself high above, looking guilty.

In normal circumstances, Novello was prepared to meet La Pascoe, or any woman, head-on, but at this prospect her spirit quailed.

'Stay there,' she commanded. 'I'm coming down.'

She descended rapidly, swinging athletically from branch to branch, and dropping the last six feet to land lightly at Rosie's side. All that work at the gym felt worthwhile, even if her prime purpose in going there was to get a personal preview of what was on offer in the wrestling department.

'You can jump a long way down,' said Rosie Pascoe admiringly. 'I can jump a long way too but not as far as that, not till I'm bigger. But I'm a good climber.'

'I'm sure,' said Novello. 'But not this tree, eh?'

'Why not this tree?'

Novello thought of saying it was a special police observation tree, but casting her mind back to her own childhood, she guessed this would only encourage the DCI's brat to become all proprietorial and take the first opportunity to get up there.

Her mind stayed in her childhood. Lots of authority figures to pay lip service to, but the only one whose word was really law had been a big girl called Tracy, the leader of her playground gang. Tracy, she recalled, had a winning way with hearts and minds.

'Because I say so,' she said. 'And in my gang, if you don't do what I say, I'll drop you face down in a cow pat.'

Rosie considered this then nodded.

'OK,' she said. 'What's our gang called?'

Gangs had to have names. Novello thought a

second then said, smiling to herself, 'We're the Uncumber Number. Don't forget it.'

'OK,' said Rosie. 'What's it mean?'

Small girls had to have reasons.

Novello gave her a potted history of St Uncumber, turning her into a sort of anti-small-boys Action Woman and omitting the gory details of her final fate. She didn't want the kid having nightmares La Pascoe could trace back to her.

Rosie listened, wide-eyed.

Then she said eagerly, 'Shall we go and find some boys to get rid of?'

Uneasily, Novello hoped this brat wasn't a literalist.

She said, 'No. First we see if we can find some food to get rid of. Cake. Uncumber liked to get rid of a lot of cake. As well as boys.'

Lunch had confirmed her fears that the two older women had reached the age when unattractiveness is measured in cellulite. To Novello, the obvious response to Feenie Macallum's supper invitation was to eat Mrs Stonelady's stew for lunch. But the dish seemed to have vanished completely (perhaps consigned to the freezer?) and the wrinklies had seemed more than content to nibble at some tasteless biscuits spread with smelly cheese. Breakfast she did not doubt would be dried apricots and guava juice.

Well, such a thin mix might be all right for antique machinery, but a late model just off the assembly line and into the showroom needed richer fuel.

There was no sign of cake but she did find a loaf of what looked like home-baked bread, some real butter and a large jar of what turned out to be the best lemon curd she'd ever tasted. She cut two half-inch slices, applied a good inch of butter and curd to one slice, placed the other on top, and pressed down till the glorious yellow goo oozed out of the sides. All the time she felt the pressure of Rosie's gaze upon her. With a sigh, she sliced the sandwich in half and pushed one section towards the girl.

'From now on you get your own, OK?' she said. 'I am not your personal caterer.'

They were just sinking their teeth into the succulent sandwiches when Ellie came into the kitchen.

'Rosie, what on earth are you eating?' she demanded.

Novello knew little about motherhood but she made a note now that if you were bothered by your kids speaking with their mouths full, you should avoid asking them questions when they were eating.

Rosie, her mouth glutinous with curd, was clearly both physically and behaviourally challenged. Novello was neither.

'My fault,' she said gooily. 'Thought she might like something to put her on till supper.'

'Put her on? There's enough cholesterol there to put her on an NHS waiting list!' snarled Ellie.

'Yeah? Sorry.'

Daphne came into the kitchen with a towel over her shoulder.

'Gosh, that looks good, Rosie. Spare a corner?'

Wordlessly, Rosie offered her the sandwich and she took a hefty bite.

'Mmm. Mrs Stonelady's curd. Heaven. I'm going for a swim, my dears. Anyone fancy a dip?'

'No, thanks,' said Ellie. 'Some letters to write.'

The prospect of seeing Feenie that evening had restimulated her guilt feelings about her neglect of her Liberata correspondence.

Rosie swallowed and tried to say something but her mother said firmly, 'You stay with me, dear. Don't want you getting a chill first day you're here.'

'Yes, Mummy.'

Over-protective, thought Novello. But maybe she had cause. None of her business anyway. She had her own protection agenda to think of. Things would be a lot easier if everyone stuck together.

'Is it really advisable to go swimming by yourself?' she asked. 'Especially in the sea.'

'I think I'll survive,' said Daphne, smiling. 'I'm a reasonably good swimmer –'

'She means she used to be the Yorkshire Overprivileged Girls Two Thousand Leagues Butterfly Champion,' interrupted Ellie.

'Sorry?' said Novello.

'Ignore her,' said Daphne. 'That is social-envy-speak for my brief membership of the county

366

under-eighteen swimming team, which is so socially non-exclusive, they even select members of police families if they're good enough. I will be all right, believe me, but if you're worried, do feel free to come along.'

'Yeah, well, I did want to take a look at the beach, you know, reconnoitre . . .'

She saw La Pascoe roll her eyes and that made up her mind.

'Mrs Pascoe . . .'

'Ellie,' said Daphne.

'. . . be sure to keep all the doors locked and try not to let Rosie out of your sight. OK?'

She saw not without pleasure the irritation on the woman's face.

'I think I'm able to look after my daughter,' she replied.

'Great. Then let's go, er, Daphne.'

Outside, the older woman strode ahead on what presumably she saw as a path but what felt like an obstacle course to Novello, stumbling over tussocks of grass, stubbing her toes against stones, and fighting off the assault of thorny branches with a malevolent life of their own.

What in the name of God am I doing here? she asked herself.

This was strictly a no-win job. Most likely there wasn't any threat, which meant all she had to look forward to was a couple of days of mutual irritation in a landscape so unattractive it merited her Irish grandmother's ultimate condemnation: *This is the kind of place a dacent woman could find herself being cheated by Protestants.*

And if by some miracle there was a threat, how the hell was she supposed to counter it? She had no authority to force the party to stick together. She supposed she really ought to have stayed close to the Pascoes at the cottage, but then if Daphne Aldermann went and got herself drowned, no doubt that would be down to her, though of course the fallout would be even more nuclear if on her return to Nosebleed she found the Pascoes, *mère et fille*, with their throats slit.

She shuddered at the prospect then assured herself firmly there wasn't much chance of that. No, if this were a real job, there would be at least two watchers, and they'd probably be men. She was a token; not a token woman exactly, more of a woman token, because she'd been selected as a token because she was a woman . . .

'Oh shit,' she said.

Ahead of her, Daphne Aldermann had fallen off a cliff.

She ran forward and looked down.

There was cause here for both relief and trepidation.

The cliff dropped away in an uninviting tumble of sandstone boulders and shale, but far from being in trouble, Daphne was descending at speed as if on a carpeted stairway.

Gingerly, Novello began to follow.

She concentrated so hard on where she was

putting her feet that she paid little attention to the beach, but when she finally reached it a quick glance north and south confirmed what she had already guessed. Not an ice cream van or a wrestler to be seen. Not even a cheating Protestant.

On the sand lay a T-shirt, sandals, a pair of shorts and a towel. Ahead, running naked into the sea, was Daphne.

Oh God, thought Novello. All this, and I've got myself a middle-aged nuddy too.

She watched long enough to confirm that at least the woman's reputed swimming prowess hadn't been oversold. Daphne ripped through the strong swell with a long easy stroke till she reached a cluster of rocks a couple of hundred yards out. Here she pulled herself out of the water, stood and waved or beckoned, then lay down on her back to soak up the sun.

Not a bad idea, thought Novello.

She lay back on the sand and closed her eyes.

She was awoken by the sound of movement close by. She opened her eyes and sat up. Daphne was towelling herself down briskly. Bit of sag and droop there, registered Novello, making a comparison with her own flat belly and gravity-defying bosom, complacently at first and then with self-reproach. Give her another two decades and two kids and what might she look like? Comparisons are odorous, her granny used to say, unless they're both the same to start with.

She realized Daphne was looking at her and

she dropped her gaze, embarrassed to have been caught running so assessing an eye over the older woman's body.

'I thought you might come in,' said Daphne. 'It's lovely. Plenty of towel for two.'

'No, thanks,' said Novello. 'You always swim nude?'

'I prefer to. Why? Does it bother you?'

Not with a fellow, it doesn't, thought Novello.

'No,' she said.

'Now I'd guess it does,' said Daphne in her pleasant easy voice. 'I'd guess that you're worried in case what you clearly find a rather uncongenial task should be further complicated by having some ageing dyke making a play for you. Please accept my assurance that I'm so straight, you could use me for architectural drawings. As Ellie keeps telling me, I am the victim of my upbringing. Life at a girls' boarding school totally removed from me any inhibition about flashing my flesh in front of my own sex, while at the same time inculcating an almost Victorian modesty under the gaze of men. Which is why I came off my rock as soon as I spotted that chap on the clifftop.'

Her head still dull with sun, it took Novello a moment to react.

Then she sat upright and demanded, 'What chap?'

'Some passing peasant, most likely, who must have thought it was his birthday. I glanced up and spotted him and then he ducked out of sight, and

I headed back for the shore. Always safest. Not to do so might imply to the simple male mind that I didn't mind being spied upon.'

Novello jumped up, took a small pair of binoculars out of her holster bag, ran to the water's edge and started scanning the clifftop.

Red stone, blue sky, sea birds soaring. The only sign of human intrusion was some kind of building perched precariously on the edge some way to the north. Bag-lady territory.

Daphne called, 'No need to get neurotic. It was probably Donald, Mrs Stonelady's son, and he's completely harmless.'

Novello ignored her. She'd caught a movement. A small adjustment of the focus and suddenly she had him sharp, just for a moment, side view, more back really, not a full profile, as he moved south along the clifftop path. Not all that big, dark hair, nothing else. She kept on watching in the hope that he'd reappear, but nothing.

Water suddenly covered her brand-new trainers as the oncoming tide rolled up the beach. You couldn't be too careful.

She hopped quickly out and returned to Daphne, removing her mobile phone from her belt.

'What's the cottage number?'

Daphne told her, adding as she dialled, 'But I doubt you'll get through. Even without the cliff, mobile signals are notoriously weak in Axness. Even the landlines aren't very reliable. Nosebleed is off as often as it's on.'

She was right. There was nothing.

Clicking the phone back onto her belt, Novello said, 'Look, I'm going to climb back up and take a look. Are you done here now?'

'I thought I'd dry off in the sun a while then head back to the cottage.'

'Good, I'll see you there.'

'Fine, but honestly, Shirley, I don't think there's any cause for alarm.'

'You're probably right, but my bosses don't like *probably*.'

She set off up the cliff. Going up was easier than coming down, though even with her gym-toughened leg muscles, she was puffing by the time she reached the top.

No sign of life along the edge running north towards Gunnery House.

She checked south too. Nothing.

Which *could* mean that the watcher, having ascertained that both non-Pascoes were safely occupied on the beach, had headed towards Nosebleed.

Feeling, without any logic, that she'd been out-manoeuvred, she set off at a trot back towards the cottage.

vii

the sirens' song

Ellie, seated on a garden chair that looked like wrought iron but yielded like foam rubber (where *did* Patrick get his garden furniture?), wearing a floppy sun hat and a long loose-fitting cotton dress, with her fingers poised over the keyboard of her laptop whose screen was displaying Chapter 3 of her Comfort Blanket story, suddenly felt like a real writer. Or at least, computer apart, like the kind of painting of a real writer that Renoir might have done in Monet's garden.

This was a considerable advance on the fraudulent feel which often stole over her in the boxroom she refused to call a study. A visiting American had told her that back home it was possible to gain membership of serious author groups as a 'pre-published writer' before you'd even set pen to paper. Ellie had laughed derisively, till she realized her friend was talking personal experience without any sign of ironic self-mockery. Her sense of hostessly responsibility, plus an instinctive sympathy with most anti-elitist ideologies, now made her sit submissively under the subsequent reproving lecture. But not all the lip-service in the world could change what she felt inside, which was that until she saw her words in print with a price tag on them she would remain a wannabe; and that if and when she finally ceased to be a wannabe, not all the out-reaching democratic arguments in the world would make her share her status with some idle plonker claiming to be 'pre-published'!

But out here, in the sun, with birds singing in the trees and Rosie close by, chattering happily to Tig and whatever other strange creatures the little dog had set free from her imagination, it seemed after all possible to think of herself as a true creator, a maker of dreams, without the hard evidence of lunches and launches and learned reviews. Perhaps, she thought, this was ESP at work, and the longed-for letter of acceptance was already dropping through her letterbox. So strong was the feeling that she went into the cottage and tried to ring home on the off chance Peter had come in since she'd left a message on the answer machine shortly after they arrived. Which turned out to be just as well as the phone was now completely dead.

Curiously, instead of irritating her, this sense of being cut off had fed her mood.

Nothing can touch me here, she thought.

But when she returned to the garden she found

she was wrong. Some electronic quirk had switched her display from the story to her unfinished letter to Bruna Cubillas. The Colombian woman's letters had rarely spoken directly of the conditions of her imprisonment, perhaps because of the fear of censorship and reprisals, perhaps because through them she was escaping to another world of domestic life with its everyday pleasures and anxieties, and she didn't want to bring her own world with her. But Ellie knew from her reading elsewhere, and from listening to those who had suffered a similar fate and made it back to freedom, that the same sun she basked in would turn Bruna's tiny cell into a foetid oven where even the cockroaches hardly had strength to crawl over the floor . . .

Angrily she punched the letter out of sight. Later. Later would do. This spirit of delight she was enjoying at the moment came so rarely that it would be churlish to suppress it. Anyway, hadn't Feenie said something about Bruna being released? If so, not much point in sending a letter to the prison. She doubted if her friend would have left a forwarding address.

She conjured up her story once more and plunged back into her revision like a dolphin into the wine-dark sea.

She'd begun this chapter with one of those extended similes the classical epicists were so fond of and she wasn't sure if it worked. Or perhaps she meant she wasn't sure how she wanted it to work – as epic simile or post-modern irony?

Or maybe simply as good honest fun! What the hell? Why should things always have to be complicated?

Let it stand!

Chapter 3

Like to the spikenard spider which casts an invisible floating web over the scented shrubs abounding the fringes of the foetid Asian swamplands in which it lives, trapping the golden bees lured there to feast on the rich exuded juices of the blossoming trees in bonds so loose that though they may not flee, they may still drink their fill and be at their sweetest when the time comes for patient Arachne to suck them dry, so Aeneas plied his guest with wine and sweetmeats, always purposing that in the end he would pay the price for the great deception which toppled Troy, but not before he had been drained of all he knew of the shifting perils of these dangerous seas.

Yet, be they never so different of race, taste, and temperament, and though they have fought long years on opposite sides, when men of arms at a camp fire share memories of battles fought, pains endured, perils survived, another invisible bond will form between them which has nothing to do with plots and schemings.

'You are truly the most resourceful of men,' said Aeneas, after listening to Odysseus's tale of how he had escaped from the cave of Polyphemus. 'And in

this instance at least, I too have cause to be grateful for your cunning, for without it, my fleet might never have come away free from the land of the Cyclops.'

'You got mixed up with them one-eyed bastards too?' exclaimed Odysseus. 'When was that?'

'About three moons after you escaped. No, do not look surprised that I am so exact. When we landed, a poor wretch came running down the beach and threw himself at our feet and prayed for mercy. He was one of yours who'd been left behind when you escaped and he was so desperate that he preferred to put himself in the hands of Trojans rather than run the risk of being eaten alive by a Cyclops.'

'Achaemenides! You're not telling me you rescued Achaemenides?'

'Yes, that was his name. It was a lucky encounter for us. He told us of your adventures, and thus forewarned we were able to make our escape, though not without a close scrape.'

'Well, I'm buggered,' said Odysseus. 'So Achaemenides survived after all. He always claimed his mother was told by the gods he was destined for great things, that he'd likely become a king one day! Well, nowt's impossible as far as that mad lot are concerned. So where's he at now? Good job I didn't run into him outside, else he'd likely have told the whole world who I was.'

Aeneas looked a little uneasy and said,

'Actually, he's not here. We had to . . . let him go.'

'Let him go? Like, you set him down somewhere and said, Off you go, lad; it's been nice knowing you?'

'Not exactly,' said Aeneas. 'The truth is when we got hit by the great storm that eventually drove us to this inhospitable place, as we rushed along before the wind which seemed at any moment like to turn us over and drive us down into the dark jaws of death, some of the men, indeed most of them, began to feel that there must be some presence among us which was offensive to the Earth-Shaker, and Achaemenides, being one of your crew who had blinded great Poseidon's son, Polyphemus, seemed the man most likely. So we held him over the side. Then, after a while, well, we . . . let him go. I'm really sorry.'

Odysseus looked grim for a moment, then his face split in a huge toothy grin and he said, 'Nay, Prince, think nowt of it. In your place, I'd have done just the same.'

'Thrown a Trojan prisoner overboard, you mean?'

'Nay. Thrown Achaemenides over! He were always a useless bugger and a right liability at sea. Know what we used to call him? Hector, after that girt brother-in-law of thine.'

'Because he was a useless bugger, you mean?' said Aeneas, ready to be offended.

'Nay! Because he was forever lolloping around, knocking Greeks over!'

Aeneas laughed, then, serious again, said, 'Alas, poor Hector. When he died, our hopes died too. A remarkable thing, though – among many other remarkable things since the debacle – I ran across his wife, Andromache. On Epirus. She's married to Helenus – you remember him? Another of Priam's sons.'

'Aye, I do. I once captured the bugger and he went into a trance and told me Troy were doomed. I thought, this one's either very clever or he's doolally, so I ransomed him quick. He's still around, is he?'

'Oh yes. He's got a nice little thing going. He's established a sort of mini Troy which he calls Chaonia.'

'I were right about him then. Bloody clever! Weren't you tempted to set up shop there too?'

Aeneas smiled. 'No, not really. I'm bound . . . elsewhere. But I'm interrupting your story. Funny how our trails keep on intertwining. Scylla and Charybdis, the Cyclops . . .'

'Aye. Bet you never heard the Sirens sing, but,' said Odysseus complacently.

'No, and from what I've heard, I understand that no man can and remain living.'

'He can if he gets his crew to stuff their ears with wax then bind him to the mast so he can't be tempted to jump over the side.'

'And that's what you did? Remarkable. You must be truly greedy for experience, Odysseus. And was it worth it? Myself, I can't imagine a song so sweet that it would cause a man steeled in war to forget all else and rush madly to discover its source.'

'You can't? Well, if I'd not been tied up, I'd have gone rushing, I tell you, no question.'

'Really? So what did it sound like, this irresistible music? Can you perhaps give me a flavour?' enquired Aeneas, faintly mocking.

'Do me best. Let's see now. It were something like this.'

And the Greek took a deep breath, threw back his head and let out a terrible rasping, gasping, raucous yell.

The din filled the cavern and before its echoes had ceased bouncing round the walls, the curtained entrance had been torn aside by Achates, and the fat Greek was surrounded by grim-faced guards with drawn swords.

'See?' said Odysseus complacently. 'Told you it worked. Brings 'em running every time.'

For a moment there was silence, then Aeneas began to laugh and the Greek laughed with him, till in a short while both men were helpless with mirth.

Unable to speak, the Prince dismissed his men with an imperious gesture. Achates paused in the entrance and looked back as though he had something to say. Then he shook his head and let the curtain fall behind him.

Aeneas refilled the goblets with red wine and the two men drank deep.

'If that was a fair example of their singing, it sounds more like an invitation to Hades than to Heaven,' said Aeneas.

'Hades? Aye, been there, done that,' said Odysseus with a shudder. 'And I'm not inclined to make any jokes about it either.'

The Prince leaned forward and looked deep into the other man's eyes.

'You are serious? You have made that journey and returned? I thought none had done that save Orpheus who braved the blackness for love.'

'Oh him,' said Odysseus dismissively. 'I got the low-down on him. Load of crap, that all-for-love business. Seems that wife of his was the jealous type and when she caught on he were using his musical charms to get his end away elsewhere, she hid his best lyre. Then she got bit by a snake afore he could find out where she'd put it, and that was why he went down below after her. But when he met Pluto and his missus, he thought he'd best go for the sympathy vote so he span that yarn about not being able to live without her. All he wanted was a quick chat – Where's me lyre? Thanks, luv, see you around – and off, but his story worked so well they said he could have her back, only he hadn't got to look back at her as he led her out of Hades. Well, there he was walking along playing his second-best lyre and all the time a few steps behind came Eurydice, and she never stopped wittering. On and on she went about his bits on the side and he needn't think this made any difference, and just wait till they got home, she was really going to give him what for. And in the end, with the daylight in sight, he thought, sod this for a lark. And he said, "Sorry, luv, didn't quite catch that," and he turned around. Bye-bye, Eurydice. It's true. Honest. On my mother's life.'

Aeneas said dryly, 'Truly I see that you are the man that all your legends claim you to be. So, what did you do in Hades? Who did you meet? What did you learn?'

'Well, funny enough, I met my old mam for a start. That were a shock. Didn't even know she were dead. Mebbe I swore on her life once too often. And I saw a lot of other women, all wives of noble husbands . . .'

'You didn't . . .' said Aeneas hesitantly. 'Did you perhaps see . . . would you know . . . Creusa, my wife, my son's dear mother, who strayed from my side as we fled burning Troy and was taken and slain by . . . say, did you see her?'

Odysseus shook his great head and said, 'Nay, Prince, I'll not lie. I didn't notice her, but there were so many, and time were short. Tell you who I did see, but. Great Achilles! Aye, he were down there, prancing round the Elysian Fields, large as life. I said to him that I were sure a great hero like him got real special treatment even down here, and you know what he said?'

'No. What did he say?' said the Prince dully, his mind still on his dead wife.

'He said he'd rather be a serf working for a landless nobody than be king of all these dead warriors. Makes you think, doesn't it? Great Achilles. Makes you think, eh?'

'Yes, I suppose it does,' said Aeneas, taking another long drink of wine. 'But you'll forgive me if I don't feel too much sympathy. If he'd never come to Troy, you'd never have beaten us. Didn't the gods proclaim it so?'

'Aye, they did.'

'And isn't it true that his mother sent him away to hide on Skyros disguised as a girl because she knew that he would die if he came to Troy? And was it not the subtle and cunning Odysseus who followed him there and found him out and made him join the Greek force? Oh, you have much to answer for, my friend, both at the start and at the end of this tragic business.'

He stared gloomily at the fat Greek, and suddenly the old soldiers' bond which had grown between them felt very weak.

'Hang about,' said Odysseus. 'You can't argue with the gods. You don't imagine any of us would have given up ten years of our lives to fight over a daft tart if we'd had any say in it? I certainly wanted no part of it, even though I'd taken an oath with a lot of other daft buggers who were wooing her to defend the rights of whichever of us got her in the end. When I heard that she'd been snatched and Menelaus was calling in our markers and going after her, I let on I was doolally and

383

went around clucking like a chicken and pecking corn. Well, that didn't work, for all my famous smartness. So I thought, right, if you can't beat 'em, join 'em, and let's see if we can't get this mad business over and done with and all be home for the winter panegyris.'

'You were still responsible for discovering Achilles, without whom none of this could have happened,' accused Aeneas.

'Come on!' protested the Greek. 'You make it sound like summat special. Well, it weren't. Any idiot could have found him out. I mean, think about it. There he was, disguised as a lass among all these other lasses. Good thinking, eh? Except that he's seven foot tall and he's got a dong like Big Ajax's spear! You know what the lasses on Skyros used to call him when he hid among them? Stiffy! And it weren't for the way he danced.'

Ellie laughed out loud at her own joke and sat back and sipped at her lemonade.

Why did she want to be a writer? friends had asked her, though rarely staying for an answer. Which was just as well as there were so many answers, mostly disingenuous, none complete.

Favourite at the 'serious' end of the market was that you were trying to make sense of, impose a pattern on, apparently senseless and disorderly human experience.

But fiction writing, as she'd indicated to Daphne

in the garden at Rosemont yesterday, was also an extension of experience, indeed at times a substitute for it, as well of course as an escape from it. Sitting here in the sunshine, laughing at her own invention, she felt she could offer one answer to the question without any prevarication.

She wanted to be a writer because a writer could do anything, go anywhere, answer any question. Here was a world of profit and delight to equal that which tempted Faustus. Here was dominion which stretched as far as doth the mind of man. Maybe as with Faustus the price to be paid was your soul, or at least that part of you which fitted you to live in the real world. For she had tasted the sweet poison and knew that more than pipes of opium or lines of coke, when you drank the waters of Hippocrene, all that was actual, people and problems, time and troubles, trees and green grass, presently departed from you and left you falling down through the clouds to land lightly on the world of your own creation. Here she was God moving through Her Garden, and if from time to time her creatures exercised their free will, why, that was part of the deal too.

'Mrs Pascoe . . . *Ellie*! Are you OK?'

Suddenly she was back in the garden of Nosebleed Cottage, summoned there by a flushed and anxious-looking Shirley Novello.

'Yes, of course I'm OK. Have you been running? You really should be careful in this heat.'

'You said you'd stay inside and lock all the doors,' said Novello accusingly.

'*You* instructed me to lock the doors, which in fact I have done,' said Ellie. 'As for staying inside, on a day like this? You must be joking!'

'Yeah, I'm full of jokes. Where's Rosie?'

'She's . . .'

Nowhere.

The birdsong persisted, but the chatter of the child's voice as she played in her own parallel universe was no longer its descant.

And now the trees and green grass did swim away from Ellie Pascoe and leave her falling down through the clouds.

'Rosie! Rosie!' called Novello. 'Where are you? *Rosie!*'

Silence. The desperate cry had silenced even the birds.

Then there came a barking, followed a moment later by Tig. And blessedly, somewhere beyond the high garden wall, they heard the girl's voice calling, 'Goodbye, goodbye,' and a moment later she came running through the garden door, in her hand a posy of small white flowers.

For a second Ellie felt a huge gratitude to Novello, as if it was the power of her summons alone which had brought Rosie back to her. But almost instantaneously this turned into an equal and opposite resentment at the unnecessary shock to her system administered by the stupid woman's sudden arrival and disruptive urgency.

Rosie was the beneficiary of this reversal. Instead of reproving her for straying, Ellie said, 'Hello, darling. You mustn't get too hot. Come and have a glass of lemonade. Are those for me?'

'Yes, the lady picked them for me and Nina.'

Novello, who had gone to the doorway and looked out, turned round and said, 'Nina? Who's Nina?'

Ellie, who was studying the wild flowers, looked up and said, slightly mocking, 'Rosie's friend that no one else can see.'

Novello frowned at her. She had the kind of strong face which a frown made even more striking, thought Ellie grudgingly.

'And the lady who picked the flowers? Does she have a name too?' demanded the DC.

Rosie considered this then said, 'Well, she had a moustache so I think she might be the lady you told me about. Cucumber.'

'Cucumber?' said Ellie, puzzled.

'Think she might mean Uncumber,' said Novello reluctantly. 'She's a saint . . .'

'Yes, I know,' said Ellie suspiciously. 'Wilgefortis. I'm just wondering why on earth you were telling Rosie about her. Not missionary work, I hope.'

'It just came up,' said Novello. 'And I'm just wondering how on earth you know about her?'

Cheeky, thought Ellie.

'As a well-known atheist, you mean?' she said. 'Well, you see, my dear, just because I don't subscribe to any of the primitive superstitions doesn't mean I can't be entertained by their more risible legends.'

Novello's face flushed with an angry offence which it would have done Father Kerrigan's heart good to see, but which made Ellie feel guilty.

Time maybe for an olive twig.

She said, 'Rosie, dear, this lady you mentioned with the moustache, is she like Nina? Or could Shirley here see her too?'

There. She'd used her first name!

The girl examined Novello assessingly over the rim of her lemonade glass, then gave her a complicitous smile as if to remind her they were in the same gang.

'Maybe she could,' she said. 'And maybe Nina too.'

Baffled, the policewoman looked to Ellie for assistance.

'Probably Mrs Stonelady,' she mouthed, then returned to her examination of the posy, the greater part of which consisted of plants with white-leaved yellow-centred florets blooming in profusion on single stalks.

'How lovely,' she exclaimed. 'And how fitting. Yarrow. I think these are yarrow.'

'Yarrow? What's that?' said Novello.

Ellie smiled into the posy, not her daughter's smile, which had been conspiratorial and inclusive, but an inward-looking and secretive smile.

'I will pick the smooth yarrow that my figure may be more elegant, that my lips may be warmer, that my voice may be more cheerful,' she murmured. 'May my voice be like a sunbeam, may my lips be like the juice of the strawberries. May I be an island in the sea, may I be a hill on the land, may I be a star when the moon wanes, may I be a staff to the weak one.'

She paused and now her gaze lifted to look straight at Novello.

'I shall wound every man,' she declared in a strong clear voice. 'No man shall wound me.'

The dog, which had been sniffing at Novello's trainers with a foot-fetishist's enthusiasm, now cocked his leg and began to pee.

Oh God, thought Novello. Trapped in a cottage called Nosebleed with a gang of skinny-dipping, poetry-reciting nutters, not to mention a weird kid and an incontinent dog.

This could be a long, long day.

viii

we galloped all three

Peter Pascoe opened the door of his house, picked up the mail from the mat and went through into the living room.

The answerphone display was on, indicating one message. He pressed the *Play* button and sorted his mail from Ellie's as he waited for the machine to start.

'Hi, it's me. Just to say we've arrived safely, quite a miracle when you consider the way Daphne drives. The bothy is lovely, makes our place look a slum, couldn't you take up growing roses? Rosie thinks it's heaven, and she's taken a shine to *your* infant prodigy, which isn't surprising I suppose when you consider what they've got in common, like grating voices and no social graces. Only joking, only *just* joking anyway, still can't see why we couldn't have had Dennis Seymour or that nice boy, Hat, no problem with sleeping arrangements, even Rosie has got her own room. So, everything's fine. You can enjoy your bachelor delights with a clear conscience. By the way, if there's anything for me from you-know-who, if it's a package, stick it on top of the wardrobe and say nothing till I get home. But if it's a letter, open it at once! Love you. 'Bye.'

Pascoe stood, looking at the slim white envelope in his hand.

Shit. He wished it hadn't come. OK, it was the letter not the package, but it might just contain a formal rejection and a request for the return postage if she wanted her script back. Did publishers do things like that? He'd never met any, not even professionally, though presumably some were penny-pinching bastards. Maxwell had been a publisher, hadn't he? And he'd certainly pinched a lot more than pennies. A good sign was that the envelope was handwritten, implying a personal interest. Or maybe they were just economizing on secretaries.

Only one way to find out.

He tore open the envelope and took out the single sheet it contained.

The letter was unambiguous but he read it three times just to be sure.

Then he shouted out, 'Yes, yes, yes, yes, YES!' like a porn movie star having a climax, and grabbed the receiver.

There are few things more frustrating than riding from Ghent to Aix and finding nobody in.

He let the phone ring at Nosebleed Cottage for several minutes before putting down the receiver.

Still, a pleasure delayed was a pleasure heightened, wasn't that what they said in the sex manuals?

The doorbell rang. It was Wield.

'Come in, come in,' said Pascoe. 'Grab a seat. What would you like to drink? Tea? Beer? Champagne?'

The sergeant looked at him curiously and said, 'Tea'll do. You're very bouncy. Tracked down Lord Lucan, or what?'

Pascoe was tempted to share his news, then thought, no, no one should hear this before Ellie, not even that doyen of discretion, Edgar Wield.

'No. That's tomorrow, isn't it? Today he just wants us to find Kelly Cornelius. How'd you get on?'

'Interesting.'

Wield described his adventures in the park, concluding, 'Then finally just when I was thinking of packing it in, I saw Old Joe, you know, the bus-station beggar who always tries to get nicked for Christmas. He was just coming into the park from the town side. He says there's a lull about teatime and he likes to take a kip in the sun before he does the homeward-bound shift. He did the same yesterday and yes, he remembered Kelly Cornelius. Good description. Lovely girl, legs all the way to heaven, was how he put it. I said I hoped he wasn't turning into a dirty old man, clocking girls' legs, and he said he couldn't help it as she was on a bike, moving at speed, with her skirt trailing round her neck.'

'Nice picture,' said Pascoe. 'So, the bike again.'

'I headed back to the cricketers then. The young lad, the gormless one I mentioned before, he was coming away. Said it was boring. I remember the feeling, standing around at long stop all day, never getting a bowl, and out first ball. I thought, mebbe not so gormless after all. This time I listened to him. He's definite not only that he saw Cornelius on a bike, but that he saw the old woman she'd spoken to by the canal on the same bike, coming from the direction of the car park, and heading up the rise towards the public bogs.'

'Before or after they spoke?'

'After. And when he saw Kelly a bit later, she were shooting down the track from the bogs. She went across the grass, which impressed him as it's against the regulations and a parky chased her. At least he assumed it must be a parky as why would anyone else bother?'

'Nice logic. Definitely not so gormless. This old woman, how old would that be?'

'I wondered about that too. At his age anyone over twenty who doesn't look like Cornelius or Michael Owen probably qualifies as old. I asked him if she was older than me, say. He thought a bit then said, mebbe.'

Pascoe was feeling an uneasiness, the same kind of uneasiness which had made him want to focus his attention on Cornelius after the attempted abduction of Ellie, and he guessed he was going to need the same obliquity of view to detect its source.

A prolonged peal at the doorbell which could only harbinger Dalziel prevented any experiment.

'Sorry I'm late. Had to go back to the factory,' he said. 'Ee, I could murder a cup of tea and a wad.'

Pascoe brewed some tea to the required strength and with some trepidation dug out the last six inches of his favourite walnut cake, a slice of which he'd been looking forward to enjoying in bed with his hot chocolate nightcap. Nothing could compensate for the absence of Ellie's warm and willing body from his side, but walnut cake, whose crumby presence she absolutely forbade in the bedroom, was a small consolation.

Wield refused, which was a good start. But the Fat Man said, 'Aye, why not?' and sliced himself a good three inches.

'Right,' he said, after washing down his first cetacean mouthful with a torrent of hot black tea. 'How'd you get on?'

Wield repeated his story, then Pascoe outlined his investigations, pausing for comment when he mentioned the car.

'Lots of blue Golfs around,' said Wield. 'Could be coincidence.'

'Coincidence is when I get into bed with Maggie Thatcher,' said Dalziel. 'More loose ends here than at a monk's wedding, and I don't like the way some of 'em tie up. And if she's got her car, why's she end up on a bike? Were that all planned in advance?'

'Not in any detail, I imagine. But she knew she

was going sometime, so she shoved her favourite photos in her bag just in case she didn't come back. When her accomplice told her about the bike plan, she jumped at it. Cool as you like, she drifts off to the shops to buy some basic female survival gear plus a knapsack to carry it in while the old bird puts the bike in the ladies. Then it's over the hills and faraway with Sempernel's men flat-footed. I think she probably enjoyed it.'

'Aye. Smart lass from the sound of it,' said Dalziel. 'Smarter than you two buggers if that's all you've managed to find out.'

Wield and Pascoe exchanged glances, then the DCI said mildly, 'I thought starting from nothing we did OK, sir.'

'You didn't start from nothing, lad. You started from knowing that she's taken off and that's where you've finished from the sound of it. All this fancy detective work you've been doing, has it left either of you with any notion where she's gone to? No, don't bother to answer. God, it's enough to drive a man to gluttony.'

As if to illustrate the depths of his distress at their incompetence, he seized the remaining chunk of walnut cake and thrust it into his mouth.

Hope the fat bastard gets indigestion, thought Pascoe surlily.

'OK, sir,' he said. 'When you've finished chewing, are you going to tell us what you found out?'

There had to be something. The Fat Man never

sneered at others' empty hands unless he himself was the bearer of trophies.

Another draught of tea, and he said, 'George Ollershaw. I knew he might be worth a look.'

'Actually,' said Pascoe, 'I think it was me who suggested you look at him. So, is he an accomplice? Could he have set up the escape? Hey, Wieldy, this old woman in the park, did the boy say there was anything odd about her, the way she moved, I mean?'

'George Ollershaw in drag?' exclaimed Dalziel in mock-outrage. 'He's a member of the Gents and a Mason!'

He bellowed a laugh, then said, 'No, it's a nice thought, but you're barking up the wrong tree. Listen and I'll tell you a story, then mebbe you'll tell me what it means. Five years ago the old Nortrust Building Society demutualized itself. This means it stopped being owned by its members, that is them as saved with it or got mortgage loans from it, and became a bank, a public company, with shares on sale on the stock exchange and paying dividends to its shareholders, most of who didn't have savings with it or take out mortgages from it. You with me?'

'As it's happened innumerable times in the past decade, I think we all grasp the principle, sir,' said Pascoe.

'Is that right? Well, I'm glad you grasp summat. It seems that Ollershaw had a lot of his money invested in the building society, so he had a vote like any other investor, but he kept in the background during the debate about the change, only coming into prominence later after it was all signed, sealed and on the point of being delivered. And now it turned out there were a problem. You see, it seems the Nortrust, like a lot of the old building societies and savings banks, had been founded way back by some benevolent buffer who felt the workers would work a sight better if they learnt the art of regular saving. That way they could take on the kind of long-term debt like a mortgage, which made them even more dependent on a regular wage, and what's more they'd have some chance of repaying it.'

This, to Pascoe, seemed a somewhat cynical way of looking at the motives of Victorian philanthropy, but he set aside the ethical discussion for a later date.

'So where is this leading, sir?' he asked.

'Don't be impatient,' said Dalziel, looking sadly at the empty cake plate. 'I'm getting there fast as me failing strength can manage. This problem which no one had spotted was that the founder of the Nortrust Building Society had provided the original building, that great black granite job on the old High Street where the bank's headquarters is now, and where our Kelly worked. Plus, as the building society prospered and needed branches all over Mid-Yorkshire, he provided these too. Very philanthropic fellow, but sharp with it. Seems that he didn't actually give these buildings to Nortrust, lock, stock, and freehold. No, he gave them on a perpetual lease with a peppercorn ground rent. But, and here's the catch, in the head lease of each such building was a clause setting out the purposes for which the building was to be used. Which is, not to labour the point, as a building society. Legally it could be argued, and with good chance of success, so I'm told, that by converting from a mutual to a PLC, the terms of the lease were broken and the freeholder was entitled to evict the leaseholder and regain full rights over the properties.'

'Let me guess,' said Pascoe. 'George Ollershaw turned out to be the freeholder.'

'Right on. Yes, our George had been quietly acquiring all these apparently valueless freeholds over the years, and he waited till the changeover to bank status was irrevocable, but before the share flotation had taken place, then he pounced. Now Nortrust had a real problem. It wasn't just that if they went to court, they might well lose and then have to renegotiate leases with George or find new premises, it was the devastating effect that news of this glitch was likely to have on confidence in the new bank and therefore its share price. It was all sorted quietly. George ended up with his pockets stuffed with share options, a seat on the board, and a hefty salary as the head of the Investment Department. At least he seemed to have proved he'd got the credentials for that job!'

Pascoe shook his head as though to dislodge a

persistent fly and said, 'Very interesting, but what's it got to do with Kelly Cornelius, sir?'

To his surprise, Dalziel said, 'Haven't the faintest idea, but it could have something to do with your missus. Distantly.'

'Ellie?'

'You've not got another in the attic, have you?'

'Could you stop being enigmatic, please,' said Pascoe forcefully. 'What do you mean?'

'I wish I knew, lad. It's just that when you get mixed up with twisted minds like Pimpernel, you start making crazy connections. Thing is, the guy who founded the Nortrust Building Society way back was one Mungo Macallum, the old-time arms king, and, more to the point mebbe, he was yon Feenie Macallum's father, and she's a playmate of your Ellie, I gather?'

'Yes,' said Pascoe slowly. 'She runs this Liberata thing, human rights, women in prison, that sort of thing . . . but I don't see how or why . . .'

But he was beginning to see something, as elusive and quick-melting as the first flake of a blizzard.

'Me neither,' said Dalziel. 'Something Ivor said to me rang a bell though. That's why I went back to the factory to dig it out. She'd checked this Feenie to see if anything was known. Only thing of interest to us was a dangerous-driving conviction a few years back. She ran this guy off the road and when our lads got there, it turned out they knew each other and he was screaming attempted murder and she was screaming natural justice! Well, he quietened down later and so did she, and it came down to dangerous driving. But thing is, the guy was George Ollershaw and for the past God knows how many years, he'd been Feenie's accountant and financial adviser.'

'Oh shit,' said Pascoe.

His vision had cleared. He was seeing an ancient sit-up-and-beg bicycle, leaning drunkenly against the *Pompon de Paris* outside his front door.

'Wieldy,' he said. 'The boy in the park, or Old Joe, did either of them describe the bike?'

'Not Joe. Too busy with the legs. But the lad said it were pretty ancient, not a racer or a mountain bike, certainly. Heavy-looking. Oh, and it was painted what he called a cacky-brown. Might have meant khaki, or mebbe not.'

'So what's on your mind, lad?' demanded Dalziel.

He told him about the bike.

The Fat Man looked pleased.

'Well, that does it, eh? Too many connections for coincidence. I think we ought to have a word with Feenie Macallum. Any idea where she lives, Peter?'

'Excuse me, I've got to ring Ellie.'

Pascoe went to the phone and dialled the number of Nosebleed Cottage.

It rang and rang but as before there was no reply.

'Oh shit!' he exclaimed again. 'Novello's mobile. I've got the number somewhere . . . Wieldy?'

Wield repeated the number without thought. Pascoe dialled.

'Unobtainable,' he said, crashing the receiver down.

'Pete, lad. No need to get your knickers in a twist. Whatever's going off here, and it's still all guesswork, Ellie and Rosie are well out of it. Good move that, dumping them out in the sticks.'

'You don't know, do you?' said Pascoe savagely. 'Of course you don't. That's why you were asking where Feenie Macallum lives. Well, I can tell you. She's got a house out at Axness. That's right. Where Daphne Aldermann's cottage is. In fact she bought it off Feenie. They're right on her sodding doorstep!'

ix

coitus interruptus

'Come in, come in,' said Feenie Macallum. 'No need to keep your dog on its lead, my dear. Carla will set him right if he misbehaves. That is one of the reasons God put bitches on the earth, to keep unruly dogs in good order, wouldn't you agree, Mrs Aldermann?'

Rosie, still wary after her earlier encounter with the old woman at her most fierce, hesitated a moment before releasing Tig, while Daphne answered Feenie's question with the blank politeness of a royal being offered a bag of chips.

Ellie said, 'You've still not sold the panelling, then?'

Feenie said, 'Not yet. I'll strip it out eventually, I suppose, but an architect friend warned me that with the bit of subsidence we've had already, in some places it's probably all that's holding the walls up.'

She gave the heavy oak panelling in question a hearty whack with her fist, setting up a disapproving tremor in her father's portrait.

'That's not a John, is it?' said Daphne, peering up at the picture.

'No, it's a painting. Want to buy it for your downstairs loo?'

'They're a handsome pair. Did they come with the house?'

Daphne in regal mode was quite undentable, thought Ellie, and the sooner Feenie caught on to this, the better. As a writer she supposed she ought to start treating such skirmishes among her friends as fodder for the next magnum opus, but while she remained pre-published, it might be as well to act as peacemaker.

'Feenie's father built, or rather rebuilt, Gunnery,' she said. 'As I believe I mentioned.'

'Ah, I see. So your father had to buy his pictures, Miss Macallum?' said Daphne. 'And his furniture too, I daresay?'

'Indeed. And his daughter has had to sell it,' said Feenie. 'Funny thing, life, Mrs Aldermann. Perhaps one day you may have to try it.'

'These are Feenie's parents,' said Ellie firmly, trying to draw a line.

'Really?' murmured Daphne, as if talking to herself. 'How interesting. I wouldn't have guessed. So very handsome.'

There was a low growl, coming, happily, not from the old woman's throat but from Carla, her Border collie, which had just trotted into the entrance then stopped dead on spotting Tig.

The two animals eyeballed each other for a long

moment, then began a slow advance till, just before the head-on collision, they each diverted a fraction and kept going till they stood side by side. Now a gentle almost oenophilic sniffing of ends began which looked like it might go on forever till suddenly Carla span round, body tense, like a goosed *grande dame*, and gave the terrier a hearty buffet to the left ear. Tig, with no pretence at chivalry, instantly replied in kind. Ellie thought, oh shit, here beginneth World War Three, as the two animals started racing round the room in parallel, hurling mouthfuls of glistening teeth at each other's throats as they ran.

'Good, that's all right then,' said Feenie briskly. 'But why don't you take them outside, child, before they destroy what little's left of the furniture. Come round the back when you're ready. There'll be some lemonade.'

She turned and led the way out of the entrance hall with Daphne in close attendance. Ellie paused to confirm what Feenie had recognized immediately, that the two dogs were simply playing. Their gambols took them out of the front door. Rosie, eager to join in, followed.

Ellie looked at Shirley Novello, who said, 'It's OK, I'll keep an eye on them.'

'Thanks,' said Ellie. 'And I'll keep an eye on those two.'

They shared a brief moment of understanding, then Novello went back out into the sunshine.

Now Ellie followed the other two through the

house. Feenie hadn't been joking when she referred to what was left of the furniture. Even with only the vague memory of a single visit more than two years earlier to go on, she was sure these wide-open spaces had once been occupied by heavy Victorian bookcases and bureaux and tables and chairs, while the discoloured squares and rectangles which marked the walls like blocked-up windows left no room for ambiguity about vanishing pictures.

Feenie and Daphne had come to a halt by a french window giving out onto a long terrace, at either end of which, mounted on concrete plinths, stood a pair of three-inch mortars.

'We can sit outside, if you don't mind marble,' said Feenie. 'Used to say it gave you piles when I was a girl.'

'Marble's fine,' said Daphne, stepping out. 'Are those things real?'

'Real, and actually used in the Great War, my father used to claim,' said Feenie.

'I'm surprised you haven't got rid of them,' said Ellie. 'They must be worth a bit to a museum.'

'Probably. But I've no desire to follow in Daddy's footsteps and make money out of selling arms. Their place is at the bottom of the sea and that's where they'll end up.'

Such certainty, thought Ellie.

Daphne was kneeling on the bench running beneath the Italianate balustrade so that she could admire the view.

'What a splendid outlook. I do so love the sea,' she said.

'So do I, in its place,' said Feenie. 'Unfortunately it seems to think its place ought to be here.'

Ellie was taking in the near view.

'Good Lord,' she said. 'There's bits missing since I was last here.'

'Yes. I think we still had the FOP then, though it was already out of bounds.'

'FOP?' said Daphne.

'Forward observation post,' said Feenie. 'The Great War broke out while the house was being restored and my father ordered the construction of an observation post on the edge of the cliff, so that a watch could be kept for German invaders. He even had an old Maxim gun mounted there, plus ammunition. That FOP went sometime in the thirties, despite all that he spent on sea defences, but he built another during the Second World War a bit further back. That's the one you'll remember, Ellie.'

'Yes, it was sagging a bit, I recall. But you've still got the Command Post, I see.'

She was looking towards the roof of the concrete and glass pavilion, visible over the rampant shrubbery away to the left.

'Yes. But the sea is chewing away at the sandstone round the granite, and I'm advised that eventually, even if a stack remains, the pavilion will go. It is already too dangerous to enter. Indeed, the local authority have made it clear that I personally will be responsible for the safety of anyone straying beyond their marker fence, so please do not be tempted. It really is very dangerous.'

Not like Feenie to give a toss for bureaucratic pronouncements, thought Ellie.

Daphne peered at the line of garishly red plastic and exclaimed, 'So that's what that is. And the danger area starts there? But it's so close!'

'Come back next year, it will be a lot closer,' said Feenie.

'Is there really nothing to be done? I'm so very sorry. Your childhood home . . . It must be devastating.'

Feenie studied her keenly for satire, found none, and said briskly, 'Don't upset yourself, my dear. While I would have preferred to sell the place and get the money, it's not unfitting that a house based on the proceeds of death and destruction should itself end up as a pile of worthless rubble. Of course, I take care to remove anything which can be turned into cash in advance of the sea's approach. The Command Post was stripped some time ago, and as you may have noticed I have already started the house down the same road. So it's not all loss. Ah, what excellent timing. I was just going to suggest a drink. That's kind of you.'

To Ellie's surprise, a woman she recognized as Wendy Woolley had come out onto the terrace carrying a wooden tray on which stood a selection of glasses, a pitcher of lemonade and a bottle of gin. She gave Ellie a shy smile then put the tray down on the marble bench.

'Mrs Woolley, Ellie you know, of course. And this is Mrs Aldermann, one of my . . .'

She paused long enough to let *tenants* hang in the air, then completed, 'Neighbours.'

'Yes. Hello. I heard you mention, I think you said the Command Post, Miss Macallum? Is that what you call the pavilion on the cliff? I was wondering if it was still possible to take a walk down there for the view . . .'

'Certainly not,' said Feenie firmly. 'I thought I'd made it clear, it is far too dangerous. Anyone penetrating beyond the council's fence does so at their own peril. Now, how are we doing for time?'

'I'll check. There are a few problems, I think, but . . .'

She started to speak in a low voice, with Feenie listening attentively.

'Who is that?' hissed Daphne in Ellie's ear. 'Mrs Danvers? Or just an ageing tweenie?'

'No. She's a member of Liberata. In fact, she's our new secretary.'

'Good Lord. And does she do the laundry too, or is that the treasurer's job?'

'She's only brought a tray of drinks in, for God's sake,' said Ellie defensively.

Wendy Woolley went back through the french door and Feenie rejoined the others, saying, 'Sorry about that. I don't entertain much nowadays and things tend to get rusty in the kitchen.'

Was this figurative or literal? wondered Ellie.

'And of course it's so hard to get the staff these days,' said Daphne.

'You find it so? Well, certainly people are getting more choosy about who they work for,' said Feenie. 'It's called human rights. I personally have no problem.'

'No? I suppose a lot depends on how willing one is to exploit one's acquaintance,' said Daphne. 'Look who's here!'

The two dogs came gambolling down the side of the house with Rosie in hot pursuit and Novello following more sedately, though looking just as hot.

The animals shot under the warning fence and Rosie would have followed had not Feenie bellowed, 'You there, child! No further!'

Instant obedience, no questioning; I really must ask Feenie to teach me the trick, thought Ellie.

'Now stay in sight and let Miss, I'm sorry I've forgotten your name, have a drink.'

'Novello. Shirley Novello,' gasped the WDC, flopping down on the marble bench. 'Jesus, it's hot out there.'

With the sun sinking down the western sky, the seaward side of the house was pleasantly shaded. Feenie, who was looking to the east with a keen eye, said, 'Yes, it does feel rather close. I think there's some nasty weather coming. Forecast was fine for another forty-eight hours, but I daresay they've got it wrong again.'

Ellie could see little in the uninterruptedly blue

sky to cause concern. True, where it met the sea, the blue smudged into gentian violet, but that must be halfway over to the continent, which had nothing to do with here.

A polite cough announced the return of Wendy Woolley, who murmured to Feenie, 'All's well. She says about twenty minutes.'

'Excellent. Do come and sit down. I don't think you've met Shirley. I was just going to pour the drinks. How do you like it, Mrs Aldermann? With or without?'

Daphne, disconcerted by this shattering of her mental picture of Wendy Woolley slaving over an open fire in some medieval kitchen, opted for *with*, as did everyone else, thus leaving unanswered the question whether *without* meant you got only lemonade or only gin.

They sat and drank and talked. After a while, Daphne and Feenie settled to a wary neutrality whose politenesses were as entertaining as its breaches. Wendy Woolley and Shirley Novello said little but seemed to be enjoying themselves, while Ellie was observing them all with what started as a novelist's sharp objectivity but after three strong *withs* mellowed into something surprisingly like affection.

Feenie suddenly said, 'It's going to be far too warm to eat inside. Let's bring the table out here. Volunteers, please.'

They all followed her into the dining room, where what proved to be a battered table-tennis table stood covered by a cloth which Ellie was sure had been half of the french window curtainings last time she was here. It was elegantly set with silver cutlery, clear crystal glasses and fine Spode side plates, all in designs rather more modern than Ellie would have expected Mungo Macallum to have chosen for his household. Daphne seemed particularly struck by them, but Feenie quickly gathered them all up into a cardboard box which she covered with the curtain/cloth, then set the four younger women one at each corner of the table, and supervised its carriage out onto the terrace. Shirley and Wendy were then sent back to bring the chairs, which ranged in style from rickety Chippendale to folding canvas.

Rosie came onto the terrace from time to time to top up her liquid level with lemonade, then shot off again to join in the games of the inexhaustible Tig and Carla. Ellie kept an eye on her until persuaded that Feenie's prohibition against trespassing beyond the marker fence was stamped in the grain, then let herself relax into the pleasure of the moment.

Daphne, leaning over the balustrade, was saying what a beautiful garden this must once have been.

'Indeed,' said Feenie. 'No expense spared. Plants begged, borrowed or stolen from Asia to the Antipodes.'

'You disapprove of that too?'

Feenie shook her head.

'Not at all. Seeds and botanical specimens are the least culpable of cargoes and usually obtained with the minimum of exploitation or despoliation. When I was a child, playing in the garden was like a living geography lesson. I could actually see and smell and touch many plants that other children could only read about in books.'

'Oh, how Patrick would have loved it,' exclaimed Daphne.

'Your husband?'

'Yes. He's a horticulturalist.'

'Is he now? For some reason I thought he must be a stockbroker. Well, well. Look, as you can see, the garden's been allowed to go to rack and ruin, partly because I had better things to do with my money, partly because it hardly seemed worthwhile trimming and spraying and pruning what was eventually going to tumble into the sea. But I do grow increasingly sentimental in age and if any time when your husband is at Nosebleed, he feels like coming out here and helping himself to seeds or cuttings, do feel free. It would be nice to think that the best of this place might survive.'

'How very kind,' said Daphne. 'He would love it, I know.'

This moment of rapprochement might have been hard for such natural combatants to sustain, but at that moment a deep cracked voice said, 'This where you got to then? Nobody tells me owt.'

Standing at the french window, bearing a broad

tray with several steaming dishes on it, was the gnarled and wizened figure of Mrs Stonelady.

That's where the stew went! thought Novello.

That's who's in charge of the kitchen! thought Ellie.

Hurriedly, Feenie threw the cloth over the table and began arranging the cutlery and glasses.

'Plates are back there if anyone can walk,' said Mrs Stonelady, setting her tray down.

Novello beat Wendy to it by a short head. When she returned, Feenie was organizing the others into their seats. She set the plates down in front of the old woman, who picked one up and dipped a ladle into the largest dish. But before she could serve, Daphne plucked the plate out of her hand, turned it upside down and examined it closely.

'Unless there has been an amazing coincidence,' she said, 'these are my plates from Nosebleed. And the cutlery too. And the glasses. And, I presume, the stew itself!'

'That's right,' said Feenie, unabashed. 'I got rid of the good stuff from here years ago, and though I'm sure you don't mind roughing it a bit, I didn't think you'd care to eat and drink off the bits and pieces I've kept for everyday. So I asked Mrs Stonelady to help me out. You don't mind, do you? We'll take great care of everything and if you're really worried, you can supervise the washing-up.'

This, thought Ellie, is make or break point.

Daphne shook her head in disbelief, then threw it back and let out a long peal of laughter.

'This beats all,' she said. 'Am I providing the wine as well as the glasses?'

'There's no need to be offensive,' said Feenie huffily. 'There are still a few bottles in my father's cellar. Perhaps you'd care to try this for a start.'

From under the marble bench she drew an opened claret bottle whose label had long since degenerated beyond legibility, but whose quality had Daphne's eyes popping with pleasure.

'My word,' she said. 'I don't know how your father was with pictures, but he knew how to choose wine.'

'He knew how to spend money,' said Feenie dryly. 'You asked experts what was the best and you bought it. Perhaps you'd care to pour the rest of us a little if you feel able to share it. Ellie, is the child of an age where she'd like a taste, or do you subscribe to that strange English custom of postponing the legitimate experience of alcohol even further than the legitimate experience of sex?'

Before Ellie could answer, Rosie, who'd reluctantly allowed herself to be drawn away from the dogs to the table, said, 'Please, Miss Macallum, I have tried it but it tasted sour and it made me silly so may I just have lemonade?'

Feenie said, 'There was a time when children waited till they were addressed before answering, but it wasn't all that good a time, and yours was an excellent answer, so stick with lemonade by all means, but take a care of Mrs Aldermann's fine glass.'

Mrs Stonelady's stew was as delicious as forecast. They mopped up the gravy with hunks of bread too freshly baked to be cut neatly, and when they had eaten their fill, they took a long rest before the promised pudding, leaning back in their dangerous chairs and sipping their wine which had changed in colour and style through at least four bottles, all anonymous, all superb.

Ellie felt as relaxed as she had done in a long time. All the pains of life, pinpricks and bare bodkins alike, seemed dreams in a troubled sleep from which she had at last awoken. She let her gaze drift fondly round the table. What a gamut of company was here! In age, in background, in temperament, in outlook, in profession, what a range of difference, yet what harmony. She experienced a surge of affection which took them all in. Even Novello. If the Ancient Mariner could bless the sea snakes unawares, why should she have a problem with the WDC? She leaned back against her creaking chair and smiled benignly at the universe.

Rosie, ever sensitive to her mother's moods, said if the pudding was going to be much longer coming, would it be all right if she went and played with the dogs?

Ellie said, 'Darling, we're not at home, we're guests of Miss Macallum. This is her table. It's her you should ask if you can get down.'

Rosie looked at the old woman fearfully and repeated her request with no great ring of confidence.

Feenie considered for a moment then her face broke into a wide smile.

'Of course you may, my dear. But don't go out of earshot else you may miss your mother's call when the pudding comes. Mrs Stonelady's doing us her bread-and-butter but in case you don't like that, I've got chocolate ice cream especially for you. Of course, you may have both if you prefer.'

Rosie, unable to keep the surprise out of her voice, said, 'Thank you very much, Miss Macallum,' and made a speedy exit.

Wine-mellow, Ellie said, 'Getting soft in your old age, Feenie?'

Feenie said, 'When you've seen as many sad children as I have, you don't miss chances to bring a smile to a young face. And let us have less of the old age. I hope I am still a long way from the point where my descendants need to book me a place in a Home. In any case, Ellie, be kind to your girl now and when your time comes, at least she'll make it a good Home.'

Like a sudden squall in a blue sky, thoughts of her father darkened Ellie's mind. She raised her glass to her lips to hide her feelings, but Daphne saw and touched her arm comfortingly, and Feenie's sharp eyes caught the interplay.

'Ellie, I believe I've said something crass. I'm sorry. Tell us about it.'

For God's sake, it's the last thing I want to talk about, thought Ellie indignantly. Then realized in fact it wasn't. Haltingly at first, then with increasing openness, she began to talk about her father's decline into Alzheimer's and her mother's stratagems for dealing with it. Soon they were exchanging reminiscences and analyses of their relationship with their parents, confiding in each other like a group of old and trusted friends. And gradually the discussion widened and lightened and eventually, at whose instigation it was impossible to say, took a distinctly raunchy turn. Maybe it was Feenie opening a bottle of superb champagne that did the trick. Whatever, all of a sudden they were talking noisily about coitus interruptus, not as a primitive method of birth control, but as a source of hilarious anecdote.

Ellie's contribution was a slightly embroidered account of an incident from her student days.

'They had those old double-decker buses on the route back to our hostel,' she said, 'and if you got the very last one it was sort of a convention that couples shot upstairs to get down to some serious necking, and the conductor didn't bother you till you came down to get off at your destination. Well, me and this chap I was dating got on one night and we found for some reason we were the only ones on the upper deck, and we sort of got carried away, and we were going the whole hog, him sitting, me on top, when suddenly I heard footsteps on the stairs and next thing the conductor's head appeared, and he just stood there looking at me, then he said . . .'

Her anticipatory laughter set the others off.

'What? What?' gasped Daphne.

'. . . he said, I just wondered, how far are you going? And I said, all the way!'

What had actually happened had been a lot more embarrassing as well as rather painful and pretty messy, but what the hell, she was a pre-published novelist, wasn't she?

If ends justify means, the hilarity her story provoked made truth a trivial casualty.

Daphne's story, typically, involved an undergraduate cousin going into Holy Orders, the dean of his Oxford college, and a punt on the Cherwell. Shirley Novello told a plain tale of an encounter with a police firearms instructor in which she was so clearly and uninhibitedly in charge that Ellie felt quite envious. Even Wendy, her eyes sparkling, came up with a rather rambling story of an encounter between a pedalo and a lilo on the Costa del Sol, though which was hosting the coitors and which the interruptor wasn't altogether clear.

Feenie had joined wholeheartedly in the laughter and Ellie, while curious to see whether she would also join in the anecdotage, wouldn't have dreamt of pressing her. But Wendy, made bold by her own confession, said, 'What about you, Miss Macallum? I bet sometime in your long life . . .'

Here her nerve or her command of diplomatic terminology failed her, but the old woman gave her an almost kindly smile and said, 'Can't match you youngsters' tales, of course. We were brought up to be a little more discreet, I suppose. But the war slackened things off a notch or two for most of us. I was a pretty fair linguist and I spent a bit of time liaising with resistance groups in Europe, heady stuff for a young girl, and it was hard to resist some poor chap who stood a fair chance of ending up in front of a firing squad before the year was out. I recall this occasion I was lying on a bed with this fellow on top of me, big brawny chap, he was, but he did seem to be taking an unconscionable time about things. Usually the other way round, isn't it? But I'd certainly had my own little moment of excitement and I was just waiting patiently for him to have his when over his shoulder I saw the door open and a German officer in full Gestapo fig, Luger in hand, stepped in. He was as surprised as I was, I think, and he said something silly like, "Hands up! Stand still!" Counterproductive really, as the shock of hearing his voice brought my friend at last to the conclusion he'd been labouring over for so long!'

This was the first time Ellie had heard a direct reminiscence of Feenie's wartime work, though there'd been hints from other sources. The habit of secrecy must be grained deep, especially when, as the old poster used to say, careless talk cost lives – literally. As she joined in the laughter, the tiny area of her mind untouched by the wine and that delicious sense of relaxation in the company of friends – perhaps the part which might one day make her a novelist – posted its own warning, not that anything she said could cost a life, but that she must be careful not to let slip anything she'd regret WDC Novello knowing in the morning.

Bollocks! some other part of her mind told her angrily. The woman is not your enemy. And aren't moments like this when you feel at one with those around you as real and as important as that other larger existence you are so eager to protect? Or rather, doesn't the one contain the other, and take nourishment from it, and even if there is a price of some small betrayal to be paid in the morning, isn't *that* the false note, not anything that is said or done tonight?

She glanced towards Shirley and would have given her another smile if their gazes had met. But the policewoman's eyes were fixed elsewhere, towards the end of the terrace where the steps ran down to the garden, and on her face the light of pleasure and amusement which still touched the features of the rest of them had died.

Ellie followed her gaze.

Alongside the three-inch mortar stood a figure, a slightly built, sallow-skinned man with a narrow moustache.

Now the others were looking too.

Daphne said indignantly, 'Oh my God, it's *him*!'

Feenie said, 'Can I help you?'

Wendy Woolley put her hand to her mouth and her eyes darted here and there around the terrace as if searching desperately for God knows what.

'Please, do not move, ladies,' said the man.

'It's the Gestapo,' gasped Ellie, reluctant to be dragged out of her happiness.

Nobody laughed.

And Shirley Novello was rising to her feet and moving towards the intruder.

'Sit down!' he commanded.

'I'm a police officer,' said Novello.

As she advanced she reached towards the leather holster pouch in which presumably she carried her ID. The soft pad of her trainers on the marble floor was the only sound which broke the silence.

Silence. It hit Ellie that she hadn't heard Rosie's voice for several minutes.

Without thinking, she yelled, 'Rosie!'

The man's head turned towards her in alarm.

Novello undid the stud on her holster with a sharp click.

The man's hand went into his jacket and came out with something in it.

Ellie couldn't believe it was a gun. It was something shaped like a gun. Something that might be mistaken for a gun. But no way could it really be a gun.

Novello lunged forward, trying to grasp his arm.

A foot more, a glass of wine less, and she might have made it.

Instead he swayed back out of her reach and the something that couldn't be gun coughed in his hand.

Novello stopped. Turned. Put her right hand to her left shoulder. Looked at Ellie with an expression of intense bafflement, as if here was a problem she didn't understand but was too proud to ask for help in solving. Removed her hand. Looked at the red stain which had blossomed on her palm like a stigma. And fell.

At the same time the terrace was struck by a wind, Pentecostal in its suddenness, and when Ellie, desperate for sight of Rosie, desperate indeed for sight of anything but the slumped body on the terrace floor, stared out across the garden, she saw that, unnoticed by the happy women as they ate and drank and span their fragile cocoon of intimacy, the eastern sky had turned flame-lurid as streptococcal clouds drove their furious infection landwards over a livid and blistering sea.

x

belly or bollocks

Gawain Sempernel sat on Ellie's bed at Nosebleed Cottage and switched her laptop on.

There was only one item under *Existing Documents* and that was called Comfort Blanket. He brought it up and began reading. He read almost as fast as his finger pressed on the *Page Down* key kept the text scrolling, and at only a slightly slower speed he could retain all that he saw. It was a useful talent which had helped persuade most of his Cambridge tutors that here was the next generation's leading classical scholar in the making. But one of them had seen the truth that his scholarship was only memory-deep and that his questing mind was more excited by modern power struggles and the Cold War than ancient feuds and the Fall of Troy. So the probes had been launched, the gentle questions put, and finally the ambiguous invitation given which had led him to where and what he was now.

Without that invitation he might have become

the scholar much of academia still thought him to be and have used those other attributes of preemptive decision-making and ruthless opportunism to steer him safe into the comfortable haven of the Master's Lodge at his old college.

Well, that was still possible. The present Master was dying and his on-the-spot heir apparent was much hated by most of his colleagues and in any case susceptible to attack on several sexual fronts, details of which Sempernel had in a private dossier. Feelers had been put out some months ago when he dined at the college. In his business there was no official retiring age, but it had become increasingly clear to him that he had risen as far as he was going to go, though not as high as he felt his abilities deserved. This galled him rather, and to some extent his hands-on involvement with this his final operation was meant to demonstrate that though his coevals might be reduced to sending out directives from the depths of comfortable armchairs in their clubs, he, Gaw Sempernel, could still hack it in the field with the best of them, before removing himself voluntarily to one of the most comfortable armchairs in the civilized world. And in addition, though he would never admit it, he who had made a religion out of rationality, there was in the matter of Patrick 'Popeye' Ducannon and his arms cache a private and personal motive. That fiasco at Liverpool Docks which had resulted in three men dead and hardly enough armoury to furnish a country gent's study had left his chin faintly eggy and, while it can't have been a major factor, it had certainly provided his enemies with a minor factor in their campaign to block his final move from the steps of the throne to the throne itself.

Occasionally as he read, his lips pursed in distaste at some jarring anachronism or sciolistic inaccuracy, but on the whole he was entertained and he laughed out loud at the picture of Achilles disguised as a woman. Just the kind of joke Odysseus might have made about the great hero, he thought, as his eyes scrolled on. And the picture of Aeneas which followed seemed somehow to come from the heart.

Odysseus saw with some relief that he'd got the Prince smiling again. Ever since he'd arrived he'd been running over in his mind what he knew about Aeneas. Ten years of warfare gave a man plenty of opportunity to get to know his enemies. They'd never actually talked directly to each other, but he'd seen the man's pale watchful face at parlays, and he'd taken note of the way he led his troops in battle, and of course he'd read the reports from the Greek spies in Priam's court. His digest of the Trojan's make-up read: strengths – great courage allied to great caution; completely lacking the foolhardiness of Hector or Achilles; bright and perceptive, not an easy man to fool; tactically very sound, would never throw

*his men at an unassailable object, but would
not hesitate to risk great losses in pursuit of a
significant gain; loyal to a fault; which fault
was one of his main weaknesses – this loyalty
preventing him from opposing the crazy policies
of old Priam and yon mad bugger, Hector, who
missed every chance of ending the war by simply
handing Helen back to her legal husband. Other
weaknesses: inflexible on what he saw as matters
of principle; not open to bribes or appeals to
self-interest; bound by some rigid notion of duty
and responsibility which he would not relax, no
matter what pain it might cause to himself or
those close to him.*

*So, how did you manoeuvre an awkward cus-
tomer like this into seeing things your way?*

*Odysseus said, 'But that's enough about me,
Prince. How about you? Tell me about yourself,
how you managed to get out of Troy, where
you're heading. Just now when I asked why
you didn't settle down with Helenus, you said
something about being bound elsewhere. Where
would that be?'*

*Aeneas looked at him doubtfully for a moment,
then shrugged and said, 'What harm to tell
you? There is a land, called Hesperia by you
Greeks but Italy by the natives, where the soil
is fertile and whence by tradition our Trojan
ancestors hailed. There I am directed to journey
and establish a new and mightier Dardanian
empire.'*

'Directed? Like, by the gods, you mean.'

'Yes. By the gods.'

'You poor sod,' said Odysseus feelingly.

'Why do you say that? Are we not all under the command of high Olympus? Even you, my friend, cannot deny the influence of mighty Poseidon in bringing you to this place.'

'Aye, but there's a difference. All I'm trying to do is get back home. Now the gods can help or hinder me as they will, but I'm heading back to Ithaca 'cos that's where I want to be, and whatever I find there, I'll get it sorted, 'cos it'll be my business, not the gods'. And if that's blasphemy, well, hit me with a thunderbolt and turn me into pork scratchings, but gods or no gods, in the end a man's got to look after himself, 'cos no other bugger will.'

Aeneas gave him a curious look in which distaste and envy seemed strangely mixed.

'It must be . . . comfortable to live a life without meaning.'

'Meaning? You want to ask Achilles about meaning. All his heroics, and now he'd rather be back on Skyros wearing a frock with all the girls saying, Come and help me with my needlework, Stiffy.'

'He too was in the hands of the gods.'

A whimpering sound, like a puppy in pain, came from the rear of the cave and Aeneas looked anxiously round and half rose. But the attendant came out from behind the curtain, gestured reassuringly, helped herself to a jug of water and returned to the ailing child's bedside.

'Aye, he was,' said Odysseus. 'And I expect that lad lying back there is in the hands of the gods too. Your son, is he?'

'Yes, my boy, Ascanius. He grew sick from the violent motion of the ship as the storm drove us here. I hoped that after our landfall, his health would return, but . . .'

'Can I take a look at him?'

'Is medicine another of your skills?' said the Prince, half-hopeful, half-mocking.

'No, but I've had plenty practised on me,' said Odysseus, with a glance down at his scarred flesh.

He went into the rear of the cave and by the light of a flaming torch held by the attendant, he studied the boy's flushed and feverish face. Then delicately he took the child's small hand in his huge paw and raised it slightly. The child's eyes opened and fixed on the man's. They stared at each other in silence for a moment, then the boy's eyes closed and Odysseus gently released his hand. He exchanged a few low words with the attendant, then he returned to his place by the fire and helped himself to more wine. Up till now, it had always been the Prince who refilled his goblet.

He said, 'So?'

'So what?' said Aeneas.

'So what're you not telling me?'

'About what?'

'About yon lad. He's got a high fever, but his pulse is so slow it's almost stopped, and his eyes are as bright as a lass's when you show her the family jewels. The nurse says the lad hasn't had any nourishment, not even medicinal herbs and such, for nigh on two days, but he's got no better and no worse. And you . . .'

'Yes? And me?'

'You're sitting here, passing the time with me. Like you were almost glad to have your mind taken off something.'

'Would not any man be glad to have his mind taken off worrying about his sick child?'

Odysseus shook his head.

'There's nowt can do that,' he said. 'No, what I've been taking your mind off is another kind of worry, some kind of decision. It probably concerns the lad, but until you make it, nowt's going to change with the lad, that's how you can sit here so calmly, glad of an excuse to let time go by without doing anything. Might as well tell me about it, Prince. How can telling an old Greek soldier make things any worse?'

Aeneas regarded him coldly and said, 'Perhaps sacrificing an old Greek villain to the high gods might make things better?'

'Nay,' said Odysseus, shaking his head vigorously. 'You thought that, you'd have done it half an hour since. Likely there's a god mixed up in it somewhere, there usually is. But this is between the pair of you.'

The Trojan sipped his wine then shrugged.

'Why not? Let us see what the craftiest mind in the civilized world can make of what I say. Two nights ago, keeping watch over my boy and praying for his recovery, I was visited by a vision. Vision! Strange term for an ancient, crook-backed and carbuncled crone, but this is what we must call one who can pass the guards outside this cave, both coming and going, undetected. She told me that this island was called Ogygia, and it was sacred to the nymph Calypso, daughter of Atlas, grandchild of mighty Uranus, most ancient of the gods, and that we had defiled it with our presence. If we left within three days, we would go unpunished. But a condition of our going was that we must leave Ascanius behind. If we lingered longer than three days, we would die. If we tried to take him with us, we would die. My time is up by dusk tomorrow. So now you know why I am glad to sit and talk with you, Odysseus. Who knows? When I first saw you, I wondered whether perhaps you too might have been sent by the gods for my aid, but now . . .'

'Now what?'

'After hearing you talk, I cannot believe the Olympians would use as their vessel one who holds them in such low regard.'

'You might be surprised,' said the fat Greek. 'You tried to make contact with this, what did you call her? Calypso?'

'Of course. My men have roamed in every direction. They've found nothing, no sign of life or habitation, hardly any vegetation even. This island is little more than a heap of slippery windswept rocks. I shudder to think what a creature must look like who chooses this for her sacred dwelling place. And as for leaving my boy to her mercy ... but what choice will I have? What choice?'

His voice rose into a cry of anguish.

This poor sod's made for pain, thought Odysseus. Give him a tree nymph, he'd not know whether to climb up her or chop her down.

He said, 'Tell you what, lad. Why don't I get a bit of shut-eye, then in the morning when things are looking a little bit brighter, you and me can take a look around to see what we can see?'

Aeneas looked at him with scorn and suspicion.

'Is that the best the wisest head in the world can offer?' he mocked. 'A bit of shut-eye and a look around? What are you really planning, oh wily one? Get your strength back then work out a way to escape?'

'Nay, lad. I've got plenty of strength for that and if I wanted an escape plan, it's all worked out already,' said Odysseus. 'Oops, sorry.'

He'd reached for his goblet and clumsily knocked it over. Aeneas started back from the rivulet of wine which ran towards him and suddenly felt his head dragged back by the hair and a keen edge of metal was drawing a line of warm blood along his exposed throat. Somehow the fat Greek had moved his bulk behind him in the blink of an eye. As to where a man he'd seen naked could have been concealing a knife, Aeneas didn't care to guess.

'See? Slit your throat, knock out nursie back there, mebbe even give her a quick bang, then I can be out of this cave so quiet them guards of yours wouldn't know till they found your body later on. Stroll round to your mooring place, got to be on the windward side of the island, so it shouldn't be hard to find. Then swim out, help myself to anything small enough for one man to manage, scuttle the rest, and I'm away and free and you don't have to worry about making your mind up any more.'

Aeneas closed his eyes in anticipation of the blade biting deeper into his throat.

Then sudden as it had come, the pressure vanished, the grip on his hair was released, and when he opened his eyes, Odysseus was sitting opposite him, regarding him over a full goblet, and saying solicitously, 'You OK, Prince? Looked like you were having a bit of a funny turn there? Mebbe you should call for help.'

Aeneas's hand was at his throat. He drew it away and looked down at his fingers, lightly stained with red. Wine not blood. And the same redness marked the sharp thumbnail of the man opposite him.

He looked towards the cave entrance, beyond which he knew that faithful Achates and his armed guard kept watch.

Then he looked at the fat smiling man sitting opposite him and he saw again the fire raging through the temples and palaces of Troy and heard again the shrieks of despair and defeat rising up from the ruins with the billowing smoke.

All down to this fat smiling man.

He smiled back and said, 'Yes, perhaps I should call for help. What time would you like your morning call?'

End of chapter. Sempernel lay back on the bed and looked thoughtfully at the ceiling. Interesting woman, this Ellie Pascoe. He felt almost sorry that he was probably going to have to put her away. Her involvement might of course turn out to be more coincidental than conspiratorial, but his long experience of looking for connections others had missed had taught him to be very reluctant about admitting accident. After keeping Peter Pascoe firmly in the picture and clearly in his sights after the 'chance' encounter with Cornelius on the Snake Pass, he was minded to concede that *his* involvement might be accidental in every sense, which meant that this family had used up its share of coincidences already.

He scrolled to the next page, eager to read on. But all that came up was:

Chapter 4

Nothing else. Damn. How like a woman to leave a man up in the air. Well, if as was distinctly possible she ended up taking a rest as Her Majesty's guest, she would have plenty of time to finish it.

There was a tap on the door, which opened before he could call, 'Come.'

Must have a word with her about that, he thought, looking at the tall, well-made woman with black hair and a strong handsome face, slightly marred by some bruising and scratches down her left cheek, who'd come in.

She said, 'Word from Wen. That pavilion on the cliff, they call it the Command Post. CP.'

'How nice to receive confirmation of what one has already intuited. Anything more?'

'No. Pushed for time.'

'Let me know soon as you hear anything further from her or Jacobs.'

The woman went but reappeared almost immediately.

'Car coming,' she said urgently.

'Well, go out and meet it, my dear.'

Pascoe, seeing the woman come out of the door as his car bumped down the lane, felt his heart leap, even though simultaneously he realized it wasn't Ellie. Same build, same colouring, same hairstyle, in fact, similar enough to deceive anyone who knew her only through description or even a fuzzy photo but, even at twice the distance, not a husband who knew intimately and loved passionately every inch of her body . . .

His mind jerked tardily to a connection he should have made long before.

What was happening to that fine high-flying detective mind which could once leap vast distances to places other minds couldn't reach? It had taken the Fat Man's hefty nudge to make him stumble over the similarities between the courtroom watcher and the fake welfare officer. Now, despite Ellie's description of the woman, and her dream of seeing her doppelgänger get out of the car and head for the front door, key in hand, he had let his anger and shared pain obscure what should have been obvious.

That woman hadn't come to his house to help abduct Ellie. She had come expecting to find the house empty and to take Ellie's place.

All this came to him in the seconds it took to pass at speed through the open gate with its ominous sign and slam to a halt, jolting Dalziel and Wield hard forward against their seat belts.

'Bloody hell, lad, you caught short or what?' exclaimed the Fat Man as Pascoe flung open the car door and shot out.

The bruising on the woman's face confirmed his identification.

'Bitch,' he said as he pushed by her. 'I hope you get blood poisoning.'

He went through the front door into the small porch. The sight of a pair of yellow wellies he recognized as Rosie's on the flagged floor twisted his gut. Then he was through into the living room.

'Ellie!' he yelled. 'Rosie!'

A door opened and a tall, thin, white-haired man with a welcoming smile on his face came towards him, hand outstretched.

'Mr Pascoe, how nice to meet you ag –'

He was driven against the wall with a crash that dislodged a parade of fine china from the Delft rack.

'Where's my wife, you bastard? Where's my daughter?'

Hitting someone, except in the extremes of self defence, was never going to be easy for a man of Pascoe's temperament but he would have done it if his drawn-back fist had not been seized in a grip like a gorilla's.

'Easy, lad,' said Dalziel. 'Have I taught you nowt? Beating someone round the head's no way to get information. No, that just knocks them silly. The belly or the bollocks, that's what gets them talking.'

As he spoke, he drew Pascoe away, their feet scrunching on shards of china, and when he got him into the middle of the room, gently but with irresistible force he lowered him onto a sofa.

'Right,' he said. 'Now you're sitting comfortable, Mr Sempernel's going to answer your question, isn't that right, Mr Sempernel?'

Sempernel slowly straightened up. The assault had clearly shaken him but he was a quick recoverer. A slight adjustment to his tie and shirt front, a hand to his handsome head of white hair, and the reel had been run back to his original entrance, even to the welcoming smile.

He said, 'Cynthia, my dear, do put that thing away before you do somebody some harm.'

In the doorway the woman was standing uncertainly, a small automatic pistol in her hand. The chances of her doing harm to anyone but herself were slim as Wield had her in an armlock which directed the pistol's muzzle towards her own left foot.

He relaxed his grip and the woman gave him an unfriendly glance then put the weapon away.

Sempernel said, 'Now that we've both got our violent underlings under control, Mr Dalziel, by all means let's sit down and talk. I take it from your presence here that you have decided to ignore my request and your superior's command not to meddle in this affair.'

'Nay, perish the thought,' said Dalziel indignantly. 'We're just down here on a social trip, see how Ellie and the kiddie are enjoying their bit of a holiday.'

'In that case, I can set your minds at rest. They seem to be enjoying it very well. They are presently taking supper with Miss Macallum at Gunnery House, which is half a mile or so up the road. Believe me, the only thing likely to sound a note of alarm in their minds and spoil what looks set to be a perfectly delightful evening would be the inexplicable arrival of yourself and your colleagues, looking anxious. I really think it would be best all round if you drove quietly home and left them in our very caring hands.'

Pascoe, his feelings back under tight control, said evenly, 'No one's leaving here until you've told me exactly what's going on, Sempernel.'

'I see. And do you propose following Mr Dalziel's advice in order to extract this information?' enquired the tall man courteously. 'I must say I should find this strange behaviour in one who, by all reports, is reckoned to fit the new user-friendly profile of policing in so many respects that great things are forecast for him.'

'You really do know how to wrap up a threat, don't you?' said Pascoe. 'But you're not so good at recognizing when a threat is empty. Yes, Mr Dalziel's technique is certainly tempting, but in this instance unnecessary. What I propose is to carry out my duty as a good cop. I have reason for suspecting that your lackey here took part in an attempt to abduct my wife, and reasonable grounds also for suspecting that you were a party to, and therefore fellow conspirator in, this attempt. These are serious offences. I shall arrest you both and take you back to Headquarters for questioning. I shall, of course, radio ahead to give warning of my arrival and it wouldn't surprise me in the least if our local media hawks who, quite illegally, monitor our radio channels, hear what is happening and are waiting with their cameras when we arrive.'

Sempernel seemed unperturbed.

He raised his eyebrows about two inches higher than Pascoe had ever managed and said, 'What say you, Superintendent?'

'Sounds like by the book to me, sir,' said Dalziel, who'd sunk into an armchair and looked ready to spend the rest of the evening there. 'Can't see owt to quarrel with there. That's how I train my lads to act. By the book.'

'You must lend me this book one of these days,' said Sempernel. 'Very well. I am nothing if not a pragmatist.'

He sat down, looked towards the woman and said, 'Cynthia, my dear, would you care to resume your guard-dog duties in case of further interruption?'

The woman nodded and went out. Wield looked towards Dalziel, who gave him a single nod, upon which he followed.

'What well-trained beasts we keep,' said Sempernel. 'Now, Mr Pascoe, first let me assure you there was never any plan to abduct your wife. Far from it. Our intelligence was that your house would be empty that day with your good lady accompanying your daughter on her school trip. What occurred was merely a botched-up attempt to extemporize when, to their great surprise, my operatives discovered Mrs Pascoe still at home. I hope that puts your mind at rest on that point.'

'At rest?' exclaimed Pascoe. 'She had a key. To my front door. She was going to masquerade as Ellie. And I'm supposed to feel reassured?'

'Well, no. Perhaps not. I take your point. But my point is that neither you nor she would have known anything about this if things had gone to plan.'

'Mebbe,' said Dalziel, who'd been looking round the room with a pointer's unblinking and questing gaze, 'if you told us about this plan . . . ah yes.'

He rose, went to a fine oak bureau, opened the cupboard to reveal an array of bottles and glasses, and said, 'Malt or blended?'

'I bow to your taste,' said Sempernel. 'The plan. Yes. Mr Pascoe, for some time now, your wife in her capacity as a member of the Liberata Trust has been in correspondence with various political prisoners, including a Colombian woman called Bruna Cubillas. Have you heard of her?'

'Vaguely. I knew Ellie wrote to these people, and sometimes, not often, got replies. But we didn't talk about it much.'

'Really? Could this perhaps be because she felt there might be some conflict with your job as an officer of the law?'

'Of course not. How the hell can you break the law, writing to someone?'

'I can think of half a dozen ways off the top of

440

my head,' said Sempernel. 'But never mind. Are you sitting comfortably? Then I'll begin.

'Bruna Cubillas . . .'

xi

spelt from Sibyl's leaves

Bruna Cubillas . . .
born in a shack in a slum on the banks of a
  drain . . .
living was pain . . .

One brother, five sisters. The other girls all died in infancy.

Did Bruna ever look up soulfully at a questioning stranger and insist, *we are seven*?

I doubt it. She might feel her life in every limb, but kids of that condition in that place almost certainly knew a hell of a lot about death.

look at her growing . . .
out on the streets where each day a new terror
  could strike . . .
What was it like?

Even if I knew the details, could I begin to understand? She probably had freedoms which I in my narrow little Welsh village in my narrow little Welsh valley could never have dreamt of, the freedom to roam at will from her earliest years, the freedom on boiling-hot days to leap naked from the concrete lip of the dock into the sordid but cooling waters beneath, the freedom to make her way from the shanty town where she lived into the heart of Cartagena, the real town next door, the freedom to beg in the street, the freedom to snatch bread or fruit from market stalls and slip her pursuers by squeezing under fences and through cracks that their adult bodies couldn't negotiate.

But my freedoms – the freedom to wear clean new clothes, to eat fresh wholesome food, to sleep between cool linen sheets, to be feted and fussed over on my birthday and at Christmas, to go on holiday with my family in the summer, to sit at a school desk among my friends and complain about being educated – these were freedoms she never knew, and probably never dreamt of. Not until her brother started talking about them.

Fidel Cubillas . . .

Known to the world – to his world anyway, that world of myth, legend, heroism, horror, ranging from Andean heights to the depths of the rainforests, which is South American subversive politics – as Chiquillo. Because of his youthful appearance. Or maybe on the same basis as they called that early A-bomb Little Boy.

443

killed his first cop with a knife driven straight
through the spleen . . .
he was thirteen . . .

Or so the legend tells us. A raid on the shanties in search of subversives, the boy wakened rudely by having the rags that covered him snatched away, the knife that was never far from his hand sleeping or waking thrust up in unthinking reflex, the cop on the ground, screaming and dying, the boy dragged to police HQ where he is beaten and sodomized, the prison where the treatment continues till he comes under the protection of a group of Farc freedom fighters. While outside, Bruna, under the protection of no one now that her fiery brother is taken away, somehow survives and grows and doesn't forget and aged seventeen is waiting when one of the irrational amnesties used to clear space in the prisons for the next intake sends her eighteen-year-old brother stumbling out into the light of day.

She nurses him to health. Miraculously his boyish looks remain, but inside he has aged and hardened to match the ancient rocks his cell was carved out of.

And now he is connected.

Over the next few years Little Boy becomes a big player in the long-running saga of insurgency, but eventually, in a land where the boundaries between terrorist/freedom fighters, cocaine kings, compliant local officials and colluding national security officers are blurred and indistinct, his un-compromising take-no-prisoners-make-no-deals attitude turns him into a liability in the eyes of the main insurgent groups. His own small but fanatically loyal following make it difficult to deal with him directly, but a hint to the government's counter-insurgent force seems set to do the trick. But in this world, even treachery is usually betrayed and Chiquillo and his men escape, not unscathed but scathed only enough to provoke the ferocity of the wounded animal.

Thus is formed PAL, short for *paliza*, meaning a beating or thrashing, a name which captures pretty well the motives and methods of a group which, though small, is soon recognized as one of the most dangerous ever to emerge from this long shadowy war. Chiquillo manages to do what the peace brokers have been failing to do for decades, unite government and anti-government elements in their desire to suppress him.

But he is as elusive as the Snark. Reports of his capture here, his fatal wounding there, are rapidly discounted by his appearance in another outrage a hundred miles away. Finally the counter-insurgents hit lucky and get a fix on the group. There is an ambush, a ferocious fire-fight, the insurgents take huge casualties, the survivors retreat, killing their wounded as they go, leaving no one alive to become a prisoner. Except one. Shot through the leg and unable to walk.

Bruna Cubillas.

Bruna has not been one of those women who

like the Amazons of old have assumed an active role in the armed struggle, but since Fidel's release from jail, she has never been far from her brother's side, devoting herself to his wellbeing even to the extent, rumour has it (a rumour which gave even the liberation priests an excuse for condemning him), of sharing his bed.

So now the government forces have a bargaining counter, or so they think.

Bruna Cubillas . . .
tortured and raped but won't talk and at least
* she's alive . . .*
can she survive . . . ?

Messages are sent into the forest, inviting dialogue. Nothing comes back but silence.

Just when it seems that perhaps Chiquillo has decided that with his group in tatters and his sister in enemy hands, his best course is to lie low for a while, PAL explodes into new life. No longer a potent guerilla force, they launch a vicious urban terrorist campaign. Bombs, assassinations, uncaring for the death of twenty innocents so long as they get the target they judge guilty. It is like the Troubles, and indeed word is that in the freemasonry of terror, they have been breaking bread with Irish extremists.

Curiously, this eases rather than exacerbates Bruna's lot. A worthless bargaining counter isn't even worth throwing away.

Then after a year a sharp-witted prison censor notes that she is developing a relationship with a bleeding heart from Liberata, one of those irritating human rights groups.

Eleanor Pascoe.

Could this be usable, long term, in getting a line on the incredibly elusive Fidel?

But it would need cooperation from the UK. Hardly seems worth the effort.

Nevertheless, eventually someone mentions it casually to Our Man in Bogota who happens to have gone to school with Gawain Sempernel.

Sharp old Gaw. Once he told me, in those dear departed days when he was still disguising self-congratulatory pillow talk as grooming me for a Top Job, that if you wanted to catch big fish, you must never miss the chance to drop another hook into no matter how unpromising a water.

And while at this time Chiquillo was of no more than academic interest to him, Liberata and its prime mover, Serafina Macallum, were certainly in his sights, and Eleanor Pascoe proved to be already tucked away in my little casket, all neat and tidy and declined to that relative silence Gaw always finds so suspicious.

Coincidence is the name fools give to the voice of God who is the Accuser of this World. Thus sayeth Gaw.

So we took over. Mrs Pascoe's letters were gradually phased out and our own, indistinguishable in style but much more insinuating in politics, were substituted. Bruna's replies, of course, were intercepted long before they reached Yorkshire, though an occasional formal note was sent to Mrs Pascoe so that she would not grow over-anxious and start agitating. Her gift of books to help Bruna improve her English was reduced by an irrational censor to the single-volume Shakespeare, and as this provided Bruna with her only example of the English language in use, gradually her letters abandoned Spanish for a kind of fustian Elizabethan.

But still they said nothing that was useful to the men hunting for Chiquillo, not even those which she imagined were being smuggled out of prison to evade the censor's eye.

In an effort to lull her into indiscretion, her lawyer was told that the authorities were minded to admit his application for release on the grounds that she was never an active participant in PAL's terrorist activities, and a date was set.

And then Gaw learned that his old enemy, Popeye Ducannon, was negotiating to sell the arms Gaw had missed in the Liverpool fiasco. It emerged that PAL, eager to become a player on the guerilla front again but barred from using the usual American arms dealers by the strict interdiction of all the major native customers, was interested and had contracted Kelly Cornelius to broker a deal.

Or perhaps it was Kelly who had contacted Chiquillo. For they seem to be long acquainted and she knows all his ways. Not too surprising in view of her line of work. But neither would it be surprising if their connection was more than professional. Kelly is . . . Kelly! And Fidel, with his boyish looks and his devil's heart, has to be a turn-on for the kind of woman who's turned on by that kind of thing.

Says I, with all the superiority of one who went for the father figure. But at least we had the devil's heart in common.

But if Kelly told Chiquillo about the arms cache, that also means she must have some link with Popeye. If so, I can't believe this one is also sexual. Does that make me sexist? I guess it does. Just because I find bulging eyes a turn-off, is that any reason to condemn a man to celibacy? He can't help his appearance.

But he needn't go out in daylight, as my old gran used to say.

Whatever, Kelly did the direct negotiation with the Irishman, but there was no way she could do more than reach a notional agreement with him. To set up security for the handover, to arrange for the arms to be shipped out of the UK, and, most difficult of all in face of the combined opposition of everyone in Colombia from the government down to the cocaine lords with the insurgent groups in between, to get the consignment safe into the hands of PAL, needed cooperation in the highest, which is to say the lowest, places. In other words, the Cojos, the Lame Ones.

Chiquillo knew how to set about this. You applied to El Cojo with a barrowload of the country's most negotiable currency, cocaine.

So far so good. Except that in the eyes of the Cojos, intermediaries, especially female intermediaries, have no standing. Chiquillo must come himself to close the deal.

He must have been desperate to agree. Or certain enough of his own superior cunning. But agree he did.

How he got here, God alone knows. Despite all the best efforts of the Colombian police and ourselves, we have not been able to find any trace of either his exit or his entrance. Which is why the release of Bruna fell so opportunely. Somehow she knew everything that was going on and when she made it clear she was heading for the UK, we knew that this was our best line onto Fidel, Popeye and the arms.

It seemed impossible that we would lose her too. But we did. Then a letter intercepted before it reached Mrs Pascoe told us that Bruna was as keen as ever to meet her friend and benefactor. And when a phone call was intercepted to the Pascoe house, our substitute readily agreed to a meeting.

Trouble was that Bruna insisted on coming to the house.

Perhaps it was simply the effect of a lifetime of caution. Nothing is certain in this life, but meeting Ellie Pascoe at the address she had been writing to for all this time reduced the chances of betrayal to a minimum.

Or perhaps it was simply that Bruna had built

up a picture in her mind of where and how her friend lived, and had an irresistible longing to see all this for herself.

All that this did was add an extra dimension to our masquerade. A dimension too far, by all accounts. Gaw has tried to keep report of the fiasco down to a minimum, but not even his famed capacity for intelligence management in the world at large could stop the tattle in the world in small. Our world.

So everything seemed to be slipping away from Gaw. Fidel had the arms, we know that. All we had were four bodies by a lake in Kielder. We didn't know where the arms were (except for this mysterious CP), where Chiquillo was, where Bruna was, where Kelly Cornelius was.

Gawain must have felt he was wandering alone in a remote wasteland with no sound in his ears but the grinding of the axe that is going to chop off his head.

Then suddenly all is well. How do I know? By nods and winks from my magical mystery machine. From words dropped by my colleagues who confuse their Sibyl with the machine she tends. But most of all because, near or far, I still can feel that surge of arrogant self-congratulation which sends your ego tumescing when the gods reveal yet again that they have marked the great Gaw Sempernel down as one of their own.

You've made yet another breakthrough, haven't you, Gaw? You're soaring high above once again,

watching all the little rodents scuttle vainly away
from the beat of your mighty wings.

> *All those looney people, you know where they*
>   *come from . . .*
> *All those looney people, you know where they*
>   *belong . . .*

xii

come to dust

One thing you had to give old Pimpernel, thought Andy Dalziel, sipping the Scotch he'd liberated from the Aldermann drinks cabinet, he might be economical with the truth, but he could tell a tale with precision and clarity when the occasion demanded.

'Oh God,' said Pascoe when the story was done.

'What?' demanded Sempernel, leaning forward.

'These letters in Elizabethan English. We got one through the door two nights ago. Archaic language. Ellie recognized it. *Cymbeline*. From the dirge for Fidele . . . *Fidel* . . .'

'Yes, probably because of her brother's real name, our letters show a particular fondness for *Cymbeline* too. But this came through your door, you say? She got as close as that?'

'Someone did.' He was looking at Sempernel with loathing. 'Where the hell were your people then?'

'Where, I might ask, were yours, Mr Pascoe?'

said Sempernel. 'I, surprisingly, have rather limited resources. I assumed that the Mid-Yorkshire constabulary would be pulling out all the stops to make sure their nearest and their dearest were fully protected.'

A keen blow. Pascoe recalled his insistence to Novello that while he was in residence, he was quite capable of looking after his family. At least this Bruna could be assumed to have a pretty friendly agenda.

'The man who attacked Daphne,' he said. 'Where does he fit into this?'

'That, we guess, would be a man called Jorge Casaravilla. The Colombians like to keep a close eye on their disaffected exiles and their main anti-insurgency agency, the *Consejo Juridico*, commonly known as the *Cojos*, has a presence in most of their embassies. Officially, of course, they are under political control, but over the years they have garnered so much power that for all practical purposes they are answerable to no one.'

'Oh aye? Must make you lot feel right at home,' said Dalziel.

'We have our checks and balances,' said Sempernel, unprovoked. 'Diplomatically, Casaravilla is a trade attaché in London, but he is in fact the Cojos' Chief of Staff in Europe. He is venal and vicious, and the nastier his job is, the more he seems to enjoy it. Officially we have been cooperating with him, our target being Ducannon and the arms, his Chiquillo. Unofficially it seems his agenda has been slightly different. The plan, I think, was for his men to return from the Kielder handover with a sad tale of an attempted double rip-off. They would claim that Popeye Ducannon was lying about the arms cache, and all that Fidel Chiquillo had brought was a bagful of talcum powder, not coke. In the ensuing argument, all the Irishmen got killed, as did Chiquillo, in proof of which they would produce his undisputed body, causing enough rejoicing on both sides of the Colombian fence to have the operation starred as an unqualified success. Jorge accepts the plaudits, sells off the cocaine, and when things have gone quiet, looks for a new market for his valuable arms cache.'

'Jesus Christ,' said Pascoe. 'And you say you work in partnership with these guys?'

'Security makes strange bedfellows, Chief Inspector. I should perhaps say that a little further down the line we had our arrangements made to take both Popeye and Chiquillo separately. The Cojos would have been politely thanked, then dismissed. We'd have had an operational triumph in capturing the arms, boosted our always over-stretched overseas finances in the form of the coke, and made lots of friends in America by handing over Chiquillo for close questioning by their anti-drugs agency.'

'Christ, you're as bad as them!' accused Pascoe.

'Believe me, it would be a mistake for you to think so,' said Sempernel earnestly.

Before Pascoe could reply, Andy Dalziel said,

'Nice line in Scotch your mate Patrick keeps, Peter. Must be doing all right with them flowers of his. Sure you won't try some? How about you, Mr Sempernel?'

The white patrician head shook and the Fat Man went on, 'Please yourself. This has been really interesting, better than owt they ever show on telly. But like they always say on the telly, there's one thing I don't understand. How come if you lot know so much, you're hanging around here? Unless there's something going on you're not telling us.'

Sempernel smiled ruefully and said, 'How I wish I could confess to such an arachnoid subtlety, with a web of plots and plans based on secret knowledge and close reasoning. The truth is far more banal. Alas, for the best-laid plans of mice and Military Intelligence, we have lost contact with almost everyone, nearly all our lines of enquiry have dried up and we are reduced to marking time and keeping an eye on your good lady, Mr Pascoe, on the off-chance that Bruna surfaces here in another attempt to make contact. Unlikely, I realize, but at least it means that Mrs Pascoe has an additional cordon of security to the one I do not doubt that you and Mr Dalziel have put in place. So you see, we're all on the same side. I'm sorry we've had this little misunderstanding among friends. I shall now withdraw with my people to hide my embarrassment. You of course will want to remain here till your womenfolk return. It would be a mistake, I think, to try and contact them at Gunnery, only causing unnecessary alarm. So good night now. I'm so glad we've cleared the air.'

He rose like a well-mannered guest, expert at judging when to take his leave.

This is a change of heart, thought Pascoe. Or at least a change of plan. When we got here he was telling us we ought to make ourselves scarce.

He glanced at Dalziel. To his surprise, the Fat Man was rising obediently, a pleasant smile on his lips, looking for all the world ready to say thanks, it's been a perfectly charming evening, I do hope we meet again soon, and let Sempernel make his departure with nothing said about Feenie Macallum and Kelly Cornelius and George Ollershaw and the Nortrust Bank and . . .

'No!' he said. 'It won't do. I think you want shut of us and as you've realized we're not going anywhere, you've decided the simplest thing is for you to leave us here.'

Sempernel looked at him with that polite smile and those ironic eyebrows while Dalziel's great slab of a face registered something which approximated to embarrassment.

'Nay, lad,' he said. 'Let's be sensible. If Mr Sempernel here says your missus is safe and it's best for us to sit here supping Scotch till she gets home, we've got no choice, have we? Except maybe . . .'

'Yes?' enquired Sempernel.

'Like I said before, if you want hard information, you choose between the gut and the bollocks.

Now which do you think we ought to go for, Pete, lad?'

How serious he was, Pascoe never found out. Very serious, he guessed, and Sempernel's expression hinted he guessed the same.

But before the Fat Man could indicate his choice, the door opened and the woman, Cynthia, was propelled into the room by Edgar Wield. She had a radio in her hand.

'Sir,' said Wield to Dalziel. 'Our friend here's just had a message. Didn't want me to hear it, but I think it's something we should all hear. Go on, luv.'

The woman looked at Sempernel.

'It's Jacobs at the house. A white Merc and a truck turned up a couple of minutes ago. Parked a little way back. Two men in the truck. Look like muscle. In the car two Latins, one white male. He's pretty certain the Latins are Jorge Casaravilla and Luis Romea. The other's definitely Popeye Ducannon. Him and Romea have gone into the house, Casaravilla and the muscle round the side.'

'A white Merc?' said Pascoe. 'That mad bastard who attacked Daphne was in a white Merc. And now he's at Gunnery House? What the hell's going on, Sempernel?'

'Honestly, nothing to worry about,' said the white-haired man reassuringly. 'Everything's under control. As you heard, I've got a man round there keeping watch. And if that's not enough, there's . . .'

'Cyn, you receiving? Over.'

It was the woman's radio.

She glanced at Sempernel who made an impatient gesture.

'Yes, I'm here. Go ahead. Over,' she said.

The man spoke again. His voice was breathless, his tone urgent.

'Tell the boss there's been a shot. I say again, there's been a shot . . .'

The voice kept on talking but Pascoe heard no more.

Fear, anger, despair muffled his senses to everything except his need to be with his wife and child. He was heading for the door in an act of instinct not volition. A table stood in his way. It would have made no difference if it had been an armed soldier or the Queen Mother.

He sent it spinning aside and neither heard nor saw the small crystal vase on it go crashing to the floor.

Then he was outside and scrambling into his car.

Behind him, voices. Dalziel's, Sempernel's, Wield's.

Pascoe heard none of them.

All he heard was a gun going off.

And a gun going off.

And a gun . . .

On the floor of Nosebleed Cottage, trampled by the feet of his pursuers, amidst shards of crystal and a spreading stain of water, lay Rosie's posy, sending up a sweet unnoticed fragrance from the florets of crushed yarrow.

xiii

faery lands forlorn

What a stupid, useless, gimcrack thing life is, thought Ellie Pascoe.

Here am I, lulled once more by food and wine and the company of people I enjoy and might even come to love, into feeling at ease with myself and the world, into believing once more that there is hope for the human race, that our history, especially if left to the tender care of women, might after all be a long and slow but none-theless steady progress towards some kind of perfect state.

And then, one shot, one loud explosion, one little piece of hot metal, brings the whole ram-shackle jerry-built edifice tumbling down.

And the scene fills rapidly with men. Demoli-tion men.

Two more had emerged from the shadows of the garden, solid muscular men who could have been brothers, though one was six inches taller than the other, guns in hand, faces smooth and blank, only their eyes showing (or so it seemed to Ellie) their eagerness to start massacring everyone in sight.

Another two came from the house onto the terrace. At least this pair weren't waving guns. One of them, wearing a Cardinals baseball cap, dark and Latinate like the man who'd shot Novello, was pushing Mrs Stonelady before him. The other, pale-skinned to pastiness, with dark pop eyes like whole plums in an undercooked duff, went to the fallen policewoman, looked down at her and said, 'Oh Jesus, Jorge, what the fuck are you playing at?'

'She said she was police. She was reaching for a weapon,' said the gunman defensively.

Popeye felt in Novello's holster and pulled out a small leather folder.

'She was telling the truth and it's her ID she was reaching for. We're in trouble here. They're like rats, they run in packs, these ones.'

He had a soft Irish accent, which grew stronger under stress.

'No,' said the gunman, Jorge. 'She is here alone to guard Mrs Pascoe.'

He jabbed his gun threateningly towards Ellie and said, 'Is that not right, Mrs Pascoe? Are there more?'

'No,' said Ellie. Her voice, to her own ears anyway, sounded remarkably calm but her body felt paralysed from the neck down. 'She's the only one. Is she dead?'

'Of course she's not dead,' said Feenie with god-like certainty. 'One round to the shoulder doesn't kill a healthy young woman. Let me see.'

Ignoring the men, she knelt down beside Novello, raised her from the floor slightly, and slipped beneath her head one of the cushions used to make the worst of the chairs more comfortable. The police-woman groaned. It was the most pleasing sound Ellie could hope to hear. Apart from Rosie's voice. No, wrong. Yes, she wanted to hear her daughter's voice to know that she was all right. But if she heard it, then everybody would hear it, including this psychopath whose reaction to any threat, real or imagined, was violence.

Feenie rose and headed into the house. Jorge and the muscle-men pointed their guns. Popeye yelled, 'No!'

The other Latin used Mrs Stonelady to block Feenie's way.

'She needs treatment,' said Feenie over the tiny countrywoman's head. 'I've got a medicine box in the kitchen.'

'I will go with her,' said the man to Jorge. 'You, old one, sit down.'

He shoved Mrs Stonelady towards the table. She sat on Novello's chair, looking completely uncon-cerned. Perhaps to her this was just another in the long line of oddities a Yorkshire lass had to expect once she got mixed up with the affairs of incomers.

The paralysis affecting Ellie's body was beginning

to fade, permitting her to realize she desperately wanted a pee. She could also have done with a drink but the two needs seemed incompatible.

In a low voice she said, 'Daphne,' and for her pains got a look of pure hatred.

Then it faded and she realized it was aimed at Jorge and had been too intense to remove in the moment it took for her friend to turn her head.

'You OK?' said Daphne.

'Silence!' shouted Jorge.

'Silence yourself, you bastard,' retorted Daphne. 'You don't scare me. This time I'm ready for you, you greasy little dago!'

Ellie made another small adjustment to her world view. There were after all circumstances in which vulgar racial abuse was not only tolerable but admirable.

But in any circumstances, dangerous.

Jorge moved slowly round the table till he was standing right alongside Daphne.

He put the gun to the back of her head.

At its touch, Daphne's body went rigid. Not just through fear, Ellie guessed, though she must be terrified, but as much through her effort of will not to show fear. If this is what private education along lines running back unbroken to days when Britannia ruled most of the known world did for you, thank God for comprehensives! Grovel! she urged her friend mentally. Whatever he says, agree. Beg for mercy. It's only in very old and very out-of-date children's books that a show of British pluck can shame a foreign villain into reluctant admiration. Nowadays, they just blow you away.

Jorge spoke. For a moment, fixed in her expectation of threat, abuse, or demands for submission, Ellie could not understand what he said.

Then he pushed Daphne's head forward with the pistol and repeated it.

'Where is the place called CP? Is it in this house? Answer!'

Now Daphne's face showed emotion. Fear, yes. But also, and principally, indignation. Silence to the death was an English nobility, but to die quiet because you'd been asked a question you actually couldn't answer was ludicrous in any language.

Ellie said, 'It's out there, on the edge of the cliff. The pavilion. They call it the Command Post. CP. See?'

'CPC?'

'No. Just CP. Command Post.'

'Show me.'

She had his full attention now and part of her, in fact quite a lot of her, wished she hadn't been so quick to divert it from Daphne. She'd read of people being traumatized, bank tellers, post office clerks, off-licence owners, policemen even, by being put under threat from a firearm, and while full of genuine sympathy, she'd never been altogether successful in suppressing a feeling that maybe some of them were being just a touch wimpish. Perhaps she'd inherited it from her father who would shake his head when anyone talked of post-traumatic stress disorder and say, 'Counselling? What good's all this counselling? In my day, you just got on with it!' Of course, her adult reaction had been reasoned if patronizing argument. It made no difference to his views, and oh, what she would give on her visits to the Home to see any sign of that old stubborn certainty in his fearful and unrecognizing face.

But now she *knew* how wrong he'd been as she looked into that gun in the hand of a man who'd shown he would use it and felt a terror which would never leave her and which dissolved what little control she had left over her bladder.

'It's there. Look. Please. I have to go . . .'

Need overcame fear. More, it overcame shame. She walked away from him and made it to the end of the terrace where she squatted beside the plinth bearing the mortar and let go. She felt the greatest physical relief she'd experienced in her life. *If it were now to die, 'twere now to be most happy . . .* Somehow the ludicrously misplaced quotation gave her strength. She looked up to find the muscle men, Big Ajax and Little Ajax, she christened them, looming over her.

'Careful you don't tread in my xanthic linn,' she said, standing up. 'Unless of course you're into golden shower.'

She returned to Jorge and pointed to the roof of the pavilion, almost invisible now in the growing darkness of the approaching storm.

'There, that's it. It's nicknamed the Command Post and that's what CP stands for.'

Suddenly lights came on in the house, throwing a golden glow over the terrace, and Feenie emerged, carrying a wooden box with a large red cross on it.

'I need to be able to see,' she said coldly to Jorge, who looked ready to object to the lights. 'What's going on, Ellie?'

'This gentleman was enquiring the whereabouts of the Command Post,' said Ellie.

'Why?' said Feenie. Her voice remained even but Ellie thought she detected something like alarm in her features.

'He didn't say.'

Feenie knelt beside Novello, produced a pair of scissors and began to cut her T-shirt.

'Careful. That cost good money,' gasped the WDC.

Plucky little trouper. Perhaps the old and the young through experience and innocence can deal with trauma. It's us poor buggers in the middle who crumble.

Wendy Woolley, without even a permission-asking glance at Jorge, joined Feenie on the floor and began to help her clean and dress the wound.

'Straight through,' said Feenie. 'May have chipped the bone but nothing more. Either a lousy shot or a very good one.'

She worked expertly.

Wendy said, 'You've done this before.'

'And worse. You're pretty handy yourself, my dear.'

The woman flushed and said, 'Thank you. What on earth's that you're putting on?'

Feenie was using her fingers to extract what looked like goose fat from a jam-jar and smearing it onto Novello's wound.

'It's an ointment Mrs Stonelady made up for me. Don't ask me what's in it. All I know is when I cut my foot chopping logs, this healed me up faster than our dear NHS could have managed.'

'Yarrow,' said Ellie. 'I bet it's yarrow.'

Mrs Stonelady glanced at her appraisingly, then nodded.

Jesus, thought Ellie. What's going on here? Trigger-happy thugs, the latest medical advances hot from the Trojan war, everyone else being brave and useful and defiant, and her own major contribution had been to take a pee in public! Thank God Rosie hadn't been here to witness that!

Rosie. Where was she?

She had a vision of the girl and the dogs suddenly racing out of the shrubbery and the jumpy bastard with the gun taking a potshot. It must be better that they knew.

The two Latins and Popeye were having a conference.

Boldly she went up to them and said, 'Excuse me. I just wanted you to know my daughter's in the garden somewhere . . .'

'Your daughter? In the garden? Where?'

Jorge had spun round in alarm, gun waving.

'No, please, she's only a child. No danger. She's

playing with the dogs. Just little dogs, no danger either. I just wanted you to know so that you wouldn't be surprised by her and start shooting . . .'

Speaking a possibility makes it more possible. She heard her voice wavering.

Popeye said, 'Never you worry, darling. Me and Luis here'll keep Wild Bill Hickok under control. Now that pavilion place, the CP, you call it, what kind of place is it?'

'It's a sort of summerhouse, I suppose. Where people could go and sit in comfort and watch the ships go by, or storms out at sea.'

'Looks like there'll be plenty of chance for that just now,' said Popeye.

He was right. The wind had dragged the turbulence of cloud right across the sky and under the darkling air the sea was flocculent with foam.

'So, this CP, is it a substantial sort of building then?'

Ellie said, 'Well I've only been in it once, but there were a couple of rooms at least. The big one, the viewing chamber they call it, you could have a dinner party there. In fact I think that was the idea. Water and electricity were laid on. Oh, and there's a cellar, for storing wine and provisions so that they didn't have to bring everything down from the house.'

Away from the subject of her daughter, she was amazed how calm she'd become. Scope here for a treatise on the nerve-soothing effects of urination. Don't take prozac, chew on a dandelion instead.

'Ellie, what are you telling them?'

Feenie had joined them and her tone was accusing. Where does she think we are? Back in the Resistance refusing to betray our comrades to the Gestapo?

'How's the girlie?' asked Popeye.

'She'll live but she needs a doctor. I hope that this is what you are discussing,' said Feenie sternly.

'Not really. I'm sure she'll survive a little while longer with you to look after her, darling. And we'll be getting out of your hair as soon as possible, then you can doctor her to your heart's content.'

The two Latins seemed content for the time being to let Popeye talk to the natives, though Jorge was beginning to look impatient.

'This pavilion, darling, can we get a truck down to it?' continued Popeye.

'Certainly not,' declared Feenie. 'Nor do I see why you should want to. Everything of any use or value was removed from it as soon as the council declared it dangerous.'

'Dangerous? What do you mean, dangerous?'

This was Jorge getting back in on the act with his gun-in-the-face technique.

Feenie wrinkled her nose as if assailed by a particularly noxious cigar.

'Dangerous insomuch as it is likely at any moment to fall into the sea. In fact, the whole garden beyond that fence is off limits for the same reason. That is why it has warning notices printed all along it. I am assured that the weight of a human being might be enough to cause a landslide. Anything like a truck would immediately precipitate an avalanche.'

This was laying it on a bit thick, thought Ellie. In any case, if there was a degree of truth in what Feenie was saying, surely the clever move would be to encourage these thugs to drive straight down there!

'Not very keen to have us visit your precious Command Post, are you, darling?' said Popeye slyly. 'Tell you what. Why don't we all take a look-see with you and your friends leading the way like the womenfolk do out in Cambodia when dada wants to take a walk. Takes a lot to make an oriental give precedence to women, but show him a minefield and suddenly he's a feminist.'

Jorge and Luis spoke to each other in Spanish too rapidly for Ellie to understand, then Jorge nodded at Popeye.

'Looks like we're on,' said Popeye. 'All right, ladies. This way if you will. That's right. Nice and easy does it and you'll be back here for the rest of your dinner before you can say Hail-Mary-full-of-grace. You've not had your pudding yet from the looks of it. Fine ladies like yourselves shouldn't have to go without your pudding. Old ones at the front. And you two, give the lady cop a hand.'

Ellie and Daphne looked towards Feenie for guidance.

She said, 'Don't be silly. She can't be moved. Have you forgotten she just got shot?'

'No, but you seem to have, darling,' said Popeye.

'Only way my friends are going to let her stay here is if she gets shot again.'

Feenie considered then nodded at the two younger women, who went to Novello. Feenie had taped a dressing round her wound and put her left arm in a sling. She looked very pale and swayed as they helped her to her feet but uttered no sound. Daphne draped her right arm round her neck and took most of the weight, while Ellie supported her left side as best she could without bringing any pressure on the injured shoulder.

'You, where are you going?' demanded Jorge.

Wendy Woolley had made a move towards the marble bench.

'I was just going to get my handbag,' she said fearfully.

Cue Edith Evans, thought Ellie. Time like this and the poor cow doesn't feel able to move without her sodding handbag!

'Leave it,' said Jorge.

For a moment it looked as if Wendy's dread of committing a social solecism was going to be stronger than her fear of the gun.

Then Feenie said, 'For heaven's sake, forget your precious bag. If you must have something to carry, carry this.'

She thrust the medicine chest into Wendy's arms and obediently, though not without one last long-ing glance towards her large sensible handbag, she fell into line behind Novello and her supporters, with Feenie and Mrs Stonelady leading the way, flanked on one side by Big A. and Little A., on the other by Jorge and Luis.

'Now just in case anyone hasn't read the script,' said Popeye who was bringing up the rear. 'If any one of you decides to make a run for it and hears a shot, don't bother to duck. It won't be fired at you, it'll be blowing a hole in one of the friends you leave behind. Let's go.'

At this hour on a summer evening it should still have been broad daylight, but the clouds which had now eaten up the blue sky entirely were so heavy and dark, shading from murrey through perse to empalling black, that they rapidly moved from the bright-lit windows of the house into a frightening crepuscular world which felt even less like England than Axness normally did. This too was once one of the dark places of the world, thought Ellie. And might be again. What was it these men wanted? And above all, where was Rosie?

Pointless and terrifying speculations, both. She concentrated on the ground at their feet, trying to pick the smoothest way for the injured woman. Ahead, Feenie had reached the warning fence. She halted and called, 'Stay!' in a loud commanding voice. What does she think we are? Dogs? Ellie asked herself as the little procession came to rest.

The fence presented little problem to an active adult who could either climb over or duck under it, but when Jorge asked impatiently why they had stopped, Feenie said in the same loud voice, 'Have you forgotten that you have shot and wounded

Miss Novello? She is hardly fit to walk and certainly unable to perform gymnastics.'

Jorge looked ready to give her an argument, but Popeye, moving to the front, said, 'You're dead right, darling. We'll soon have this out of the way.'

He produced a knife, pressed a catch which released a vicious-looking blade and began sawing at the fillet of red plastic.

The Ajaxes were uneasily examining the threatening sky as if minded to open fire on it while Luis and Jorge talked together incomprehensibly fast, but with body language suggesting it was a less than amicable discussion.

Probably debating what to do with us later, thought Ellie. With everyone's attention otherwise engaged, it occurred to her that this might be a good time to make a run for it. Except of course no one was going to run, not with Popeye's threat hanging over their heads . . . but why not? Why should it be *of course*? Why trust the implied promise that if they all stuck together and did what they were told, no more harm would come to them? She thought of those long columns of the doomed and dispossessed, outnumbering their captors by thousands, who'd let themselves be marched quietly to their deaths during this century, and centuries before, when if they'd turned and fought and run, some at least would have escaped, some must have survived who were driven down to death. *Driven down to death* . . . that or something like it was the stock phrase Homer used in the *Iliad*. Not a euphemism in sight there when it came to being killed, nothing for anyone's comfort. Blood, guts, pain, despair, it was all there. No joyful embracing of heroic death. These heroes saved their heroism for living. When it came to dying, as often as not they turned and ran, they screamed, they abased themselves and begged for mercy, they offered bribes and prayers. In the whole of the poem, while there are plenty of reproofs for those who try to hold back from going out to confront the enemy, no one ever gets blamed for doing their best to avoid death on the battlefield.

If Hector could turn tail and run when he saw Achilles raging towards him, why shouldn't I let go of plucky little trouper Novello and head for freedom? For if these men are truly capable of killing one of the others because I have escaped, then they are capable of killing the lot of us once they've got what they're here for.

As these thoughts synchronized through her head, historical, literary and practical indistinguishable from one another, she looked around for the best exit route. Whichever way she ran except forwards, there were yards of open ground before she reached cover and Big Ajax and Little Ajax would have all the time in the world to pick her off. The only area which offered immediate concealment was the shrubbery, but that was beyond the fence and involved running past the Latinos which would be somewhat counterproductive. Still not knowing whether it was common sense or even commoner fear which was making her think of escape, she looked longingly at the jungle of rhododendrons which the ever rising wind was whipping into a maelstrom of branches and leaves and shredded blossom, everything on the move so that it seemed a wonder it didn't all take off like in *The Wizard of Oz* and go spinning into the vast inane.

Except for one small patch of paleness straight ahead which didn't move, now visible, now not, as the swirling veil of greenery moved over it and away.

She stared. Found the focus. And saw Rosie crouched there, looking right at her, one arm around Tig, the other tightly gripping Carla.

Oh shit! she thought. What to do? Rush forward and scoop her up? Or hope that no one else noticed her? But they must do when they resumed their forward progress, they were right in the way.

And even if Rosie somehow managed to remain hidden, how long were the dogs going to remain under constraint, particularly Carla, who must be bursting to leap out at her mistress . . .

Stay!

That was why Feenie had suddenly started bellowing at them. She too had spotted the lurking trio and realized that her own dog was the greatest danger. Realized also that a few more steps would bring them right up to the girl's hiding place, so caused the delay with the fence. And then she'd gone on to let Rosie know what had happened to Novello.

That was good thinking. Rosie's instinct to hide probably derived from her reluctance to be caught having disobeyed the injunction not to go beyond the fence. Now she would know there was something seriously wrong.

'There we are,' said Popeye, laying the severed ends of the plastic barrier on the ground. 'Let's go.'

They began to advance once more.

To Ellie it seemed they were heading straight for the spot where her daughter lay concealed. Again, a vision of Rosie making a sudden movement and Jorge taking a potshot came into her mind. But Feenie was ahead. She had to trust in Feenie. They entered the shrubbery, following an old overgrown path. Ellie couldn't help glancing sideways at the place where the trio had been crouching. There was no sign of life, human or canine. She let out the breath she hadn't realized she'd been holding and felt it stretch her lips into a huge smile, which Popeye happened to catch as he glanced at her. He looked puzzled to be in receipt of such a display of happiness. She didn't care. With each step beyond the spot her spirits rose. Whether Rosie would or could do anything to bring them help she didn't know. Great if she could, but all that really mattered was that her child wasn't going to be part of whatever lay in wait for them at the pavilion.

She'd been sure that Feenie was grossly exaggerating the instability of the ground earlier, but now it seemed to her that she could actually feel it moving beneath her feet. She knew, of course, it was partly ocular, deriving from the sense of a world in disintegration that the raging shrubbery gave her, and partly down to the difficulty of maintaining balance when leaning into a strong gusting wind, especially when you were concentrating on keeping someone else upright, but it still felt like walking across the deck of a ship in a tumultuous sea.

No, correction. As they got closer to the edge of the cliff, she became more and more aware of what was happening to the sea. She could feel its spray in the air, hear it exploding against the cliff face, and now she could see it surging below into ever-changing mountain ranges of green and black water. This was designer God's original computer program, projecting how the wilder reaches of His world would look. Now the Andes, now the Rockies, all building up to His Himalayan masterpiece. No one would be walking across the deck of any ship in these seas.

They were almost at the Command Post now. Set on a narrow stack of granite, Feenie had said. How narrow was narrow? This felt like one of those land-hungry storms which wasn't going to go away empty-mouthed.

Feenie was opening a door. She turned and bellowed that they were here and would they please be careful in case there were any broken windowpanes or other potential sources of damage.

She had to shout to make herself heard above

the wind, of course, but what she was shouting was so inconsequential . . .

Last time she had shouted unnecessarily it had been to quieten Carla and warn Rosie . . .

There's somebody inside the pavilion, thought Ellie.

They went inside, stepping into a small anteroom with three doors off it, one to either side, one (a double door this) straight ahead. The side doors, Ellie recollected, led respectively to a lavatory and to a small kitchen, which in turn had a door opening onto the steps down to the storage cellar.

Feenie stepped forward and flung open the double door which led into the viewing chamber.

'Oh, my God,' said Daphne.

It was a moment of terror and sublimity. It was like stepping through a door and finding yourself on the peak of Kanchenjunga. It was like floating through an airlock and looking down at the Milky Way. It was most of all like opening a magic casement on the foam of perilous seas in faery lands forlorn.

The wall before them comprised a single pane of reinforced glass running the whole length of the building. Beyond it was nothing but air and sea. And such air, and such sea, the one fit domain for Valkyries and Harpies and flying dragons and golden rams and randy swans and all the wailing souls of the newly dead, the other for Sirens and Krakens and Scylla and Charybdis and the victors and the vanquished of toppled Ilium and the drowned and the shipwrecked sinking into their happy graves to the music of old Triton blowing his wreathed horn.

Ellie stared, speechless. Beside her, Shirley Novello forgot her pain and wondered if she had come to the bounds of living. Big Ajax and Little Ajax uttered their first sounds, grunts of awe, and pressed forward to get a closer look. Even Jorge, pistol dangling forgotten in his nerveless hand, seemed completely rapt.

'Impressive, isn't it?' said a voice behind them. 'Oh, I do like to be beside the seaside.'

Ellie turned.

A woman had appeared from somewhere. Presumably, since the door was open, from the kitchen. In her hands was a short-barrelled automatic weapon like the ones everyone – terrorists, freedom fighters, police ARUs, kids robbing post offices – seemed to carry nowadays. The woman was young, slim, dark, and very beautiful.

Ellie was sure she'd never met her but equally sure she'd seen her before, and very recently.

'You can drop the guns if you like. Or even if you don't,' said the woman.

Big Ajax and Little Ajax looked enquiringly at Jorge.

Jorge glared accusingly at Luis. Ellie guessed that at school when teacher demanded who'd put the drawing pin on her chair, Jorge was pretty quick with the accusing finger. Always someone else's fault. Daphne's fault that she got her nose mashed,

Novello's fault that she got shot, all our faults when he finally got round to massacring us . . .

'Now!' said the woman with sudden force.

Slowly, Jorge stopped and laid the gun on the floor, with Big A. and Little A. following suit.

'That's better,' said the woman. 'Now we can all sit down and talk this thing through.'

Sounded good to Ellie. Except, it struck her, that they were one short of *all*.

Popeye hadn't come into the pavilion with the rest of them.

He came now, quietly, knife in hand, moving far more rapidly than Ellie's warning scream.

His left hand seized the woman's long black hair, dragging her head back, while his right set the gleaming blade against her exposed throat.

'Hello, me darling Kansas,' he said. 'How're you doing? Give your gun to Luis here. There's a good girl.'

She didn't look like a good girl. She looked like a girl who'd like to be very bad indeed. But obediently she released the weapon into Luis's hands.

'Right,' said Popeye. 'Now we can relax and enjoy ourselves.'

He let go of her hair and put the knife away.

She turned her head to look at him.

'Uncle Paddy,' she said. 'I knew it had to be a mistake when I heard you were dead.'

'Reports slightly exaggerated, darling.'

'Well, I'm really glad to hear it,' said the woman.

She sounds as if she means it too, thought Ellie. Uncle Paddy? Kansas? Which, Toto, I've a feeling we're not in any more. What the hell is going on? And where have I seen you before?

And then it came to her in one of those flashes of utter clarity.

She recalled precisely where and when she'd seen these beautiful features.

But when the clarity started to fade, she found its aftereffect was to leave her understanding even more benighted than before.

xiv

a face from the past

'What the hell is a painting of Kelly Cornelius doing hanging in Feenie Macallum's hall?' asked Andy Dalziel.

By the time Peter Pascoe skidded to a halt before Gunnery House, he'd regained some measure of control, and when he saw the front door gaping invitingly open, he approached it comparatively cautiously. Then he heard rapid footsteps on the gravel drive and turned to see a man running towards him with something black and metallic in his hand.

Pascoe ducked low, drove his right shoulder into his attacker's gut, straightened up to lift the man's winded body high in the air, and speared him head first into the gravelled drive.

The object he was carrying went spinning away. It wasn't after all a gun, more like a radio, but Pascoe didn't pause to investigate. If this guy was one of the five who'd just turned up, that left only four and the way he felt at the moment, odds like that were in his favour.

He went through the front door low, like the hero of a TV action movie. This faintly mocking self-awareness was perhaps an index that reason was beginning to reassert itself, but if there'd been another open door, he would probably have kept going. Instead, once he'd established the large entrance hall was empty, he saw there were three doors off it, all closed. He paused to make a decision, and reason took the chance to get its messages through to his muscles.

A second or two later it was reinforced by the restraining arms of Andy Dalziel, who had done considerable violence to the engine of Sempernel's car in pursuit.

'Easy, lad,' said the Fat Man. 'They're out of the house now, lucky for you. Getting yourself shot's not going to help any bugger, is it?'

'We outnumber them. Andy, there's only four of them left. Has someone got a hold of that guy out there? He'll tell us what's going off.'

He spoke with the certainty of a medieval torturer.

'I fear not, Mr Pascoe,' said Sempernel, coming through the front door.

'Shit. The bastard hasn't died on us, has he?'

'Happily not. The bastard is in fact one of my operatives whom I'd advised on the radio of your approach and instructed to intercept you before you came to harm.'

'Oh God,' said Pascoe, remembering the vicious

force with which he'd speared the man into the gravel. 'Is he OK?'

He broke free of Dalziel and went to the doorway.

The man was sitting on the ground, leaning back against a car. He looked dazed, and his forehead and left cheek were tessellated with gravel.

'I'm sorry,' said Pascoe. 'I thought . . .'

Then the grazed and bleeding features began to tug at his memory. Surely this was the man he'd seen with the Fraud Squad super in the court, the man who matched Ellie's description of the male half of the couple who'd tried to lure her out of the house with their story about Rosie being sick . . .

'Bastard,' he said. 'I wish I'd broken your neck.'

He turned back to Dalziel, and found him standing rapt before the life-size painting hanging on the wall opposite the main door.

And . . .

'What the hell is a painting of Kelly Cornelius doing in Feenie Macallum's hall?' the Fat Man asked.

Pascoe looked.

Dalziel was right. There she was, standing next to a fellow who could have modelled for Ozymandias, Kelly Cornelius to the life, that combination of classic bone structure and vibrant life, like Galatea feeling the first strong pulse of warm blood through soft flesh as Aphrodite's breath quickens the cold ivory.

What did it mean? thought Pascoe. What did any of it mean?

He said to Sempernel, 'What's going on? Have there been any more shots? Who was firing? Where are those men who arrived? What are we doing standing around here? What in the name of God has happened to my wife . . . ?'

'Do take it easy, Mr Pascoe,' said Sempernel. 'You are an amazingly impetuous young man. If you had stayed to hear Jacobs's whole message, you'd have learnt that when he first thought he heard a shot, he went to investigate before reporting in. There was a deal of activity on the terrace at the rear of the house. Eventually he saw a party of ladies amongst whom he recognized your wife . . .'

'He would, wouldn't he? The bastard's seen her before.'

'Indeed. As I was saying, he saw them process through the garden towards some kind of summerhouse on the cliff –'

'So there wasn't a shot?' interrupted Pascoe.

'I'm afraid there probably was,' said Sempernel gravely. 'Jacobs observed your wife and her friend, Mrs Aldermann, supporting your officer, WDC Novello, whose arm appeared to be in a sling.'

'Shirley? Oh Christ. And what about my daughter? Did he see Rosie?'

'He didn't mention her but that doesn't mean she wasn't there. Jacobs had to observe from some distance, naturally . . .'

'He'd have seen her. If there was bother, she'd not have strayed far from her mother. How the hell can you let something like this happen to innocent people?'

'Sometimes it's hard to separate the innocent from the guilty, Mr Pascoe,' said Sempernel significantly. 'And sometimes it's distance rather than closeness which lends accuracy to the view.'

Pascoe was looking at him like a man who feels that language has gone as far as it can and maybe it's time to reopen older and more direct channels of communication.

Dalziel, entertained by this unsuspected propensity for violence in his henchman, had no philosophical objection to witnessing Sempernel taking a punch on the nose, but felt with the Preacher that there was a time for every purpose under heaven and this long streak of owl-shit's comeuppance could wait.

'Shouldn't we be doing something cleverer than standing around here when there's a looney with a shooter who could show up any minute?' he said reasonably.

'It's all right, Superintendent,' said Sempernel rather patronizingly. 'I dispatched my Cynthia to take over watch duties while Jacobs is recovering. I believe your sergeant, who seems something of a doubting Thomas, has accompanied her to take the lie of the land for himself.'

'He gets that from me,' said Dalziel, sniffing the air, which carried a faint but not yet unpleasant burning smell. 'Think I'll take a quick look inside just to make sure there's no one lurking.'

Sempernel didn't look happy, but the Fat Man had already opened one of the doors and was moving out of sight into the body of the house.

'Do take care,' called Sempernel. 'And please do not show yourself on the terrace. Hello, what have we here?'

Through the front door into the hall ran a small patchwork dog, barking excitedly at Pascoe and jumping up at his legs.

'He seems to know you, Chief Inspector,' said Sempernel.

But Pascoe did not hear. He was lost and away, recalling Wield's account of going to tell Elsie and Tony Dacre that their missing daughter was dead and inadvertently letting Tig run into the house ahead of him as so often he must have done to announce the return of his young mistress.

Sick with foreboding, he went to the doorway and looked out. Echoing fate once more had Edgar Wield hot on the small dog's heels, but now Pascoe's heart soared as high as it had plummeted low when he saw that it wasn't bad news the sergeant was bearing, but Rosie, high on his shoulder.

'Look what I found!' cried Wield.

He swung the child down and she came running to her father, who caught her up and hugged her so tightly she cried out.

'I'm sorry, darling,' he said, releasing her. 'Are

you OK? No one's hurt you, have they?'

'Only you,' she said without malice. 'But Shirley's been shot, I heard Miss Macallum say so, but not shot dead, she's got a sling and she's walking, only Mummy and Daphne are helping her, and we had Mrs Stonelady's casserole, and there's bread and butter pudding and chocolate ice cream for me, only I got down to play before the pudding while they were all talking, and I wouldn't have gone under the fence but Carla went and Tig followed and I think they must have been chasing a rabbit, so I went to fetch them back, and I hid when I heard someone coming, and Miss Macallum spoke very loud so I knew not to come out, but they would probably have found me when they came through the fence only the lady with the moustache took me by the hand and showed me where to hide and I stayed hidden till I heard someone else and looked out and saw it was Wieldy.'

She paused for breath.

'Who,' said Sempernel softly, 'is the lady with the moustache?'

'The lady who gave me the flowers for Mummy,' said the girl, with the natural exasperation children display when adults ask them to explain what is obvious. 'Uncle Andy, what on earth are you eating?'

Dalziel had re-entered, in one hand a large bowl, in the other a matching spoon.

'Hello, is that my favourite girl or is it a garden

gnome?' he cried. 'Come here, luv, and give your Uncle Andy a kiss.'

She ran up to him and reached up to kiss his stooped head, then examined the contents of the bowl with great interest.

'Bread and butter pudding, bit charred, just the way I like it,' Dalziel explained. 'Custard were ruined but. Some things you can burn a bit, like tatie pot and traffic wardens, and no harm done. Not custard though. That's why I had to put chocolate ice cream on it.'

'That's mine!' cried Rosie indignantly.

'Nay, finders keepers. You can try a spoonful if you like.'

His gaze met Pascoe's over the child's head as she helped herself to a large dollop of choc ice and he went on, 'Bit past your bedtime, isn't it, luv? Tell you what. Why don't you go back to yon cottage with the funny name . . .'

'Nosebleed,' said Rosie indistinctly.

'Aye, that's the one. Wieldy will take you, right?'

His gaze was still on Pascoe. He wants Rosie out of here, as do I, thought Pascoe. But he knows I won't go while Ellie is still in danger.

'My pleasure,' said Wield. 'There's that story I didn't finish yesterday.'

'What about Mummy? I want Mummy,' said the girl. Then, quick to avoid giving offence to those she loved, she looked round and said, 'And you can come too, Wieldy, and finish your story.'

'That's settled then,' said Pascoe. 'You go on

489

with Wieldy, darling, and Uncle Andy and I will go and fetch Mummy. OK?'

'OK,' she said, with the insouciance of one who had not yet learned that there were things in the world which not even her father and Uncle Andy could guarantee. 'What about Carla?'

'Carla?'

'The other pooch,' said Wield. 'Miss Macallum's dog.'

He snapped his fingers and a black and white sheepdog which had been lurking in the background came trotting forward.

'Tig and her are best friends,' said Rosie. 'Miss Macallum won't mind.'

Is this menagerie going to keep on growing? Pascoe asked himself. What happens if I get mixed up in a case involving wolves?

'Best I think if Miss Macallum's dog is out of the way,' murmured Sempernel, coming close. 'They can be so unpredictable. Especially the female of the species. Mr Pascoe, I have no desire to cause your daughter stress, but if perhaps Sergeant Wield could get out of her as detailed an account as possible of what she witnessed, it might assist us in our deliberations.'

'You heard that, Wieldy?' said Pascoe. 'But go very easy, eh?'

'I'll only use the rubber truncheon if I've got to,' said Wield.

Pascoe, reproached, said, 'Sorry. She couldn't be in better hands.'

He watched as Wield drove away with Rosie and the two dogs, then turned to Sempernel and said, 'So what happens now?'

'Aye,' said Dalziel. 'I were wondering that. Normally I'd have whistled up a couple of our ARVs by now. Shot fired, policewoman hurt, armed suspect on premises, hostages taken . . .'

'No, not hostages,' said Sempernel. 'Until they know we're here, the ladies are merely captives, not hostages.'

'That's grand,' said Dalziel. 'I'll remember that in future. How to avoid hostage situations, just don't let on to the crooks that you know about them. And if folk didn't let on they'd been burgled, or if corpses kept it to themselves they were dead, we'd really knock the burglary and murder rates on the head.'

'I meant that we have time to deliberate our next move, Superintendent. The situation is static until we set it in motion.'

'Wrong,' said Dalziel. 'I've got a wounded officer out there who's not getting any better without proper treatment, and is likely getting a lot worse. Plus my colleague here's got a wife out there who he'd prefer to have back in one piece. So unless you can convince me that you've got a better idea, I'll just get on with calling up the cavalry. Mebbe you'd care to start by being a bit more honest with us. So far you've been lying through your teeth about why you're here, and if removing your teeth's the only way to stop you lying, I'll do that too. So, like Shakespeare says, who's doing what and with which and to whom?'

Sempernel smiled thinly and said, 'First let me deploy what little force I have. Jacobs, you fit for service now? And just as important, is your radio fit for service?'

The man was back on his feet. He'd recovered his radio which he now raised to his damaged face.

'Seems OK,' he said.

'Good. Go and keep watch on their vehicles. Eventually they'll have to come for the truck. Let me know as soon as that happens.'

Jacobs moved away. Pascoe didn't know whether he felt sorry or not to see his new ally limping.

'This truck,' said Dalziel. 'What's it for?'

'Transport, what else? Somewhere round here, Mr Dalziel, as I suspect you have guessed, Popeye Ducannon's cache of arms is hidden, plus, almost certainly, the cocaine which Chiquillo brought to pay for them. Before you wax indignant, let me say that if we had thought there was any prospect of either the drugs or the arms disturbing the even tenor of criminal life in Mid-Yorkshire, we would of course have tapped into your expertise. But Mr Trimble, your Chief Constable, was persuaded that the fewer people who knew about their existence, the less chance there was of any leakage. Particularly as until a little while ago we were unsure ourselves of their precise location.

492

We didn't want to spark off some kind of lowlife treasure hunt.'

Pascoe said, 'You're telling us that this stuff's hidden in Gunnery House? And you knew this back there when you were shooting us all that shit about Ellie being completely safe?'

'Not in the house,' said Sempernel, feeling it best to ignore the second part of the question. 'In something called the CP, which stands for Command Post, which I have reason to believe is the nickname given by the Macallum family to the pavilion on the cliff where Mrs Pascoe and her friends are now, I regret, situate. The good news is that there's no way for anyone to move out of there without passing us here.'

Pascoe digested this, then said in the softly reasonable tone which sometimes made people underestimate him, 'Great. So the best plan is to let them do just that. Pass us here, I mean.'

Sempernel's eyebrows took off like Harrier jets.

'Let them go past us? I do not see how that is even a possible plan, let alone the best!'

'You don't? Well, maybe that's because you've been playing with yourself so much, you've gone blind,' snarled Pascoe. 'Any idiot can see that it's better to let these guys drive away with their gear rather than keeping them trapped in there with my wife and the others as hostages. They've got miles of narrow empty road to negotiate before they get anywhere. You can block them off and take them out any time, no one else at risk.'

'Sound sense to me,' said Dalziel.

'You think so? I'm afraid you do not yet understand the nature of the people we are dealing with,' said Sempernel. 'They will undoubtedly take some of the ladies with them when they go, giving themselves bargaining power in the event anything goes wrong along the way, and also giving those left behind an extra incentive not to contact the authorities.'

'What do you mean, an *extra* incentive? What other incentive do they have?'

'The natural reluctance criminals feel against incriminating themselves.'

Here we are again, thought Pascoe. The sly slur. Damnation by circumlocution.

He said politely, 'Could you please tell us in direct and unambiguous terms which of the women in the pavilion you believe to be criminally involved here?'

Sempernel, to his credit, started strong.

'Feenie Macallum,' he said. 'She is the founder of and leading light in Liberata –'

'I know who she is,' interrupted Pascoe. 'And you're telling me she's a crook? Bollocks.'

Sempernel stayed serene.

'As I'm sure one so distinguished in his profession must know, one of the problems for large-scale criminals, particularly drug traffickers, is that they tend to get paid in dirty money which they need to render clean. To this end many of them use the services of professional launderers, usually hi-tech experts with skills equally valued in legitimate financial circles whose mandarins, I fear, are often quite happy to have large sums of dirty money passing through their systems so long as they can throw their hands up in horror if things go wrong and demonstrate that there is none of the dirt under their fingernails.'

'Listen, sunshine,' said Dalziel, scraping the bottom of his pudding bowl. 'When I'm finished eating, if I've not heard summat significant, I'm going to start filling Axness with wall-to-wall flashing blue lights. So get a bloody move on.'

'You're talking about Kelly Cornelius,' said Pascoe. 'And you think she's here too, don't you?'

'I'm certain of it,' said Sempernel. 'Her escape, as you've clearly worked out, was connived at by Miss Macallum. When I tell you that one of the many ingenious routes by which people like Cornelius channel their dirty money is via charities working in the Third World, you'll begin to see the connection. Indeed, some of these charities have been set up precisely for this purpose.'

'But Liberata's always broke,' protested Pascoe.

'Your wife tells you that, does she? Well, well. No, don't look so angry, Mr Pascoe. I make no accusation. Yet. But she is here at Gunnery House. And Kelly Cornelius is here too. And would you be surprised to learn that as at close of business yesterday, Liberata's account, which your wife assured you is in the red, stood in excess of three million pounds sterling?'

'This is getting as close to an accusation as I want to hear you get without a lot more evidence,' said Pascoe softly.

'Interesting,' replied Sempernel with matching softness. 'You don't, as many husbands would, simply assert the impossibility of your wife's being mixed up in anything illegal. Instead you require evidence. Could it be that you feel, as indeed her track record suggests, that she might in certain circumstances think the end justifies the means?'

'Cut the crap,' said Pascoe. 'Evidence.'

'Very well. My evidence, I admit, though highly suggestive, is purely circumstantial. Her Liberata cases seem to be concentrated in South America, and in Colombia in particular. Kelly Cornelius works specifically for several Colombian groups, freedom fighters or terrorists depending on your stance, whose main source of income is usually cocaine, which is why they need her services. As I told you at the cottage, it was Cornelius who brokered the arms deal, and it was she who got Miss Macallum to take Bruna under Liberata's wing, and as you know, Miss Macallum entrusted her to Mrs Pascoe's care. Of course, this might have been quite innocent, and your wife's involvement could be purely attributable to chance.'

He didn't bother to conceal that this was the merest of sops.

Pascoe spat it back in his face.

'And I suppose chance has put her in the hands

of this bunch of terrorist thugs?' he sneered. 'I'd say chance has a face like a knackered horse and white hair, Mr Sempernel.'

Dalziel felt like applauding. All these years of Pascoe coming across with the manners of a high-class waiter, while all the time he'd been learning how to spit in the soup with the best of them!

He said, 'The lad's right, Gaw. You knew all this, why'd you not do summat about it earlier?'

'Because while we knew a little, there was a lot we were guessing, and some important things we didn't know at all. Viz, where the arms were hidden. And we still don't know what happened to Chiquillo or where his sister is. But one mystery has I think been solved.'

'And what's that?'

Sempernel turned to look up at the portrait of Mr and Mrs Mungo Macallum.

Outside the storm suddenly wrapped its arms round the house and tried to drag it out of its foundations. The wind caught the front door, hurled it shut, dragged it open again . . . shut . . . open . . . sending the lurid light of the cloud-smudged sun flickering across the painted figures till it seemed to Pascoe that the man glowered out at them with real hatred, while the woman's lips curved in a mocking smile.

'Whatever the business relationship of Cornelius and Macallum,' said Sempernel, 'it's quite clear it's based on a very close blood relationship, wouldn't you say, gentlemen? In fact, I think I would care to wager that there must be a direct line of descent. Mother and daughter, perhaps? No, the ages do not accord. Grandmother and granddaughter is more likely. What do you think?'

'I think we're wasting fucking time,' said Pascoe. 'For God's sake, let's do something!'

Sempernel regarded him almost pityingly.

'Action is transitory,' he said. 'A step, a blow, the motion of a muscle, this way or that. 'Tis done and in the after vacancy, we wonder at ourselves like men betrayed. Never let the strain of inaction alone be your stimulus to action, Mr Pascoe. But I think your wish may after all be my command. What news, my dear?'

The woman, Cynthia, had come back into the hallway. The sounds of the rising storm had multiplied outside, but the storm within had deafened Pascoe's ears to mere weather. Now the sight of the woman standing before them like an undine, dripping water to the flagged floor, her black hair enamelled to her skull, her sodden clothes clinging so tight against her body, scarcely any curve or crevice went unmoulded, seemed to him like an irrefutable authentication of the pathetic fallacy.

'Jacobs says there's movement. Two of them at least heading for the truck.'

'Excellent. This confirms the stuff is here. They must be ready to load. Let's go and give Jacobs a hand, shall we, gentlemen?'

He paused in the doorway and looked back.

'Yes, definitely grandmother and granddaughter, I'd say.'

But no one was listening.

xv

bloody glass

'Cornelia is my granddaughter,' said Feenie Macallum.

'Cornelia?'

'Cornelia Kelly. Known to her friends as Corny, and therefore to some inveterate punsters as Kansas. When she decided her nefarious activities required that she be born again, with singular lack of ingenuity she merely reversed her names and became Kelly Cornelius.'

The women were sitting on the floor against the wall at one end of the pavilion's long room. There was nowhere else to sit. The room was devoid of furniture save for a single dilapidated wooden chair which stood in the centre like a symbol of authority. The two Latinos and Popeye had gone clattering down the steps which led from the kitchen into the cellar. Big Ajax and Little Ajax were standing by the window staring out with wonder like a pair of kids at a firework display. Ellie tried not to look out, but from time to time her gaze was drawn irresistibly towards the view. The storm had no rain in it yet and the view through the glass was terrifyingly clear. It was like sitting on a magic carpet hovering a few feet above Hades. What made it worse was that the worst was yet to be. Away to the east, beyond the livid gloom shot through with angry reds and diseased magentas which filled the narrow space between lowering sky and boiling sea, an inexorably advancing wave of darkness was visible. When it got here . . .

She dragged her eyes away and said, 'Feenie, I never knew you'd had a child . . .'

'No need to sound so surprised. I wasn't always a dried-up old stick, you know.'

'I'm sorry. I didn't mean . . .'

Feenie laughed and said, 'Of course you didn't. In fact, it was almost certainly that chap I was telling you about. I had taken some elementary precautions, but the shock of hearing the German's voice caused him to explode so violently, everything went. Nine months later I gave birth in a stable. Fortunately it was a girl, otherwise I may have established a cult.'

Jorge had commanded them to sit down and be quiet. Daphne, who seemed to be nursing a grudge against the Latino quite unbecoming in the daughter of an archdeacon, had ignored him completely as she busied herself making Shirley Novello comfortable. The WDC was now lying with her head on Daphne's lap. Her eyes were closed and her cheeks pale, but she was breathing naturally. Daphne had demanded water, Jorge had waved his gun (he now had the automatic weapon taken off Kelly Cornelius) and screamed once more that they must remain silent or be shot, Popeye had said very reasonably that there didn't seem to be much point in requiring the prisoners not to talk when even if they yelled at the top of their voices, there was no one to hear them, and even if there was, they wouldn't, because of the noise of the storm. Luis had added his support for this viewpoint, a bottle of mineral water had been fetched from the kitchen, and Jorge had subsided with Spanish mutterings and a promissory baring of the teeth at Daphne.

Then the two Latinos and Popeye had vanished, leaving the women in care of the two Ajaxes.

It occurred to Ellie that a group of men in similar circumstances would probably by now have elected an escape committee. Her reaction whenever she saw a Colditz movie was, why did these scions of the officer class bother with escape when they were safely out of the war and living in conditions which, though not ideal, weren't much worse than those prevailing in many of the boarding schools they sent their kids to?

She recognized now that she might have to moderate her position slightly, but for the moment there didn't seem much point in starting to dig a tunnel or build a glider, so instead she'd turned her attention to the young woman who'd almost rescued them.

On learning her identity, she recalled a certain mildly suspicious languor which had modified

Pascoe's manner whenever Kelly Cornelius was mentioned. Now she saw why. But any jealous pang she might have felt was soon subsumed by the interest of establishing the link between her and Feenie. As an unpublished author, she knew a great story when she heard one. Also, anything which took her mind off here and now was very welcome.

'So what happened?' she demanded eagerly. 'I mean, having a child behind enemy lines in the middle of a war! It's incredible.'

'I could tell you things far more incredible,' said Feenie shortly. 'I nursed her for a couple of weeks till my friends found a family who could take her in.'

'You mean, you left her?' She tried not to sound shocked.

'There was a war on. I had work to do. If I'd got caught, I would certainly have been tortured and shot. Not much future for a child in those circumstances.'

'And after the war?'

'After the war, she was behind the Iron Curtain. I used to go to see her. Fortunately I had some standing with the authorities there, but they refused to let her out. What could I offer her in the decadent west which she was not already enjoying far more abundantly where she was?'

It wasn't quite clear if she was quoting straight or ironically.

'Did your father know about her?' asked Ellie.

'I told him eventually.'

'How did he react?'

Feenie was silent for a while and when she answered her voice had an unfamiliar overtone of regret.

'Badly. But that was my intention. Our relationship was degenerating fast by then and I told him merely to provoke him. I let him believe I'd abandoned her there deliberately because I did not want her to be brought up in England. I told him she would never learn anything from me about her grandfather, she would never even know he existed. It was cruel. I meant it to be. I thought he deserved it. Well, we learn what a rough measure desert is when it's meted out to ourselves.'

'She means she got me,' said her granddaughter, smiling at the old woman affectionately. 'I'm a terrible trial to her.'

Wendy Woolley, who'd been busying herself with what looked to Ellie like a hussively obsessive tidying-up of the medicine chest, said unexpectedly, 'Why? Because you're a common criminal?'

Kelly laughed, a melodious chortle which rippled through her body in a way which Ellie guessed made men eager to set her laughing.

'Not the common bit. Gran doesn't object to a little necessary illegality in a good cause, but she draws a rather old-fashioned line.'

Feenie came back in as if she didn't much care for this line of development.

'My father died shortly thereafter, so he never

met his granddaughter. He would have done, you see, as I was very close to getting her out by then. But by the time I managed it, he was gone. His death meant I had the money to see that my daughter got a good education. We were never close, too much time had passed for that. But we kept in touch and saw each other from time to time. I think in the end I got her understanding.'

'You got her respect, Gran,' said Kelly gently. 'And if you had pressed, you could have had her love.'

'Perhaps. But there was no time for that,' said the old woman with a harshness which didn't quite hide her pain.

All the love that she withheld from her daughter she has lavished on Kelly, thought Ellie, feeling slightly ashamed that in these circumstances what she regretted most was not having a recorder.

'And your father?' she said to the young woman. 'Irish?'

'South American-Irish,' she said. 'Juan Antonio Kelly. Not that nationality meant too much to him, as long as the causes were right. He was a great man for causes, which I suppose was why he married Mama. She had causes in her blood too. Must be in the genes. I sometimes think I could have done without that particular inheritance. Causes can really get in the way of having a good time, can't they?'

She smiled at Ellie as if detecting a possible ally. But it wasn't tea and sympathy all round.

'Excuse me,' said Wendy Woolley with the determination of the timidly righteous. 'You *are* the woman I've read about who's accused of embezzling the money from Nortrust? What kind of cause was involved there, please?'

She's well-informed. Must read papers I don't see, thought Ellie, who'd been surprised how little news coverage there'd been even locally about Cornelius.

'The best,' said Kelly, smiling affectionately at her grandmother. 'Love. Is there a better cause?'

'So you were in on it too, were you, Miss Macallum?' said Wendy in a tone of shock and disapproval.

Feenie looked at her with surprise not so much at the question as at its source.

'Against my better judgement, but needs must when the devil drives.'

'But Feenie, why?' demanded Ellie. 'For Liberata, was it?'

'For Liberata and all my other activities,' said Feenie wearily. 'So much to do, so little money left to do it with. As you could see up at the house, I'm pretty near the end of my realizable assets. I have so many commitments, so many promises to keep.'

Daphne, who'd been listening with growing disbelief, let out a snort of indignation.

'So you decided that what *you* do is so important you could steal other people's money?' she sneered. 'Well, well. How *terribly* highly you must value yourself, Miss Macallum. Below St Francis

506

but above Mother Teresa, would that be about right?'

Feenie took this with a faint smile, but Kelly turned angrily on Daphne.

'What do you know about anything? Who the hell are you anyway, with your snooty accent and hundred-quid hairdo?'

'Takes a one to know a one,' said Daphne with spirit. 'As to who I am, among other things, I'm a customer of the Nortrust Bank, so I suppose I'm one of the victims you and your grandmother have been robbing.'

'No, there aren't any victims. The bank owed my grandmother that money,' retorted Kelly.

'It's all right, dear,' said Feenie.

'No, they can say what they like about me but not about you,' said Kelly. 'So listen in, Miss Twinset and Pearls, but be careful. I may shock you so much you'll mess your silk drawers. I move money around for certain groups in South America. Dirty money, you'd call it. But it's dirty work these groups have to do, a bit like your housemaid cleaning your grate.'

'For someone who looks so young, you really are awfully dated, my dear,' murmured Daphne. 'But do get on with your interesting exposition.'

'One good route for cleaning it up is to pass it through a charitable organization. I've always been interested in Liberata, as a cause, I mean. In fact, I've used my South American contacts to get the names of women Liberata could help, sometimes women I knew personally, and I've passed them on to my grandmother. So naturally I thought of using its account in one of my laundry operations. I say naturally because something always gets left behind and I'd have seen to it that Liberata got a real benefit. Only there was a problem. Some of the organizations I act for have their financial basis in the cocaine industry. Sometimes it's used directly instead of currency, but mostly it has to be sold to get the money to buy whatever's necessary to keep the struggle going. And that's the money which needs to be cleaned up.'

'Cleaned up? You could shovel it into a furnace and the ashes would still stink!' interrupted Daphne.

'Hey, I'm surprised you don't get on better with Gran,' said Kelly. 'That's the way she thinks. She wanted nothing to do with my little proposal. In fact, we had a serious falling-out. I felt I'd disappointed her and I wanted to make it up to her. Then I saw the Nortrust Bank advertising for a systems expert and suddenly I saw the way. You see, I knew they owed her.'

'Ollershaw. George Ollershaw.'

The words were spoken so softly it took a moment to trace them to their source.

It was Shirley Novello, face still pale as death, eyes hardly open, lips hardly moving. But nothing the matter with her ears. Good cop. Always working. Peter will be pleased, thought Ellie.

'Right,' said Kelly. 'How do you know that?'

'Financial adviser . . . ran him off the road . . . could've killed him. I saw the file. Should have made the connection . . .'

Suddenly Ellie did make a connection – between the skimpy pants she'd found at Nosebleed and Cornelius. Feenie must have had to get her out in a hurry when Mrs Stonelady told her Daphne and friends were on their way. Presumably Feenie had informed her granddaughter there was a cop, and a cop's wife, in the party.

So why was Kelly talking so freely?

The good answer was because she was confident of being long gone before Novello was in a fit state to use any of it against her.

The bad answer was because she didn't have much hope that any of them would be in a fit state for anything when this came to its end.

How close was that end? From time to time there were noises beneath them. Popeye, Jorge and Luis down in the cellar, she presumed. When they returned . . .

Look on the bright side. Every time she thought about Rosie wandering around alone in the increasingly wild weather, her stomach churned. She longed to see her, hold her, comfort her. But if she'd been given the power to transport her to her side, she knew it would have been an act of huge selfishness to use it. The blacker things looked in here, the better off Rosie was at the mercy of nothing worse than wind and rain.

And that was the bright side!

She shook these thoughts out of her mind and said, 'Feenie? Is this true?'

'Not in law, maybe, but I was certainly cheated out of money by Ollershaw, and Nortrust ultimately benefited. So yes, I felt entitled.'

'Could you explain that for the benefit of us poor citizens who are bound by more conventional notions of legality?' said Daphne sweetly.

Ellie recalled some of the doubts she knew Peter still had about Patrick Aldermann and wondered if any of them had ever impinged on Daphne's consciousness. You could know a lot about people, but there were always no-go areas.

Feenie gave a succinct account of her dealings with George Ollershaw, concluding, 'So that's the story, Mrs Aldermann. You must decide for yourself if I had a grievance.'

Daphne, who would hold up long supermarket queues to dispute a possible ten-pence overcharge, nodded vigorously and said, 'I should think you had! You say you ran him off the road? You should have waited till he got out of his car and finished the job!'

'That wouldn't have got Gran's money back,' said Kelly. 'My plan did. I worked out that Ollershaw's little fiddle had done Gran out of at least three million pounds, including interest, and that's the amount I took Nortrust for. And I left all lines leading back to dear old George. The more they dig, the worse it's going to look for him. The only way he's going to keep out of jail is by paying it back out of his own personal savings.'

'Bravo,' said Daphne, completely converted. 'And the three million, I take it, is somehow going to end in Liberata's account as a genuine charitable donation?'

'You got it,' said Kelly. 'And I assure you that the law's got more chance of finding Lord Lucan than they have of tracing that money back to Nortrust.'

She and Daphne were smiling at each other like old chums now and Ellie, feeling an irrational urge to interpose her own body, said rather sourly, 'If you'd got things tied up so neatly, why were you doing a runner when my husband caught you?'

'Your husband? Of course. You're the policeman's wife. And in answer to your policeman's question, something came up. Nothing to do with Nortrust. I needed to get somewhere safe with people I knew who would help sort it out.'

She glanced shamefacedly at her grandmother, who said, 'I think these good people who have been led into peril by your irresponsible behaviour deserve the whole story, don't you? A story which, incidentally, I knew nothing about until this afternoon.'

Kelly grimaced like a child finally obliged to confront an unpleasant task she has been putting off. She was one of those rare women whose beauty survives the expression of no matter what emotion, thought Ellie enviously. I bet that red-eyed and snively she'd still get the fellows horny.

'Gran, I'm really sorry,' she said. 'Like I told you, I wouldn't have done it but it was an emergency. I'm sorry.'

'Would you please stop being sorry and start being clear?' exploded Daphne. 'I thought all this Nortrust stuff was leading up to an explanation of why we're sitting here at the mercy of these lunatics. You mean there's something else? Something worse?'

Simply and directly, Kelly told them about PAL and Fidel Chiquillo and Popeye's arms cache and the deal with the Cojos and the shoot out in Kielder. Rapt though she was by the narrative, Ellie had time to observe the rapid dissolution of the brief rapport between Kelly and Daphne, who believed that terrorists in general and Irish terrorists in particular should be hung by their balls till their scrotums snapped.

'Fidel suspected the Cojos might try a double-cross,' concluded Kelly. 'So we had a contingency plan. I knew no one ever came close to this place any more, and Feenie was out of the country, and I thought we could get things turned around long before she came back. But Fidel was wounded, so that was going to take a little time, and then . . .'

She glanced uncertainly at Feenie, who replied with a glower which defied her to be reticent, then went on, '. . . and I got this warning message, don't know where from, telling me it was time to go, and when I told Fidel, he said no point in hanging about to see what happened, I should make a run for it, head back to South America where in any case I could be useful contacting his friends to make new arrangements for receipt of the arms shipment. But unfortunately . . .'

'You met my husband on the Snake,' said Ellie. 'How unlucky for both of you.'

'Oh, I wouldn't say that. I must admit I was really knocked over when I found he was a cop, though. He's such a dish.'

She flashed a smile, congratulatory, almost conspiratorial. From another woman it might have stirred jealous resentment, but somehow Ellie felt simply complimented.

She smiled back, then Daphne threw in some cold water by saying, 'So what you're saying is we're up to our necks in trouble because this terrorist friend of yours brought a truckload of IRA arms here and you hid them in some cellar beneath our feet?'

'That's right. But don't be frightened,' said Kelly, brightly reassuring. 'They won't go off unless someone's smoking down there.'

'Ha ha,' said Daphne, stung by the accusation of fear into what Ellie thought of as her brisk Girl Guide Commissioner manner. 'In fact, I was just wondering how you and your wounded friend managed to unload the arms. Must have been an effort even for someone as wirily built as yourself.'

It took real expertise to find something downputting to say about Kelly's figure. Perhaps, thought Ellie, for whom this was turning into something of an apostatizing experience, there was something to be said for private education after all.

'I had help. Mrs Stonelady's Donald.'

The old countrywoman had been sitting still as a stone on a mountainside and scarcely more noticeable since their arrival. Now all eyes, except for Novello's, which were once more firmly closed, turned to her.

Feenie said, slightly accusing, 'Mrs Stonelady?'

'I does what's asked and says nowt,' declared the woman. 'If they didn't turn off my bread-and-butter, it'll be ruined.'

This seemed a pretty fair assertion of both philosophy and priorities, thought Ellie. Oh for such certainties!

Wendy Woolley, as though in a classroom, half raised her hand and said, 'Please, I have a question.'

'Yes?'

'What happened to the cocaine? And your friend, Fidel?'

Before Kelly could reply, there was a noise from the doorway and the three men returned from the cellar. Luis was carrying a bulky leather grip.

The two Cojos were as usual engaged in animated conversation. They spoke too low for Ellie to catch what they were saying, and in any case they were rattling away at a speed which would have made it impossible for someone at her level of colloquial Spanish to understand more than the occasional very basic phrase.

Popeye seemed to be in the same or perhaps an even less seaworthy boat. He looked from one of the Colombians to the other, shook his head as if in puzzlement that such a cacophony could actually make sense, took a swig from a bottle of water he was holding, then came wandering across to the women.

'How are you doing, ladies?' he asked. 'Anyone like a drink?'

He offered the bottle. Ellie took it, wiped the top, and drank, then passed it on to Feenie.

She took a pull, then said, 'What's going on?'

'You'd need to be a United Nations interpreter to know that,' said Popeye. 'But in any case I don't think it's anything you need to be bothering your old grey head with, lady.'

The old grey head gave him a coldly assessing stare which chilled Ellie, but the Irishman's eyes had already slid from the grandmother to the granddaughter.

'I see you found the left luggage,' said Kelly pertly.

'That's all I'm here for, darling. Getting what's rightly mine. You'll not dispute that, will you?'

'I won't. But you don't imagine those two are going to let you keep it, do you?'

'Now why shouldn't they? It's mine, they know that. Whose the weapons are is between Jorge and your friend, what's-his-name? Chiquilla, is it?'

'Chiquillo,' said Kelly precisely.

'Of course. Sorry, darling, I was never very good

at the old linguistics, hard enough coping with English,' said Popeye, giving her a broad smile which she didn't return. 'But while we're on the subject of Chiquilla, sorry, *o*, I ought to warn you. Those two are seriously pissed off because your friend wasn't here to greet them. Sooner or later they're going to start asking you where he might be. If you know, I would seriously advise you to tell them, sooner rather than later, which might be too late. I'll do what I can for you. Blood's thicker than water, they say. But that works against you too, you see. One of those two goons your guy killed was Jorge's brother.'

Kelly said, 'And the two men he killed were your friends. For God's sake, Uncle Paddy, how can you stomach working with these people when they killed your friends?'

'Now I don't know that, do I? All I heard were a lot of shots and when I opened my eyes and decided I wasn't in heaven, there were bodies everywhere and the only person officially alive was our unpronounceable friend, which has to mean something. Jorge told me that it was him that must have planned the double-cross, and then he went all the way and killed his own people too. Makes sense.'

'No, it doesn't, and you know it,' said Kelly forcibly. 'Tell me this. Did you find Jorge or did he come looking for you?'

'Bit of both,' said Popeye, smiling slyly. 'He thinks he found me, but I wanted to be found.

When you've been nearly killed and totally ripped off, you've got to be ready to deal with anyone who can help you get your pension fund back, wouldn't you agree? As a businesswoman, that is.'

'Maybe. But as a businesswoman, I'd be very careful about my long-term investments.'

'Is that right? I'll remember that. Getting back to your own long term, me darling Kansas, when Jorge starts asking, I'd have my story ready. Tell him the plain truth. That's what I did. Told him everything I saw and heard as I lay there pretending to be dead because I didn't know what your friend would do if he knew I wasn't dead.'

'And what did you see and hear, Uncle Paddy?'

'Well, I heard him ringing someone, you, I expect it was, and talk about hiding the stuff in the CP, which is here. And I saw him take his shirt off. Oh God, even in my condition that was a shocking sight to see, truly shocking.'

'Why?' said Kelly urgently, her eyes riveted on Popeye's face. 'And what did you tell Jorge?'

Popeye met her gaze blankly for a moment then smiled a slow sly smile.

'Why? It was such a terrible wound the poor creature had, a killing wound, I reckoned. I could hardly bear to look at it. That's what I told Jorge, that if your friend made it here, it must have been on willpower, and I couldn't see how he'd survive the trip. My bet is he died after he got here, and you wrapped the body in a blanket and weighted it down with rocks and tipped it into that sea out there. That's what I told Jorge. But he'll need to be persuaded. Think you can manage that, Kansas?'

Now it was Kelly's turn to peer into the Irishman's face as if in search of something she wasn't certain of finding.

Then she nodded and said gently, 'Thanks, Uncle Paddy. I think I can manage that. You take care of yourself now.'

It was like being at a play, *Cymbeline*, say, which was constructed like a wildebeest, no part matching any other, and you'd no idea of the plot, and you'd missed the first two acts, and you had a seat behind a pillar, and the people around you were coughing and eating popcorn noisily.

What the hell was going on here? wondered Ellie.

'Don't fret over me,' laughed Popeye. 'Harder to kill than a crab louse on a baboon's ballocks, that's what they say about me in the Vatican. Hello, looks like it's showtime.'

The two Cojos seemed to have reached a decision, and Jorge was beckoning Popeye imperiously to join them.

As he moved away, Daphne whispered to Kelly, 'Is he really your uncle?'

'Strictly speaking, no. But when one Irishman meets another he's going to do business with, first thing they do is try to establish a family connection.

When my dada met Paddy years back, they worked out that their great-grandmothers had been second cousins or some such thing, and after that he became Uncle Paddy to me.'

'So no relation of yours, Miss Macallum?'

Feenie looked at her like a Fundamentalist confronted by Darwinism.

'Not many of my relatives have given me cause for pride,' she said sourly. 'But at least I can boast that I do not count Mr Ducannon amongst them.'

'Come on, Gran, he's not that bad,' said Kelly spiritedly.

'Then how come he's so chummy with those monsters?'

'Doesn't look all that chummy to me.'

She was right.

Popeye was making some point very forcibly, with Jorge and Luis looking pretty unconvinced.

They made some attempt to keep their voices down but as tempers rose, so did the sound level. Soon it became clear that Popeye had asserted his moral right to be identified as the owner of the coke and his legal right as one who has met his share of a bargain to move on out.

Wise move, thought Ellie. In the little red book of law-breaking, it said that before a crime, time was your friend, but after a crime, time was your enemy. Or, more simply, plan very carefully, run very fast.

Hard to run fast when you had a lot of heavy crates to lug out of a cellar and load into a truck.

Much easier when all you had to carry was a case full of coke.

Luis was objecting on the grounds that Popeye would need transport and their vehicles weren't going anywhere till they'd got the arms loaded.

Popeye responded that there were at least three cars parked around the house and he was quite capable of helping himself to one of these, thank you.

Then Jorge said, 'No. It's better that we stick together. We need you to help us with the crates. Then we all leave together.'

Not much of rational argument here, but something about the way he spoke gave the message that beyond this, words would not be the medium of debate, and Popeye, with the wisdom of long survival, shrugged and smiled and said, 'OK. No sweat.'

'*Bueno!*' said Jorge, suddenly very friendly. 'We are all partners here, agreed? Now, why don't you and Luis go to fetch the truck as close as you can get? I will start these two strong men bringing the crates up from below.'

'Doesn't need two to bring the truck,' objected Popeye.

'Not to drive, but this ground is not too safe and the weather is making things worse. It may need one to walk ahead making sure. To get bogged down now would be disastrous, no?'

'Good point,' capitulated Popeye. 'So let's be off then, Luis.'

The two men went out.

As if to signal their departure, a tremendous jag of lightning cracked the eastern sky and the window seemed to dissolve as the onshore wind hurled the first cataract of rain at the flexing glass.

Jorge went and stood against it, looking out, like some mad scientist in one of the old horror movies, trying to draw strength directly from the elements. When he turned, his gaze ran over the huddling women, then settled into a focused stare. Ellie had no difficulty pinpointing its object, and even less reading his mind.

Kelly Cornelius.

He'd got Popeye out of the way. Maybe he'd even fixed with Luis to get the Irishman permanently out of the way.

Now he was going to go to work on Kelly to discover the whereabouts of the elusive Chiquillo. And in the intensity of his gaze, Ellie saw that it wasn't just desire of revenge that was going to inform his questioning. There was desire of another sort there too. So far, God be thanked, in all the shifting mass of menace which had rolled across the terrace from the moment of the shot, there had been no sexual element. But that, she saw, from the shine of his eyes and the swelling of his crotch, was over.

For an irrational moment she felt a huge resentment directed at Kelly. Why the hell did she have to be so fucking attractive? Everything about their demeanour had said that these were men in a hurry, keen to get their loot loaded and be far away from this remote and frightening neck of the woods. To them Axness must look like a trap ready to close. Would Jorge's keenness to locate Chiquillo have kept him here long? Possibly not. Chiquillo, if still alive, would keep. But for Jorge, interrogating Kelly was going to be an absolute pleasure, not just a means to an end. Kelly would resist . . . he would want her to resist. She recalled the easy unthinking way he'd dealt with Daphne and Novello. When he'd finished with Kelly, chances were she'd be dead.

And once he'd killed one of them, what were the others but dangerous witnesses?

'You,' said Jorge to Little Ajax. 'Watch them. If they move, shoot.'

And to Big Ajax he said, pointing at Kelly, 'You, bring her.'

He set off to the door, confident in his commands being obeyed.

Big Ajax moved forward.

Ellie scrambled to her feet. Images were jumbling in her brain. Horatius jumping onto the bridge. Spartacus attacking the head of gladiator school, Lytton Strachey telling the tribunal that if he saw a horrid Hun about to ravish his sister, he'd try to interpose his own body.

Why did men get all the best stories?

She said, 'No.'

She didn't know what she expected, except of course support. Horatius got his two chums,

Spartacus got an army of revolting slaves, even Strachey probably got a quickly suppressed laugh.

All she got was a headmistressly rebuke from Feenie.

'Ellie, don't be silly. Sit down!'

True, Daphne made a token effort to rise but when Feenie's hand pressed down on her shoulder, she subsided without much resistance. Woolly Wendy kept her head and eyes as low as a grazing sheep, Mrs Stonelady didn't even register that anything out of the ordinary was passing. Only Kelly stood up, looked at her grandmother, smiled, and said, 'It's OK, Ellie. I'll be fine.'

'Fine? No! We can't let this happen!' cried Ellie.

And as Big Ajax reached his arm forward to grasp Kelly, Ellie seized it, bent her head, and sank her teeth into the ball of his thumb.

She had some recollection from the sensational literature of her childhood that this caused such a distracting pain that a nimble heroine could usually find time to make her escape.

Big Ajax must have read other books. He dragged his hand out of her mouth and swung it at her face with a force that sent her crashing against the window. Then he took Kelly's arm and pulled her, unresisting, through the doorway.

Ellie removed her face from the glass. The storm outside seemed to be raging in her head. The now almost continual lightning flashes lit up the window with such intensity that the rain streaming down the glass looked red as blood.

Then as her head cleared a little she realized it *was* blood, hers, on the inside.

She put her hand to her nose, which hurt like hell, and turned to face her cowardly companions, expecting to see their faces dark with guilt.

'Now we're a matching pair,' said Daphne, not without satisfaction. 'Perhaps at last I'll get a little sympathy.'

xvi

a palomino pony

Uncle Paddy . . .
Popeye . . .
the Pop-Up Man . . .
Patrick Ducannon didn't mind what people called him, so long as they stayed a long pace short of the truth of him.

He was a great survivor, that was certainly part of the truth, but his famous hair's-breadth escapes from death were only a part of that part. It was good to be lucky, but early on in his career as a Volunteer, he'd decided that a man who relied on luck alone in this line of work was very soon going to be dead lucky. However, it didn't harm at all to let the world at large think that this indeed was what he relied upon, as it distracted their minds from other possibilities.

There was for instance the question of his linguistic ability. In fact, he had an excellent ear for languages and could speak good colloquial Spanish, but he saw no reason to let people know that he'd got beyond basic tourist level – not even when the people happened to be his 'niece' and her friend, Chiquillo, and certainly not when they happened to be Jorge Casaravilla and Luis Romea.

Hearing what people said, when they didn't think it mattered you could hear, was a very useful aid in helping a man spin out his good fairy's gift of luck.

So he knew for certain what Kelly had guessed, that the two Cojos had no more intention of letting him walk away with the bag of coke than he had of joining the Orange Order.

It was simply a question of when and where they decided to get rid of him. Jorge would have shot him at the CP in front of the women, no problem, but Luis had argued that it was better if he simply disappeared, no witnesses, no body. Then no one could contradict their report that he'd taken off with the grip, and there'd be no question of sharing the money from the drugs with any of the innumerable *manazas* or big hands reaching out of the murky swirl of political protection surrounding the Cojos.

It was good reasoning and Jorge had been persuaded. But Popeye had a feeling that Luis, though no doubt ruthless enough in a good cause, i.e. his own profit and protection, lacked Jorge's total indifference to, bordering on positive enthusiasm for, the use of violence as a first resort. He guessed that if he took the chance now of having a quiet word with the man and saying, 'Look, I've been thinking, and on the whole, I reckon I'd be better off out of this, so what I'm going to do is help myself to one of the women's cars and take off into the night and you and Jorge can do what you like with the gear back there, OK?' he wouldn't get an argument.

On the other hand, he would be going home empty-handed when what he wanted to be going home with was his pension fund. This kind of stuff was very wearing and he'd been at it far too long now and he felt he deserved a few years in the sun some place where all the colours green and orange meant was leaves and fruit on the trees in his garden.

So, a quiet word with Luis or not? In fact, just at the moment it wasn't a real choice as the storm raging around them made any kind of word, quiet or noisy, a waste of breath. The only good thing was that the gale was at their backs, blowing them inland, like a pair of skiffs caught too far out at sea by a sudden tempest and driven landwards at such a speed and with such a lack of control the oarsmen do not know if the breakers ahead marking the shore signal their salvation or their grave.

Not a comfortable thought for a good Catholic boy to be having, especially a good Catholic boy who hadn't been to Mass for longer than a good Catholic boy in his line of work ought to regard as sensible.

The storm wasn't just affecting the way he was

thinking, it seemed to have had a strange trans-mogrifying effect on the terrain they were crossing, changing it from the overgrown and extensive but nonetheless conventional garden they'd passed over not all that long ago to something more like an Amazonian jungle. Suddenly he recalled the Englishwoman, the policeman's wife, the one who'd taken a leak on the terrace, saying something about her little daughter being loose in this. He hoped to heaven the child had found shelter. Her mother must be worried sick. On the other hand, if she was a sensible woman, and she looked pretty sensible, she'd have the wit to work out that the little girl was a sight better off out here in the rain than in there in the warm with mad, bad, dangerous Jorge who was definitely one Ave short of a Rosary.

Through the driving rain and the surging shrub-bery he glimpsed lights ahead and his heart hic-coughed in shock till he realized they must be the lights of the house. The women had been having a good time there, eating, drinking, laughing at the unimaginable kind of things women prob-ably laughed at when left to themselves, then Jorge had come sweeping in like Cromwell and his Ironsides at Drogheda, and the laughter had to stop. There'd been a fine smell of cooking about the place and the memory made Popeye realize that he was extremely hungry. Maybe there'd be something left of the feast for them to forage. He plucked at Luis's sleeve and gestured first at his mouth then towards the house, but the Colombian shook his head and forked off right towards the outbuildings where they'd parked the Merc and the truck.

Shaking his head at this new evidence of Latin stupidity, Popeye followed. Thick sandwich washed down by a mug of coffee liberally laced with whiskey (or even whisky) would armour a man against this terrible night, surely even Luis must feel that? Could the poor bastard be so terrified of Jorge that he didn't dare to deviate even slightly from his orders?

Still grumbling to himself, he followed the other into the ruined barn where the truck was hidden and was still so absorbed in his grumble that it took him a long moment to realize that his question had just been answered. What Jorge decreed was law.

Luis was standing by the truck with his automatic pointed straight at Popeye's head.

'Ah, come on now,' said the Irishman. 'This is a joke, isn't it? Don't muck about, let's get the truck down to the pavilion.'

'Stand still!' commanded the Cojo.

'I'm standing, I'm standing. Listen, if this is about the coke, forget it. I was going to suggest anyway, why don't I just take myself one of the women's cars and head out of here? That's all I want really. I wouldn't be here at all in the first place if Jorge hadn't come looking for me and twisted my arm, you know that. I'm just a plain businessman, win some, lose some, cut your losses. I'd written the coke off as a bad deal till Jorge found me. He's a persuasive fellow, that one, but that doesn't mean he's always right. So what do you say? Close your eyes for a minute and I'm gone. You can tell the man I ran off into the night, and to be sure, isn't it a hell of a good night to be running off into?'

He was getting to him, he could see that. He'd been right about Luis. Takes a one to know a one, and like himself the man was no natural born killer. He too had probably got into his line of business by chance and drift and a readiness to take the nearest way when no road led him anywhere he passionately longed to be.

He smiled almost affectionately at the man and thought he saw the beginnings of a response dawning in his eyes and on his lips.

Then there was a sound like a cough which someone couldn't quite suppress in church during the holy silence at the Elevation of the Host, and it was as if dawn's rosy fingers touched the Colombian's chest and poked right through to his heart.

He actually seemed to smile, or perhaps it was just a mortal rictus, then he let out a deep sigh, and Luis Romea, whose father ran cattle and bred fine horses on the *llanos* close where the Orinoco flings its wide curve towards the distant Atlantic, and who dreamt of wearing the gay tunic and bright braid of an army officer till consumption touched his left lung, leaving him ready prey for recruitment into the Cojos because this seemed to a young

530

man just another branch of the public service he yearned for, but whose service later brought him many sleepless nights when he lay with damp and open eyes, remembering a young boy on a palomino pony making imaginary cavalry charges across the high grassy plains to bring relief and justice to long-sieged cities – this Luis Romea, who might have been a good man, heard his pony neigh somewhere near, and closed his eyes, and died.

Popeye Ducannon span round and looked at the slightly built, thinly moustached figure who stood framed in the square of the hayloft loading window above him and cried, 'Is it you then? I knew you must be near. Why the hell did you do that? I was getting to him!'

'Too long, you took. Besides, it is one less. Come now, for there are others nigh. Come away. Come away.'

With a last regretful look at the crumpled figure lying in front of the truck, Popeye scrambled up a pile of rubble and, following his rescuer through the gap, lowered himself into the turbulent darkness without.

Two minutes later, united for once in impatience, the small party laying siege to the barn decided to investigate.

Sempernel's operatives, Cynthia and Jacobs, came first, crouching in the doorway and sending their torch-beams prying into the darkest corners.

'Shit,' said Jacobs when he spotted the body. 'Cover me.'

A moment later Cynthia came out and said to the trio pressed hard against the outer wall, 'All clear. One dead. Romea. No sign of Ducannon.'

If it is a mark of greatness to be able to react to any eventuality as if it were both expected and welcome, then Sempernel was great.

'Excellent,' he said, striding into the barn and looking down at the shot man. 'A falling-out among thieves. This suits us admirably.'

Pascoe shook his head in mingled fury and wonder.

'This suits us admirably?' he parodied. 'Would you care to parse that? No, don't bother. Andy, we've got a wounded officer, Ellie's a hostage, and now we've got a dead body. Isn't it time we stopped letting this fucking idiot call the shots and took control?'

He doesn't mean *we*, thought Andy Dalziel, recognizing the desperate fear in the younger man's voice. He means me. He wants me to pull a sodding rabbit out of the hat. Only I've looked in my hat and there's nowt there but sodding rabbit shit.

If this hadn't been personal, if Ellie hadn't been one of the women imprisoned in the pavilion, he'd probably have said, 'Listen, lad, it were you who skived off to go on that hostage-negotiating course, you're the sodding expert here, why don't you read your notes and tell us what we ought to do now?'

But sarcasm wasn't an option. He knew what he ought to do. He ought to get through to Mid-Yorkshire Control and ask for every Armed Response

Unit within hailing distance to be dispatched hell for leather out to Gunnery House. That would keep his nose clean whatever happened. But as a lad, to his mother's vast irritation, he'd never seen much point to using a handkerchief when his gansey sleeve was so much more handy.

He stopped, picked up the dead man's baseball cap and tried to fit it on his head where it lay like a tea cosy on Ben Nevis.

'Right,' he said. 'They're obviously expecting a truck. Let's take them a truck. Jump in the back all them as is coming.'

'Superintendent, this is stupid,' said Sempernel at his most commanding. 'I absolutely forbid it.'

'What're you going to do? Shoot me? Pete, you coming?'

'Not in the back,' said Pascoe, plucking the cap from the Fat Man's head. 'Anyone sees me in the cab might just about take me for this guy. You've not got the figure for it. Sorry.'

He didn't wait for a reply, but climbed into the cab, and Dalziel didn't try to offer an argument but lowered the tailgate and scrambled in with surprising agility.

'Right,' he said. 'Any more for the *Skylark*?'

The two security operatives looked at their leader, who once again displayed his capacity to ride the wind even when it was blowing a gale.

Smiling benevolently, Sempernel said, 'Looks like you're calling the shots, Superintendent. Come on, you two. Give me a hand here, will you?'

And pushed from behind by his underlings, and pulled from above by Dalziel, Gawain Sempernel mounted with some difficulty and prepared to ride forth to do battle.

xvii

a formal complaint

Ellie's nose was split, not broken, as Feenie established by taking a firm hold of its bridge and waggling it around.

'Je-sus!' exclaimed Ellie. What a break would feel like if this wasn't one, she didn't care to imagine.

She accepted the offer of a smudge of Mrs Stonelady's yarrow ointment because it seemed silly to miss the chance of being anointed with the same salve that had, allegedly, done such good service under the walls of Troy, though from her memory of the flesh-ripping, bone-shattering, gut-spilling injuries described by Homer, the sight of Achilles approaching with a small jar of gunge can't have been all that reassuring.

It had a pungent peppery smell (good, her nose was still functioning) and stung a little at first, but quickly established a mild local anaesthetic effect.

As these ministrations were taking place, part

of her mind was glad of the distraction from the pictures another part was running of what might be happening to Kelly, and her ears still strained for the sound of screams, but no sound came, or at least nothing loud enough to penetrate the din of the storm which was now beating its giant fists unrelentingly against the plate-glass window.

She couldn't take any comfort from the absence of cries. Maybe Jorge had taken Kelly down to the cellar, or simply gagged her, though this would be a bit counterproductive if he was attempting to get information out of her about the disappeared Chiquillo.

'What are we going to do about Kelly?' she whispered to Feenie as the old woman examined her dressing critically.

'Whatever we can,' said Feenie, glancing significantly towards Little Ajax, who had seated himself on the single rickety chair which spread its legs under his bulk, like a weightlifter taking the strain. 'And preferably without any more amateur heroics, please.'

For a second, Ellie's pain was blanked by angry resentment. Not to be backed up in her gesture of defiance was bad enough, but to be rebuked for it was past bearing.

'For God's sake,' she hissed. 'We can't just sit here . . .'

'Yes, we can,' said Feenie. 'We can sit and look defeated. Let our friend there get used to the idea that as a group we offer no threat, then it will be even harder for him to imagine that any single part of the group can be remotely dangerous.'

This sounded like total defeatism to Ellie. She wanted to reply angrily, then pulled herself up. Feenie was very old. She looked at her now and for the first time saw just how old. She'd got so used to seeing her as the energetic embodiment of positive action against the world's injustices that to adjust the focus and glimpse the ancient bag lady that others saw was a disjunctive shock. Worse, that lined and sunken face was now smeared with tears and her whole body seemed to be caving in, like a worked-out mine with the tunnel props decayed or removed.

Wendy Woolley put a protective arm around her and pressed the ancient head against her shoulder, glaring accusingly at Ellie, then murmuring comforting words in the old woman's ear. After a while Feenie whispered something back in tones too low and broken for Ellie to catch, then Wendy looked towards Little Ajax, raised her free hand in the schoolroom manner Ellie had noticed before, and murmured, 'Excuse me.'

Either he didn't catch it or, like a sadistic teacher, preferred to ignore it, sitting on his chair of authority, looking straight ahead.

She repeated slightly louder, 'Excuse me. Please.'

Now she had his attention. They knew this because the pistol dangling from his hand came up to cover them.

Wendy said, 'Miss Macallum needs to go to the toilet.'

Little Ajax stared at her blankly. Was he foreign? Alien? Or just thick? wondered Ellie.

Wendy went into the English middle-class speech mode which does for any or all of the three.

Speaking very loudly and distinctly she said, 'Old lady want toilet. You understand toilet? To relieve herself. Pee-pee. Understand pee-pee?'

Little Ajax shook his head, whether to indicate he didn't understand pee-pee or didn't give a toss wasn't clear.

Wendy slowly rose, lifting the almost strengthless figure of the old woman with her.

'Toilet,' she said firmly, pointing to the door. 'Pee-pee.'

Now Little Ajax understood something and didn't much care for it. Angrily, he shook his head and the gun started waving with increased menace.

'It is necessary,' declared Wendy, beginning to move forward.

To Ellie's eyes, the man seriously considered shooting her but finally compromised by putting his impassable bulk between the advancing couple and the door.

Wendy urged the old lady another step forward, paused, studied the gun which was now aimed unwaveringly at her chest, and said, 'All right. But she must go. Over there in the corner then.'

As she spoke she did a little mime which managed to be at the same time explicit and as delicate as the circumstances permitted.

Oh God, thought Ellie, recalling her own experience on the terrace. What indignities our bodies put us to.

It was hard to read any emotion on Little Ajax's face other than the aggressive menace for which it seemed specially cast, but a look of which might have been relief at the reaching of an acceptable compromise touched his eyes as he nodded agreement.

Wendy led Feenie to the corner by the window furthest away from the sitting group. Feenie squatted down, gesturing Wendy away with a last pathetic attempt to preserve some of her dignity. Wendy came back towards the group, stopping as she passed the guard and angrily indicating that he shouldn't watch with another mime, this time shielding her eyes. Almost shamefaced, Little Ajax averted his gaze.

Wendy walked on another pace, then halted again and swung round to face him, her body stiff with indignation.

'I just want to tell you that this outrageous behaviour will not go unreported,' she said. 'I shall take the first opportunity offered me to write to my MP and make a formal complaint on behalf of Miss Macallum and the rest of us. You may rest assured that any further inconvenience which may be visited upon us will be added to the already lengthy list of matters for redress. Do you understand me, my man?'

Was the woman stark staring mad? wondered

Ellie. Her own heroics might have been futile but this was positively surreal!

Then she saw what she hadn't noticed at first because all her attention was focused on Wendy.

Feenie was upright and moving forward, no longer the pathetic broken geriatric of a moment ago, but with something predatory in her pace and on her features.

Little Ajax's attention was even more focused on Wendy's scoldings, but something in the atmosphere, or in someone's eyes, gave him warning.

He began to turn.

And Wendy Woolley pounced, leaping forward to drive her knee into his crotch (my move! thought Ellie), at the same time grabbing his gun hand at the wrist and forcing it sideways.

Little Ajax's finger squeezed reflexively on the trigger. A stream of bullets lashed against the window. The glass crazed where they hit but didn't break. Someone screamed. Ellie wouldn't have taken bets it wasn't her. Then she realized it could have been Wendy. Blood was bubbling from her thigh. She must have been hit by a ricochet. She hung on gamely but Little Ajax seized the chance of her distraction to hurl her from him. She crashed to the floor beneath the window. Still crouching under the pain to his balls, he brought the gun round to bear on her head. Ellie was still in that it-all-happened-so-quickly state which in the past she'd sometimes mocked as a good excuse for doing nothing. But even if her body had obeyed instantly her commands to get up off its arse and give assistance, she couldn't have got anywhere near the action in time to influence the outcome.

But Feenie could. And did.

It was neat and undramatic and final.

Her left arm went round Little Ajax's bull neck, her right hand rested against his jaw, she made a sharp twisting movement, there was a click, and when she moved away, the body folded slackly and crashed down on the rickety chair, reducing it to kindling.

'Oh my,' said Daphne, round-eyed. 'And I argued with her about money.'

Ellie was on her feet now, hurrying forward to give what help she could to Wendy Woolley. But her reaction was in its own way just as astonishing as Feenie's intervention. Instead of lying there, gritting her teeth against the pain till somebody did something to her bleeding thigh, she had crawled forward, grabbed the gun which had fallen from Little Ajax's hand, and was now expertly removing the ammunition clip and checking it out. She didn't look happy with what she found, and began searching through the dead man's clothing.

As Ellie knew from personal experience, kneeing a guy in the balls required no special training, but this smelt strongly of expertise.

Feenie thought so too.

'I was beginning to wonder about you, my dear,' she said. 'What are you? A security plant?'

'I suggest we discuss it later,' said Wendy. 'Shit. This idiot didn't carry any reserve ammo. And this clip has got only one round left in it. Sounds like a good recipe for poker.'

'Bezique is more my game, dear. Mrs Aldermann, would you care to listen at the door and yell out if you hear anything? I don't think we need worry too much that we've attracted attention. If we can't hear what our friend Jorge is up to, then he certainly won't be able to hear us. Let's have a look at that leg, Mrs Woolley. Ellie, fetch the medicine box, will you?'

She cut the woman's skirt to reveal the wound, which she examined critically for a moment then said, 'More buttock than thigh, fortunately. I can see some metal in there. Best to get it out. There should be some tweezers in the box, Ellie. Thank you. Would you mind putting that gun down, Mrs Woolley? I should hate to be shot dead with our one remaining bullet, and this might hurt a little.'

It must have hurt a lot if the sweat pouring down Wendy's face was any indication, but apart from one gasp, she bore the pain in silence.

Finally Feenie applied Achilles's salve and bound up the wound, saying cheerfully, 'We're going to need another batch of your ointment, Mrs Stonelady, if things go on like this.'

The old countrywoman had been studying the recumbent Little Ajax with some interest.

'This here's a dead 'un,' she opined finally. 'You've done for him, missus.'

'Yes, I know,' said Feenie. 'In my prime, I could have just laid him out, but age reduces the options, I'm afraid. Now it's all or nothing, and in the circumstances, it had to be all.'

From the doorway, Daphne said, 'That German officer, the one who interrupted you when you were . . . you never told us how that turned out.'

Feenie smiled.

'Much the same, my dear. As this one here did with age, poor Fritz confused nakedness with harmlessness. But this is no time for trips down memory lane. Mrs Woolley, or whatever your name really is, how close are your people?'

Wendy didn't prevaricate.

'Close,' she said. 'They've been watching the house.'

'How many?'

'Only three.'

'Marvellous. First time in my life I've wanted to be haunted by spooks in droves and we're down to three,' said Feenie. 'What are they likely to be doing?'

'I don't know,' admitted the woman. 'Hoping to hear from me, for a start.'

'And how might they do that?' said Feenie hopefully.

'They can't. They could have done if you'd let me bring my handbag, which contains both my radio and my gun.'

'My fault, is it? I'm sorry but I'm not psychic. What was the last thing you told them?'

'I told them I'd heard you talking about the Command Post. They'd been speculating what CP stood for.'

'So they've probably got a pretty good idea of the situation here and could have rustled up some extra help?'

Wendy Woolley shook her head.

'My boss isn't a man to involve more people than he feels absolutely necessary,' she said. 'And if he thinks he can get what he wants by simply sitting and waiting, that's what he'll do.'

'And what does he want, this boss?'

Wendy hesitated.

Ellie thought, she's screwing him! Which means she knows exactly how he ticks but still feels she owes him some loyalty.

She said, 'Showtime, Wendy. If we can't tell the truth here, when the hell can we tell it?'

The woman nodded.

'You're right. Above all, Gaw wants, in fact he *needs*, a successful operation. Which in this case means securing the arms, the cocaine, Popeye Ducannon and Fidel Chiquillo. The survival of the rest of us would be a bonus but he can live without it.'

'He's that cold-blooded?'

'Well, yes, but he is genuinely convinced most of you have stepped over the line anyway,' said Wendy defensively.

'What line?' asked Ellie.

'The line between the good of the state and

common humanity,' said Feenie savagely. 'In the eyes of security, there are no degrees of guilt. So, ladies, it doesn't look like the US cavalry will be attending on this occasion. We must do what we can for ourselves.'

And what is that precisely? wondered Ellie.

Simplest would be to sit and wait till the door opened and hope to take one of the men out with their single bullet and bluff the other into submission with the empty gun. Even if you said it quickly it didn't sound good, plus it would mean leaving Kelly to her fate. Also, if they hung around too long, the odds against them would double when Popeye and Luis came back with the truck. However sympathetic the Irishman might be, he'd made it clear his first priority was to retrieve his pension-fund cocaine.

No, they had to take the initiative.

She consulted her feelings and found to her surprise that the prospect quite invigorated her. The news that there were other security people in the offing had cheered her up greatly. Not that it sounded as if they'd be much help in the short term, but with luck, Rosie would have found her way back to them and be in their safe-keeping. And with Peter at least sixty miles away, that meant that she had no one to worry about but herself.

Which is what that selfish little corner of her being which she'd hoped to sublimate into the creation of fiction had wanted, wasn't it?

Well, now she'd got it. Now was the chance to see just how creative she really was.

'I've got a plan,' she said.

xviii

the US Cavalry

In prospect, driving the truck to the pavilion had seemed to Peter Pascoe an easy matter with the real problems starting once they arrived.

After five minutes, *if* they arrived seemed a better way of putting it.

Presumably somewhere there was a proper service track dating from the days when the pavilion had been Mungo Macallum's hospitality suite from which his house-guests could watch the elements at their most dramatic whilst feasting off the fat of the land.

Now those same elements had turned the air into a whirling mulch of debris and rain which absorbed the headlights' amber beam like a pub champion downing a yard of ale, so that even if he knew where the track had been, he doubted if he could have followed it. The only directional aid he had was to head straight into the storm's blast which from time to time was so strong it threatened to push the truck backwards. The screen was a river in flood across which the wipers spasmed slowly like dying eels, and the ground beneath the wheels had become so saturated that the vehicle's weight was trying to dig its own grave.

To stop could be fatal. Slowly, blindly, Pascoe sent the truck inching forward, lurching over unseen and unidentifiable obstacles with a series of jolts that tossed him all over the cab. Pascoe almost pitied the security trio behind him. Bouncing around in a small space with Andy Dalziel was probably as dangerous as being trapped below decks on an old sailing ship with a loose cannon sliding around.

The only real navigational aid he had was the occasional flash of lightning which momentarily lit up the sky before leaving it even darker than before. He could only hope that such a moment of illumination would occur a few yards before they reached the edge of the cliff their present course must inevitably bring them to.

This is England, he kept on reminding himself. This is Yorkshire. But whatever his mind told him, his senses and his imagination knew that he was in some land of myths and monsters, light years away from all the certainties and securities of home.

I am Theseus sailing to slay the Minotaur, I am Perseus speeding on the *talaria* to rescue Andromeda from the dragon, I am Flash Gordon with a lot less than fourteen hours to save the universe . . .

'Bloody hell!' he said.

He was Childe Roland too.

The lightning had flashed up the world again and there right ahead, crouching blank-eyed and ominous as the Dark Tower, was the Pavilion by the Sea.

What now?

He didn't doubt that those in the back would all have their own notions on how to proceed. Well, he didn't need them. This was his show. What did Childe Roland do when he finally came to the Dark Tower?

Dauntless his slug horn to his lips he set, and blew.

Good thinking. Get those within to come out where he would have them dazzled in the head-lights' beam.

And then, what?

Would he be able to use the gun Sempernel had reluctantly given him and shoot a man down like a lamped deer?

Yes, he assured himself. No problem. Choose between Ellie and my precious conscience? No competition!

Yet, pile these self-assurances high as he could, he still felt deep down beneath them a pea of doubt.

One way to find out.

He leaned all his weight on the horn and blew.

It made a pretty satisfactory noise even in these conditions but it evoked no response from the pavilion.

He tried it again and again he waited.

This time he thought he saw a movement through the small window in the door facing him, but no one came out.

He blew the horn a third time.

Nothing.

He sat a little longer. Where were they? And almost as puzzling, where were those buggers in the back? He couldn't believe that either Fat Andy or Gawain Sempernel would sit for long waiting for an insubordinate subordinate to give them permission to alight. He hoped their rough ride hadn't left them too bruised to move!

He opened the door with difficulty, fighting against the wind which was a heavyweight puncher even here in the lee of the pavilion. Out of the truck, it became a wrestler who seized him gleefully and sent him spinning round to the rear and would probably have spun him all the way back to the house if he hadn't grabbed at the tailgate.

Which was down.

For God's sake, surely they hadn't already got out and gone blundering off into the storm?

He leaned against the tailgate and peered in. The lightning flashed. No, they were all still there, sitting upright, looking towards him.

But not moving. And not talking.

The next flash told him why.

They were all neatly trussed and gagged, like meat rolled and dressed for the oven.

He prepared to vault in and release them but there was something cold and hard pressing against his neck. He could feel it all the way through to his brain and to the pit of his stomach.

'You are welcome, good master,' said a soft voice. 'Will you not step inside?'

xix

I shall wound every man

As creative plans went, Ellie's wasn't Pulitzer stand-
ard, though weird enough to win the Booker in one
of its dafter years.

'We've got to stop Jorge and Big Ajax doing
whatever they're doing to Kelly and get them back
in here,' she said.

'Who?' said Daphne.

'Big Ajax,' said Ellie, recalling that her nick-
names existed only in her head. 'That's Little Ajax
on the floor. And when they come in, they've got
to be distracted enough for us to take them out.'

'Take them out?' said Daphne. 'As in NATO
bombers taking out an anti-aircraft battery?'

'That sort of thing. Now here's what I suggest.
Wendy, you get up against the wall there next to
Shirley . . .'

She flashed a smile at Novello who was looking
so pale she was almost translucent but whose eyes
were bright and taking everything in.

'. . . and look terrified. You'll have the gun. Put

your arm around Shirley and keep it hidden behind her. How good a shot are you?'

'In normal circumstances, excellent.'

'Don't overdo the false modesty,' said Ellie. 'Your job will be to deal with Big Ajax, OK?'

'I'd have said that Jorge was the more dangerous,' objected Wendy.

'Possibly. But Big Ajax has got a neck like an elephant's leg and I'm not sure if Feenie can pull the same trick with him that she managed on Little Ajax here.'

Feenie, who'd been listening with close attention said, 'You're right, my dear. I was just about at my limit with this one. But I reckon that, given a firm standing, I could lever that little runt Jorge's head right off his shoulders.'

'I can't believe I'm hearing this,' said Daphne. 'I've eaten too much lobster and am having a weird nightmare.'

'You ain't heard nothing yet,' said Ellie, now really fired up. 'This bit you're going to love. Daphne, I want you to pull your knickers round your ankles, your skirt up round your bum and lie on the floor just about here.'

'You what? You realize you're talking to the President Elect of our local WI? If you feel pulsating pudenda is the best bet for distracting horrible Jorge, why don't you flash yours?'

'Don't worry, I'll be doing my bit,' said Ellie, tearing at her T-shirt and ripping down her bra. 'And if it's your modesty you're worried about, it's OK. He won't be able to see a thing because you'll have Little Ajax here on top of you. There we go. Do I look like a woman wronged?'

She stood before them, her breasts spilling out of the ruins of her T-shirt.

'No, you just look like Cher at an awards ceremony. What was that you said about *him* being on top of me?'

'I think,' said Feenie, 'that what Ellie is suggesting is a scenario in which Little Ajax has run berserk, sexually speaking. Attacked her, shot Mrs Woolley, and is now ravishing you. Jorge will certainly not be pleased. May I suggest, my dear, that we can both add to his displeasure and also add a little verisimilitude to Little Ajax's extraordinary behaviour *thus*?'

As she spoke, she went to the grip, opened it, took out one of the plastic bags, ripped it open and scattered the white powder on the floor.

'There. Now, Mrs Aldermann, if you don't mind, time is of the essence. I could render you unconscious if that would make things easier for you, but I think in the circumstances at least one of you ought to be moving.'

It was hard to tell how serious Feenie was. Absolutely, was Ellie's guess. And Daphne's too, for she now let herself be arranged in the proposed tableau, her resistance reduced to repeating over and over, 'I do not believe this . . . I do not believe this . . .' as they eased Little Ajax's body on top of her.

'His trousers need to be down,' said Ellie.

'Yes, of course. At my age you forget such details,' said Feenie as together they dragged the dead man's trousers down over his buttocks.

'That's fine,' said Ellie. 'Daphne, dear, could you writhe about a bit and shriek? Give the impression that Little Ajax is having a good time and you're not?'

'You've got that half right,' said Daphne. 'Oh God. How's this?'

One thing you had to give these public-school girls, once you persuaded them to take part, they didn't hold back.

'Excellent. But don't tire yourself out. Relax till the curtain goes up. So here's the scenario, ladies. I shall rush out of the door, sobbing and sighing and crying rape. My guess is they're down in the cellar. I'm going to make a lot of noise because I want them to hear me coming so they don't start blasting away out of sheer surprise. If all goes well, Jorge and Big Ajax will come rushing in here to see what the hell's going on. The picture they'll get is that Little Ajax has been snorting coke and has got ambitious to screw us all. Jorge will rush across to him to beat him senseless, Big Ajax will remain standing at the door. Wendy will blow his head off and Feenie will break Jorge's neck. Any questions?'

From the floor, Daphne said, 'I've been in many amateur dramatic productions and my experience is, as Sod's Law, or maybe it's God's Law, states, something always goes wrong. What do we do then?'

'Improvise,' said Ellie. 'Anything else.'

Feenie said, 'One suggestion. I am normally totally opposed to drug abuse in any form, but I think on this occasion a little artificial stimulus to our perceptions and reactions might be useful.'

She stooped, dipped a finger into the spilled coke put it to her nose, and sniffed. Then, taking a handful, she went round the others like a priestess round her acolytes, offering each of them it in turn.

Mrs Stonelady shook her head, but all the others partook.

Ellie sniffed long and deep.

It felt good. She felt good.

She looked down. She looked good.

Her breasts were firm, her nipples engorged.

She said, 'I shall wound every man, no man shall wound me.'

Then, screaming hysterically, she opened the door and staggered outside.

XX

Liberata liberata

It was like stepping into a black hole.

She must have got used to the light coming through the huge window in the main chamber, adjusting as it thickened with the onset of evening and the storm. By contrast the anteroom through which they had entered the pavilion was in darkness, accentuated rather than diluted by the dull grey square of the window in the door.

The door.

The door that led to the outside world.

It would be easy to open it and run free into the night. The storm would make it almost impossible for them to find her. She could salve her conscience by sticking her head back into the big chamber and inviting the others to follow. Except of course that two were wounded and Kelly Cornelius was in the hands of Jorge and Big Ajax.

Curiously, these pros and cons didn't enter her mind in the form of a debate. There was never a second when she seriously considered escape. Perhaps it was the coke, perhaps her own adrenalin, but the only reason she thought about them at all was that, in stark contrast to the darkness around her, her brain was lit with the clarity of a tropical noon.

Nor did her thoughts occupy any significant portion of time. She didn't need either thought or sight to register that the anteroom and the kitchen were empty, and she was staggering down the steps into the cellar, sobbing and wailing, without the slightest perceptible physical pause.

There was light down here, shed by a pair of hurricane lamps, the kind of light sought by horror-film directors for dungeon scenes, and there was enough horror here for the most gothic of tastes.

The low ceiling room was full of boxes and chests, presumably containing the arms that Popeye had sold to Chiquillo. Across one of these lay Kelly Cornelius, naked, her face and body pied with blood, her arms twisted above her head by Big Ajax while Jorge knelt before her with his pistol barrel thrust deep between her legs.

Don't react, Ellie told herself. You're in shock, you've got nothing left for anyone else, you're so deep in shock you'll even ask animals like these for assistance.

Jorge had dragged the pistol out of Kelly's body and was pointing the bloodstained muzzle at Ellie.

'Help me . . .' she sobbed, 'oh help . . . he's gone mad . . . please . . . please . . . please help . . . or he'll kill everyone . . .'

Jorge looked for a moment like he might think

it wasn't such a bad idea. Then he started jabbering in Spanish so rapid she couldn't pick out more than the odd pronoun, and came towards her, pushing at her with his weapon. Behind him, Big Ajax hauled Kelly to her feet. Ellie was able to register with relief that she still had enough strength to take a couple of staggering paces before Jorge spun her round and prodded her back towards the stairs.

So far so good, she told herself. But the big test was yet to come. Daphne was probably right, Sod's or God's Law would be invoked and something was bound to go wrong – Wendy might miss, Feenie might not be able to cope with Jorge as easily as she thought – and as the only able-bodied woman available (Mrs Stonelady didn't count and Daphne could hardly be expected to hurl Little Ajax's bulk to one side and join the fray), she had to be ready to lend a hand wherever it was most needed.

What would happen if Sod and God combined and *everything* went wrong she didn't care to con-template.

They were back up the stairs, Jorge was pushing her through into the viewing chamber and the show was on the road.

It looked good, she thought, not without a *soupçon* of self-congratulation; in fact, it looked just like she'd envisaged it, a disaster zone – the ripped coke package trailing powder over the floor – Wendy cowering against the wall next to Novello with her wounded leg prominently displayed – Mrs Stonelady sitting as still and as harmless as a garden gnome – and Feenie looking about two hundred years old, teetering in helpless protest over the *pièce de résistance* of Daphne (what a trouper!) screaming and thrashing under the bulk of Little Ajax which she was flinging around in a facsimile of frenetic fornication which Ellie suspected was well outside his range in life.

And Jorge's reactions were straight out of her script too. With a high-pitched cry of rage he threw Ellie aside and ran to the couple on the floor, where he began beating Little Ajax over the head with his gun.

Ellie moved to the centre of the room to make sure she wasn't interfering with Wendy's line of fire. But when she looked towards the woman, she didn't see a gun, only a look of anguished frustration on her face. A glance over her shoulder revealed the cause. Big Ajax was standing as precisely on his allocated spot as an old pro actor on his chalk mark, but he had his arms wrapped around Kelly and was pressing her hard against his body, clearly enjoying this chance to cop a feel. If she were anything like as good as she claimed to be, surely Wendy would have no difficulty in putting a bullet into that broad skull, thought Ellie. At the same time, she could see how the idea of missing and blowing a hole in the person you were trying to rescue might give even the crackest of shots a moment of self-doubt.

But it was now or never. Jorge's rage could not blind him much longer to the fact that even a sexually absorbed Little Ajax ought to be showing just a little more response to having his head beaten to a pulp.

Ellie glowered at Wendy and hissed, 'Do it!'

The woman began to withdraw the gun from behind the recumbent Novello.

And at that moment, like the sound from without a tilt-yard which announces the arrival of a new contender to enter the lists, a horn blared, long and hard, and light poured through the anteroom window and spilled over into the viewing chamber.

It was the truck horn and headlights. Luis and Popeye were back. The odds had swung against them dramatically.

There was a moment when they might still have done it. If Wendy had shot Big Ajax . . . if Feenie had attacked Jorge . . . but they both froze, waiting for the other. Then the horn sounded again and Big Ajax, still with his arms round Kelly, retreated into the anteroom and the moment was past.

The only plus was Daphne, who must be a wow in her local dramatic society, thought Ellie.

Sensing Jorge's attack on Little Ajax's head was winding down, and seeing puzzlement replacing anger on his face, she had let out one huge last scream, rolled the body off her and scrabbling to her knees sobbed, 'Oh thank you, thank you, thank you, you've killed him, I think you've killed him, thank you,' then hurled herself at the dead man,

561

beating his face with her fists in a marvellous simulacrum of fury.

The Cojo felt Little Ajax's pulse, dropped the limp hand in disgust and turned to snarl, '*Es muerto,*' at Big Ajax in the anteroom. That got his attention. There was a pause, then a crash as the big man let Kelly slump to the floor. Now he was unprotected as he strode back into the viewing chamber, but the clear shot offered was useless as Jorge had moved away from Feenie to check just how much of his precious coke had been lost from the grip.

Outside the horn was sounding a third blast. It went on even longer this time before it fell silent.

Big Ajax stooped, grunting with the effort, to check Little Ajax out. It was rather touching really. Perhaps they were related. Daphne kept up her posthumous attack on his head. Another house point to the archdeacon's daughter. It wasn't a good idea to let either of these two get close enough to that end of Little Ajax to work out how he'd actually died. But Big Ajax was no respecter of female priorities, or maybe he knew something about Little Ajax's sexual proclivities that no one else did.

He pushed Daphne aside and stooped to examine his comrade's head and neck. When he rose his gaze went slowly round the room, then he stepped close to the window to take a look at the pattern of bullet strikes.

He knows something's wrong, thought Ellie as the big man turned from the window and let his gaze move systematically over the room once more.

Oh shit! He's looking for the gun!

Now his own weapon was raised and ready and as he moved to join Jorge, he was keeping everyone in the room in plain sight.

The two men began to speak together, or rather Big Ajax spoke and Jorge listened, anger returning to his features.

Thank you Sod and God, raged Ellie. Just for once couldn't you have stayed out of things and let us mortals sort our fates out by ourselves?

At that moment they heard the outside door open and Popeye's voice said, 'Oh Jesus, Mary mother of God.'

He's seen Kelly, thought Ellie. Perhaps the sight of what Jorge's done to her will get him on our side. She felt a new stirring of hope and moved slightly so that through the doorway she could see the two new arrivals stooping over the bloodstained figure on the floor. They spoke together then, to her surprise, it was Popeye who straightened up and came into the viewing chamber. Behind him she could see a rear view of the baseball-capped figure of Luis still stooping. He was taking his coat off to make a pillow, then peeling his shirt off also to wrap around Kelly. This unexpected concern from the Cojo turned her stirring of hope into a positive tremor. If they were both horrified by what Jorge had done to Kelly, maybe . . .

Popeye was so wet he'd have made a drowned

rat look dry. So much water was still cascading off his coat he could have modelled for one of those stormcloud symbols on the weather forecast. But there was nothing stormy in his demeanour.

He looked at Jorge, smiled broadly, and said, 'You look like you've been having fun. Me, I've just been getting wet. Jesus, but a man could drown out there standing up. I swear the ground's boggier than Connemara and I was just telling Luis here that I reckon we could be in trouble when we've got the truck fully loaded.'

Ellie's hope died away. Not even a token remonstrance about the treatment meted out to his 'niece'! All the bastard was worried about was his sodding drugs.

Why should she have expected more? Popeye was a realist. Jorge was calling the shots here, and with that little psycho, she guessed there would be only one outcome. She should have taken her chance to run. Being loyal to the others had made her feel good but she saw now it meant being disloyal to Rosie and Peter. There had to be priorities, and just because the two most important people in her life were away and safe didn't mean she was entitled to act exactly as she wanted, perhaps not even in the pages of her fictions. Hostages to fortune weren't just a man's prerogative. And it was now small consolation to think that Smartass Novello had been right and this after all had been her own adventure, nothing to do with Peter's job, and all the trouble tracking to their door was down to little old Ellie.

And yet she could not see how she might have acted differently.

She noticed that Jorge was looking at Popeye with speculative surprise. As if he hadn't expected to see him return? If Popeye got that message too . . . but she was grasping straws.

Jorge made a dismissive gesture and returned his attention to Big Ajax who was still talking.

When at last he fell silent, Jorge slowly raised his weapon, holding it at arm's length, and moving towards Feenie till it was almost touching her head.

'Luis, get yourself in here,' he called. 'Now, ladies, the one who has the gun has three seconds to hand it over or you start dying, the oldest first. *Uno . . . dos . . .*'

'For God's sake!' screamed Daphne at Wendy Woolley. 'Either give him the gun or shoot the bastard!'

And at the same moment, Luis came through the door.

Or rather the man wearing Luis's baseball cap came through the door.

His appearance hit Ellie with shock.

Beneath the long peak of the cap she saw a narrow hollow-cheeked face with a thin moustache. She knew she'd seen it before but that wasn't the source of the shock.

Naked to the waist, having used his outer garments to minister to Kelly, his torso was skinny to the point of emaciation with a long half-healed wound running along the lower right ribcage.

And he had breasts.

Not large, scarcely bigger than a couple of Cox's pippins, but definitely indisputably breasts.

Jesus Christ, it's St Uncumber come to save us! thought Ellie.

And as if that was indeed her purpose, with an animal cry of rage, the ambiguous newcomer hurled herself at Jorge.

She had a gun in her hand. Perhaps it jammed. Or perhaps her anger was such as could not be satisfied except by direct physical contact. If that was the case, she might have paid dear if Feenie hadn't seized the opportunity offered by Jorge's distraction to grab the man's gun hand and twist the little finger till it broke with a crack like a dry twig.

Jorge screamed, the gun fell, and then the avenging fury was on him, driving him back against the window beyond which the storm blustered and raged as if in frustration at being debarred from the mortal struggle within.

At the same time, Popeye had produced a pistol and started firing at Big Ajax.

The Irishman didn't look at home with the weapon and in fact seemed to be firing with his eyes shut. But such a large target was hard to miss and most of his rounds seemed to strike home, till Big A.'s chest was a cirque of blood.

Yet still he stood there, showing no pain, like that

Balder, son of Odin, whose mother Frigga obtained from all things, stone and metal and wood, a promise that they would never hurt her son, save only the mistletoe which in the end killed him.

He was, though, finding it difficult to bring his own weapon to bear. Each time his huge right hand tried to raise it, he took another shot from Popeye and the muzzle remained pointing harmlessly down. Then the Irishman's gun fell silent.

All this took only a few seconds, yet to Ellie it seemed as drawn out as the climactic shoot-out scene in one of those spaghetti westerns Peter loved to watch on the telly.

And now, as Popeye desperately began to search his pockets for more ammunition, Big Ajax finally brought his gun up to waist level, the wavering barrel trembled to a halt, and his trigger finger began to squeeze the trigger.

With a scream of *something*, she didn't know what, and with no conscious thought at all, Ellie flung herself forward, scooping up en route the splintered leg of the chair Little Ajax had wrecked, and drove it into the bloody target of the gunman's chest.

It must have been mistletoe. He went over backwards at the merest touch and lay quite still.

She stood over him, feeling shock and triumph in equal parts, then looked around.

Crazy laughter tried to struggle up from her belly at what she saw. The two wounded women, Shirley and Wendy, huddled against the wall –

Daphne, her clothes torn and dishevelled, curled up like a woodlouse behind the protective bulk of Little Ajax's corpse – St Uncumber wrestling with Jorge in front of the storm-beaten window with Feenie hovering over them, like some demented harpie waiting to snatch her prey – Mrs Stonelady still sitting in a corner like a curious garden gnome – and herself, naked to the waist, triumphing over her fallen foe with a bloody stake in her hand – it was like the climax of some crazy gothic movie – *Reservoir Maenads*, co-directed by Tarantino and Ken Russell.

But it wasn't over yet. And it still might not end happy ever after.

For Uncumber was losing. Whatever deeply felt emotion fuelled her hate, it wasn't enough to compensate for long the weakness caused by her unhealed wound and the deprivations suffered by her emaciated body.

As Ellie watched, the Cojo punched her hard in the throat and drove her off him, flinging her backwards, and her flailing arms caught at Feenie and brought her crashing down too.

Now Jorge rolled to the side and came up clutching his gun.

Ellie had no doubt of his intention now. No more Mr Nice Guy, he was simply going to kill them all.

She looked desperately at Popeye, but his search for new ammo had been in vain.

She screamed her fury once more at Sod/God for letting them get so close.

Then from the corner of her eye she saw Wendy Woolley finally draw the hidden gun from behind poor pale Shirley Novello, take aim, and fire.

Upright, unwounded, in the unthreatening depths of the security practice range, she might have been a crackshot.

Here she was just good enough to get close, and close got you no cigar.

The bullet missed Jorge's head by a fraction small enough to make him flinch before it flattened itself against the window.

Then he smiled and levelled his weapon down at Feenie and St Uncumber.

Cue God or Sod, thought Ellie desperately. Only direct divine intervention can save us now.

And behind Jorge, Mungo Macallum's precious reinforced glass which had hitherto withstood all that man or nature could throw at it, decided that this last bullet was a bullet too far.

The storm outside, as if sensing this weakness and tired of being upstaged by the battle within, hurled its full force at the crazing glass. It bent, it bulged, it broke with an explosion which seemed to rumble forever like a huge cannonade, and with a scream that didn't need a Greek poet or pantheon of gods to make it sound triumphant, the raging wind and the turbulent sea came in.

xxi

an elfin storm

There was a moment when Ellie thought that they must all simply drown in the viewing chamber which had now become an aquarium tank.

She had a sense of bodies struggling and thrashing, and no sense whatsoever of up or down, then the waters ran through the open door into the anteroom and went cascading like an Alpine torrent down the stairs into the cellar.

She shook her head and eyes clear and looked around. She had time to take in only one thing. Jorge with his head almost severed from his body by a shard of glass was lying across the leather grip out of which trailed lines of sodden coke for the fishes to snort.

Then the storm came back as if the sea had merely withdrawn to take a longer run at them. This new blast of wind and rush of water was even stronger than before, picking everyone up and crashing them against the rear wall. Ellie heard herself scream in agony. What it did to those already in pain she dreaded to think. But at least when the waters once more went bubbling down the cellar stairs, they were all near the doorway.

'We've got to get out of here!' she yelled.

In times of crisis, cliché comes into its own.

She grabbed at Novello whom the waters had rolled to her side, picked her up in what she guessed must now be known as a fireperson's lift, and staggered to the door. She glimpsed Mrs Stonelady helping Wendy Woolley, Uncumber and Popeye were already in the anteroom lifting Kelly, and Feenie and Daphne were rolling along with their arms round each other, like a pair of happy drunks out on a night's carouse.

The sea came back again, this time bearing them all with it through into the anteroom. By now the cellar must have been too flooded to carry all the water away and a foot or so remained swirling beneath their feet, giving the impression that the floor and the whole building were moving. From somewhere deep down there came a fearful grinding and bumping noise as if some Kraken was stirring in its sleep. Then a memory from her childhood reading told Ellie what it was. The coffins floating in the vault in *Moonfleet*! This had to be the cases of arms being tossed around by the water in the cellar.

Behind them in the doorway, the bodies of Jorge and the Ajaxes came crowding, as if they too even in death were eager to flee this fearful place. Feenie and Daphne with the equal insouciance of a former

Resistance fighter and an archdeacon's daughter thrust them back into the viewing chamber and closed the door. Then someone got the outer door open and the beam of the truck's headlights shone fully in and they passed out into the open air. It was wild and it was wet and it tasted like nectar in Ellie's gaping mouth.

One thing which hadn't changed, though, was the sense of movement beneath her feet. And there was no moving water here to create an illusion. She looked at Feenie and saw her stagger slightly too.

'Quickly, get the wounded into the truck!' ordered the old lady. 'I think this bit of Axness is saying goodbye!'

Ellie carried Novello round to the back. Popeye lowered the tailgate then climbed inside to help her slide the wounded policewoman aboard. Next came Kelly. Uncumber clambered in after her, and knelt by her side, murmuring comfort in Spanish, then kissed her before climbing out. To Ellie's expert eye, it didn't look like a particularly saintly kiss. While this was going on, Ellie helped get Wendy Woolley aboard too. She looked more pallid than she'd done at any time since the ricochet hit her, as if now the worst was over, her body could admit its pain.

During all this activity, Ellie had been aware of vague figures deep in the truck's shadows, sitting in Buddha-like stillness, but it took a great flash of lightning to show her what her straining eyes had dismissed as delusion.

There were four . . . no, five people in there, bound tight, their faces half hidden by something taped over their mouths. Despite this she recognized two of them instantly, yet needed another flash to make her believe her recognition.

One was Andy Dalziel.

The other was Peter.

Oh Christ, why was he here . . . ? Had something happened to Rosie . . . ?

His eyes were riveted on her face but she couldn't read his thoughts in them.

Seizing hold of Popeye's arm she dragged herself aboard, took hold of the tape across her husband's mouth and pulled it clear.

He gasped, 'Rosie's safe.'

That was why she loved him. Even here, even now, in circumstances when only a couple of words were possible, he knew exactly the couple of words she wanted to hear.

And only a couple of words *were* possible, for Feenie was yelling, 'Everyone who can walk, get out. NOW!'

She touched Peter's lips with her fingers then jumped out and stepped aside just in time as the truck began to reverse. Feenie made no attempt to turn, judging that time was of the essence, also that reverse gear was her best bet for getting across this boggy ground.

She was right in both respects.

The fit survivors trotted alongside, one hand on the side of the truck, like security men alongside a presidential limousine, their feet sinking deep in the sodden ground.

From time to time Ellie risked a glance backwards. The headlights picked out the classical frame of the pavilion, only it wasn't quite so classical any more. There was a definite list to starboard. Or was it larboard? She pounded on for a few more yards, then looked back again. Now it was definitely moving. Her fascination at the sight nearly cost her dear. Her foot slipped in the mud and she might have gone under the wheels if Uncumber, who was just behind her, hadn't reached forward and grabbed her arm and pulled her up.

'Thanks,' she gasped. Then with a matter-of-fact certainty which surprised her she said, 'It's Bruna, isn't it?'

'*Si*. And you are Ellie, fair mistress Pascoe. I told you when you have quite forgot to look for me, a door shall open and there shall I be.'

'Did you?' said Ellie. 'I don't remember that. But Fidel . . . Chiquillo . . . your brother . . .'

'Buried long years ago deep in our forest glades where none may disturb his rest,' said the woman.

This made little sense. Nothing was for real any more. But why should it when you couldn't even trust the ground beneath your feet.

She glanced back once more. Bruna smiled, but Ellie was looking beyond her.

Damn! She'd missed it. Wasn't it always the way? Peter swore that the most certain way to get England to score was for him to pop out of the room for a pee.

Where Mungo Macallum's pleasure pavilion, his Command Post, had once loomed, turning nature into an after-dinner entertainment, there was now only empty space.

No, not empty. Filled with a triumph of cloud and sea and wind and sky.

Then they were on slightly firmer ground, passing over the red plastic warning fence, and there ahead, its line of festal light showing clear, was the terrace and the life she had left a million years ago.

The next hour passed in a dream. She and Peter were united, and after they had spoken on the phone with Wield at Nosebleed and been reassured that Rosie was fast asleep in bed with Tig's head beside her on the pillow and Carla's body across her feet, they had shared stories and embraces and, surprisingly, much laughter, as though time was already lacing what had so nearly been tragic with comedy.

She and Bruna too embraced and shed tears, but had little time for more than a bare outline of the Colombian woman's tale. Her brother had been fatally wounded by the security forces and when he died, his closest comrades, recognizing that PAL relied almost entirely for its clout on Chiquillo's charismatic reputation, persuaded Bruna to take his place. The masquerade had been completely successful, and when finally a carefully laid security ambush had left her cornered, she had been able to reinforce the legend of Chiquillo's almost magical elusiveness by reverting to being Bruna and letting herself be taken and thrown into jail.

'And then Kelly – sorry, Corny – got her gran to put you on Liberata's mailing list,' said Ellie. 'You've known Corny a long time?'

She spoke casually, but Bruna smiled and said, 'We are lovers since first we met many years ago. When I lay in durance, it is she who helps to keep Chiquillo alive by . . . but I do not think these things are for your ears. You have your life which in prison I longed to make mine, and in it there is no place for all these killings.'

And finally Ellie couldn't resist asking, 'I'm sorry, but your moustache, it looks very real.'

'It is in grain, it will endure wind and weather,' said Bruna. 'Before when I pretended to be Fidel, it was false so that those who glimpsed me would be deceived. But in prison, the guards . . . I need not tell you what the guards like to do . . . and slowly my body puts on a new case, my breasts grow small, and this real hair grows on my lip, so that in the end I become a thing that these men do not desire. But now I am at liberty, I return slowly to being a woman again.'

So, St Uncumber after all, thought Ellie.

Of course, the medical explanation was fairly straightforward to one who had mugged up the physiology of anorexia for her Women's Studies course. Serious starvation, whether self-induced or given a kick start by a prison diet, could inhibit the release of hormones from the hypothalamus, resulting in hypogoñadism which in mature females is often the cause of virilism. *Sic probo.* But for once in her life, Ellie found herself eager to embrace the supernatural explanation.

Bruna went off to check on Kelly, and Ellie returned to helping Feenie and Mrs Stonelady, who were busying themselves providing dry clothing and hot food.

After some first aid, the injured Shirley Novello and Wendy Woolley had been driven to hospital by Daphne who, in a very short time, had contrived to look as if she was going on a photo-shoot with *Country Life.*

Feenie had tried to insist that Kelly should go too, but Popeye had assured her that arrangements for her treatment were all in hand, and it was true that Kelly, though clearly still in much pain, had been hugely reinvigorated by the appearance of Bruna.

Journey's end in lovers meeting every wise man's son doth know.

Andy Dalziel too seemed little affected by his experience and had taken upon himself the task of dispensing alcohol to any who needed it. The only words he exchanged with Ellie at an early stage were, 'Good to see you, lass, but like my old dad used to say, if it's not on the market, don't put it on the stall.'

Ellie had been baffled till Pascoe murmured, 'I think he's a little disconcerted by your deshabille,' and fastened the buttons on the jacket he had draped round her shoulders.

Then Bruna came to find her and said, 'Ellie, the farewell time has come too soon, but here we must not stay. I shall write to you again, this time in such a way these wicked schemers cannot intercept. My best love to your little daughter whom I met.'

'The lady with the moustache,' said Ellie. 'She wasn't fooled.'

'Children see plainly,' said Bruna. 'One day perhaps we all shall see as children.'

She flung her arms round Ellie and they embraced. Then she kissed her on the lips and turned and went.

Ellie followed her to the front door. Popeye was in the driving seat of the white Mercedes, the two women, close entwined, in the rear.

The storm was still raging, but now as she watched the white car vanish into its damp embrace, it seemed a magical protective thing.

She went back inside.

Pascoe said, 'So they've gone then.'

'Yes. Peter, I know that they must be on all kinds of wanted lists. Thanks for not trying to stop them.'

'Who, me? When my great superior is sitting on his bum, supping Scotch and doing nowt? I wouldn't have dared!'

'By the way, weren't there more of you than just you and Andy trussed up in the back of that truck?'

'Were there? Perhaps we'd better ask him.'

But when they joined the Fat Man they found Feenie was already raising the question.

'Superintendent,' she said. 'What on earth happened to those other friends of yours in the truck?'

'I don't rightly know,' said Dalziel. 'Pete, lad, didn't I tell you to untie them?'

'Don't think so, sir,' said Pascoe.

'I'm sure I did. But if you didn't, then they must still be in there. Bloody hell. He won't be best pleased, not if I know old Pimpernel!'

This was an understatement.

Sempernel did not rage, but his anger was visible in every stiff movement of his body, every controlled syllable of his speech.

When he learned that Popeye had driven away with the two women, his stillness and his silence were even more eloquent.

And finally he snapped when he was unable to get any of the telecommunication equipment in the house to work.

He said, 'Mr Dalziel, Mr and Mrs Pascoe, Miss Macallum, what has happened this evening is not yet totally clear, but I should not like you to think that you can interfere with Her Majesty's security services with impunity. I already have information enough to bring all your futures into doubt. When my investigations are complete, I would anticipate that your troubles are just about to begin.'

He swept out, followed by his acolytes.

'Didn't follow a word of that,' said Dalziel cheerfully.

'I think, as Bruna might have put it,' offered Ellie, 'that he was saying, I'll be revenged on the whole pack of you.'

'He couldn't do anything, could he?' said Pascoe uneasily. 'I mean, you never know what these people have in their files.'

'Stop worrying, lad. I've got this feeling that dear old Gawain's going to find his files are a bit like himself, fading with age. Any road, I'm sure he's far too much of a gent to offer poor mortals like us a threat. But just to put your mind at rest, I'll be sure and ask him next time we meet.'

'And when do you anticipate that might be?' enquired Pascoe.

Andy Dalziel took out a huge khaki handkerchief and started wiping his fingers which somehow seemed to have got a bit oily.

'I reckon in about two minutes when he finds his car won't start,' he said.

xxii

spelt from Sibyl's leaves

Morgan Meredith . . .
lost in a dream where she walks and she doesn't
  need wheels . . .
how good it feels . . .

Meredith. A good name. To make it even better, I used to insinuate at Cambridge that I was related to George, the novelist. More than insinuate. Gradually I created a web of circumstance, of family tradition and anecdote, of heirlooms and letters and manuscripts in boxes in our attic.

'Fascinating,' said my tutor. 'Perhaps a good subject for your Ph.D. should you feel that way inclined.'

And I smiled, thinking myself the great deceiver, Morgan le Fay, swinging out of the sixties with my skirt round my bum, the world at my feet, dancing to a Beatles beat, confident that every kind of first in every area of experience was in my grasp.

And my tutor smiled too, more impressed by

my powers of deceit than my academic potential.

Then his dear friend Gawain Sempernel, alumnus of our college and respected classical scholar, visited the university to give a lecture on *Homer in the Eighteenth Century* and when my tutor invited me to meet him, I thought it was my scholastic brilliance that was being acknowledged.

Much later, and much too late, I realized he was in fact merely Gawain's pander, supplying him with likely lads and lasses for his closer examination.

Of course in our case *pander* proved more than just metaphor.

Lovers beneath the singing sky of May we wandered once.

He put it so well, my unrelated relation. Except that our version of Modern Love was far beyond what he could imagine even at his most cynical and disillusioned.

We two were rapid falcons in a snare.

Half right. Gawain means *hawk of May*, I expect you know that. And you were a veritable bird of prey, Gaw. I have felt your talons.

As for me, certainly I acted like a falcon for a while, with the singing sky my element.

Perhaps my high-flying days were already numbered. Perhaps like the wren on the eagle's back, I felt you had strength for two. Certainly when the aches started, and the lassitude, and the air grew thin and hardly able to bear me up, and I went to the departmental doctor for a check-up, I did not hesitate to come fluttering to you to share his dusty answer.

MS. Multiple sclerosis.

How loving, how sympathetic you were.

How quickly, how subtly you acted.

I said we must part. You said it made no difference.

Neither of us meant it, in that at least we were one.

And gradually you eased us apart, almost imperceptibly, and in such a manner that when I did perceive it, I almost believed it was my decision.

But not quite. Or rather not forever. For by creating me (to universal applause) your Sibyl in her cavern, you gave me access to areas of information where the truth of you was writ plain.

It's no use letting your creature talk to the gods unless you accept that the poor thing must hear what the gods have to say.

Apollo offered the Sibyl at Cumae anything she wanted and she asked for eternal life but forgot to include eternal youth and good health. Centuries later there she still was, now so reduced and wizened that they put her in an earthenware pot and she uttered her prophecies, dangling helplessly from the roof of her cave.

My pot is made of steel and leather and has four wheels and my fate is less tragic than hers, for I can still move, though where I should move to is a question beyond Apollo's wisdom. The end of my service here is in sight and soon I must go rolling into the greyness which swirls between me and the final dark, while you, my hawk of May, are all set to go out in a blaze of glory, to end your days in the sybaritic comforts of the college where we met.

Or perhaps not.

For you are teetering on the brink of fiasco, Gaw.

Oh yes, I know you have often been here before, and always those broad strong wings of yours have opened at the last minute and you have soared away, safe and high above the smoke and stir of this dim spot which men call failure.

But this time, Gaw, this time . . .

What have you got to show for your efforts, your assurances, your boasts? What have you bought with your overspent budget?

Well, what you certainly don't have to show is any arms, or any drugs. Full fathom five in the North Sea they lie, buried beneath tons of breakaway Yorkshire, or washed out on the long tides to Dogger.

And what of Fidel Cubillas, the famed Chiquillo? And his sister, Bruna, whom you bragged to have dancing like a puppet on your string? Or Patrick Ducannon, Popeye, whom you used to call a living Irish joke? Or Kelly Cornelius, laundress extraordinaire?

You don't seem to have these either.

Which seems to leave . . . what?

Slim pickings that will require all your ingenuity to fatten up as an offering on the altar of your reputation.

Liberata and its founder Serafina Macallum. A charity used as a cover for terrorist money laundering and its notoriously subversive founder. Yes, that could be a tasty morsel.

Then there's Eleanor Pascoe, long-time left wing agitator, active supporter of said trust and a proven contact with said terrorists. Married to one Peter Pascoe, an officer of the CID well placed to assist and advise in matters of criminal evasion. Well worth slicing up and laying out for close examination.

And finally (and there's nothing insubstantial about this one), you prod forward the sacrificial ox, Detective Superintendent Andrew Dalziel, flouter of authority, skater over thin ice (always a dangerous pursuit for a fat man), already marked down as a possible security risk, in a close sexual liaison with a known and active dissident, who wilfully disobeyed your commands, connived at your protracted physical restraint and permitted the major suspects to make their escape.

Yes, there's something there, certainly, which properly dressed might be acceptable to our masters who, knowing that you are going, could be happy to connive at letting you go quietly.

And yet, and yet, to revert to my avian metaphor, these are fragile twigs for you to be perching on, my Gaw, though many times in the past I have seen you launch yourself to safety from perches even more insecure.

But not this time, I think. For even you, my hawk of May, can't get a purchase on twigs that crumble to nothing beneath your talons. Not even you can point at complete blankness and persuade our masters that your hawk-eyes see culpability. For the time has come for your Sibyl to scatter her leaves.

Look at them flying . . .
Drifting away on the wind which blows hard
from the west . . .
Never to rest . . .

Feenie Macallum . . . I press *Delete*, and there she goes.

Ol' Man Dalziel . . . for all his bulk, he too flutters to nothingness just as quickly.

Eleanor Soper . . . Ellie Pascoe . . . all her family . . . there they go too.

Edgar Wield . . . back to the safety of his beloved Eendale.

In fact, let me rake up all my Sibyl's Leaves and scatter them onto the deleting gale . . . Popeye and Feenie and Chiquillo and Kelly . . .

(Oh Gawain, are you grieving over Goldengrove unleaving . . . ?)

So now it is as if they had never been.

Poor Gaw. What shall you prey on now that nothing remains of your prey?

Now you know that silence where the birds are dead yet something pipeth like a bird.

That's me, Gaw.
Sibyl
piping in your head forever and flying again at
last too
oh you shall all know the moment of my flight
when I open up my magic box and reach inside
and grasp the living heart of my mystery
and feel its power surge through my veins for
the last time
and high and low in this mighty building all
screens go dark together . . .
then you shall know I am far away, riding on
the west wind with all the other leaves,
flying only the wind knows where . . .

all us looney people where do we all belong . . .
all us looney people . . . where . . .

EPILEGOMENA

Oh my fair Ellie
This missive I trust will reach you for Uncle Paddy knows
all the byways and sly ways to slip behind the watching
eyes, if eyes still watch as keen. Too little time we spent in
talk but now I know from Corny's tale and Paddy's too
that what I had sampled in your loving letters is the true
taste of you, a heart to care, a spirit to dare. Always I will
recall you as first I saw you clear, upright in that dreadful
place, one whose rags shamed gilded arms, whose naked
breast stepped before targs of proof. My fight I know is not
your fight but I could wish I had a thousand such in my
command, for then we would see such changes! For the
present time, we rest till all our wounds be healed. Paddy
says he longs to say farewell to all the wars, but he knows
much of use to us, and besides he lacks the wherewithal
to comfort, so we shall see. Mayhap our paths will cross
again. Mayhap one day when you have quite forgot to
look for me, a door shall open and there shall I be. Till
then rest happy, my Ellie Pascoe, and know that I remain
as faithful in friendship as in my brother's name.

From the London Times.

AWARDS

**To Gawain Clovis Sempernel for public service –
MBE.** (On his retirement from the Civil Service we
understand that Mr Sempernel is to take up the post
of Her Majesty's Honorary Consul in Thessaloniki
where he plans to conclude his lifelong undertaking
of translating Homer into Latin hexameters.)

OBITUARIES

Meredith Morgan: *civil servant; passed away quietly
at home, after a long illness, bravely borne; greatly
missed by her friends and colleagues at the Department of Information Technology.*

Chapter 4

*Young Dawn's rosy fingers stroked Odysseus's
cheeks and he was instantly awake.*

*But he didn't open his eyes straightaway. Instinct
told him he wasn't alone, and instinct was confirmed when he turned over as if in uneven slumber
and allowed the thinnest sliver of light under his
left eyelid.*

*Squatting close by his head, eyes fixed unblink-
ingly on his face and sword point poised unwaveringly over his throat, was Achates.*

'I know you're awake,' murmured the man.

'And I know who you are. Which means every instinct of my brain and belly urges me to kill you. Only the Prince's command prevents me and I'm sorely tempted for once in my life to disobey him. You know what stops me, Greek? You're shit, that's what. You're not worth breaking wind over, let alone my oath. I look at him and I look at you and what do I see? Two men adrift on the great seas, undergoing equal perils over many years. But there the resemblance ends. For my Prince has still got the greater part of his people with him, his father, his son, his officers, his men, their families. While you, you sad fat bastard, are alone. Where are your companions, Greek? Where are your friends, all those poor trusting idiots who sailed with you so many years ago from rocky Ithaca? All gone, all driven down to death by the mighty god whose rage you have so far evaded but only at the cost of all your companions. If you do ever manage to reach your home shore and climb the shingly beach to your mighty stronghold, it will be their bones you hear crunching beneath your feet. But my master, the Prince, when he reaches the promised Lavinian shores, will have his whole race with him, intact, to conquer and colonize our new land. The gods have promised it shall be so. The same gods that you defy and profane and cheat and wheedle and deceive in your efforts to stay alive. So I will obey my Prince, for his commands come ultimately from on high. But at the first sign of treachery, be sure I will plough a trench across that great gut of thine and not relent until I have dug out your heart. So think on, Greek. Take care of what you do and what you say this day, for Achates's sword will never be far from your back.'

He fell silent and after a moment Odysseus opened his eyes fully, sat up, yawned, stretched and said, ''Morning, chuck. Any chance of some breakfast?'

Half an hour later Aeneas watched impatiently as Odysseus cleaned his third platter of stew.

'Come, man,' he said. 'I don't know what good this little look-around you talk about can do us, but I do know that time is fast running by.'

'Plenty of time,' said the Greek, glancing up at the watery sun which was now clear of the horizon and doing her best to show her face through a veil of tattered clouds, but it was a losing battle and what little warmth dwelt in her fitful rays was washed away by the damp wind gusting off the grey sea. 'Two things a man should never neglect in the morning, his bowels and his breakfast, else he's bound to be caught hungry or caught short later in the day.'

He stood up and belched melodiously.

'Well, that's me breakfast taken care of. Now for me bowels.'

He wandered off out of sight behind a rock, followed by the vigilant Achates. When he returned, Aeneas, who was wrapped against the wind in a *cloak of heavy fleece, combed till it was fine as gossamer thread and dyed the rich blue of the ocean under more temperate summer skies, offered him a matching garment.*

Odysseus smiled and shook his head.

'Lovely weather like this, I'd be sweating cobs in yon thing,' he said, pulling out the skirt of his light tunic and pirouetting. 'This'll suit me fine. So let's be off. Best not bring your poodle though. With luck we'll be visiting a high-class lady and a face like his could frighten the land crabs.'

Aeneas turned to Achates and somewhat apologetically ordered him to stay in the camp.

The captain's features showed no emotion but he fixed his eyes on Odysseus once more and breathed, 'Remember what I promised.'

'Oh aye. You'll need a long sword, but. Right, let's be off.'

He strode away, setting such a sprightly pace that it was all the younger man could do to keep up with him.

'What's your hurry?' he gasped. 'Where are you heading?'

'Nowhere. Anywhere. Lovely morning like this, it just feels so good to be alive,' said Odysseus.

The Trojan looked up at the grey skies and down at the boulder-strewn ground whose only hint of colour came from patches of pustulant lichen. He drew his cloak more tightly about him with a shudder. Apart from the occasional evasive scutter of a crab, nothing moved. There wasn't even any vegetation to be agitated by the strengthening wind.

'If this is your idea of a lovely morning, I dread to think what it must be like on Ithaca,' he said surlily. 'Why are we doing this, Odysseus? I'm warning you, if you think you can gain anything by wasting my time, you'd better think again.'

'Waste your time, Prince? I'd not dare!' exclaimed the Greek. 'Hello. What have we here?'

They were approaching a great mound of boulders, black and menacing, which looked as if they'd been piled by some monstrous traveller as a waymark. From out of a dark cleft between two of the stones emerged a figure, clad in filthy rags, and female from the length of her snagged and clotted hair. She leaned heavily on a staff almost as warped and twisted as her own skinny frame. Her toothless mouth opened in a silent cackle and from the left side of her hooked nose one bright eye fixed itself on the two men as they approached, while the other orb, whose pupil was a clouded grey, roamed uncontrollably hither and thither as though in search of some message from the heavens.

'That's her, that same foul hag who visited me in the camp and warned me of my fate,' said Aeneas. 'No use to parley with her. We must force her to take us to her mistress, the nymph, Calypso. Only face to face can we make a plea that may . . .'

But Odysseus wasn't listening.

To the Trojan's amazement, the fat Greek was running ahead, and incredibly, when he reached *the noisome creature standing by the rocks, he flung himself onto the ground, grasped the hem of her foul robe and pressed his face against her filthy claw-like feet. Aeneas, inured though he was by hard experience against terrible sights, found himself gagging at the sight of the man's mouth sucking on those greeny-yellowy running sores.*

'For Athena's sake, Odysseus, remember what you are, man,' cried the Trojan. 'A prince of royal lineage with the blood of gods in your veins! How can we hope to meet with the nymph on equal terms if you abase yourself like this to what must be the vilest of her creatures?'

But Odysseus only looked up and said, 'Prince, bow down straight off. Even if you're daft enough to reckon you're above paying homage to divinity, at least be a man and give beauty the tribute it deserves.'

'Beauty!' exclaimed Aeneas. 'I've seen camels' backsides more beautiful than this. She makes Achates look like Lady Helen. Vile hag, take us at once to your mistress or I'll test the depths of your divinity with my sword.'

His weapon was out and at the creature's throat, but Odysseus leapt to his feet and knocked it aside, then, abasing himself once more, said humbly, 'Forgive this Trojan fool, lady. Grief and loss and wonderment at your great beauty have driven him quite mad. I beg you to enthrone yourself in your bower here and listen to the humble supplications of us poor mortals.'

The hag stooped and took the Greek's great head in both claw hands and raised it till she could look deep into his eyes.

'Tell me, Odysseus, what is it you see here?' she demanded in a voice more like the screech of some bird taught to mimic human tones than a real woman's voice.

'I see noble wisdom and gentle mercy compounded in a face of such loveliness it raises a man's great desire above even his awareness of his minute desert.'

'Desire? You desire me?' The hag opened her mouth wide to show her rotting gums as she cackled her derision. 'Then feast your lust, thou most cunning of Greeks. Will you not at least vouchsafe me a kiss?'

Her gaping maw looked to Aeneas like the entrance to Hades. He shuddered to the depths of his being at the thought of coming into contact with those chapped and spittle-flecked lips, of feeling that serpent-scaled tongue darting into his mouth.

But Odysseus was standing upright, in every sense as his light robe was inadequate to conceal. His arms went around the harridan, his mouth crushed down on hers while his hands pushed through the rents in her disgusting robe and caressed her sharp and calloused buttocks as though they were the soft pink orbs of a girl.

And suddenly, even as Aeneas raised his sword to bring an end to this obscenity, that's what they were, he stepped back in wonderment as the *hag's skew and ancient frame straightened into the shapely form and slender limbs of a young woman and the hideous sunken features filled out and glowed with vigorous health and an unearthly beauty.*

Nor did the wondrous alteration end here. The dark rock cleft from which she had emerged opened up into an airy cavern richly furnished within and overhung without by a rampant vine, heavy with ripening grapes. Bielding woodlands of alders and aspens and sweet-scented cypress grew all around, their branches melodious with chirruping birds. Four springs of the purest water ran bubbling under the trees and across neighbouring meadows, whose green and undulating grass was starred with many-hued violets. It was a scene to make even a god marvel.

Aeneas sank to his knees, speechless.

The divine nymph, Calypso (he could not doubt that this was she) was laughing and pushing the ardent Greek away.

'Odysseus, I had heard that you were ready to assail by cunning or by strength any foe who stood in your way, but I had not thought to find you quite so bold as this.'

'Lady, I cannot see a foe before me, and it was your own invite that led me on.'

'Perhaps. But you say you saw me as I am now, not as this poor creature beheld me?'

'Eyes that have looked on the dead in Hades have had all human scales removed,' said Odysseus

seriously. 'From eyes that see as clear as mine not all the magic in the world could conceal divine beauty like yours.'

'You say so?' said Calypso, looking both amused and pleased. 'And what is it you want of me that you so rudely disturb my repose?'

'What do I want, lady? Well, I'd rather bring that up in private. Wouldn't want to embarrass the lad here, if you understand me.'

'This is effrontery beyond punishment!' exclaimed the nymph.

'I'm glad to hear you say that,' said Odysseus. 'How about reward, but?'

She shook her lovely head, not in denial but in mock-amazement, and said, 'Well, I will attend to you a while before I decide your fate. Come into my bower.'

She went into the cavern. Odysseus glanced at Aeneas, winked, and followed. The Trojan took an uncertain step after them but the encircling vine trailed its grape-heavy stems before him, sealing off the entrance.

Baffled, he retreated and sat on a mossy bank facing the cavern. After a while he felt so warm that he shook off the heavy fleece cloak, and when he looked up he saw that the sky too had been transformed and it was now a flawless vault of the deepest blue with the pulsating orb of the sun almost directly overhead.

Time passed. He marked its passing by the slow declension of the sun down the western sky. The

lower it got, the more agitated he became. What-
ever was happening beyond that vine, the nymph's
decree was still in force, and that gave him till
sunset to flee the island with all save his son, or
stay and be destroyed.

At last, with by his estimate barely an hour
to go before the sun lipped the horizon, his
patience ran out and he rose and strode towards
the cavern entrance with sword outdrawn. But
before he reached it, the vine raised itself to the
lintel again and Odysseus emerged, adjusting
his tunic.

'How do, lad,' he said cheerfully. 'Sorry to keep
you waiting. Eeh, for Priapus's sake, put that thing
away. Waving it around like that all the time will
get you into bother.'

Behind the Greek the vine was descending once
more but not before Aeneas glimpsed in the depths
of the cavern a low couch spread with soft furs
and dishevelled silks on which reclined a long and
lovely figure aglow with the soft pink freshness of
a spring dawn.

Aeneas said accusingly, 'I'll sheath my sword,
Greek, when I know the truth of what has passed
between you two in there.'

'And you a grown man? Use your imagination.
A gent doesn't tell, specially not when the other
party's a bit of a goddess. Come on. We'll need to
move. Not much time.'

Odysseus strode away. Infuriated, Aeneas began
to follow. Then the fat Greek turned round and

said, 'Best not forget thy cloak. Don't want to catch a cold, do you?'

Aeneas suddenly realized he was shivering. The wind had sprung up again, and looking up he saw that the sky was once more overcast and darker than ever with the onset of dusk. He glanced back. The cavern with its protecting vine, the rich woodlands, the crystal springs, the verdant meadows, all had vanished and been replaced by the desolate landscape of grey and black rock.

He seized his cloak and hurried after Odysseus.

'Where are we going?' he demanded. 'This is not the way back to the camp.'

'Bugger the camp,' said Odysseus. 'We're heading for that little bay where you sheltered your fleet. Soon be sunset and that's the deadline for getting off this place, remember?'

The sword was out again and Aeneas cried, 'What? You think to save your skin by flight?'

'No, it's more sailing I had in mind,' said Odysseus. 'Hurry, or you'll not make it.'

'You are quite mad,' said Aeneas quietly. 'Do you really think I am going to sail away with you and leave my son and my father and all my comrades to their fate? Goodbye, Greek. I only regret I do not have the time to kill you.'

He turned and began to run back the way they'd come.

'Where are you going?' yelled Odysseus.

'Back to the camp to face whatever fate awaits me,' called the Trojan over his shoulder.

'But there's no one there!' bellowed Odysseus. 'They've all packed up and gone.'

His voice carried enough conviction to stop Aeneas in his tracks.

'What do you mean?' he demanded. 'Gone where?'

'Down to the bay to get the ships ready, of course. Don't you buggers ever listen to anyone? No wonder you lost the war. Come on!'

But still Aeneas did not move.

'They have left my boy?' he said brokenly.

'Don't be daft. He's down there too. But they'll be leaving you if you don't get a move on. Come on. Run! Imagine Achilles is after you. I've never seen anyone run as fast as you lot when the Big Man was on the rampage!'

They ran, with Aeneas soon too breathless to ask further questions. And at last they were descending the windy path to the bay where the Trojan fleet lay.

The Greek had not been lying. The strand and the sea were alive with activity. On the ships, sails were already being hoisted in preparation for departure. And best of all, as they reached the shore, Achates came hurrying towards them holding young Ascanius by the hand.

At sight of his father the boy broke free and rushed into the Prince's fierce embrace.

'My son, my son,' he cried. 'Why are you not in your nurse's care?'

'Don't fuss so, Father,' said the boy impatiently.

'And do hurry. Everyone's waiting for you. I'll go and tell Granddad you're here.'

He pushed himself free then looked up at Odysseus.

'Who're you?' he demanded.

'Me? Friend of your dad's. Name of Odysseus.'

'Don't be silly. Odysseus is a villain and my father would kill him. Also he's ten feet tall with a lion's head and a serpent's tail and you're just an old fat man. Now do hurry, Father.'

The boy sprinted away.

'Nice lad,' said Odysseus. 'Need to work on his manners, but.'

Achates had reached them.

'Good, you're here,' he said. 'I got your message and we're just about ready to sail.'

'My message?'

'Yes. That old hag. The one you gave your ring to for authority. Here, you'd best have it back.'

He gave Aeneas a ring. The Prince looked at his hand in amazement to notice for the first time the ring was missing.

'How can such things be?' he asked Odysseus. 'And the nymph, she never left the cavern, for I kept watch.'

'That's one of the advantages of being divine,' said the fat Greek. 'Can be in two places at once. I should know. She were all over me.'

'Will you come aboard now, Prince?' said Achates. 'We are ready, and your message was most insistent we must be afloat by sunset.'

'Right. Fine. We'll be with you in two minutes.'

Achates turned away, paused, and glanced at Odysseus. No emotion showed on those craggy features but he nodded once then moved away.

'That 'ud be a thank you, mebbe?' said Odysseus.

'Do you deserve a thank you? No, I'm sorry. Of course, you must do. What is happening here must have something to do with what happened back there. But no time to talk about it now. We must hurry aboard and once safe at sea, then we can relax with a bottle of wine and, gentleman or not, you can tell me exactly how you contrived to persuade the nymph to change her mind.'

'Yeah, well, I'd love to. Except I won't be coming. I'm stopping on here a bit. Best all round. I mean, first storm and your lads 'ud be all for tossing me overboard.'

'No!' said Aeneas strongly. 'However you worked it, you have done me and my family such service here that I swear to the gods that nothing on earth or above it will make me withdraw my protection of you.'

'Nay, lad, I'd be careful how you chuck them oaths around,' said Odysseus kindly. 'I reckon you're one of them poor sods whose strings the gods will be forever pulling, and there's no arguing against them. So I'll stay. You push off now. Enjoy the rest of your trip.'

'But how will you leave, you who are so desperate to get home?' said Aeneas. 'At least let me take you to an inhabited island where you can find a new ship and a crew to sail it. Or failing that, let *me leave you with one of our shore boats, so when the weather turns fair you can resume your voyage yourself.'*

'No, don't bother. I'll be all right,' said the fat Greek lightly.

The Trojan stared at him long and hard, then said suddenly, 'You can't leave, can you? That was the deal you did. Calypso decided that she'd much rather have the great Prince Odysseus as her consort than a slip of a boy like Ascanius. She said she'd let him go if you stayed in his place. I'm right, aren't I?'

'Summat like that. No need to go on about it. Good grub, nice billet, plus all the extras.'

Odysseus smacked his lips lecherously and gave a broad smile.

But Aeneas still regarded him doubtfully.

'Back there,' he said, 'when you first saw her, tell me true, what was it you saw? A lovely woman in a beautiful setting or a nauseating old crone by a pile of rocks?'

Odysseus shrugged.

'Not what you see that counts,' he said. 'It's what you know is there.'

'Yes, but such an act of faith . . .' He shuddered at the memory of the Greek caressing those foul and ancient feet.

'You'd have done the same, if you'd thought on. For your boy.'

'Yes. But would I have done it for your boy . . . ?'

'It were my boy I were thinking of,' said Odysseus.

'My boy that I've not seen since he were younger than thine . . .'

He turned his face away, but not before Aeneas had glimpsed the tears in his eye.

'How long did you have to agree to stay here?' he demanded.

'Oh, a fair bit.'

'Forever, isn't it? She wants you forever. Face it, man. You're never going to get home!'

'Forever's a long time,' said Odysseus. 'Likely she'll get tired of me afore too long. Look, you'd best be off. They're waiting for you and the sun's nearly set.'

Aeneas reached forward and grasped both the Greek's hands in his.

'Goodbye, friend,' he said fervently. 'I'll never forget you.'

'Oh yes, you will,' said Odysseus.

'No, I swear it . . .'

'There you go again. Always waving your sword and swearing. Gets you nowhere. What I mean is, she, the nymph Calypso, has fixed it so you'll forget. You and all your men. Your meeting with me on her island will be forever wiped from your memory and when the bards start singing our stories, no man will ever relate what has happened here.'

'Can she do such things?'

'Oh aye. Very ingenious lady. Only she's not infallible, see? She says that no man will ever sing our story. Mebbe, though, in the future, some bint will have a stab at telling it.'

605

'A female bard?' said Aeneas doubtfully. 'Could such a thing ever be?'

'Anything's possible,' said Odysseus. 'Couple of thousand years from now, only the gods know what the world's going to look like.'

'I have heard,' said Aeneas slowly, 'that some of your Greek thinkers believe that the spirits of some great men may be reborn to walk the earth again in later years. What do you think of that?'

'Like I say, after what I've been through, I'd say owt's possible.'

'Then it may be that after many centuries you and I will meet again, Odysseus.'

'Aye, but how would we recognize each other?'

'Well, that's easy. I would look for a fat man who pays no heed to appearances but acts on what he knows is there.'

'And I'd look for a skinny lad who's always trying to walk in two directions at once and spends more time waving his sword than using it.'

The two men embraced. Then Aeneas broke free and ran down to the waiting boat which pulled off immediately, bearing him out to the ship that bore his princely pennant.

It was almost dark now. Only a pale-pink line between the lowering sky and the choppy sea showed where the sun was sliding beneath the horizon. Odysseus watched the boat come alongside the ship. Even before the men had scaled the waiting ropes and reached the deck, the sails were breaking out and the vessel was under way.

He stood and watched as the sails caught the wind and the Prince's ship began to follow the others which were already heading out to sea.

Rapidly the growing darkness and the spume and swirling rain swallowed them up but his eye still strained to follow them and in his mind he was out there too, not with the Trojan fleet but at the prow of his own ship, his body soaked with sweat and salt water, feeling the timbers creak and strain under the heavy swell, hearing the sails crack and his crew groan as they heaved at their oars, and recognizing in their groans not dismay or fear but simply the honest effort of men who know that every long pull takes them a few yards nearer home.

But he had no ship, and he had no comrades, and no movement he could make in any direction was going to take him an inch nearer home.

Desolate and alone, he turned from the choppy, wind-tossed, dark and longed-for sea, and found himself instantly in another world.

The sky above was clear, dark purple pricked with a million stars and bossed by a full golden moon which lit up the scene like a thousand torches. The gentlest of balmy breezes ruffled his hair like a woman's fingers.

The steep rocky track down which he and Aeneas had run at risk of their lives was now a wide green path gently ascending between sweet-scented shrubs. At the end of it he could see a figure standing, Calypso smiling and beckoning, clad only in her long tressed hair.

> *Strange, he thought, how at the same time
> a man's heart could be so heavy and his flesh
> so light.*
>
> *He put his hand under his tunic, gave him-
> self an anticipatory scratch and began to move
> forward.*
>
> *The path was sown with camomile and as he
> advanced the bruised herb gave off its sweet fra-
> grance at every heavy tread.*
>
> *Bit like life, he thought. If you work at it. A bit
> like life.*

So that's that, all done and dusted.

I never thought there'd be a Chapter 4.

I mean, now that I'm a soon-to-be-published novelist – well, OK, not all that soon, but I've been lunched by an editor (who looked about three years older than Rosie!) and I've got a signed contract and soon, very soon, my infant editor assures me I should be getting a cheque! – now that I've got all that, who needs a Comfort Blanket?

Also, the Chapter 4 I had mapped out wasn't anything like this. No, it was going to be pure farce shading into fiasco, with Achaemenides, the Trojan twit, dumped overboard by Aeneas's crew, being washed ashore on the island half-drowned and being nursed to health by Calypso who mis-hears his delirious answer to her enquiries about his identity and thinks he says he's Achilles. So he gets to be a kind of king like his mother forecast and Aeneas and the rest of them get to leave the island as the nymph reckons they're superfluous to requirements now she's got old Stiffy himself, and Odysseus cons the Trojans into thinking he knows the best route to Italy, only he gets them sailing in the opposite direction and eventually they hit Carthage . . . something like that.

But first of all I found that, while I might not need my Comfort Blanket any more, I couldn't leave it unfinished.

I bet old Penelope got stuck into that tapestry of hers after all the blood had been rinsed off the palace floor and things started to settle down.

And secondly, I sort of lost my way. Or found it.

I'd set out to do a bit of gentle piss-taking, to portray these men, these *heroes*, and their epic pretensions, their crazy notions of duty and courage and honour, their absurd rivalries and their loyalties equally absurd, as essentially laughable.

Instead they've come out sort of . . . noble?

Maybe that was what male nobility is, the flip side of male stupidity.

Or maybe now that I've spent some time in that world of action, and bonding, and physical fear, and surging adrenalin, and moral ambiguities, and blood and death, I've got a different perspective.

At times I found myself (and I observed the

others), behaving just like these invented men in my mock epic.

And at times, many times recently, I've seen my real man behaving like . . . a woman?

Perhaps that's the message of the millennium.

Bisexuality is the new rock 'n' roll.

Whatever, here I am, journey over. Or at least safely harboured and able to rest before the next stage.

And I've got my ticket to ride, I'm a real novelist now; no, more than that; a real person who happens to be a novelist. And upstairs, though Peter doesn't know it yet, is a boxroom which he is going to turn into a study, with floor-to-ceiling bookshelves, busts of Dickens and Austen, the odd literary award scattered casually around . . .

I've told Mum all about it, of course. My triumph, I mean. Not my tribulation. Though I have this irrational suspicion that in a few years' time they may seem to have changed significances.

Mum was delighted. She said, 'Wait till I tell your father.' I nearly said, 'What's the point?' but, thank God, or Sod, I didn't.

Instead I said, 'No, I'll tell him myself next time I see him.' Which was a couple of days later. And I did.

He said, 'Splendid, absolutely splendid,' just as he would have done a few years back. And he smiled. Then he went back to being that puzzled, slightly uneasy stranger I'm growing used to.

I've told Mum I'm dedicating my book to him.

And when she cried, I cried too. Sentimental? And why not? But selfish too. I don't know how many years I've got of visiting that stranger, but every time I look at my book I shall hear that old familiar voice saying, 'Splendid, absolutely splendid,' and see his smile.

Perhaps that's the real, the only important meaning of my book.

But I promise myself I'll never even hint at such heresy in my Booker acceptance speech.

I look across the room at Peter asleep on the sofa, Rosie on his knee with her arms twined round his neck, Tig on one side of him also asleep, his head against the girl's trailing leg. (Carla, thank God, is still at Gunnery House, but Rosie has promised she'll take care of her next time Feenie goes on her travels. Sufficient is the evil . . . !)

I observe the little tableau closely but not with a novelist's selective eye. That's not for my family. For other people, yes; strangers. And even, yes, from time to time, some of my friends.

But not my family.

Comfort Blanket was a one-off. Peter would be entertained, no doubt, by Aeneas, but ever after he'd be looking at me and wondering if the tape was running.

So it's oblivion via the recycle bin for you, my creatures, then I can cross the room and get into that tableau.

Just two more words to type before I press the *Delete* key. How reluctant I am to type them. How I would love to keep on coming back, and tweaking and twisting and revising and reshaping forever and ever and . . .

But I'm a real writer now and there's a yet-to-be-built shelf in that boxroom-soon-to-become-a-study which will stand empty till it is filled with books bearing my name.

So if I want to see those other two words, Ellie Pascoe, repeated ad infinitum, or at least till the end of the shelf, I've got to get used to typing this awful pair.

The words which ought to give us real writers the greatest pleasure, but somehow manage to give the greatest pain.

The End